THE
GOD
MACHINE

✦ Book 3 ✦

THE GOD MACHINE

✦ *Book 3* ✦

EMERGENCYCOMPLAINTS

Podium

This is a work of fiction. Names, characters, places, and incidents are either products of the author's imagination or used fictitiously. Any resemblance to actual events, locales, or persons, living, dead, or undead, is entirely coincidental.

Cover design by Iromonik

ISBN: 978-1-0394-5513-9

Published in 2024 by Podium Publishing
www.podiumaudio.com

THE
GOD
MACHINE

✦ Book 3 ✦

CHAPTER 1

The last two months of Luke's life had been beyond boring. There was really only so much of staring at empty, open water he could take, and he'd hit that limit weeks ago. Other than a brief break from the monotony when *The Silk Lady* had docked at an island port to make repairs for a week, there'd been nothing to see and nothing to do.

Luke had used that opportunity to hunt down some local wildlife, both to butcher some meat and to finish grinding out the last bit of XP he'd needed to level up to 42. He'd gotten one of the locals to prepare it for long-term storage and brought three large barrels back to *The Silk Lady* to be consumed on the remainder of their voyage.

That, more than anything else, had convinced the sailors to stop glaring at him and Zea. He suspected finally having the holes in their deck repaired also helped. Either way, things had gone smoother after the repairs, and the true enemy of the trip had been unrelieved, everlasting boredom. Zea spent all her time working on various projects and ignoring him.

"Land ho!" someone called from above.

"Oh, thank God," Luke muttered.

He wasn't the only one excited about it. Most of the crew perked up at that, and no less than four different sailors jumped up onto the riggings to scramble upward. Luke was half-tempted to take a look himself, but he knew he'd just be getting in people's way, so he stayed sitting in his customary spot near the stairs leading up to the poop deck, as he'd learned it was called. He'd asked no fewer than six different people if that was really the name before deciding they were either telling the truth or the entire crew was in on pranking him.

Luke took a set of dangerously steep stairs down below deck to the room he shared with Zea. She was sitting in her usual spot in the corner, working at her portable enchanter's bench. Luke was constantly amazed when she managed to finish another project despite the rocking motion of the ship. She'd spent some of her remaining AP on agility and perception, and apparently that had been enough to overcome the handicap of engraving runes on things while sailing across the ocean.

"They spotted land. We'll be there soon."

"Fucking finally," Zea said. "I am so sick of being on this boat."

"Really? You got a lot done with the downtime," Luke said.

"Sure, but it was boring."

"Yeah . . . That's true." He'd given up on his own project ideas before he'd even gotten started and donated the black snake leather to Zea. The AP was better spent on buying the **[XP Reset]** bloodline skill for her. Once she was done with her work and had everything set up, she'd be wanting him to do that immediately. They hadn't discussed it yet, but it was pretty clear. Things had started to cool down between them now.

He wasn't really sure what to do about that, or even if he should do anything. Every time he tried to say something, his tongue got tangled up in his mouth and everything came out wrong. It was just easier to change the subject, and the fact that Zea let him said something about how she felt too. Neither wanted to talk about it, at least not while they were stuck sharing forty square feet of space for weeks on end.

"So . . . I guess we'll be back on solid ground here in a few hours," he started.

"Yeah. Maybe a day. Depends how high the guy who spotted land's perception is."

Luke brushed that aside. "And we should probably figure out what we're doing to do."

"I figured we'd take a day or two to get situated and resupply, then follow the road that's closest to going in the right direction," Zea said.

"We?" Luke asked.

"Well, yeah. You're not trying to get rid of me, are you?"

"No! I just . . . I thought, you know . . ." Luke trailed off.

Zea blinked and frowned at him. "You thought what?"

"I—Never mind, I don't know what I was thinking."

Zea nudged the bag in the corner with her foot and said, "Please, after all the effort I put into making all of this, you think I'm just going to give up now?"

She'd made a whole bunch of things over the last two months, but she hadn't shared what those things were, and Luke hadn't pried. Part of her plan had always been to make a lot of money in a hurry before he reset her level for her. He'd just assumed that was what she'd been working on.

"What did you make?" he asked.

"I am so glad you finally asked. I expected the curiosity to get the better of you six weeks ago. First, you might recognize this."

Zea pulled out a length of chain about three feet long. "I had to cut off the end to recycle it after we used it on the ship, but I managed it. This is functionally magic armor. You wrap this chain around yourself, let the ends connect, and it'll absorb hits for you until it runs out of mana."

"Wait, really?" Luke eyed up the metal. "That's so cool!"

"Damn right it is. But it probably won't last more than . . . I don't know . . . ten hits maybe? Depends on how hard the hit is and some other stuff."

She reached into the bag and dug out what looked like a fishing line with a bunch of bones strung up across its length. "Finally got that whip I wanted finished," she said. "But, uh, can't really show that off in here."

He'd seen how much damage the shortened version she'd used a few months ago could do. There was no doubt in his mind that anything with less than 40 stamina would be ripped to shreds by the new whip. That would certainly make it easier on Zea to take out monsters on her own when they went out hunting, but at the same time, she'd been pretty definitive that she was done farming XP until Luke had a way to prove he could reset it.

Oblivious to Luke's thoughts, Zea dug around in the bag. "Let's see, where is it . . . Ah! Here we go. This is for you."

"My shirt?" Luke asked, taking the folded-up piece of cloth Zea shoved in his hands. It was a nice shade of blue, a bit long once he held it up to look it over, and with sleeves that came down to his elbows. He'd bought it as part of a spare set of clothes a few months ago but hadn't gotten into enough fights to warrant needing it yet.

"A tunic, technically," she said. "More importantly, it is an enchanted tunic. It is self-regenerating. If it gets torn, it will knit itself back together. If a piece gets ripped off, it will regrow that part. It's also self-cleaning, to an extent. Of course, the more it needs to do this, the faster the runes wear off, so you should still make an effort to take care of it."

"Holy shit, that's amazing!"

Keeping clothes in one piece had been a challenge for Luke since arriving on Aros, and more than once he'd had to go without. Even if it was just a shirt, it would be so much nicer to not have to worry about one piece of clothing being destroyed in combat.

"You're probably going to want these too," Zea said, holding out the matching black trousers. "Same deal."

"So I could just, like . . . wear these all the time, sleep in them even, and never have to change them or clean them or sew up any cuts or tears."

"I would prefer if you bathed regularly," she said dryly. "For all our sakes."

"Er, right, yeah. I knew that."

"Right. Yeah. You did. Anyway, there's a few bombs in here too. What else . . . Oh! These are fun." Zea held up a wooden jar full of what looked like a few dozen smooth, flat river stones. Each one was the perfect shape for skipping across a lake. "They're all enchanted with an electric payload that will lock up muscles for a few seconds. On something under fifty pounds, it should fully paralyze the target. On something your size, it'll only lock up a limb, maybe disrupt a heartbeat if you get them on the chest. Won't do much against the skull, unfortunately."

"You made all of this in two months?" Luke asked, slightly overwhelmed.

"Some other stuff too. I've got a better temporal-stasis enchantment on our food bag now. It should be good for at least a year before it runs out of power. I put a warming enchantment on my cloak with some of the leftover supplies from your second purification ritual. Hmm, here's an enchanted pen for copying out a map when we find one. Oh yeah, and I made these!" Zea held up two squares of parchment with some sort of complicated runic design on them.

"And, uh, what are those?" Luke asked.

"Temporary runic markers, for the next time we inevitably end up separated. We'll apply these to our skin somewhere, preferably where a captor won't immediately find them, and when we need to find each other, we can just put our thumbs right here on this rune that looks like a circle. The whole thing will start getting warmer as the marks get closer to each other."

Luke hadn't gotten a temporary tattoo since he was six, back when his mom was still alive and he occasionally managed to beg a few quarters off her at the grocery store. But that was exactly what Zea's runic marker reminded him of when she slapped it onto his hip, muttered something, and carefully peeled the parchment back off. It was blank, and the tattoo stood out as stark, sharp black lines against his skin.

"Wish we'd had those four months ago," he said. "Would have saved us some grief."

"Yeah, I should have poured some AP into **[Rune Forging]** a long time ago. Oh well, live and learn."

"You know, I really thought we were parting ways once we got off the ship," Luke said.

"Why?"

"Well, you know, you were kind of . . . I guess I figured you were avoiding me? You didn't ever really want to talk; we haven't, uh, you know, in weeks."

Zea rolled her eyes. "You still haven't reset my level yet, so you're stuck with me. I've just been busy building us an arsenal so we can tear this place apart and go get your family back. It's tiring work doing so much enchanting. Also hammocks suck for fucking in."

"I see that now!" Luke said. "Sorry I just assumed instead of talking to you about it. I didn't want an awkward monthslong boat ride."

"Ugh. You're a dumbass sometimes. Whatever. Why don't you go find out how many hours we have left, and I'll try to get this last piece done."

"What is it going to be?" Luke asked curiously. He shot a glance over at her enchanting table and found what looked like a rough strip of snake leather half covered in runes. It had been hacked off the main chunk so badly that little strands came off it every few inches. "You should have had me trim that for you. I've got the **[Leatherworking]** ranks."

"I did it this way on purpose," she said. "This is my secret weapon."

"What does it do?" he asked.

"Oh, it'll be fun," Zea told him with a grin.

"Is this going to get us in trouble?"

Zea shrugged and her grin got bigger. "If it does, it'll be worth it."

Name	Luke Bennet	Zea Stenter
Level	42	35
XP	255178/273479	146001/157276
AP	42	4
Bloodline	SysAdmin III	None
Strength	61	7
Agility	70	30
Stamina	66	27
Perception	55	21
Skills	Butchering (4)	Arcano Dynamics (3)
	Counter (3)	Bartering (2)
	Deception (1)	Bloodline Purification Ritual (2)
	Detection (2)	Cadence (3)
	Disguise (2)	Cold Reading (1)
	First Aid (1)	Cooking (1)
	Leatherworking (2)	Dagger Mastery (1)
	Life Surge (2)	Deception (1)
	Mace Mastery (5)	Disguise (2)
	Ostari (1)	Engraving (4)
	Peripheral Awareness (2)	First Aid (1)
	Power Strike (2)	Gem Cutting (1)
	Stealth (1)	Ghost Script (1)
	Survivalist (2)	Goldsmithing (2)
	Sword Mastery (1)	Keen Instincts (1)
	Tactical Foresight (2)	Lock Picking (1)
	Thalian (2)	Mana Manipulation (3)
	Torturer (1)	Mana Sight (3)
	Twitch Reflexes (3)	Mending (1)
	Unarmed Martialist (4)	Metallurgy (1)
	Wood Carving (1)	Neyardic (3)
	Analyze (BL)	Ostari (1)
	Remote Access (BL)	Painting (1)
	XP Mask (BL)	Rune Forging (3)
		Sleight of Hand (1)
		Steady Hands (2)
		Stealth (2)
		Streetwise (2)
		Temperature Acclimation (2)
		Thalian (3)
		Whitesmithing (1)

CHAPTER 2

The first thing they did upon disembarking *The Silk Lady* was to take a few minutes to just wander around and get a feel for the most prominent language. Neither of them had any firsthand knowledge of the eastern continent and only had System's insistence than the locals spoke a language called Eledarn and that Consortium Standard was the dominant trade language between the various clans that controlled the eastern continent.

Luke had the AP to buy both languages, but Zea could only afford one. They'd decided to see if Consortium Standard was widely used outside of the business and transportation sectors before committing the AP to picking it up, both because Zea didn't want to level anymore and because Luke needed about 500 AP to pick up the rest of his bloodline skills. Wasting a big chunk on languages that would only be useful for a week or two didn't strike him as a smart move.

"I want a place to sleep that has an actual bed, and I want a bath," Zea told Luke. "We've got fifty-two gold left, and I have no idea what the exchange rate is for local currency. So our priorities right now are figuring out the local dialect, getting some money, and locating some hospitality."

[Detection] spent the next ten minutes going crazy while they walked. People on the eastern continent, at least the ones who lived in Naldrin, seems to be on average a lot shorter than literally every human he'd met prior to getting off the ship. Consequently, foreigners stood out since they were half a foot taller than just about anyone else. Zea was still the shortest person in a mile radius, but the difference was less pronounced since there were plenty of other people under the five-foot mark.

If that was the only difference, it might not have been a big deal, but the overwhelming majority of the locals also had silver-white hair. It was like the whole city had one hair stylist, and the guy was the biggest anime nerd ever. There was a word for that . . . Started with a *W*.

"Webabo . . . Weed . . . Web . . . something," Luke muttered.

"What?" Zea asked.

"Huh? Oh, nothing, just trying to remember something from back home."

"Mm-hmm. Is it, you know, relevant to our situation?"

"Nah, not really. So, time to pick up a new language, you think?"

"Yeah. What's your AP floating at right now?" Zea asked.

"Still 42. I figured I needed to bank it for bloodline skills, so I didn't spend any after my last level up."

Left unsaid was that he'd been planning to upgrade **[Leatherworking]** to rank 4 but ended up giving the raw material to Zea instead. There didn't seem to be much point in wasting the AP if he had nothing to work on. On the bright side, it was always nice to have a cushion in case he needed a new skill immediately.

"Take Consortium Standard as a language skill and we'll see how far it gets us? If it's working for you, I'll pick it up too."

"Sure," Luke said. He navigated through his system interface to the skill store, found **[Consortium Standard]** under the languages section, and bought rank 1 for 5 AP. His brain skipped a beat as it got slammed with new knowledge, and suddenly he could understand most of what was being said around him.

"Oh yeah, that's the dominant language here," he told Zea. "Seems to have a lot of overlap with the local dialect, enough that if you were fully fluent in one, you could probably communicate with someone speaking the other as long as you're patient."

"Figured, but let's get away from the docks where all the foreigners are and see if the ratio shifts once it's just native Naldrinians talking to one another."

They walked deeper into the city, deep enough that people with dark-colored hair quickly shrunk to the minority and the street signs stopped being in two or three different languages. The streets weren't exactly crowded, but they were comfortably full, and everything was just a little bit too narrow to Luke's mind. That combined with the architecture utilizing some sort of clay blocks instead of wooden planks for buildings, most of which were two or even three stories tall, gave the city a somewhat claustrophobic feel for Luke.

The farther away from the docks they got, the less **[Consortium Standard]** was able to translate for Luke. There were occasional open squares where he still heard it and various ground floor shops that had signs written in multiple languages. He could read parts of those, but most of the idle background chatter from everyday people not looking to sell anything was in another language. That didn't mean the citizens of Naldrin couldn't speak Standard just because they weren't. There was an easy way to test that.

"Excuse me," Luke said to a young woman minding a small fruit stand on the side of the street.

"Hello," she said, giving him what he would have called a customer-service smile. "Are you interested in some fruit?"

"No, well, yes, but . . ." Luke held up a silver coin. "I don't have any of the local currency yet. Do you know where I can get my money changed over? And then perhaps an inn, one with a bath."

"I can make change for you," she said hesitantly. "But . . . maybe it is better to go to a money changer. That way you know you are not getting taken advantage of. There is one over in the commerce square that could help you. It's a big, wide building with a blue-tiled roof."

"Oh! Yeah, I saw that. Over that way, right?" Luke asked, pointing behind him and to the left.

"Right. Over there."

Luke thanked the woman and led Zea back toward the commerce square. He stopped once more to ask for directions, even though he knew where he was going, just to see if a random person who wasn't trying to sell anything would also understand him.

"Okay, I think we can safely assume that most people here are bilingual. It would be better to speak both languages, especially if we were going to stay for a long time, but Standard should be good enough for our purposes," Luke said.

"Hopefully System was right about it having spread to other . . . What did he call them? Provinces?"

"I think so, yeah."

Zea purchased the skill as well and took over the bargaining and haggling, which was just fine by Luke. It wasn't that he had anything against a bath and a bed to sleep in, but if it had just been Luke, he'd have had System point him in the direction of the God Machine and started walking. It wasn't like he had a car anyway, so roads were optional. If the eastern continent was anything like the western, something would try to kill him within an hour or two of getting away from civilization, he'd kill it, and then he'd eat his fill of badly cooked meat before moving on.

Thank God his high stamina protected him from getting food poisoning.

Luke just kind of trailed along, only vaguely interested in watching Zea work. She exchanged half their gold for the local currency, some sort of oval thing with a groove carved down the middle and a hole in one end. A bunch of them were strung together into something like a necklace, which, now that Luke knew to look for them, he saw people wearing everywhere.

Zea promptly cut the string and dumped the coins into her own pouch. After that, they did a quick lap around the square to restock some of their supplies and found an inn on the south side of the city near the shore that had been built so that the entire first floor was a bathhouse. Luke had to admit after that she'd been completely right. It was worth the time and effort to get cleaned up before he put on his new set of enchanted clothing.

After renting a room and depositing their road supplies, Zea dragged him back onto the streets. "Where are we going?" Luke asked as he allowed himself to be tugged down the stairs and past the doorway leading back into the bathhouse.

"We're on a whole new continent. There's a culture here we know nothing about, and for probably the first time in months, nobody wants to kill us. We're going to eat new foods and listen to new music and visit new places. Then we're going to get a good night's sleep before it's back to endless walking tomorrow."

Well, he certainly couldn't argue with that.

"I have no idea what I'm eating," Luke said.

"Me neither. It's . . . It's not very good."

They'd ordered some kind of meat-and-vegetable dish that came with its own sauce to dip the chunks into, but the sauce was extremely bitter, and in Luke's opinion at least, the food tasted better without it. There was also the matter of the eating utensil they'd been provided with, which looked something like a cross between a knife and a paddle.

It took a few tries to get it right, but a glance around the restaurant showed that it was designed to be used while holding the plate at an angle to scoop a chunk of food up after it had been sliced off the main portion. What exactly the eastern continent had against a simple fork, Luke couldn't tell.

It was tempting to just eat with his fingers, but Luke restrained himself. As far as he was concerned, this was a date, and it was long overdue. He wasn't going to ruin it with poor manners.

"Want to go somewhere else?" Zea asked.

"Sure," Luke said. They'd paid for the food in advance, so there was no bill to settle. They simply abandoned their table as they'd seen several other people do and exited through the front door. It was early evening now, and the streets were lit with lanterns using some sort of scented oil that made everything smell vaguely floral.

"Looks like there's some kind of show going on over there," he said, pointing toward a square a few hundred feet away. There was a crowd of people there, all facing toward a raised platform with ten people standing on it. Each of them was wearing a matching uniform, though some were more highly decorated than others. Nine of the men were in their forties, and the last one was perhaps in his midtwenties.

Luke and Zea wandered into the square and slid across the back of the ground to an out-of-the-way section where they wouldn't be blocking anybody's view. Luke was one of the tallest people there, and Zea was so short that it was easier for her to just jump up on top of a large crate and sit there. "What kind of a show do you think it is?" she asked.

"No idea, but it looks like it's about to start."

Across the square, a new man was just climbing up a few steps onto the platform. He turned to address the crowd, but unfortunately, he wasn't speaking Consortium Standard. "Damn," Luke said. "I'm getting maybe half of this. I don't think it's a show though, more like a ceremony, maybe."

The man who was speaking paced back and forth in front of the other ten. He thanked them, of that part Luke was sure. The words were the same between the languages, but what exactly he was thanking them for, Luke couldn't tell.

It was about then that Luke noticed how quiet everything had gotten. The city was full of energy and noise as people went about their lives, and that was still present in the background. But here, in this one square, nobody in the crowd said a word. They just listened, silent, and waited for the man up on the stage to finish giving his speech.

The middle-aged man on the far left and the young man on the right stepped forward out of the line and met in the middle. The younger man said something—Luke thought he was thanking the other man—and they clasped hands.

Then the younger one's free hand blurred, and a knife sliced through his counterpart's throat.

Name	Luke Bennet	Zea Stenter
Level	42	35
XP	255178/273479	14001/157276
AP	37	4
Bloodline	SysAdmin III	None
Strength	61	7
Agility	70	30
Stamina	66	27
Perception	55	21
Skills	Butchering (4)	Arcano Dynamics (2)
	Consortium Standard (1)	Bartering (2)
	Counter (3)	Bloodline Purification Ritual (2)
	Deception (1)	Cadence (3)
	Detection (2)	Cold Reading (1)
	Disguise (2)	Consortium Standard (1)
	First Aid (1)	Cooking (1)
	Leatherworking (2)	Dagger Mastery (1)
	Life Surge (2)	Deception (1)
	Mace Mastery (5)	Disguise (2)
	Ostari (1)	Engraving (4)
	Peripheral Awareness (2)	First Aid (1)
	Power Strike (2)	Gem Cutting (1)
	Stealth (1)	Ghost Script (1)
	Survivalist (2)	Goldsmithing (2)
	Sword Mastery (1)	Keen Instincts (1)
	Tactical Foresight (2)	Lock Picking (1)
	Thalian (2)	Mana Manipulation (3)
	Torturer (1)	Mana Sight (3)
	Twitch Reflexes (3)	Mending (1)
	Unarmed Martialist (4)	Metallurgy (1)
	Wood Carving (1)	Neyardic (3)
	Analyze (BL)	Ostari (1)
	Remote Access (BL)	Painting (1)
	XP Mask (BL)	Rune Forging (3)
		Sleight of Hand (1)
		Steady Hands (2)
		Stealth (2)
		Streetwise (2)
		Temperature Acclimation (2)
		Thalian (3)
		Whitesmithing (1)

CHAPTER 3

Oooooh shit," Luke said.

Nobody in the crowd was panicking or screaming, so obviously they'd been expecting something like this. Blood spurted into the air, and a chorus of voices rose up, all saying the same thing. Then the man on the stage died, and his murderer's lips moved in some silent prayer. Even with his perception at 55, Luke couldn't make out what the man said.

"What the fuck is going on here?" Zea whispered harshly as she grabbed at Luke's arm. "Maybe we should go."

"I think we're alright," Luke said. "This isn't something weird to these people. It's cultural, some kind of tradition."

"How the hell can you tell?"

"Well, because I've been dealing with this kind of stuff since I got here. Something weird happens, and I have to figure out from context if everyone else thinks it's just another day or if I should be worried. This is expected. Look at them all. They came here to witness this. They knew what they were going to see."

Luke was pretty sure he knew what was happening, but just to be sure, he started spamming **[Analyze]** on everyone on the stage. They were organized in order of descending level, with the strongest person still alive being level 51 and the weakest being 44. The young man was level 26.

The ritual repeated itself after the corpse was removed, with the next man on the left stepping forward and the young man murdering him. That pushed him up to level 27. By the time the process was finished and the last body had been taken away, the man was level 29.

Luke watched it silently, and when Zea saw that he wasn't going to leave, she settled down too. Once it was over and the crowd began to disperse, they walked back to the inn they'd taken rooms at. It wasn't until they were a few blocks away that Zea finally spoke, her voice dripping with disgust. "That was absolutely barbaric."

"What? Why?"

"Slaughtering people like that," Zea said. "Just . . . What, killing them to funnel XP to someone? What the fuck kind of civilized society does that?"

"They were all high level," Luke said. "Some of them were over level 50. The uniforms . . . I think they were some sort of military force."

"Probably. There's a reason we rotate soldiers off the front lines when they start getting into the high 20s," Zea said. "It's so we don't have to have shit like this happening in the middle of our cities."

"You don't know if this is a normal occurrence. Maybe something special happened here. Maybe those guys held some choke point against thousands of enemies and saved entire towns from being destroyed."

"I fucking doubt it," Zea said. "That wasn't a temporary stage they set up. And even if that was the case, they wouldn't be funneling it all into that one guy. How many years of his life did he give up right there for some extra XP?"

"I don't think it was about the XP," Luke said. "There are plenty of easy ways to farm XP. They don't need to kill their own for a minor level bump that they could get with a few weeks of dedicated monster hunting."

"No, it's about the sacrifice. They served the motherland well, fought off her enemies, became an impenetrable wall for her citizens to shelter behind, but now the sickness of the mind is upon them, and it's time for one last act of service, time to die. And here's a symbolic passing on of the duty to the next generation by making some guy get up in front of a crowd to murder the veterans in job lots. Fucking savages."

If he'd wanted to fight about it, Luke would have pointed out that Zea was making a lot of assumptions there, some of which were suspiciously specific and made him think she'd encountered exactly that kind of behavior in the past. But at the end of the day, Luke didn't know anything about Naldrin's culture, certainly not enough to defend it, and he didn't feel like playing devil's advocate for a group of people he had no association with.

The whole experience did prompt him to start using **[Analyze]** regularly, and he quickly noticed a pattern. "There are a lot of people in this city over level 20," he said. "A few over level 30 as well. And you know what, maybe it's just the district we're in, but do you see a single person who's more than fifty years old?"

Zea frowned and said, "That's weird."

"Hey, System," Luke said. "What's the average level for a monster on the western continent, and what's the average level on the eastern continent?"

"17 and 31," System said.

"How about the average level for people?"

"14 on the western continent, 29 on the eastern."

"Everything and everyone is stronger here," Luke said. "We shouldn't expect things to go as easily as they did back on the other side of the ocean."

"Maybe, but without the church actively hunting us down, it should be less stressful."

Luke snorted. "There is that," he agreed.

They turned off the street and climbed the stairs back up to their room. "We'll have to see how the hunting is out in the wilderness," Luke said. "I need to gain 3 levels for [XP Cycle], then another one for [XP Reset]. Then 5 levels for [Inflict Status]. Or . . . maybe 4 levels? I'd have to do the math. Either way, I'll be right around level 50 just for that, assuming nothing else comes up."

He skimmed through his skill list on his status and for probably the hundredth time considered changing the order back. He'd switched it over to read alphabetically, but he'd gotten so used to the old version of a few broad categories roughly sorted by order of acquisition that the new list was actually harder to read to him.

"Couple combat skills left to max out before I start getting into advanced skills," he said. "But I probably won't need them once I have [Inflict Status]. If possible, I'd like to just grind that out and call it good."

"What about [Matter Generation]?" Zea asked.

"Ah, your gold farm. Right. Uh, I guess I have nothing against the idea, but it's kind of low priority, you know?"

"You know I could make you some incredible weapons if you could just create me anything I wanted, right?" Zea asked.

Luke shrugged. "Sure, but it's not like I can take them with me after I get to the God Machine."

In truth, his final level was going to be largely dependent on how much resistance he encountered on the way. While he doubted he'd just stroll right up to the place, he didn't think he'd be killing enough monsters to put on levels without going out of his way to make it work. Now that they had the time and resources, Zea could churn out enough bombs for him to decimate a few anthills before they really got going.

"The fastest way to pick up [Matter Generation] is to have you make bombs for me to use at the nearest anthill," Luke said. "Or I guess maybe some other concentration of bugs. Wasps or bees maybe? I don't know if I want to risk it with something that can fly."

"I could do twenty or so bombs with the funds we have left," Zea said. "That would probably be enough to hit level 50, right?"

"Maybe. System, how much XP would I need?"

"182928," System told him.

"Really, that much? Damn, that's way more than I was expecting. Do you think there are enough anthills within, I don't know, let's say a hundred miles of the city?"

"There are no anthills in that radius," System said.

Luke glanced over at Zea, who shrugged back. "Lucky for the people who live here, I suppose," he said. "Okay, where is the nearest anthill then?"

"About four thousand miles west of here."

"You mean back across the ocean? Are you trying to tell me there are no ants on this continent at all?"

"There are certainly some small colonies," System said. "But the ones you are referring to, with hundreds of thousands of ants, have all been wiped out by people seeking to do exactly what you are. At some point in this civilization's history, various species of insects used to be farmed in contained fields to allow for rapid accumulation of XP. The practice died out after it was determined that too many resources had to be invested into the closed ecosystem to justify the XP gains."

"Meaning that naturally occurring anthills became valuable and guarded resources," Zea said. "Probably closely monitored for size and regularly culled by whoever is overseeing them."

"Correct."

"But that would mean those anthills still exist today," Luke pointed out.

"They were destroyed centuries ago during what local history books refer to as the Night of the Brightest Fire, which is a misnomer, as the event actually lasted two years. According to the story, the world burned for so long that the smoke blocked out the sky and left nothing but the fires to see by. Many of the strongest humans in the world died during this event, which led to a need to replace them with fresh soldiers to fight on the front line."

"I'm confused here. What were they fighting?"

"I do not know," System said.

"How could you not know?" Luke asked. "You know, well, everything."

It wouldn't have surprised him if System had told Luke that it didn't have access to the information. That happened all the time, though less now with the two bloodline purifications Luke had undergone. It was pretty rare for System to just not know something though. Luke couldn't even recall a specific time that had happened off the top of his head.

"There are many logs of people dying during this time period, but their XP was returned in full to the God Machine without the normal portion being transferred to the cause of their death. This does happen sometimes, for example if someone were to die due to some sort of accident such as falling from a great height, but there has been no other instance of so many people all dying in such a short time frame due to unknown causes."

"We're getting kind of off topic, don't you think?" Zea cut in. "The point of this is that there are no massive anthills on the eastern continent for us to exploit, so there's no reason to spend all our funds on bombs. You'll have to level the old-fashioned way."

"Not the end of the world," Luke said. As far as he knew, he wasn't on any sort of a time limit. His family would be just as dead in a year as they were right now, and it would be the exact same amount of effort to bring them back either way. Probably. He should check on that.

System wasn't always forthcoming with information, and it wouldn't be the first time Luke had assumed he had a solution to a problem only to hit a snag once he went to implement it because System had neglected to mention something vital that a normal person would have brought up during the initial discussion.

He was getting better with volunteering information, but it wouldn't hurt to revisit some assumptions Luke had made when he'd first arrived on Aros just to confirm everything was going to work out the way he was planning. If he ended up needing another bloodline purification after he reached the God Machine, it was better to find out now.

"So, let's talk about the God Machine itself," Luke told System. "Specifically, I want to discuss what I can and can't do there and if I'm going to need to take any steps prior to reaching the physical location."

"Of course," System said. "What would you like to know?"

"To start . . ."

Name	Luke Bennet	Zea Stenter
Level	42	35
XP	255178/273479	14001/157276
AP	37	4
Bloodline	SysAdmin III	None
Strength	61	7
Agility	70	30
Stamina	66	27
Perception	55	21
Skills	Butchering (4)	Arcano Dynamics (2)
	Consortium Standard (1)	Bartering (2)
	Counter (3)	Bloodline Purification Ritual (2)
	Deception (1)	Cadence (3)
	Detection (2)	Cold Reading (1)
	Disguise (2)	Consortium Standard (1)
	First Aid (1)	Cooking (1)
	Leatherworking (2)	Dagger Mastery (1)
	Life Surge (2)	Deception (1)
	Mace Mastery (5)	Disguise (2)
	Ostari (1)	Engraving (4)
	Peripheral Awareness (2)	First Aid (1)
	Power Strike (2)	Gem Cutting (1)
	Stealth (1)	Ghost Script (1)
	Survivalist (2)	Goldsmithing (2)
	Sword Mastery (1)	Keen Instincts (1)
	Tactical Foresight (2)	Lock Picking (1)
	Thalian (2)	Mana Manipulation (3)
	Torturer (1)	Mana Sight (3)
	Twitch Reflexes (3)	Mending (1)
	Unarmed Martialist (4)	Metallurgy (1)
	Wood Carving (1)	Neyardic (3)
	Analyze (BL)	Ostari (1)
	Remote Access (BL)	Painting (1)
	XP Mask (BL)	Rune Forging (3)
		Sleight of Hand (1)
		Steady Hands (2)
		Stealth (2)
		Streetwise (2)
		Temperature Acclimation (2)
		Thalian (3)
		Whitesmithing (1)

CHAPTER 4

First, I want to revisit my initial assumption. Can my family be brought back from the dead?" Luke asked.

"They can," System confirmed.

"And I could do that right now, if I were at the command console of the God Machine?"

"That is correct."

"I don't need to upgrade my bloodline again?" Luke pressed.

"You do not. You will have full access to all bloodline skills at the command console."

"And they'll come back just like how they were before? No zombies or undead of any kind. No spirits or whatever. I'm talking about flesh and blood, just like the day they disappeared. I want them ready to walk through the doorway back to Earth."

"That is the state they will appear in, if you so desire. Alternatively, you could resurrect them at the level they died at. Their final statuses remain in the system's archives for use as templates to reconstruct."

"Probably not necessary," Luke said, "but I suppose it's good to have options. Next question! Getting back home. Can I teleport us all back to the doorway in Tenebrous Valley?"

"As you currently are? You could not."

"What would I need to do in order to make that happen?" Luke asked.

"You would need to add all the skills required to learn to cast a powerful teleportation or gate spell. Would you like them listed?"

"I don't know. When you say I need to add them, do you mean by grinding out levels for AP?"

"No, you could restructure your current build at the God Machine or simply add enough XP to your total to gain the AP needed if you'd prefer."

"Okay," Luke said. "To make sure I understand this correctly, I can't currently teleport anyone, even if I was at the God Machine, but while I was there, I could make alterations to my status that would allow me to? It would just be a matter of doing it?"

"That is correct," System said.

"So there is nothing I need to do in preparation prior to reaching the God Machine to accomplish my stated goals of reviving my family or teleporting them across the world to the doorway back to Earth?"

"There is not," System agreed.

Luke glanced over at Zea. "That seems pretty airtight to me. How about you?"

"System seems sure," she said.

Luke wanted to agree, but some niggling doubt in the back of his mind made him keep pressing. "If there's nothing I need to do, what about anything I might want to do? Something that might make it easier, for example."

System shook his translucent blue head. "Nothing you do prior to reaching the God Machine will have any measurable impact on your goals. You would save yourself only a few seconds at best for each skill you obtain during your travels."

"Okay. What about Zea? Would I be able to teleport her to wherever she wants to go as well?"

"I do not have enough information to answer that question," System said.

"What more information do you need?" Zea asked.

"The most pertinent information is the destination," System explained. "Many teleportation spells have limitations both in range and familiarity with the selected location. More powerful spells can often work around these issues but not always. Some locations are impossible to travel to using this type of magic."

"It would be reasonable to assume I could go to most locations?" Zea asked. "Like, for example, Luke could send me back to Valtira the city, even if he couldn't teleport me to a specific room at an inn he's never been to."

"That is mostly correct, though with a powerful enough scrying spell used in conjunction with a gateway spell of sufficient range, he could in fact open up a path for you to a room at an inn he's never been to in Valtira."

"That's specific enough for me," Zea said. "I am assuming it won't be an issue for him to acquire the skills and spells needed directly from the God Machine once we get there?"

"It would not," System confirmed.

"I think that about covers any concerns we had," Zea said to Luke. "Unless you can think of something?"

"Nothing comes to mind. Thanks for the help, System."

Satisfied that he would in fact be able to resurrect his entire family at the God Machine, Luke dismissed System and settled down for the night. In the morning, the work would begin anew, and he couldn't deny that he was somewhat excited for it. It wasn't that they'd made no progress over the last few months, but sitting on a ship while it moved had left him with an excess of energy. Soon, they'd be moving under their own power again, overcoming obstacles and defeating monsters.

"It might be worth it to get back on a ship that's going down the coast to a southern city," Zea said.

"God, no. No more ships. I'd rather walk."

"Even if it's safer and faster to sail?" Zea asked.

"I have plenty of time," Luke said. "I'm kind of surprised you'd want to get back on a ship so soon anyway."

"I got a lot done over the last few months. Most of it was to help you, but with another month or two, I could get myself set up quite nicely."

"Fair enough. So I guess the plan is to get to the God Machine, reset you to level 1, bump you back up to . . . I don't know. Level 10? 15? Something like that, and send you back to wherever you want to be?"

"More or less," Zea said.

A few months ago, their plans had been much more nebulous. Luke didn't even know for sure if Zea was going to accompany him across the ocean, and he wouldn't have blamed her if they'd parted ways back in Sicanti. She'd decided to commit to the journey, and at this point, they were only a few months from ending it.

That was largely thanks to her. He didn't think he would be even half as far as he was if he'd been on his own. Hell, without Zea, he most likely would have died in an inquisitor cell back in Valtira. No one else in his family had made it to the God Machine, though to be fair, he didn't know for sure if they'd all been trying. Curt hadn't even made it out of Tenebrous Valley. There was no telling what goals his other family members had been working on.

"I wonder if the people on the other sides of these walls think we're crazy," Luke mused. They'd kept the conversation quiet, but anyone with a perception over 15 or 20 would still have been able to hear what to them would sound like Luke talking to himself for half an hour.

"Eh, who cares? We'll be back on the road tomorrow anyway since you shot down sailing."

"I suppose that's true."

Zea scooted across the bed and snuggled close to Luke. "If anyone is listening," she whispered, "we might as well give them something to listen to."

Luke snorted. "Maybe if you take off that cloak first."

Zea's seductive look transformed into a pout. "I like my cloak! It keeps me warm."

"I thought that was my job," Luke said.

"It was, and then I enchanted my cloak. Now I don't need you for that anymore."

"Is that so?" Luke said. "I guess I'd better work extra hard at all those other things I'm good for before you decide to enchant something else to replace me there too."

"Yes, you should," she told him quite seriously.

They were out of the city before the sun rose, much to Zea's annoyance. Neither of them really needed the sleep anymore; Luke could and had gone multiple days in a row without sleeping and then been fine to keep going after an hour-long nap. As much as Zea wanted to sleep ten hours a day, it wasn't necessary, and this time, Luke stood his ground about getting moving instead of lazing in bed.

"I know we're on another continent and all," Luke said as they walked, "but things look surprisingly different. Different trees. Different animals. Even different-colored grass. The houses all look different. The roads look different. The people look different. Okay, I guess that last one was expected."

"All of them should have been expected," Zea muttered darkly as she stomped along next to Luke.

"I know for a fact that your stamina is 27, that you can go two days without sleep, and it won't even slow you down. How is it that you're this grumpy after getting a full six hours?"

"That's my prerogative," Zea told him.

"Fine, fine. I get it." They kept walking in silence for another thirty seconds. "You know what hasn't changed though?"

"What's that?" Zea asked tiredly.

"Bandits. Fucking bandits everywhere you go."

"Huh?"

Luke pointed down the road. "See that tree dropped across the road a mile away?"

Zea squinted and followed Luke's finger with her eyes. "Eeehh. Maybe? Not saying you're wrong, but your perception is over twice as high as mine."

"It's there. What do you think the odds are that a tree came down on this road that's wide enough for wagons and goes directly into a major port city? I mean, Naldrin is barely ten miles back."

"Stupid bandits to do it so close to the city," Zea said.

"I suppose I could be wrong, but it seems pretty suspicious to me."

A few minutes later, they approached the tree. A single glance was enough to confirm that it had been dropped by an ax. "Knew it," Luke said. He stopped next to the trunk and looked around, then laughed and waved at a wide-eyed man hiding in a tree a hundred feet around the road. "There's their spotter."

"Uh, should we be doing something about that?" Zea asked.

Luke shrugged. "You think they'll try to attack us?"

[Analyze] put the man at level 18, which was respectable but not dangerous to Luke. Most of his skills were only rank 2 or 3 as well. There could very well be stronger people in the band, but by the time the spotter was able to fetch them, Luke and Zea would be long gone.

He reached down with both hands, grabbed the tree right at the end, and heaved. It shifted in place, and branches started snapping as he hauled it off to one side. "There, see. Road's clear. We can be on our way."

They glanced over at the spotter as they walked by. The man had some sort of green-and-black mask and a cloak to help him blend in, but **[Detection]** drew Luke's eyes right to him. He watched them go silently, probably confused about the lack of XP he felt from them.

"You think they'll come after us?" Zea asked.

Luke shrugged. "Let them. I'm not going to go out of my way, but I'll put them down if they try."

"Funny. I remember you having a very different attitude the last time we ran into bandits," Zea said.

"Well that was a different situation. We needed XP and money, and I was concerned about your safety," Luke told her. "Now, they're a nuisance that I'll take care of if I have to, but I'm not going to waste a few hours hunting them down for no real gain."

Zea considered that for a few seconds, then shrugged. "Okay, fair enough. We probably should get a move on at least. They might be annoyed about you hauling that tree out of the way."

"I suppose that's true. Plus it's not like it's a bad thing to get to the next stop sooner. System said we're going to be on this road for about seven hundred miles, so I figure a bit over a week as long as we don't get sidetracked."

"Come on, when do we ever not get sidetracked?"

"It doesn't *always* happen," Luke said.

"Ten gold says those bandits come after us."

Luke was about to respond when he caught some movement out of his peripheral vision. "No bet," he told her as he reached for the mace hanging off his back.

Name	Luke Bennet	Zea Stenter
Level	42	35
XP	255178/273479	14001/157276
AP	37	4
Bloodline	SysAdmin III	None
Strength	61	7
Agility	70	30
Stamina	66	27
Perception	55	21
Skills	Butchering (4)	Arcano Dynamics (2)
	Consortium Standard (1)	Bartering (2)
	Counter (3)	Bloodline Purification Ritual (2)
	Deception (1)	Cadence (3)
	Detection (2)	Cold Reading (1)
	Disguise (2)	Consortium Standard (1)
	First Aid (1)	Cooking (1)
	Leatherworking (2)	Dagger Mastery (1)
	Life Surge (2)	Deception (1)
	Mace Mastery (5)	Disguise (2)
	Ostari (1)	Engraving (4)
	Peripheral Awareness (2)	First Aid (1)
	Power Strike (2)	Gem Cutting (1)
	Stealth (1)	Ghost Script (1)
	Survivalist (2)	Goldsmithing (2)
	Sword Mastery (1)	Keen Instincts (1)
	Tactical Foresight (2)	Lock Picking (1)
	Thalian (2)	Mana Manipulation (3)
	Torturer (1)	Mana Sight (3)
	Twitch Reflexes (3)	Mending (1)
	Unarmed Martialist (4)	Metallurgy (1)
	Wood Carving (1)	Neyardic (3)
	Analyze (BL)	Ostari (1)
	Remote Access (BL)	Painting (1)
	XP Mask (BL)	Rune Forging (3)
		Sleight of Hand (1)
		Steady Hands (2)
		Stealth (2)
		Streetwise (2)
		Temperature Acclimation (2)
		Thalian (3)
		Whitesmithing (1)

CHAPTER 5

Two people stepped out of the bushes. Both had the silver-white hair Luke was seeing everywhere now, and both were well armed. Luke counted four swords between the two of them plus a pair of belt knives. One of them had a sheath strapped to his leg with another knife, and the other had her hair up with a pair of what looked like needle-sharp stilettos.

[**Analyze**] told him they were levels 37 and 35 with a bunch of combat, survival, and tracking skills, both strong enough to be a threat, names of Ruca and Val. Both of them tracked his hand movement to his mace, and the man held his hands up. He said something that Luke couldn't understand, then, seeing the look on Luke's face, tried again in Standard.

"Peace, friend. We're not here for a fight, not with you."

"Bandits sure are picky on this side of the world," Luke said.

"Maybe they're just smarter over here," Zea replied.

"Maybe we're not bandits," the strange woman said, her voice sharp.

Luke gestured back down the road toward the downed tree he'd moved. "Explain that?"

"That's not meant to waylay travelers. It's for a caravan with a load of . . . human cargo," the man said.

Luke could see Zea's sudden scowl in his peripheral vision. "You trust your bowels to a neighbor's latrine?" she asked incredulously.

The two silver-haired natives blinked at her and then started speaking in rapidly in what Luke assumed was Eledarn. "Uh," Luke said, switching back to Thalian, "I don't think you said whatever you were trying to say."

"I said, 'You're pretty trusting to just tell a couple strangers all of this.' Why? What did you hear?" Zea asked.

"Um. Not that. Maybe I should pick up rank 2 of **[Consortium Standard]** and do the talking for now."

"Ugh, yeah. Probably a good idea. I'll have to rank it up again. Wait, what am I saying? You've infected me with your XP-based solutions to all your problems."

Luke took a few seconds to navigate the skill store in his system menu and spent 15 AP on the language upgrade, then said, "Sorry, my friend here is still only at rank 1 with the language. She was trying to ask why you trusted a couple of strangers with this information."

Val frowned and asked him, "Did you just spend AP on a language skill? That's ridiculously wasteful."

Luke shrugged. "I'm in a hurry. I had some AP to spare."

"The better question is how you have any AP at all," Ruca said. "You don't feel like you have any aura. I've met toddlers with more power than you. That's actually part of the reason we came out to meet you."

"To interrogate me about my skill usage?" Luke asked. "We haven't even been introduced and you think I'm going to share a piece of my build with you?"

"No, no, of course not," Ruca said. "We came to make sure you aren't demons."

"Why would you think we're demons?"

"Strange monsters have been appearing lately, far to the south. Rumors have just recently reached this province, rumors that say that the creatures look like monsters, but they are not. They are not part of the system, either. They have no XP, and you are rewarded with none when you kill them."

Luke glanced over at Zea, who just shrugged back. There'd only been one enemy on the entire planet Luke had encountered that the system hadn't given him XP for killing, and they were pretty sure that had been the direct result of divine intervention turning Adrevald Lath into a member of the walking dead. Undead and demons weren't the same thing in Luke's mind, but it was possible there was a translation problem.

"What do the demons look like?" Luke asked. He assumed they were shaped like people, since the two not bandits thought he and Zea could be a pair of them.

"All sorts of things, if the stories are to be believed. Some are small, barely the size of your head. Others are big as houses. They come in every shape and size imaginable and with a lot of strange abilities, things our own skills have no parallels for. The only thing that's consistent about them is that the system doesn't acknowledge when they die."

"What even the fuck is going on over here?" Luke asked softly.

"Do you think . . ." Zea trailed off, but Luke didn't need her to say it. It was entirely possible this was more bullshit from the Pantheon, but if so, it was really widespread. Their previous approaches had been far more targeted. Then again, all their attempts to kill Luke on the western continent had failed, so maybe they'd opted for a new strategy this time.

"Well, I hope you're convinced we're not demons," Luke told the two not bandits. "Good luck with your liberating of the slaves. We've got places to be and people to see, so we'll be going now."

"Hmm. Yes, we've got our own work to see to as well. Someone has moved our tree out of place. If only that person would be so kind as to put things back the way he found them."

Luke glanced back at the tree, already a mile behind him. He could go back and put it into position, but that would leave him open to an ambush. More importantly, it would leave Zea vulnerable to an attack, and she was not strong enough to fend off either of these two people. "I'm sure your group can handle it. You got it there once already."

Val scowled at him, but Ruca nodded. "I understand. Smart of you not to trust strangers. We'll leave you to your travels. Best of luck."

"You as well. Thanks for the warning about demons."

The two pair split there, with the not bandits going back toward their ambush site while Luke and Zea kept running south. After a few miles had gone by, Luke said, "System, tell me about these demons. Is this the Pantheon's doing?"

"I'm afraid I don't have any information on this subject," System said, appearing out of nothing and floating through the air to keep pace when Luke. "If such creatures do exist, they are not part of the God Machine's system, and thus, I have no authority over them. I can confirm that there have been a high number of deaths on this continent that led to full XP being returned to the God Machine without any going to another creature."

"Does that happen often?" Zea asked.

"It is not infrequent. Usually it's seen in accidental deaths, sickness, or old age. The number of creatures dying with no apparent cause has increased a thousandfold in the last two months."

"Shit. So people are dying in droves, rumors are there's demons roaming around, and they've got no system connection, just like Lath. Divine bullshit again."

"I am not able to speculate on the actions or motivations of the Pantheon," System said, for probably the hundredth time. Some things never changed.

"We should assume this demon outbreak is relevant to us," Zea said. "They could be actively hunting us, either individually or cooperatively."

"That would suck. How many do you think there are?"

"Hundreds? Thousands? Maybe more." Zea frowned. "Numbers are less important than individual levels. Or not levels but whatever their equivalent is. You know what I mean."

"Right, but we have no way to measure that. **[Analyze]** didn't work on Lath after he got disconnected from the system or whatever it was."

"Other bloodline abilities might not work either. Most of them revolve around controlling the target through its connection to the system," Zea said.

Luke came to such an abrupt stop that he almost tripped. "Shit. I don't even have the level-reset skill yet, and it's already useless."

"Not useless. It would work against everything that's not one of these demon monsters. Who knows how many problems you can just blink away with that skill?"

"200 AP would go a long way toward increasing my stats, maybe putting some skills together into advanced versions, which would probably help a lot more against the demons. Whether they exist outside the system or not, I'm pretty sure if I beat one to a pulp, it'll still die."

"We're getting a little ahead of the cart," Zea said. "We don't know how much of a threat these demons are. All we've got are some rumors from two people lying about not being bandits. These things might not even be real, and if they are, maybe they're the equivalent of a level 20 monster."

"Maybe," Luke said. "But System did say there were a bunch of dead people, way more than usual. Even if those guys are wrong about the demons, there's still something going on."

The two started moving again. Their plan was to cover about a hundred miles on the road before the end of the day, but Luke was secretly hoping to get farther. Now that he knew there was a threat in their way, he was eager to cut their travel time as much as possible. He suspected he was going to need those extra days to hunt monsters.

Without knowing how strong he needed to be, the only solution was to put on as much XP as possible. Some of the AP would need to go to **[XP Cycle]**, but after that, the more he spent on raw stats and skills, the better. For all he knew, the demons out there could kill level 100s.

Actually, now that he thought about it, that was a good question. "System, what's the highest-level person who died without any of their XP going to anyone else?"

"Level 70," System said immediately.

"Can you tell me how that person died?"

"Apologies, but I cannot."

"Damn. Well, probably safe to assume it was either XP madness or a demon," Luke said.

"How could someone even survive at level 70?" Zea asked.

"I mean, XP madness doesn't kill a person," Luke said. "It just makes them go crazy, and then someone else has to kill them. If you made it to level 70, especially if you were a combat specialist, it wouldn't be easy for anyone to put you down."

"There's no use speculating," Zea said. "We don't know if their death was demon related. If it was, then no matter what we do, we're fucked. Anything strong enough to kill a level 70 is going to be way beyond us. The only thing to do is stay away from it."

"Not easy to do if we don't know where—wait, there's something on the road."

They slowed to a stop, and Luke peered ahead. The road curved around a screen of trees a mile away, but something long and red moved there. The gaps between the branches were small, making it hard to get a good picture of what he was seeing. It had a bunch of segments, and it wasn't until the wind blew the smell into his face that he understood what he was seeing.

"Horses. Wagons. People," Luke said.

"Do you think it's the caravan our new bandit friends are waiting for?" Zea asked. It wasn't hard to read her expression and know that she didn't care for the idea of a slaver wagon train.

"I don't know. Better question is, if it is, should we do something about it?"

"*Can* we do anything about it? We'd be legally in the wrong, but let's say we ignore that. How strong are the guards? Is it physically possible for us to take them out? If we can, do we have the ability to take care of the slaves?"

"Why would we need to take care of them?" Luke asked.

"Slaves are usually kept in bad shape when they're being transported. Dehydrated. Starved. Sometimes deliberately made sick. It reduces the chances of having successful runaways."

Luke gave her an incredulous look. "Your world is really fucked up, you know that?"

Zea shrugged. "As an escaped slave myself, I'm inclined to agree. But to get back to the question, if it is a slave caravan, what do we do about it?"

"I don't know. I guess we should get more information first. Let's go scout it out."

Name	Luke Bennet	Zea Stenter
Level	42	35
XP	255178/273479	14001/157276
AP	22	4
Bloodline	SysAdmin III	None
Strength	61	7
Agility	70	30
Stamina	66	27
Perception	55	21
Skills	Butchering (4)	Arcano Dynamics (2)
	Consortium Standard (2)	Bartering (2)
	Counter (3)	Bloodline Purification Ritual (2)
	Deception (1)	Cadence (3)
	Detection (2)	Cold Reading (1)
	Disguise (2)	Consortium Standard (1)
	First Aid (1)	Cooking (1)
	Leatherworking (2)	Dagger Mastery (1)
	Life Surge (2)	Deception (1)
	Mace Mastery (5)	Disguise (2)
	Ostari (1)	Engraving (4)
	Peripheral Awareness (2)	First Aid (1)
	Power Strike (2)	Gem Cutting (1)
	Stealth (1)	Ghost Script (1)
	Survivalist (2)	Goldsmithing (2)
	Sword Mastery (1)	Keen Instincts (1)
	Tactical Foresight (2)	Lock Picking (1)
	Thalian (2)	Mana Manipulation (3)
	Torturer (1)	Mana Sight (3)
	Twitch Reflexes (3)	Mending (1)
	Unarmed Martialist (4)	Metallurgy (1)
	Wood Carving (1)	Neyardic (3)
	Analyze (BL)	Ostari (1)
	Remote Access (BL)	Painting (1)
	XP Mask (BL)	Rune Forging (3)
		Sleight of Hand (1)
		Steady Hands (2)
		Stealth (2)
		Streetwise (2)
		Temperature Acclimation (2)
		Thalian (3)
		Whitesmithing (1)

CHAPTER 6

The caravan consisted of twelve wagons. The one in the lead was completely enclosed, more like a huge, overgrown carriage than a wagon, with two men sitting on the bench in the front. The next two were the ones Luke pictured whenever anyone said words like *pioneer* or *prairie*, the ones with canvas stretched around ribs to make a kind of roof, with the oval-shaped opening on the back end. Supply wagons.

The remaining eight were something completely different. They were more like giant wooden crates on wheels, sealed up except for six-inch-wide slats going across the sides near the bottoms. Luke could see feet and ankles, dirty and crusted with filth, through those slats. Stains running down the wood and across the wheels told him exactly how often the human cargo was let out. Considering there were no doors on any of sort on a single one of those wagons, it wasn't hard to picture excrement being pushed out of those slats. Or food being passed in.

The slaves had been literally boxed up like freight, transported in conditions that would make anyone sick as a deliberate tactic to work against any stats they might have. Luke counted over a hundred feet in those eight prison wagons, and considering how wide each one was, he doubled his estimate. Even then, he wouldn't be surprised if he was still too low. There wouldn't be enough room for anyone to do more than sit down and huddle upright when they tried to sleep.

It was torture. Luke knew because his skill told him so. **[Torturer]** was listing out all the benefits to putting a bunch of people in a situation like that, everything from sleep deprivation to malnourishment to various foodborne illnesses that most likely resulted in dehydration and weakness. The fact that the skill thought of those as benefits left a bad taste in Luke's mouth, but it did mean he knew exactly what kinds of problems he was looking at when he broke those wheeled crates open and let everyone out.

Getting to that point was a different issue. Each slave wagon had four guards perched on top, all armed with crossbows. Each wagon had a driver, and five more guards on horseback rode near the front wagon, the one that looked like an oversize carriage. Each of those guards had a bow on their back and a full quiver on their waist.

"Forty people," Luke said. "Most of them are between levels 15 and 25, but those guys riding the horses are all over level 30. That one on the front wagon next to the driver is level 42."

"I bet the caravan master is inside that front wagon. He could be high level too," Zea added, pointing to the carriage-style wagon.

"I hate to say it, but we might be in over our heads with this one," Luke said. The easiest thing for them to do would be to just get off the road and let the caravan pass them by. Legally speaking, they would be committing banditry if they attacked the slavers, and their appearances were so distinctive that unless they killed literally everyone who wasn't a slave, it was practically guaranteed to cause problems.

Hell, even the slaves might talk about who rescued them and inadvertently give the authorities descriptions. Or they might get recaptured and the infor-mation forced out of them. Pulling the hood up on his cloak wasn't going to make it less obvious that Luke was three to six inches taller than just about everyone he'd met since the ship had docked.

The smart thing to do was to walk away. As shitty as the situation was, it had nothing to do with them, and Luke wasn't thrilled with the idea of close to forty people shooting at him all at once anyway. Most of the guards would do minimal damage at best, probably less than that if this enchanted chain worked as advertised. Between his very real armor and that magic barrier, he might just be able to rush through a cloud of crossbow bolts while they bounced off him.

Then again, he might not. It was just as easy to picture himself making it ten feet before he fell over, writhing in pain while he bled out from a few dozen holes as it was to picture himself leaping on top of the slave wagons and laying people out left and right.

There were also the ethical considerations. Slavery was legal. The guards were just doing their jobs. It didn't even mean they supported slavery, though likely they hadn't given it much thought. He was viewing that from his own position as a person raised in a society where slavery was very much consid-ered a bad thing, and anyone who actively supported it was a bad person by association.

The whole thing made his head hurt. He'd liked it better when he didn't think so much about stuff. Luke from six months ago would have spared a moment to consider his approach, then charged in. On the other hand, that Luke would have undoubtedly died if he'd tried it.

As much as Luke wanted to bust open those boxes full of suffering, he didn't think it was possible, and certainly not without causing himself a lot of problems down the road even if they were successful. He was under no illusions that, assuming a successful assault, the guards would all stand around waiting for him to kill them instead of running for their lives.

There were good reasons to attack. There were good reasons to stay out of it. Luke wanted to help the slaves, but he didn't think he could. He glanced over at Zea and opened his mouth to say that they should get away from the road until the caravan was past them, then he noticed her rubbing at the slave mark tattooed behind her ear. He wondered if she'd ever ridden in a prison wagon like that.

"Looks like the bandits were telling the truth," he said instead.

"Looks like," she agreed.

"You think they know what they're getting into? Three's not a lot to take on this many guards."

"Probably more of them back in the trees."

Luke nodded. "Possibly. I wonder if they know how big the caravan is. We could go back and tell them. Or . . . Go back and help."

"How fast could you get back there if you went ahead?" Zea asked.

"Five miles or so, if I went as fast as I could? A few minutes. But where are you going to go?"

"I'll follow behind, be maybe ten minutes later catching up. I'll still beat that caravan, and those guys are probably going to need every advantage they can get to fight a caravan this big."

Luke glanced back at the caravan, still a ways down the road and moving slowly. "Are you sure you want to get involved?" he asked.

"I know it's going to make things harder for us," she said. "And not just missing a few hours or a day. Even if things go well, this is probably going to come back around to bite us in the ass. But . . . Look at them. I can see those feet in there. I know you can too. Who has ever deserved something like that?"

"I agree with you," Luke said. "It's not right. I hope every one of those slaves is freed, but at the same time, that's an awful tough nut to crack. Even if we manage it, do you think those guys have food and shelter for . . . What? A hundred people? Hundred fifty?"

"Better than the alternative," Zea said.

Luke nodded. "Suppose so. Alright, follow as fast as you can."

And he took off running back north.

* * *

The tree was more or less back in place, though it was half-diagonal across the road instead of across like it had been before Luke moved it. The guy watching the road was still there, and when he caught sight of Luke, he flinched so hard he almost fell out of the tree. Luke tossed a quick **[Analyze]** on him again, just because he couldn't quite remember the guy's name. The system was happy to tell him it was Wilby.

By the time Luke got over to him, Wilby had caught his balance and managed to climb down to the ground. "You okay there, man?"

"Yeah . . . Fine. Fuck, you're fast." Wilby shook his head. "Did you forget something?"

"No, just backtracked to tell you guys that your caravan is on its way in. It's five miles or so south of here. So, like, you know, you guys should get all your bandits together and get ready to hit it. There are about forty guards that I counted, plus I wouldn't put it past the wagon drivers to pull out a crossbow and take a shot at you."

"Forty?" Wilby repeated, his face going pale. "Fuck me. Shit. That's way too many."

"Thought it might be. We've got an hour, maybe an hour and a half, before they're here. You want to gather up your people and I'll lay out what the caravan looks like for you?"

Wilby let out a shrill whistle, and a moment later, a second one answered it. About two minutes after that, the pair from earlier appeared. Ruca raised an eyebrow at Luke but didn't say anything.

"This guy says he spotted the caravan. Forty guards," Wilby said in Consortium Standard, probably for Luke's sake.

Val let out a string of curses, shifting through at least three different languages and lasting long enough that Ruca pushed past her and asked, "Are you sure?"

"Counted them myself," Luke said. "Hope you've got at least twenty guys over level 25 and ready to throw down with the regular guards because there were five guys riding horses all over level 30 and one guy at level 42."

The volume of swearing coming from Val started rising. Ruca glanced at her and said one word in the language Luke didn't know, and she cut off midtirade. He turned back to Luke and said, "It's just us."

"What do you mean, 'just us'?" Luke asked. "Please tell me there are more than just the three of you."

Ruca grimaced, and Wilby stared at the ground. Val gave him a glare. None of them spoke.

"Fuck," Luke said. "How the hell did you think three people were going to be enough to stop a caravan. I mean, shit, this guy's only level 18!"

"We didn't think it would be this well defended," Ruca admitted.

"Well I suggest you reconsider your plans. Three of you are not enough to take out this group."

"Not an option," Val said immediately.

"They have her family," Ruca added, seeing Luke's surprised look.

"Shiiiiiiiitt," Luke said. He'd been counting on them having the man power to even the odds. If Luke fought the high-level guy one-on-one, he thought he could win. If that guy had thirty people backing him up, it wasn't long odds, it was suicide. There was no winning this with a group this small, even if most of them were high level.

"Someone's coming," Wilby said.

"She's with me," Luke told him, not even bothering to glance down the road. He could see Zea running along as fast as her legs could carry her. He was actually a bit surprised she'd caught up that fast. Within a minute or so, she came to a stop next to the four of them.

"You told them already?" she asked in Thalian.

"I did."

"And their band is getting into position?"

Luke shook his head. "It's just these three."

Zea's head whipped around to look at the three not bandits. "Are you fucking stupid?" she asked them.

"Hey!" Val took a step forward, only to have Ruca put a hand on her shoulder.

"Her family is in one of those wagons," Luke said.

"Oh." Zea looked around. "Shit."

"That's what I said. I don't suppose you've got anything in your bag of wonders to help."

"Against that many people?" she asked, incredulous.

"If we can blow up the lead wagon with all the higher-level guards around it, we might be able to handle the rest," Luke said.

"Might work," Zea agreed with a sigh. "Still risky. Let me see what I have."

Name	Luke Bennet	Zea Stenter
Level	42	35
XP	255178/273479	14001/157276
AP	22	4
Bloodline	SysAdmin III	None
Strength	61	7
Agility	70	30
Stamina	66	27
Perception	55	21
Skills	Butchering (4)	Arcano Dynamics (2)
	Consortium Standard (2)	Bartering (2)
	Counter (3)	Bloodline Purification Ritual (2)
	Deception (1)	Cadence (3)
	Detection (2)	Cold Reading (1)
	Disguise (2)	Consortium Standard (1)
	First Aid (1)	Cooking (1)
	Leatherworking (2)	Dagger Mastery (1)
	Life Surge (2)	Deception (1)
	Mace Mastery (5)	Disguise (2)
	Ostari (1)	Engraving (4)
	Peripheral Awareness (2)	First Aid (1)
	Power Strike (2)	Gem Cutting (1)
	Stealth (1)	Ghost Script (1)
	Survivalist (2)	Goldsmithing (2)
	Sword Mastery (1)	Keen Instincts (1)
	Tactical Foresight (2)	Lock Picking (1)
	Thalian (2)	Mana Manipulation (3)
	Torturer (1)	Mana Sight (3)
	Twitch Reflexes (3)	Mending (1)
	Unarmed Martialist (4)	Metallurgy (1)
	Wood Carving (1)	Neyardic (3)
	Analyze (BL)	Ostari (1)
	Remote Access (BL)	Painting (1)
	XP Mask (BL)	Rune Forging (3)
		Sleight of Hand (1)
		Steady Hands (2)
		Stealth (2)
		Streetwise (2)
		Temperature Acclimation (2)
		Thalian (3)
		Whitesmithing (1)

CHAPTER 7

Ruca watched, his hands clenched tightly around the hilts of his swords, as the slave caravan approached. The mounted guards at the front caught sight of the tree and called a halt well back from it. Ruca silently cursed as the front wagon came to a stop a few hundred feet away. The tree-over-the-road trick always worked in the stories, but in this case, they'd have been better off with nothing. The timing might have been tighter, but they were few enough in number that they probably could have done just fine. It wasn't like it took a lot of work to organize just a handful of people.

"Told you," Val mouthed silently. He scowled back at her, but his heart wasn't in it. They'd been expecting one or two wagons, maybe ten guards. Not this. Ruca knew he could take just about anyone in a duel but not while a few dozen other people shot crossbows at him. They were completely fucked unless the strangers came up with something.

Val wasn't going to walk away though, not with her sister in one of those wagons. They were just hoping her parents and her nephew were in there too. The alternative was that they'd been killed. Unfortunately, the refugee they'd spoken with outside of Kanna had only seen what had happened to Tirana, not anyone else.

It had been nothing short of pure, unadulterated luck that they'd managed to figure out who'd attacked Kanna and taken slaves, tracked them to the next province over, and determined which slave caravan Val's sister was on. It would be a minor miracle if her whole family was here and a full-blown one if they managed to survive raiding the caravan to find out.

The guards were making no effort to mask their presence, and Ruca could feel the power emanating from them. The only one who could match him was the man seated at the very front of the caravan, the one with a thin sword sheathed and leaning up against his shoulder and a shield on the bench next to him.

In reality, however, what he expected to happen was his opponent to shift their battle to put Ruca's back to the crossbowmen on the other wagons, who would promptly put dozens of bolts into him. Neither of them had an answer to that, and Wilby couldn't possibly outshoot that many enemies. Ruca had no doubt he'd get four or five, but they'd shoot back, and the slave wagons would make for better cover than some tree branches anyway.

Then there were the foreigners. It was only the fact that they *were* foreign that made him trust them even slightly. It was clear they were fresh off the boat, so much so that one of them had actually wasted 15 AP just upgrading a language skill. That didn't do much to inspire a lot of confidence in their competence, but any damage they did was another distraction that would keep the people Ruca actually cared about alive for a few more seconds.

"What's the plan?" Val whispered.

"Wait for them to move the tree, attack whomever they send to do it. Once the real fight starts, we need to take out the ranged combatants first. I'll hold off the ones on the horses, you start breaking open wagons. Hopefully most of the prisoners will still be strong enough to run for it."

It was a simple plan with a lot that could go wrong. It was also the best he had. Wilby was on the other side of the road, near the tree itself. His part wouldn't change, as long as he kept his nerve. He'd always been a bit squirrelly, but he'd invested heavily into perception and tracking skills, and since he was from Kanna too, it was hard to deny him a place beside them.

"Come on, come on. Do something already," Ruca muttered. The guards were all hanging back, none of them willing to walk into the obvious trap. Smart of them, but someone was going to have to move into the kill zone eventually. They were far enough back that he couldn't make out the conversation, but he suspected they were busy arguing about who exactly it was that would be doing that.

"Wait," Val said. "Did they have spare mounts?"

She pointed, and Ruca saw a horse tied to the lead wagon with no rider. He counted their numbers and said, "Shit, one of them disappeared."

"Counterambush?"

"Probably."

This was all falling apart, and they hadn't even started fighting yet.

"Sure was nice of them to deliver someone to us," Luke said, standing over the dead body of one formerly stealthy guard. He'd been expecting something like this when he'd noticed that this one's skill set was nothing like the rest of the guards. He had too many ranks in **[Stealth]**, **[Tracking]**, **[Assassination]**, **[Torturer]**, and **[Deception]**. Whatever this guy did for a living, guarding a slave caravan was outside his normal line of work.

"You think they'll send out another one?" Zea asked.

"Nah. This was the only guy I saw with the skill set for stalking people through the woods and killing them. I think they're relying on him to pick us off one by one."

"How do you want to play it then?"

Luke considered the caravan for a moment. "Doesn't look like they're going to take the bait. Too bad about them not getting close enough to set off those bombs. Circle around from the back and start taking out the assholes with the crossbows? If I burn **[Life Surge]** right at the start, I bet I can kill at least two groups before they even start shooting."

"Yeah, and then the other six will kill you."

Luke patted the enchanted chain he was wearing like an oversize belt. "This'll keep me safe, right?"

"Uh . . . Probably not," Zea said. "I mean, sure, it absolutely will for the first ten or twenty shots, and then it'll start to degrade rapidly. Depending on how good their aim is, it might not even last through the opening salvo."

"Oh. I thought it would be stronger."

It wasn't like he'd expected to just charge into an army head-on and be completely invincible. He hadn't even really thought it would last this entire fight, but he figured he could take out two or three wagons before it gave out.

Honestly, as long as the high-level guards around the first wagon were busy elsewhere and there wasn't some dude who was level 50 lurking inside it, Luke was confident he could clear all the crossbow-wielding guards off the tops of the slave wagons. The great thing about crossbows was that it didn't matter how much strength the guys holding them had. Agility might help them land a hit, but the damage was always going to be predictable, and Luke knew he could take it. He just needed to protect his face from lucky shots.

Of course, the high-level guards weren't being taken out. The ambush had failed simply because they hadn't placed the bombs far enough back. All they could do at this point was wait for the wagons to start rolling forward again, which didn't look like it was going to happen anytime soon.

They waited twenty minutes before someone in the caravan finally got impatient. Two of the guards with the highest strength stats rode up to the tree and dismounted while two more covered them with drawn bows. Unfortunately, at no point in time did they get close enough for all four of them to be caught in the blast, and the highest-level guy they really wanted never left the caravan.

"Want me to take them out? Two's better than nothing," Zea said.

"Seems kind of wasteful. Think you could get both of them with just one?"

"Hmm. If that guy takes two steps to the right, I can."

"Okay," Luke said. "I'm going to head for the back of the caravan. Give me thirty seconds before you set one or both bombs off. I'll use them as a distraction."

"Got it. Good luck. Don't push it if they all focus on you. Do what you can and get back behind cover."

Luke nodded and set off at a jog. He wove through the trees, probably visible if anyone with high perception happened to be looking in the right spot, but there were only three or four guys in the whole caravan with the raw stats, and he was hoping his lack of XP presence would keep any of them from even glancing his way. The not bandits weren't doing much to hide their own XP and should serve as attention bait for him.

He was halfway there when he heard the twang of a bowstring and one of the guards yelling out in surprise. Something heavy hit the ground, presumably the body of one of the two guards who'd been tasked with moving the tree. Immediately, a chorus of cries came up from the caravan.

Luke cursed silently. That was not the distraction he needed to get close. Hopefully, Zea would still be able to draw some attention with one of the bombs. He'd wanted to be on top of the wagon and killing the first four guards before anyone realized what was happening.

Luke reached a spot where he'd have a good angle to rush the back wagon, but the guards were all alert and looking around now. Of course, the trees were the only place to hide, so more than a few were watching for someone to emerge. Wilby had completely ruined the element of surprise.

Then the bombs went off. Everybody turned to look at that, and Luke couldn't blame them. Loose dirt went fifty feet straight up, and the concussive force stripped a chunk of branches on the fallen tree bare. A body arced up with the explosion, maybe still alive. It was hard to tell.

[Analyze] came back with nothing, proof positive that whoever'd been hit was dead. Even figuring that out was more time than Luke should have spent looking. With a thought, he triggered **[Life Surge]** and took three great, bounding steps to clear the trees, then hurled himself a hundred feet through the air to land on top of the wagon.

Either it was less sturdy than it looked, or the force of the impact was greater than Luke had expected. Wood gave way under his feet as he landed in the middle of the group of guards, but he was too well coordinated for that to slow him down. His mace spun in a bloody arc, crushing the skulls of all four guards in less than a second and flinging their bodies to the dirt below.

He pulled himself free of the hole he'd made in the roof of the wagon and had a brief instant to see confused faces looking up at him before the smell hit him and made him gag. It had already been bad prior to his impromptu ventilation, but this was on a whole different level. As much as he wanted to heave his guts out, there were still seven wagons ahead of him that he needed to clear out, and some of the guards had noticed him.

He had at best two seconds before the first bolts were flying in his direction. [Tactical Foresight] pointed out which guards were quickest to aim their weapons, mostly those in the next wagon ahead of him. The ones near the front of the caravan were still looking at the crater left by the explosion, thankfully.

The one on the left in front of him was his next target. He was the calmest out of the four, smoothly bringing his crossbow around to aim at Luke while the other three scrambled to react to a threat from an unexpected direction. They wouldn't be fast enough to stop Luke.

The wagon wasn't stable ground, but the distance was only about twenty feet instead of a hundred. Luke crouched, then leaped to the next wagon.

Name	Luke Bennet	Zea Stenter
Level	42	35
XP	257714/273479	146232/157276
AP	22	4
Bloodline	SysAdmin III	None
Strength	61	7
Agility	70	30
Stamina	66	27
Perception	55	21
Skills	Butchering (4)	Arcano Dynamics (2)
	Consortium Standard (2)	Bartering (2)
	Counter (3)	Bloodline Purification Ritual (2)
	Deception (1)	Cadence (3)
	Detection (2)	Cold Reading (1)
	Disguise (2)	Consortium Standard (1)
	First Aid (1)	Cooking (1)
	Leatherworking (2)	Dagger Mastery (1)
	Life Surge (2)	Deception (1)
	Mace Mastery (5)	Disguise (2)
	Ostari (1)	Engraving (4)
	Peripheral Awareness (2)	First Aid (1)
	Power Strike (2)	Gem Cutting (1)
	Stealth (1)	Ghost Script (1)
	Survivalist (2)	Goldsmithing (2)
	Sword Mastery (1)	Keen Instincts (1)
	Tactical Foresight (2)	Lock Picking (1)
	Thalian (2)	Mana Manipulation (3)
	Torturer (1)	Mana Sight (3)
	Twitch Reflexes (3)	Mending (1)
	Unarmed Martialist (4)	Metallurgy (1)
	Wood Carving (1)	Neyardic (3)
	Analyze (BL)	Ostari (1)
	Remote Access (BL)	Painting (1)
	XP Mask (BL)	Rune Forging (3)
		Sleight of Hand (1)
		Steady Hands (2)
		Stealth (2)
		Streetwise (2)
		Temperature Acclimation (2)
		Thalian (3)
		Whitesmithing (1)

CHAPTER 8

There were countless skills in the system, including those that helped with crossbow use. The one that concerned Luke was called **[Rapid Reload]**, which helped the user pull new bolts, place them, and reset the crossbow far more quickly than they otherwise could. Between that and a decently high agility stat, it was easy to fire three or four bolts a second.

Roughly a third of the caravan guards had that skill, not that it would do them any good if they didn't already have their weapons pointed his way. Unfortunately, the one guard who was on the ball *did* have **[Rapid Reload]**, and he wasn't shy about using it. The first bolt pinged off the head of Luke's mace. The second one got swatted out of the air. The third one cracked against Luke's shoulder, deflected by either the armor itself or the enchanted chain Zea had given him. He wasn't entirely sure.

The fourth bolt went straight up, along with the crossbow itself and the guard's body. It had taken less than a second to leap from one wagon to the next, and though it would have been easier to smash the guard straight down, Luke had some concerns about injuring the slaves in the wagon under his feet. He opted for a vertical swing going upward instead, and a brief one-note ding in his mind confirmed that the blow had killed the guard.

That extra fraction of a second gave the other three guards an instant to retaliate, but they were too slow to hit Luke, especially when he was already within arm's reach. They had enough time to start yelling before he killed all three of them.

It didn't really seem fair. Luke was used to overpowering opponents through raw stats and a build focused almost exclusively on combat, but this was on a whole different level. It was like beating up toddlers. Most of them were barely half his level, and none of them had the durability to survive more than a single blow.

On the other hand, they did have numbers, and now that the rest of the guards were aware he was there, they took turns shooting at him. The ones on the next wagon dropped to a knee and started firing, and the ones behind them shot over their heads. By the time Luke got the triple ding of successful kills on the second wagon, there were dozens of bolts in the air heading his way.

He dove off the back side of the wagon just in time for the bolts to zip by overhead like a swarm of huge, angry hornets. Luke twisted as he fell to land on his feet, crouched down and facing the last wagon in the caravan. The driver stared back at him, wide-eyed and low to the ground with his arms held up to shield his head.

Luke took a beat to consider what to do. The driver was unarmed and making no attempt to change that. He was young, younger than Luke at least, and obviously terrified. The boy wasn't a threat, not right now. Luke could ignore him and continue his assault safely. But the boy was a driver for a slave caravan, and there was no pretending anyone didn't know what was inside those wagons. He'd knowingly helped transport more than a hundred people kept in conditions deliberately designed to leave them sickened and weak.

Luke had killed a lot of people since he'd arrived on Aros. The system even kept track for him every time he killed someone else. The number was over sixty now, which meant he was either a serial killer or a mass murderer; he wasn't sure which. He'd been able to justify every one of those kills. He was defending himself or attacking someone doing something evil like banditry. Even the mercs had been a military force trying to abduct him. He'd lost a little sleep over it, but all things considered, Luke thought he should feel a lot worse than he actually did about killing so many people.

He didn't know if this boy deserved to die. Was he complicit? Had he been coerced into helping? Did he even think he was doing something wrong? A lot of people used the law as a guide to morality, and slavery was allowed by law. Luke suspected there were some laws about how exactly those slaves were acquired that might have been violated here based on what Ruca and Val had told him about why they had to hit this particular caravan, but was this kid a part of that initial raid, or was he just someone who'd been hired to drive a wagon down a long stretch of road after the fact?

For that matter, how guilty where the eight guards he'd just killed, and was it his place to determine that? Luke had already established that he didn't care if he was legally in the wrong, but the whole thing reminded him of something Curt had gone on a long rant about once, something about the contractors on the Death Star. Luke had kind of always hated *Star Wars*, mostly because he'd gotten sick of all the jokes about his name very early on in his life, so he hadn't paid much attention.

He realized his mind was wandering and brought himself back to the present. The boy in front of him was no threat, and while Luke didn't know if the driver deserved to die, he did know it was a lot harder to bring someone back than it was to end their life. If he had the power, he'd capture all the guards and drivers instead of killing anyone.

But he didn't, and at the end of the day, he was making a conscious decision to kill the people preventing him from freeing the men and women trapped in the prison wagons. If the driver came after Luke, he would die. Until then, Luke would ignore him.

He just hoped the kid wouldn't suddenly discover his courage and put a bolt through the back of Luke's head.

The plan had been to clear the first three wagons before being driven back and forced to take cover, but they'd both acknowledged that pulling that off would be more luck than anything else. That was why they'd come up with phase two, though Zea had expressed some concerns about her ability to pull off her part.

It wasn't that far from the cover of the trees to the road the caravan was on. Luke could cross it in an instant, and he was strong enough that he'd literally leaped the gap. Zea had a strength of 7, which was still quite strong compared to what Luke considered a baseline human to be. He knew she could throw the distance; the question was whether she could do it quickly and accurately. She'd been doubtful, but Luke had faith in her.

That was why he was tracking her behind the trees, a feat done entirely by hearing and made far more difficult than it would have been if the guards would stop yelling. He knew she was in position and readying her ammunition. Any moment now, he would need an explosive burst of speed to make it up to the next wagon roof.

There! A dozen small stones flew through the air in a steady stream, hurled one at a time as hard as Zea could throw them. Their speed was abysmal, at least by Luke's current standards. More than a few of the guards noticed them and had time to avoid them, but better than half were struck by the magic rocks. The enchantments discharged, sending arcs of electricity out from the points of impact and locking up limbs long enough to give Luke an opening.

He jumped straight up and then forward. A few guards reflexively fired their crossbows, but Luke was anticipating that. His initial forward jump only took him about four feet across the top of the wagon before he landed, juked left, and jumped again. Only one guard on the next two wagons had managed to dodge Zea's bombardment and was fast enough to reload her crossbow.

Luke raised an arm to guard his face and felt the bolt skip off the metal gauntlet on his hand. His foot smacked into the back of the wagon, causing him to stagger forward a step when he landed, but now he was too close to be stopped by a crossbow. The woman who'd shot at him was the first to die, and only one other guard was in good enough condition to pull a shortsword to defend himself with. Luke killed him next, then dropped straight down when he heard the click of a crossbow behind him.

The driver of the second wagon was apparently much more proactive in defending the caravan than the one at the very back. Luke scooped up a dropped shortsword and hurled it down at the driver, who immediately adopted a panicked expression and tried to leap out of the way. He was far too slow, and even though Luke lacked any sort of weapon-throwing skill, he had plenty of strength for power and agility for accuracy. The weapon struck the driver hilt first with enough force to smash the man backward into the wagon. He crumbled down onto the bench and lay there, limp but alive.

Luke hadn't been trying to spare the driver's life. Unlike the boy from the first wagon, this guy had tried to kill him. It was only the man's good fortune and a decently high stamina stat that kept him from dying. If not for the other guards already recovering from Zea's attack, Luke would have jumped down and killed the driver. As it was, he barely had time to finish off the two guards on the roof with him.

Another wave of paralyzing stones came from the trees, but this time the guards were ready and started firing back. Zea cut her attack short as she ducked behind cover, but between the stones that hit and the guards splitting their attention, Luke had an opening to jump forward to the fourth wagon.

Unfortunately, they weren't just waiting for him to move up and slaughter them one group at a time. Fully half of the guards from the front half of the caravan were on the ground now, and he wasn't facing just one or two groups firing at him. Some of them had been drawn to the front of the caravan, where Ruca and Val were engaged in some sort of hit-and-run battle with the level 42 guard and a few of the ones on horseback, and that fight was going very poorly for the bandit side.

But that still left ten armed and alert guards who hadn't been disabled by Zea's enchanted stones or distracted trying to stop her. Luke wasn't going to get another opportunity to sneak up a wagon and dispatch more of them. Every inch of ground he claimed now was going to be soaked with blood, and a lot of it would be his.

He had his armor. He had Zea's chain. **[Life Surge]** was filling him with strength and speed. He had twenty levels on his opponents. The next few seconds were going to suck, no doubt about it, but he'd learned that in this world, absolute strength trumped numbers. Everyone who didn't break ranks and flee was going to die unless one of the horsemen circled back to get in Luke's way.

All he had to do was survive the next few volleys of bolts. He trusted in his preparations and in Zea's support in keeping them from overwhelming him. The air filled with bolts from the guards, most of whom had skills to fire two, or even three, before the first had reached Luke. He ran straight at them.

Name	Luke Bennet	Zea Stenter
Level	42	35
XP	260652/273479	146232/157276
AP	22	4
Bloodline	SysAdmin III	None
Strength	61	7
Agility	70	30
Stamina	66	27
Perception	55	21
Skills	Butchering (4)	Arcano Dynamics (2)
	Consortium Standard (2)	Bartering (2)
	Counter (3)	Bloodline Purification Ritual (2)
	Deception (1)	Cadence (3)
	Detection (2)	Cold Reading (1)
	Disguise (2)	Consortium Standard (1)
	First Aid (1)	Cooking (1)
	Leatherworking (2)	Dagger Mastery (1)
	Life Surge (2)	Deception (1)
	Mace Mastery (5)	Disguise (2)
	Ostari (1)	Engraving (4)
	Peripheral Awareness (2)	First Aid (1)
	Power Strike (2)	Gem Cutting (1)
	Stealth (1)	Ghost Script (1)
	Survivalist (2)	Goldsmithing (2)
	Sword Mastery (1)	Keen Instincts (1)
	Tactical Foresight (2)	Lock Picking (1)
	Thalian (2)	Mana Manipulation (3)
	Torturer (1)	Mana Sight (3)
	Twitch Reflexes (3)	Mending (1)
	Unarmed Martialist (4)	Metallurgy (1)
	Wood Carving (1)	Neyardic (3)
	Analyze (BL)	Ostari (1)
	Remote Access (BL)	Painting (1)
	XP Mask (BL)	Rune Forging (3)
		Sleight of Hand (1)
		Steady Hands (2)
		Stealth (2)
		Streetwise (2)
		Temperature Acclimation (2)
		Thalian (3)
		Whitesmithing (1)

CHAPTER 9

The chain's magic held through the volley of bolts, and Luke charged up the length of the caravan at top speed. Guards fell one after another, but Luke paid for the momentum. He couldn't dodge all the bolts, probably not even most of them, and he wasn't trying to. What he was doing was relying on his armor and Zea's skill at enchanting things to keep him safe, and he knew neither of those was foolproof.

He killed six guards in the few seconds he had to act with impunity, and the commotion he caused doing it drew the attention of even more of them. They weren't just holding their ground either. No, most of them were on the move, darting around wagons or running for the trees. Some were just trying to play tag with Luke, and he had to run them down or let them take free shots at him.

For the most part, the drivers ducked their heads and tried to stay out of the fight. Most of them realized immediately that Luke wasn't coming after them and did their best to stay out of his way. Some of them cowered on their benches with the reins still in their fists. Others scrambled to put the wagon between themselves and Luke. He noted one who even crawled under the wagon, which seemed like a stupid idea to him because horses were still animals, and those wagons were not remaining perfectly still, especially not if the fight got too close to them.

Things were proceeding more or less as expected until a stray bolt struck a horse in the flank. That set it off and caused its partner in the harness to panic with it. The two of them reared up and lunged forward, barely missing the wagon in front as they galloped off the road and away from the fighting. Unfortunately, while the horses cleared the gap, the wagon didn't. It crashed into the one in front of it and, perhaps aided by the horses still dragging it, bounced up onto two wheels and then tipped onto its side with a great crash.

Screams of pain and surprise came out of the slats on the sides of the wagon as the occupants were all thrown to one side and piled up on one another. If Luke hadn't been busy crushing the clavicle of a particularly boisterous guard who'd abandoned his crossbow in favor of trying to duel Luke with a sword, he would have flinched just from the sound alone. As it was, all the crash really did was highlight a need to start freeing the slaves soon. Even if the attack failed, some of them might still escape.

It was callous to think it, but it would also give the guards more targets to aim at. Luke was pretty sure the chain wrapped around his waist was about to fail, and he wouldn't be able to take every hit soon.

On the other hand, he was a little busy, and it wasn't like the wagons were designed to be opened. Each one was a fully sealed rectangular box made of thick wood and banded with steel. Luke was pretty sure the proper way to open them involved some sort of bolt cutter to snip the bands and a big fucking pry bar to take the back wall off like it was a giant crate. They did not look very smashable, not without seriously injuring the people inside.

Besides, when the one wagon had tipped over, Luke was pretty sure he'd heard chains rattling. If everyone was shackled together and to the wagon itself inside, it was going to be even harder to break the slaves free. The only way the bandits were going to have enough time to start freeing people was if all the guards were dead or captured, and killing was a lot easier than arresting.

Light sparked across the chain as runes flashed in a wave before going dark again. Luke was no expert, but he was pretty sure that meant he'd exhausted all the magic the chain had stored. That was confirmed a moment later when a bolt slammed into his pauldron and stuck there, its head an inch deep past the metal and lodged into his shoulder.

"Shit," Luke said. He'd lost count of how many guards he'd taken out, but the fight was about to get a lot more painful. He ripped the bolt out and cast it aside so that **[Life Surge]** could patch him up.

A quick glance around showed him twelve of the thirty-two guards still alive and willing to fight. Some might have fled, but he didn't think so. He'd also ended up killing three of the drivers, with the remaining nine either hiding or knocked out. Luke was past the point of going easy on them now.

Of the five horsemen, Luke had killed one in the forest, and it looked like two more had been killed fighting Ruca, Val, and Wilby. One of the remaining two was fighting with Val while the leader and Ruca crossed blades, and the final one was charging at Luke at full gallop, a heavy spear held in hand. There was still no sign of the caravan master, or whoever it was in the front carriage wagon.

Luke used **[Analyze]** on the horseman charging at him, just to refresh his memory. Level 20s were one thing, but a mistake against someone over level 30 could be decidedly more fatal. The man, Acrom Wellind according to the system, was level 34 and had invested rather heavily in strength and stamina, almost completely ignored his other two stats, and had a variety of skills that focused on staying power and the use of a variety of heavy weapons. Luke suspected he might be going for some advanced merger of his weapon skills but needed another ten levels of AP to get everything to come together.

There was also a throwing skill in Wellind's build. Considering the double-bladed battle-axe on the guard's back, Luke didn't really need **[Tactical Foresight]** to predict what was about to happen. Rather than running him down and skewering him with the spear, Wellind's arm snapped out, and the spear shot the twenty feet through the air toward Luke's stomach. Wellind immediately rearmed himself with the battle-axe.

Luke was already pivoting out of the way before the spear passed the front of the horse. It came at him faster than he'd expected and scraped across his armor but left Luke unharmed. The horse followed in a split second later, and even though Luke hurled himself backward, he still got kicked as the beast passed by. The guard's axe swiped at Luke's neck, but Luke dodged it easily by moving with the momentum transferred to him by the horse's kick.

The man bent forward and grasped the quivering haft of his spear as his horse ran by and pulled on the reins to bring it around to face Luke again. If the rider had been the only threat, Luke was confident in he could win. Wellind just didn't have the raw power to take Luke down. But there were still seven guards paying attention to Luke, and they'd only pulled their shots long enough to make sure Wellind didn't get hit by accident. Now that the horseman had ridden past Luke, they started their barrage back up.

"How are you fucks not out of ammo by now?" Luke yelled at them, though not in a language any of them understood. The hostility in the tone came through clearly though, and they responded by shooting at him again.

He let **[Twitch Reflexes]** guide him out of the way of as many as he could and spun to square off against Wellind again when he heard the horse start to run his way. Then, so abruptly he'd almost forgotten it was coming, **[Life Surge]** failed. Luke stumbled a step, just one, before he regained his balance.

In that single step, Wellind's spear flashed forward and caught Luke's hip. The armor probably helped, at least judging by the tortured screech the metal gave off when the spear dug through it, and then hot, wet agony radiated up into Luke's stomach and down toward his knee. He was flung from his feet and rolled to a stop thirty feet away.

"Fuuuucck me," Luke groaned. He needed to get back on his feet before something came along and finished him off, but for some reason, his leg didn't want to respond to his brain's commands. He had seconds at most before Wellind came around for another lap and probably less than that before one of the guards put a bolt in him.

There was no time to wait for his natural regeneration to heal the hip wound, no time to bandage it up. If his leg wasn't going to work, he'd just have to do a lot of hopping around. Maybe he could get behind one of the wagons or, better yet, back to the trees. That was going to put his back to the guards and all but guaranteed he'd take a few more hits, but it was better than dying on the ground here.

Ding.

Luke paused in the act of climbing up to one knee. There was no mistaking the ding of a kill notification. It wasn't even a real sound, just something he heard in his head, like the phantom buzz of his phone vibrating, only to find nothing when he checked it. Well, maybe that was a bad example, since he never mistook the system ding for anything else.

Luke craned his neck to look around and saw Wellind's now-headless body sprawling across the ground as it fell off the horse he'd been riding.

"The fuck?"

Zea's heart leaped into her throat when Luke took that spear to the hip. It wasn't hard to guess what had caused him to stumble, and even if the guard hadn't realized why it had happened, he'd recognized the opening immediately. Getting knocked down had actually saved Luke from a pair of crossbow bolts, and the guard had paused for a second to yell at the two idiots who'd almost shot him.

Before she'd realized what she was doing, Zea was charging out from behind cover, the handle of her razor-prong whip grasped firmly in her hand. She needed no special skill to control it, just a simple investment of kinetic energy provided as she swung it forward and harnessed by the enchantments to activate the weapon's devastating cutting properties.

Her path took her at an angle to cut the horseman off. If the horse had been a high level, she never would have made it in time, but the man had been using the beast's momentum to put some weight behind his attacks, not for its foot speed. The average level 1 horse was much faster than a level 1 human, and especially a level 1 dwifkin, but it was difficult to level a horse up very high, and depending on the breed, much of its AP went toward stamina and strength, not agility.

Zea got in range with seconds to spare. The whip reached out in front of her, already primed and ready to strike. It stretched the entire length, a solid twenty-five feet now, and, driven by her will, coiled once around the horse rider's neck. The coil of whip tightened, and the head was sliced clean off. The horse kept running, heedless of its rider's death.

Luke was still trying to get off his back when the horse rider's body hit the ground. He looked at the corpse, surprise evident on his face, muttered something she didn't quite catch, and glanced over at her.

"Move!" she yelled at him as she rushed in his direction. She knew it wasn't his fault, that he'd have a hard time even standing upright, but if he just sat there, the remaining guards were going to kill him. She reached his side and did her best to drag him back upright, at least as high as she could reach.

"Come on," she said, tugging him toward the trees.

"We can't," Luke told her. "They'll die."

Name	Luke Bennet	Zea Stenter
Level	42	35
XP	268521/273479	148271/157276
AP	22	4
Bloodline	SysAdmin III	None
Strength	61	7
Agility	70	30
Stamina	66	27
Perception	55	21
Skills	Butchering (4)	Arcano Dynamics (2)
	Consortium Standard (2)	Bartering (2)
	Counter (3)	Bloodline Purification Ritual (2)
	Deception (1)	Cadence (3)
	Detection (2)	Cold Reading (1)
	Disguise (2)	Consortium Standard (1)
	First Aid (1)	Cooking (1)
	Leatherworking (2)	Dagger Mastery (1)
	Life Surge (2)	Deception (1)
	Mace Mastery (5)	Disguise (2)
	Ostari (1)	Engraving (4)
	Peripheral Awareness (2)	First Aid (1)
	Power Strike (2)	Gem Cutting (1)
	Stealth (1)	Ghost Script (1)
	Survivalist (2)	Goldsmithing (2)
	Sword Mastery (1)	Keen Instincts (1)
	Tactical Foresight (2)	Lock Picking (1)
	Thalian (2)	Mana Manipulation (3)
	Torturer (1)	Mana Sight (3)
	Twitch Reflexes (3)	Mending (1)
	Unarmed Martialist (4)	Metallurgy (1)
	Wood Carving (1)	Neyardic (3)
	Analyze (BL)	Ostari (1)
	Remote Access (BL)	Painting (1)
	XP Mask (BL)	Rune Forging (3)
		Sleight of Hand (1)
		Steady Hands (2)
		Stealth (2)
		Streetwise (2)
		Temperature Acclimation (2)
		Thalian (3)
		Whitesmithing (1)

CHAPTER 10

Fuck that," Zea said. "You're going to get yourself killed if you don't retreat."

"I'll be alright," Luke said.

Zea glanced pointedly at his hip, where blood was staining his pants and the armor that Wellind's spear had pierced. The armor was digging into his skin now, but that was still better than what would have happened otherwise. It felt like the spear had stopped at the bone instead of shattering it and passing through, a fact that Luke was fully willing to attribute to the metal the spear had needed to punch through first.

It also meant that the damage was somewhat superficial, at least by his standards. It would be almost completely healed by the time the sun rose tomorrow if he did nothing but sit on his ass for the rest of the night. If he tried to fight on it, that might introduce complications, but he was confident those would only prolong his recovery time, not stop it.

There was one other option. Back-to-back uses of **[Life Surge]** kicked his ass hard, but he'd experimented, and it was possible to do. The second one wouldn't last as long, and the side effects would be a lot like when he'd come down from using **[Life Surge]** before he'd upgraded it. With thirty seconds on the clock, he could finish off the rest of the guards, probably including the two still alive on horseback. Then Val could help Ruca with the guy he was dueling.

If it weren't for the danger all the crossbowmen presented, Luke would have gone straight for the level 42 guy first. A single glance was all it took to convince him that those dozen or so remaining guards were the biggest problem. The only reason Ruca and Val were still alive was the guards' hesitation to fire into the melee and risk hitting their own allies. Both of them were doing their best to control the positioning of the fight so they could maintain some cover from the guards.

"If you double up on a **[Life Surge]**, you're going to be completely at their mercy when it wears off," Zea said. "Even if you manage to end the fight, we do not know these people. They might decide we're loose ends and murder us both just to make sure there's no possibility of us turning them in."

"If I don't do it, they'll both be killed, probably that kid with the bow too, and all these slaves are staying in their torture wagons."

Zea cursed quietly and looked around. "How can I help?"

Luke shook his head. The conversation had taken barely fifteen seconds, but that was long enough for at least one of the guards to grow a pair and inch around to get a good angle on Luke and Zea. In the next few seconds, he'd be getting shot at again and so would she if she stayed. Zea could not take the kind of punishment Luke could, nor was she nearly as well protected.

"Hide," he told her as he activated **[Life Surge]** again, not half a minute after it had expired. He was on his feet before she had a chance to reply and darting forward. The guard who'd been inching closer to get a better angle flinched at the sight of Luke barreling down on him, and the bolt he reflexively fired went wide.

Luke took the man's head off with a one-handed swing that struck the base of the guard's skull. It exploded upward in dozens of fragments and a fountain of blood, but by the time the remains splattered across the grass, he was already gone.

Bolts from three different crossbows slammed into him. Luke made no attempt to dodge, not now. The clock was too tight for that. There'd be time to heal after, but only if he killed every enemy still standing in the next twenty-eight seconds.

They weren't willing to stand there and let him, of course. They ran, they hid, they shot blindly behind them in desperate hope that he'd be struck somewhere critical. Luke killed all but two of them. One got too close to where Zea had retreated back into the trees, and he saw her whip snake out from between the branches to kill him. The other ran in the opposite direction after throwing down his weapon.

It was surprising to Luke that only one guard actually broke and fled the battle. He would have expected them to scatter much sooner, though he supposed that quite a few of them had tried to flee and been run down. It was very possible another ten or fifteen would have survived if he'd made no effort to chase them, but it was also possible they'd circle around and come back for more. The only reason he hadn't chased the last one was because he'd left his weapon behind.

If he'd had the time, he'd have collected the weapons to keep the remaining drivers from picking them up, but killing the rest of the crossbow-wielding guards had left him with only ten seconds left and two enemies still alive. Neither was retreating, and Luke couldn't blame them. Ruca was on the ropes, and Val was barely keeping the horseman at bay.

Even now, if Luke did nothing, the way he saw things playing out was the level 42 killing Ruca, then both enemies ganging up on Val to kill her too. All the attack would have accomplished was killing a bunch of guards and freeing no one. If Luke could take out the big guy in the next ten seconds, he thought they had a good chance of winning still.

[Analyze] confirmed Luke's memory of his level and also gave him a name for his next target: Fuhlan Sentros. He was pretty well-rounded with all his stats in the low 50s or high 40s, plus a wide assortment of dozens of skills, at least four of which were designed to empower his use of a shield and sword together.

The easy solution was to hit Sentros hard enough that he wouldn't get a chance to use a single one of those skills. In fact, it was really the only solution. The man's build seemed designed to drag out fights using a hefty arsenal of defensive skills. Luke did not have time for that. He rushed in from behind, trying to keep in Sentros's blind spot even though he knew the man's perception was too high to be fully successful.

Maybe Sentros thought that Ruca was the bigger threat because Luke was the one who'd taken out the low-level guards instead of fighting the power-houses. Maybe it was the lack of XP coming off Luke that threw him. Or maybe Ruca just tied up his focus so much that he really didn't see Luke coming.

Whatever the reason, Luke was already within striking distance before Sentros reacted, and as fast as the man was, he couldn't get his shield square into place before Luke brought his mace down. [Power Strike] surged down the weapon and tore through the side of the shield, then cracked down on the man's arm itself.

Squealing metal mixed with agonized screaming, and Ruca was quick to take advantage. Both of his blades slipped into Sentros, though not deep enough to kill. The guard slipped sideways, utilizing one of his skills to create some distance, and Luke didn't pursue. Hopefully the damage to his shield and the broken arm would weaken Sentros enough to give Ruca the advantage.

Six seconds remained.

One of the reasons Luke had chosen to go after Sentros first was that the other guy was on a horse, which meant he did a lot of moving around. If Luke went after him and he tried to run away, Luke would have to run down the horse. That was doable but not under the time constraints he was operating with.

However, if the guy just happened to think it was a good idea to abandon his battle with Val to come help out his boss, well, it would be stupid not to take advantage of that. That was why when the guard rode over and attempted to get between Luke and Sentros, Luke leaped straight in the air and came down with a two-handed smash aimed right at the guard's skull.

The man's reaction was a good one. He leaped off his horse to get out of the way, and Luke was forced to abort the attack or possibly rip an innocent animal into two pieces. Despite his best efforts to be gentle, Luke landed on the saddle with both feet, and the horse's legs shook trying to keep it upright.

Luke leaped off and moved to finish the guard, but Val beat him to it and stabbed him in the throat. There was no ding, but then again, Luke hadn't actually hit him. The missed XP wasn't a big deal to him, but he'd grown used to knowing, not guessing, that his enemy was dead. In a world with so many different skills, he couldn't put it past someone to claw their way back to life even with a sword going through their throat.

Three seconds remained.

Sentros was now sixty feet away. Luke could get there in under three seconds. He could do it under one if no one interfered. Ruca was in the way, but Luke could go over top of him. His feet dug into the hard-packed dirt of the road as he sprinted forward and jumped over the two fighters. Luke swung his mace low, relative to himself, and even though he wasn't in a good position to put a lot of strength behind the attack, it was aimed at Sentros's face. The guard raised a shield to block.

The attack was deflected, spinning Luke in the air as his momentum was reversed. **[Unarmed Martialist]** had plenty to say about that, and Luke lashed out with a double kick to the back of Sentros's head as he went by. Sentros staggered forward a step, somehow still in control enough to deflect an attack from Ruca.

One second remained.

Luke was going to pay for it in a moment, but he sent a **[Power Strike]** into his mace and jabbed forward with both hands to stab it into Sentros's back. At the same time, Ruca came in from the left, leaving their opponent only one way to dodge. He leaped to the right, trying to keep ahead of Ruca's blades, and found Val there to meet him.

Twin blades pierced joints in his armor, and Ruca followed up the attack to stab him elsewhere. Sentros tried to twist away, but the pair of them literally pinned him to the ground. With no one left alive to come to his rescue, he had just seconds of life left.

That was good because **[Life Surge]** ran out right there. Luke's mace hit the ground, and it was all he could do to keep himself from dropping to his knees. He was barely conscious of Sentros's final moments, and it wasn't until he heard the ding in his head that he realized the fight was over.

As long as Ruca and Val didn't betray him here, it would be fine. They didn't seem like the type, but he'd only known them for an hour or two. If they tried something, he would need Zea to keep him safe. Hopefully she had a few of those paralysis stones left. Even if she didn't, Luke knew her pretty well. She was off making something with **[Ghost Script]** right now that would save his ass.

Whether he was about to be betrayed or not turned out to be a moot point. In all the chaos and confusion of the battle, with all the slaughter and blood, and with the deep, deep exhaustion using **[Life Surge]** twice in a row had left him with, Luke had forgotten one thing.

The door to the lead wagon opened with a slow creak, and someone stepped out of it.

Name	Luke Bennet	Zea Stenter
Level	42	35
XP	273279/273479	148271/157276
AP	22	4
Bloodline	SysAdmin III	None
Strength	61	7
Agility	70	30
Stamina	66	27
Perception	55	21
Skills	Butchering (4)	Arcano Dynamics (2)
	Consortium Standard (2)	Bartering (2)
	Counter (3)	Bloodline Purification Ritual (2)
	Deception (1)	Cadence (3)
	Detection (2)	Cold Reading (1)
	Disguise (2)	Consortium Standard (1)
	First Aid (1)	Cooking (1)
	Leatherworking (2)	Dagger Mastery (1)
	Life Surge (2)	Deception (1)
	Mace Mastery (5)	Disguise (2)
	Ostari (1)	Engraving (4)
	Peripheral Awareness (2)	First Aid (1)
	Power Strike (2)	Gem Cutting (1)
	Stealth (1)	Ghost Script (1)
	Survivalist (2)	Goldsmithing (2)
	Sword Mastery (1)	Keen Instincts (1)
	Tactical Foresight (2)	Lock Picking (1)
	Thalian (2)	Mana Manipulation (3)
	Torturer (1)	Mana Sight (3)
	Twitch Reflexes (3)	Mending (1)
	Unarmed Martialist (4)	Metallurgy (1)
	Wood Carving (1)	Neyardic (3)
	Analyze (BL)	Ostari (1)
	Remote Access (BL)	Painting (1)
	XP Mask (BL)	Rune Forging (3)
		Sleight of Hand (1)
		Steady Hands (2)
		Stealth (2)
		Streetwise (2)
		Temperature Acclimation (2)
		Thalian (3)
		Whitesmithing (1)

CHAPTER 11

The man who stepped out of the wagon wore a midnight blue robe trimmed in silver. He had long, dark hair pulled back from his face and tied into a braid that was thrown over one shoulder and pale, sallow skin. A sneer rode on his lips, and he regarded the exhausted trio with anger in his eyes.

"Well," he said, his accent somehow crisp and snooty at the same time as he dragged out the word. "This has been a disaster. On the bright side, I won't have to pay all these guards now, and I'm close enough to the city to make it there without any further issues."

"Ha," Val said. "All I see is one last corpse I need to make."

Luke knew he didn't cut an imposing figure at the moment. It was all he could do to keep from dropping on the spot, but Ruca and Val could still fight. The man didn't look scared. If anything, he looked bored. He couldn't be that high a level, or someone would have said something, not unless he was some eastern-continent version if an inquisitor with XP-dampening skills.

[Analyze] would cut right through that. Luke just needed to pull himself together enough to activate the skill, which was turning out to be harder than he'd expected. Double **[Life Surge]** had really done a number on him. It took him four attempts to trigger the skill, and he did not like what he saw.

[Name: Torwin Melathese]
[Level: 36]
[XP: 165421/171264]
[AP: 0]
[Strength: 5]
[Agility: 9]

[Stamina: 31]
[Perception: 8]
[Skills:]
[Athame Focus (3)]
[Mana Sight (5)]
[Mana Manipulation (5)]
[Fractured Mind (5)]
[Blood Adaptation (4)]
[Telepathic Focus (4)]
[Reanimation (5)]
[Reconstitute (4)]
[Life Surge (1)]
[Ritual Caster (2)]
[Soul Scaffold (3)]
[Eledarn (3)]
[Old Ganish (2)]
[Consortium Standard (3)]
[Tirvok (3)]
[Cooking (4)]
[Butchering (5)]
[Cleaning (3)]
[Steady Hands (3)]
[Torturer (2)]
[Anatomy: Humanoid (2)]

Luke only recognized a few skills off the list, **[Life Surge]** being the big one. But the general trend was obvious. Torwin was a magic user of some kind and, from the looks of it, a particularly gruesome one. He had the fashion sense to fit right in with those weird LARP people who ran around pretending to be vampires at the park near his family's old apartment too.

Really though, with a skill called **[Reanimation]**, it seemed pretty obvious to him what they were dealing with. The other two had no way to know though, and Luke didn't have a way to tell them unless he wanted to make them curious how he knew. Maybe if he was in top form, he would have considered it, but then again, they were going to find out soon enough anyway.

"Corpses? What do you know about them, you stupid little girl?" Torwin asked, scorn dripping from his words.

He gave a theatrical twirl of his hand and pointed at the body of the nearest guard. Luke had killed the man in typical fashion, by crushing his skull with one swift, decisive blow. The fact that the guard's brains had splattered across the road and his eyes were hanging out of the sockets did not in any way stop him from crawling back to his feet.

"Necromancer," Val hissed. "Abomination."

"Yes, yes, I've heard it all before. Behold my rebuttal," Torwin told her. His finger jumped from corpse to corpse, and five more guards stood back up. "Now, it's not that I need to speak for them to obey my commands, but it does make for a better show, don't you think? No? Well, it's not like your opinion matters. Kill them all."

Ruca and Val surged forward to meet the undead, but Luke didn't have the strength left to pick up his weapon and fight. He could only watch helplessly as the zombies ignored blows that would have crippled living opponents. The two bandits were pushed back one step at a time, slowly at first, then faster as new zombies joined the battle.

They weren't like the ones in the movies. There was no groaning, no stiff limbs, no shambling gait. The guards moved just like normal people, though thankfully without all the strength and agility the system had granted them in life. That was the only reason the bandits hadn't been overwhelmed immediately, but they were tired, and Torwin just kept making more zombies.

Luke needed to use **[Life Surge]** again. Torwin was a soft target. He was close, and he was physically weak. 31 stamina wasn't enough to survive even a single blow from Luke's mace. It was the aftermath that Luke was scared of. There was a very real possibility that the skill would kill him. If he didn't use it, they were dead anyway.

He tried to activate **[Life Surge]**, but the skill wouldn't respond. "System . . . Why . . . isn't it . . . working?" Luke gasped out through ragged breaths, though he was afraid he already knew the answer.

"The strain on your body would be too great. You would die immediately."

There was nothing Luke could do to influence this fight. He couldn't even save himself. The first zombie to come at him was going to kill him.

It didn't take Zea long to figure out what she needed to do. A fucking necromancer of all things had slithered out of that carriage. She'd been expecting some sort of pampered merchant or nobleman, given the accommodations. The man obviously lived in the carriage while he traveled. That he'd been a magic user had been a nasty surprise.

And of course there was no inquisitor around now that someone who actually deserved a little attention from the church had shown up. After months of being hounded by them, here in front of her was finally a threat worthy of some time in a confessional. The irony was not lost on Zea.

The necromancer didn't seem to realize she was there, which made sense when she factored in the fact that she was still under the effects of Luke's **[XP Mask]** skill. She also hadn't joined in the main fight, had in fact only come out of the trees for half a minute to save Luke after that horse-riding guard with the spear had caught him just as **[Life Surge]** had worn off.

There were no windows in the carriage either. It was a perfect recipe for obliviousness. It also meant that Zea had the opportunity to sneak up behind him and kill him. With any luck, the zombies would go down as soon as their boss died. If not, well, at least there wouldn't be any more of them.

The necromancer seemed to have some kind of sixth sense for where the guards had died. He would point at them, often at ones behind him that he'd unerringly target despite not so much as glancing in that direction, and another one would rise up to join the fight. Zea decided to take advantage of that by circling around to the back of the caravan and working her way forward. Given the man's position in front of the lead wagon, she figured she'd need thirty seconds to run all the way to the front.

That plan went out the window when she saw the first driver. He let out a startled yelp as she walked by, scaring her so bad that she almost yelled too. She'd been so focused on the necromancer that she'd forgotten Luke had spared the people who hadn't fought back. Noble of him but also very stupid.

She should have noticed him before she got there. Zea's perception was at 21. It had been simple negligence on her part that she hadn't paid attention. **[XP Mask]** worked both ways, and she couldn't feel anyone else's XP either. She'd known that, but it was still a hard thing to see someone and not be able to feel their presence.

Regardless of why it happened, the guy's yelping was going to get her caught. There was nothing she could do but kill him to shut him up, and she expected a new corpse appearing on the battlefield would catch the necromancer's attention even more than his yell had. If she couldn't hide, it was going to be a game of speed now.

Not for the first time, she wished she'd put just a few more points into strength. Zea took off in a sprint, still quiet thanks to her high agility but not nearly as fast as she wanted to be. Luke could have done it in two seconds. It took her twenty times as long. More shouts followed her from various drivers, but Zea ignored them and powered ahead.

"Who's this?" the necromancer said, his head tilted as he turned to regard her. "You don't have an aura either, just like that useless fellow over there. What are you hoping to accomplish?"

Zea did not have Luke's combat skills. Maybe if she did, she would have reacted in time. The guard standing up in front of her was too slow to catch her before she went by, but he was a distraction anyway. A crossbow bolt slammed into her back, right between her shoulders, and Zea's run turned into a stumble that ended with her falling to her knees.

It hurt. Holy fuck it hurt more than anything else she'd ever felt. It hurt so bad that at first, she didn't even realize a second bolt had pierced her back lower down near her waist. Waves of pain rolled through her, paralyzing her. She couldn't even scream her pain, it was that bad.

For all that, her mind kept working. She knew if she didn't move, they'd shoot her again. If she didn't reach that necromancer, more undead would keep rising. She'd die. Luke would die. Those bandits would die. The slaves . . . Well, they'd probably wish they were dead by the time they reached the end of their journey.

Zea struggled back to her feet, two bolts jutting out of her back as she moved. She heard the distinctive twang of another bolt being released and jumped to the left, closer to the wagon. Fresh agony lanced up and down her back, but she pushed past it. There was no time for that, not right now.

The necromancer was almost in range. She'd reach him, and she'd kill him, and then she'd help Luke. The stubborn jackass had pushed himself too far this time and certainly wasn't going to be taking care of himself anytime soon.

Another guard rose up, this one directly in front of her. Zea had anticipated that move, and her razor-prong whip snapped out to dismember the moving corpse in seconds. It fell to pieces in front of her at the exact same time the one crouching on the roof of one of the wagons fired another bolt. Her strategy of hugging the side of the wagons to get a bit of cover paid off, and the shot went wide.

She rushed forward the last fifty feet and raised her arm to swing the whip at the necromancer, who was still regarding her with an expression of amusement. At the last instant, just before the enchanted razor-prong shards could lash out, something struck her from behind.

Zea was hurled to the ground and nearly blacked out from the pain of the bolts stuck in her being jostled. She pulled herself together and rolled, an action her back did not appreciate at all and that drove both bolts deeper into her body.

Looming over her was the undead she'd dismembered just seconds ago. All the pieces were back in place, but now there was some sort of dark light coming from the spots where the limbs connected back together. Zea didn't hesitate to swing the whip again, knowing as she did that no damage she inflicted would be permanent, not as long as the necromancer was still breathing.

She just needed it to drop for a few seconds, which it thankfully obliged her in doing. She wasn't going to give the necromancer a chance to put the body back together again, not when she only needed to stand back up and strike him.

As the guard's body dropped, she saw the other one, the one with the cross-bow, jump down from the wagon he'd been perched on and raise the weapon to point at her. Really, he couldn't get a better shot. The undead that had been blocking her line of sight was in pieces at her feet, and she was still on her back on the ground, the bolts digging into her muscles as they twisted sideways under her weight. There was no way the guard could miss at this range.

The undead pulled the trigger, and the bolt shot through the air.

Name	Luke Bennet	Zea Stenter
Level	42	35
XP	273279/273479	148271/157276
AP	22	4
Bloodline	SysAdmin III	None
Strength	61	7
Agility	70	30
Stamina	66	27
Perception	55	21
Skills	Butchering (4)	Arcano Dynamics (2)
	Consortium Standard (2)	Bartering (2)
	Counter (3)	Bloodline Purification Ritual (2)
	Deception (1)	Cadence (3)
	Detection (2)	Cold Reading (1)
	Disguise (2)	Consortium Standard (1)
	First Aid (1)	Cooking (1)
	Leatherworking (2)	Dagger Mastery (1)
	Life Surge (2)	Deception (1)
	Mace Mastery (5)	Disguise (2)
	Ostari (1)	Engraving (4)
	Peripheral Awareness (2)	First Aid (1)
	Power Strike (2)	Gem Cutting (1)
	Stealth (1)	Ghost Script (1)
	Survivalist (2)	Goldsmithing (2)
	Sword Mastery (1)	Keen Instincts (1)
	Tactical Foresight (2)	Lock Picking (1)
	Thalian (2)	Mana Manipulation (3)
	Torturer (1)	Mana Sight (3)
	Twitch Reflexes (3)	Mending (1)
	Unarmed Martialist (4)	Metallurgy (1)
	Wood Carving (1)	Neyardic (3)
	Analyze (BL)	Ostari (1)
	Remote Access (BL)	Painting (1)
	XP Mask (BL)	Rune Forging (3)
		Sleight of Hand (1)
		Steady Hands (2)
		Stealth (2)
		Streetwise (2)
		Temperature Acclimation (2)
		Thalian (3)
		Whitesmithing (1)

CHAPTER 12

There was no time to think, not with the bolt all the way in the air. If she had, Zea never would have tried to stop it with her whip. The bolt was so small and moving so fast. It would be impossible to hit it out of the air, even with her perception of 21 helping her follow its path.

She didn't think; she just moved. The whip slashed up, impossibly thin but directed by her will to exactly the point where she needed it. The bolt came into the range of the razor-prong aura, and Zea knew exactly what would happen even as she watched it play out. She'd missed. The bolt passed by the aura, one side of it shaved down, and kept right on going. It was on target to strike her directly, right in the chest.

Then it wobbled in the air. With bare feet to go, it lost its trajectory and started to tumble. Instead of taking a sharp piece of metal between the ribs, Zea felt the bolt strike her flat on the side. It hurt, and she'd probably have a nice bruise there for a few hours before her stamina healed it up if she survived the fight, but it wasn't debilitating. More importantly, the quiver on the guard's hip was empty.

She could still fight as long as she could power through the pain in her back. It didn't seem so bad now, which probably wasn't a good sign. Things were going numb, and her heartbeat was pounding in her ears, but she didn't have the time she needed to parse that. Instead, she scrambled to her feet and darted past the still-reforming undead she'd already cut down.

There was a look of comical surprise on the necromancer's face when her whip lashed out and coiled once around his shoulder. Zea pulled, sawing off his arm. The severed limb hit the ground with a meaty thump, and blood started drizzling out, but the stump on the necromancer didn't have so much as a trickle of blood coming out of it.

"Well, that's annoying," he said.

Before Zea could follow up, a hand grabbed hold of her leg. The undead behind her pulled her off-balance and threatened to drag her off her feet, forcing Zea to pay attention to it instead of the necromancer. She should have gone for the decapitation strike instead of dismemberment, but she hadn't expected him not to bleed, and she hadn't exactly had a lot of time to aim.

The whip sliced through the wrist of the offending hand, and Zea turned to finish the necromancer off for real this time. The man wasn't even paying any attention to her, despite the damage she'd done. Instead he had a pensive look on his face as he considered his arm on the ground. Before Zea could attack again, she heard the click and twang of a crossbow being fired again.

She glanced over to see a different guard, one of the ones from closer to the front of the caravan who hadn't made it off the roof of his wagon before Luke killed him, pointing a crossbow in her direction. The bolt was already in the air and too close for her to dodge it. Zea jerked to the side and cried out as it tore through her elbow. The handle of her whip went tumbling through the air.

Another guard stood up, this one missing an arm. That didn't stop it from raising its crossbow and firing one-handed, but Zea ducked around one of the supply wagons for cover. For a change, there were no bodies near there, which didn't mean that some of the ones walking around weren't going to come after her, just that she didn't have to worry about one popping up off the ground.

It was hard to stay on her feet, hard to think. Her right hand was worthless now, the elbow completely shattered and nothing below that moving at all. There were still two bolts in her back, and even without all of that, using the whip put a great deal of mental stress on her. There had to be a solution, but she couldn't think of it.

The undead were closing in, but she had an answer to that problem, at least. It was going to be tricky to get them all in range, considering so many of them were using crossbows and had no reason to group up. Finding the optimal time to attack might be impossible. She'd have to settle for getting a clear shot at getting her whip back so she could finish hacking that necromancer apart.

The first guard came around the wagon, but he was clumsy compared to her. Even with her injuries, she easily kept out of his grasp. Then a second one appeared. And a third came around the other side of the wagon. Zea half expected a fourth overhead, but the wagon's canvas roof stretched over a ribbed frame made that impossible.

It was a small condolence since the only way to escape was to run farther away from the caravan, where she'd be out in the open. If she was going to end this fight, she needed to get back to the necromancer and finish him off.

Zea reached into her pocket and brought out what looked like a balled-up strip of leather, loosely held in shape with a few rough stitches. It wouldn't take much force to snap the threads on it, certainly not more than she could produce by throwing it into the crowd of zombies.

They just needed to line up right for her to use it.

Torwin couldn't decide if he was annoyed or amused about the whole thing. On the one hand, he stood to make back quite a bit of money by not having to pay all the guards he'd hired for his caravan. The slaves were far more valuable, but it didn't hurt to make a little extra profit.

But he'd hired those guards for a reason, and that reason was that necromancy wasn't legal this far north. They weren't too far from Naldrin, where he'd planned to unload the whole cargo, but getting them the last leg was going to be a pain. Reanimated undead lacked the abilities they'd had in life, no matter how fresh the corpses, and he could only compensate for so much.

Perhaps he should have stepped in sooner and tried to save some of them, but if he'd done that, then there'd be even more witnesses to take care of. No, in this situation it was all undead or no undead. He'd already sent a few to take care of the remaining drivers, annoying as it was. Now he'd need to drive the whole caravan himself for however long it took for another town to come into view, then stage the area to make it look like his guards had died fighting off bandits so that he could hire a new crop.

At least the payment would be significantly lower with most of the journey already behind him.

Absently, he reached down to pick up his severed arm. **[Blood Adaptation]** was keeping him on his feet and **[Fractured Mind]** kept him from feeling any pain at being . . . disarmed . . . but he should use **[Reconstitute]** to attach it again soon. It wasn't easy to use it on himself, not nearly as easy as commanding an undead to pull itself back together, but he wasn't a master necromancer for nothing.

The girl who'd attacked him, some sort of mixed-blood creature, he thought, was frantically trying to keep herself out of his minions' clutches, but with so much raw material just lying around for him to work with, it was a simple matter to add a few more to his numbers. The other three were also on the verge of collapsing, their pathetic attempts at killing that which was already dead doomed to failure.

Torwin stripped the sleeve of his robe down his severed arm and slipped his own torso bare, leaving the loose robe hanging around his belted waist. The tricky part here was making sure he lined it up just so. With the undead, it didn't much matter if the limb was off a few degrees. He was much more discerning when it came to himself. Two ranks in **[Anatomy: Humanoid]** were sufficient to confirm he had the limb held to the stump properly, and **[Steady Hands]** kept it still while he used his magic to reattach it.

At least the girl had made a clean job of it. He'd had a hand hacked off once with a rusty old cleaver by a little boy whose father he'd been doing an experiment on. That had been tricky to put back, what with all the filth in there and the jagged nature of the wound. It had taken him the better part of an hour to fix that little mishap, but this time, it barely took twenty seconds. Torwin made a mental note to collect that strange whip she'd used later. He might keep it for himself if it proved easy to wield, and if not, it would likely sell for a heaping pile of gold.

"Much better," he murmured as he flexed the fingers on his freshly reattached arm. Each one worked correctly, confirmed one by one, and his wrist retained full range of motion. Nothing was wrong in the elbow, and while the shoulder was a bit bruised, it wasn't pulling or tearing. All the muscles, veins, and nerves seemed to be functioning perfectly.

"Now then, what to do with you lot? Killing you would be too easy, but I do have a schedule to keep, after all. Hmm, I wonder."

The distinctive twang of a crossbow caught his attention, not because it wasn't a familiar sound in this battle, but because he knew exactly what his minions were doing at all times, and none of them had fired at that particular moment. Then he took an involuntary step forward as something tugged at his neck, and he had a momentary glimpse of the tip of a bolt sticking out beneath his jaw.

"How peculiar," he tried to say, but his throat wasn't working. Hesitantly, he reached up behind him with a hand and felt the smooth wooden shaft piercing the back of his neck. That explained that then. **[Blood Adaptation]** would keep him from bleeding out, but this was a step too close to decapitation for him to be comfortable with.

Torwin was no longer torn between amusement and annoyance.

Luke's arms quivered from holding the crossbow, and he was so weak that the minuscule recoil was almost enough to rip it out of his hands. The pain was worth it, though. He'd put a bolt right through the necromancer's throat. That ought to be enough to kill the bastard.

The zombies weren't collapsing, but maybe without their boss around, they'd stay down once they were cut up this time. He glanced back at where Ruca and Val were surrounded by a circle of undead, both fighting back-to-back and slashing at any that got within range. It looked the same as it had the entire fight to him.

Then the necromancer grabbed the bolt from the front and pulled it all the way through his neck. He turned around and stared down at Luke with smoldering anger. "This is no longer amusing," he spat out.

The bloodied bolt was cast aside, the necromancer took a breath, and the wound sealed up right before Luke's eyes. The man's whole body jerked to attention, like someone had run a current through him, and he got a wild grin on his face. Luke knew that look. It was one he was all too familiar with himself.

The necromancer had just activated **[Life Surge]**.

Name	Luke Bennet	Zea Stenter
Level	42	35
XP	273279/273479	148271/157276
AP	22	4
Bloodline	SysAdmin III	None
Strength	61	7
Agility	70	30
Stamina	66	27
Perception	55	21
Skills	Butchering (4)	Arcano Dynamics (2)
	Consortium Standard (2)	Bartering (2)
	Counter (3)	Bloodline Purification Ritual (2)
	Deception (1)	Cadence (3)
	Detection (2)	Cold Reading (1)
	Disguise (2)	Consortium Standard (1)
	First Aid (1)	Cooking (1)
	Leatherworking (2)	Dagger Mastery (1)
	Life Surge (2)	Deception (1)
	Mace Mastery (5)	Disguise (2)
	Ostari (1)	Engraving (4)
	Peripheral Awareness (2)	First Aid (1)
	Power Strike (2)	Gem Cutting (1)
	Stealth (1)	Ghost Script (1)
	Survivalist (2)	Goldsmithing (2)
	Sword Mastery (1)	Keen Instincts (1)
	Tactical Foresight (2)	Lock Picking (1)
	Thalian (2)	Mana Manipulation (3)
	Torturer (1)	Mana Sight (3)
	Twitch Reflexes (3)	Mending (1)
	Unarmed Martialist (4)	Metallurgy (1)
	Wood Carving (1)	Neyardic (3)
	Analyze (BL)	Ostari (1)
	Remote Access (BL)	Painting (1)
	XP Mask (BL)	Rune Forging (3)
		Sleight of Hand (1)
		Steady Hands (2)
		Stealth (2)
		Streetwise (2)
		Temperature Acclimation (2)
		Thalian (3)
		Whitesmithing (1)

CHAPTER 13

Luke was so exhausted that he didn't think he could fight back even to save his own life. The necromancer might have been content to ignore him since he hadn't been a threat before the crossbow incident. Now the blue-robed man was staring daggers at him, and Luke was wondering if there was anything he could buy with 22 AP that would save his ass in the next ten seconds.

Zea was dealing with a half dozen undead chasing her after she'd been disarmed and basically lost a hand. Ruca and Val were still trapped in a circle of zombies and slowly getting more and more tired. Even superhuman levels of stamina had limits, and it looked like the bandit duo was about to find them. There was no one there to help him.

It was a little late to worry about people thinking he was crazy now, and since System understood him in every language anyway . . . "System, is there any skill I could buy that I can actually use right now?"

"There are quite a few," System said as he appeared. "Most of them fall into the passive category, such as sensory- and mental-enhancement skills."

"Are they any that are going to keep that guy from killing me in the next few seconds?" Luke clarified.

"I'm afraid that is unlikely," System told him. "If you had a higher AP budget, a few of your bloodline skills would aid you, but lacking that, the situation does not appear to be weighted in your favor."

"Thanks for the heads-up," Luke said. "Shit."

"What language are you speaking?" Torwin asked him, still talking in Consortium Standard. "I've never heard anything like it before."

"Go ask your mom," Luke told him. "I taught her a few words the other night."

"You . . . My mother has been dead for twenty years," Torwin said, confusion evident on his face. "And I refuse to believe some ruffian like you has mastered the art of necromancy to such an extent that you can communicate with the spirits of the dead."

Luke couldn't help himself. He started laughing. "I guess it doesn't translate over well. Let me try again: go fuck yourself."

That got through to the man. "How droll. Very well, I'm on something of a short clock, thanks to your little stunt. Time to die."

There was a tearing sound and a roar, which surprised both Luke and Torwin. The necromancer flinched and spun in place to look back at the caravan, where Zea was cackling and the zombies who'd been chasing after her were being crushed in what appeared to be long, thick, leathery tentacles. There was no animal attached to them; it was just a ball of dozens of them knotted around one another and going in every direction.

There were currently four zombies caught up in the tentacles, but even as Luke watched, the knot of them started slapping against the ground and dragging themselves toward Torwin and Luke. It was deceptively fast too, especially considering its size. Those tentacles were half a foot thick at the base and probably fifteen feet long.

Instantly, undead started swarming it. Fourteen zombies rushed toward their master in attempt to shield him with their bodies, including six from the crowd surrounding the bandits. The tentacle ball snatched them all up indiscriminately, and the more zombies that were tangled up inside it, the slower it got.

New zombies rose up from farther back in the caravan to take the places of the ones caught up in Zea's insane tentacle-monster thing, including the boy Luke had spared in the initial assault. His neck was clearly broken, not that it mattered to him anymore. Torwin must have decided he couldn't leave witnesses.

An arrow thunked into Torwin's chest and drove him back a step. He blinked and looked down at it, then shot Luke an incredulous glance. "Your little group just keeps getting bigger. How many more of you are there hiding in the trees?"

The only answer was another arrow, this time in Torwin's leg. He rolled his eyes, reached down, and yanked out both of them. A trio of zombies started toward the trees in the direction the arrow had come from.

"Time to wrap this up," Torwin said. "I'm going to want a break here soon, and I'd prefer you were all thoroughly dead by then."

In English again, Luke asked System, "If I just dump my AP straight into stamina, would it help me right now?"

"Somewhat," System said, "though you should not expect to operate at anything close to full strength."

"I just need to hold out long enough to outlast his **[Life Surge]**."

"I think this will be rather poetic, though I'm sure you won't appreciate it," the necromancer said as he leaned down and picked up the bloodied bolt Luke had shot him with. Then Torwin strode forward, picked up the crossbow from where Luke dropped it, and fitted the bolt into place.

Luke dumped all his AP and felt vitality flood through his limbs. It was a bare fraction of what he normally worked with, but the sheer exhaustion weighing him down to immobility washed away. His mace was behind him, only a few feet but out of easy reach. He'd do this with his bare hands instead.

[Twitch Reflexes] told him exactly when Torwin pulled the trigger, and he was already pushing himself out of the way. Luke bounced up from the ground and spun to get his feet under him, then lunged forward to grab at the necromancer.

"Unhand me, you brute!" Torwin cried out as he tried to jump back. As weakened as Luke was right now, he was still stronger than a man who'd barely spared a few points for his stats. Luke got a grip on the necromancer's robes and pulled him forward to wrap his hands around the man's neck. Torwin's stamina was too high to beat him to death, but Luke could still choke him out. Probably. The guy had some sort of blood-manipulation skill, so even that wasn't a given.

As long as Luke could keep Torwin pinned down for a few seconds, **[Life Surge]** would wear off, and the necromancer would be easy pickings. Hopefully his zombies would go with him, and none of them would kill anyone in between now and then.

"I . . . said . . . let go!" Torwin gagged out as he slapped at Luke. The attacks were weak, more distracting than anything, and Luke ignored them. He kept pressure on Torwin's throat, right up until the moment a zombie barreled into his side. The undead monster didn't have the system enhancing his physical stats anymore, but he was still a full-grown man, and Luke was running on fumes.

The three of them ended up in a heap, the guard flailing wildly at Luke and Torwin scrambling to escape Luke's implacable grasp. Luke saw the exact moment **[Life Surge]** ran out. Torwin's face sagged, and his limbs lost all strength, but it did nothing to weaken the undead clawing at Luke. All the zombies kept right on attacking, and in fact a second one joined the pile.

With one grabbing each arm, they managed to pry Luke's hands off Torwin's throat. Try as he might, Luke was in no shape to compete with the full strength of a zombie clinging to each arm, and they hauled him off the necromancer, who lay on the ground, hair disheveled and chest heaving.

"You should know that my control over blood extends beyond my own body," Torwin said as he sat upright. "My minions are going to take you apart, piece by piece, and you'll stay alive for all of it. I won't let you die until you've been chopped up, joint by joint, and your belly's been sliced open so I can pick out your organs."

"You're wrong," Luke said.

"I don't think so. As soon as I finish with your friends, you're going to be my project."

"No, I don't think you understand," Luke told the necromancer. "You're not going to do any of that."

"You're hardly in a position to tell me what I can or ca—"

The loop of Zea's whip flashed by, settled itself around Torwin's neck, and squeezed. The necromancer's head popped off in a spray of blood, and the body slowly fell backward. *Ding. Ding.*

All around the caravan, the zombies fell to pieces, in some cases literally. Without their master's magic to hold them together, the wounds they'd taken during their postmortem battle proved too much.

"Holy shit," Luke said, looking around. "That was fucking wild. Glad it's over now though."

He took two staggering steps to get clear of the zombies, found a relatively clean stretch of grass, and promptly passed out on it.

The bandits weren't in much better shape than Zea, with the exception of Wilby. He'd run out of arrows early on in the fight, and it wasn't until the necromancer took the field that he'd found an opportunity to sneak in close and recover some spent ammunition. Zea couldn't much blame him for staying out of it, considering his relatively low level. He hadn't done much good against the necromancer anyway. That guy's skills had been creepy.

Her elbow was shattered, utterly and completely fucked. Without magical healing, she'd be crippled for the rest of her life. On the bright side, they could afford it with their share of the spoils, though that had its own issues to be resolved after Luke woke up. But with that having been said, it fucking hurt, and it wasn't getting healed up today. Luke still hadn't woken up from where he'd passed out. She could already picture him demanding all the food as soon as he opened his eyes.

That at least she could accommodate. Ruca had pried open all the slave wagons, revealing row after row of sick, malnourished humans sitting around in their own waste and shackled together in long lines. The four of them had done their best to break the chains and lead everyone out into open air. Zea had raided the food wagons, and they'd turned the roadside into an impromptu camp while Val and a protesting Wilby had gathered the bodies of the dead guards and hauled them off for burial in a mass grave in the woods.

Zea fully planned to claim any and all money looted off the dead. She'd spent a fortune in enchanted armaments for this fight, and she couldn't even begin to work on replacing any of it until she got her arm fixed. Even cooking was unexpectedly challenging with only one hand.

While the food cooked, some of the former slaves who knew how to do such things drove the wagons off the road and took care of the horses. They had everything set up in a ring around their impromptu campsite, though there were far too many people to fit in that ring. Wilby led them off to a nearby stream in groups of ten so that they could get cleaned up, and slowly, the slaves started to look like people again.

They were still sick, still weak, but they were clean, and they got their first real meal in weeks. Fortunately, none of them had been marked yet. Or maybe slavers didn't do that on the eastern continent. Either way, they were lucky enough that they could still live lives as free men and women. The mark behind Zea's ear was going to prevent that forever. Even after the magic in it died, she'd need to be careful that no one saw it.

She was sitting on the grass and cradling her broken arm in her lap when Luke walked up. "Finally awake, huh?" she said.

"Yeah. Lot of people here."

"I suppose."

"What do we do now?"

"We don't do anything. Those three bandits will take it from here. I'll try to get some money to recoup our losses from this fight, but I suspect the bandits are going to fight me about it. I can already hear that woman telling me they need it for the people here."

"Well, she's not wrong," Luke said. "These guys are going to need a lot of help."

Zea shrugged and wiggled her arm. "They're free now. We accomplished our objective. I'm pretty keen on getting this fixed as soon as possible."

Luke looked at it with a grimace and said, "Yeah. Move ahead and hope to find someone or backtrack to Naldrin, you think?"

"Figure we'll ask the bandits there what's down the road. If there's a city coming up, no point in going back."

"Fair enough. Ready to go find 'em?"

"Yeah, help me up," Zea said, holding her good hand out to Luke. He took hold and pulled her to her feet, and the two of them walked off together.

Name	Luke Bennet	Zea Stenter
Level	43	35
XP	273559/293811	148551/157276
AP	43	4
Bloodline	SysAdmin III	None
Strength	61	7
Agility	70	30
Stamina	88	27
Perception	55	21
Skills	Butchering (4)	Arcano Dynamics (2)
	Consortium Standard (2)	Bartering (2)
	Counter (3)	Bloodline Purification Ritual (2)
	Deception (1)	Cadence (3)
	Detection (2)	Cold Reading (1)
	Disguise (2)	Consortium Standard (1)
	First Aid (1)	Cooking (1)
	Leatherworking (2)	Dagger Mastery (1)
	Life Surge (2)	Deception (1)
	Mace Mastery (5)	Disguise (2)
	Ostari (1)	Engraving (4)
	Peripheral Awareness (2)	First Aid (1)
	Power Strike (2)	Gem Cutting (1)
	Stealth (1)	Ghost Script (1)
	Survivalist (2)	Goldsmithing (2)
	Sword Mastery (1)	Keen Instincts (1)
	Tactical Foresight (2)	Lock Picking (1)
	Thalian (2)	Mana Manipulation (3)
	Torturer (1)	Mana Sight (3)
	Twitch Reflexes (3)	Mending (1)
	Unarmed Martialist (4)	Metallurgy (1)
	Wood Carving (1)	Neyardic (3)
	Analyze (BL)	Ostari (1)
	Remote Access (BL)	Painting (1)
	XP Mask (BL)	Rune Forging (3)
		Sleight of Hand (1)
		Steady Hands (2)
		Stealth (2)
		Streetwise (2)
		Temperature Acclimation (2)
		Thalian (3)
		Whitesmithing (1)

CHAPTER 14

They found Ruca and Val sitting around a small campfire with another woman who could have been Val's twin, except thirty pounds lighter and with a sunken, sickly visage. Her arms were covered in sores, and the skin around her wrists was an angry, abraded red. Ruca was sitting on a large wooden box, and the women had a section of tree trunk that looked like it was left over from the harvested firewood.

"There he is," Ruca said. "Man of the hour right there. We would not have pulled this rescue mission off without both of their help, but he really took the fight to 'em. How many did you kill, my friend?"

"I didn't keep track," Luke said. "Enough that I got a level out of it."

"Ancestors honor your sacrifice," Val and the other woman said in sync. Luke got the feeling it was something these people said a lot, like saying, "Bless you," when someone sneezed. Or maybe more like saying, "Amen," at the end of a prayer. It felt religious to him.

"Speaking of sacrifice," Zea said. "We're here for our share of the money."

"Your share?" Ruca asked, tilting his head. "I'm sorry, but there is no share."

"Don't give me that herosh dung. There's no way none of those guards didn't have a sock under the floor to—wait, that's not right."

Zea turned to Luke and switched back to Thalian. "Tell him that the guards definitely had money on them and that the caravan master would have had even more in his wagon. We earned at least half, and by rights it should be half of what's left over after we factor in the healing services I'm going to need and all the supplies I wasted. I spent probably fifteen gold on materials alone making all of that, not even talking about the weeks it took me, and if a healer charges less than ten for this arm, I'll be surprised."

After Luke told the two of them what Zea wanted, Val snorted and said, "That's too bad. We don't have any money for you."

"It's going to take every coin to get these people healthy and back home," Ruca added.

"That's not our problem! We helped free them, we deserve a cut of the spoils," Zea said. Her right arm flopped limply around, drawing attention to the broken elbow.

"We should get that in a sling," Luke said.

"Later. We're talking about something more important right now."

Ruca sighed and said, "I appreciate that you've risked life and limb to help us. I'm sorry that you were injured in the process, but that does not change the fact that getting these people back to their homes so they can resume their lives is our first priority. The caravan didn't have enough money for that. Even with two wagons of food, considering how much these people need to regain their health, we're going to need every bit of cash to feed them on the long trip back."

"You just said I was your man of the hour, that you needed my help for all of this," Luke said. "Seems a little bit ungrateful not to deal fairly with us. We're not even asking for half, just enough to replace the supplies we spent and to cover the healing we need."

Ruca leaned forward and spread his hands. "I understand how you feel, but the fact remains that we just don't have enough to give any away. We don't have enough for what we need. It's expensive feeding this many people."

Luke was only half listening to Ruca's excuses. When the bandit had shifted in place, the box he was sitting on had shifted slightly with him. It was faint, but Luke had definitely heard the sound of metal clinking against metal inside it. Now that he looked at the box, he saw it was black wood with funny little symbols etched into it. There was a latch on the left side and a pair of hinges on the right, brass by the looks of it. It had probably come straight out of the necromancer's wagon.

"He's literally sitting on the money," Luke told Zea. "Wilby's gone, maybe off hunting, so it's just these two. I could take them both pretty easily if we want to push it."

"Can you? Wasn't that guard the same level as you? The one they were fighting while also dealing with all the other guards?"

"He was, but he was also heavily invested in a defensive strategy. That's why the fight dragged on so long, I think."

"We need the money," Zea said. "I am not okay with just being a cripple for the rest of my life as thanks for our good deeds."

"Do we have enough left to cover the healing?"

She considered that for a second, then shook her head. "Probably . . . Hard to say. I don't know how much it'll cost here. If we were back on the western continent, I'd say yes, but we definitely don't have enough to replace all the shock stones, armor chains, and the tentacle ball I used, not to mention all the new damage to your actual armor, not if you want to have enough to live on for the next month or two."

"I'm okay with not getting reimbursed for that," Luke said. "We'll make do, and they're not wrong when they say they're going to need a lot of money to take care of more than a hundred people. But if we don't have enough money for your arm, we're getting some money for that."

Maybe it was something in their tones that warned the two bandits, or maybe it was just that they weren't speaking in a language that everyone shared, but either way, things had grown tense. Val at least was expecting a fight, and it looked like Ruca wasn't far behind. He was still sitting calmly on the box, but he'd shifted his weight to get his feet under him. If it came to it, he'd be up in an instant.

"Okay, look, here's how it is," Luke said. "I get that you have a use for that money, and I agree that it's a good one. We don't want half, even though it wouldn't be unreasonable if we did. I'm willing to forego the cost for everything we used in the fight, but the money for the healing is nonnegotiable."

"With respect, my friend, you're in no position to make demands," Ruca said. "We've already given you our answer."

"Mmm. You're sure that's how you want it?" Luke asked as he threw out **[Analyze]** on Ruca and Val just to make sure nothing had changed. To be safe, he also scanned everyone else nearby to confirm that most people were under level 20 and roughly half of them were in such bad condition that they had actual debuff lines in their status. The crossbows from the guards had been distributed among the healthier of the former slaves, but they didn't have the skills or stats to assist with aiming and reloading. The quivers were also far emptier, with most people having three or four shots at most.

"Please don't do this," Luke said.

"You're welcome to a bowl of soup," Ruca said. "If you want to travel south with us, we won't turn you away."

Zea snorted. "Travel at a glacial pace while we hunt monsters to put meat on the table and defend your refugee caravan the whole time? For free, no less. No thanks."

Ruca nodded. "Fair. You've done more than enough, and I appreciate that."

"But you won't give us a cut of the money."

"I cannot."

Luke had been eyeing up a skill he'd seen used against him a few times in previous fights. There were a few different versions of it, but he was looking at the basic, bare-bones one, **[Burst Step]**. If he'd had this before the battle with the caravan started, things would have gone much smoother. As much as he wanted to save the AP for his bloodline skills, he thought it might be time to spend a little, just to make sure he lived long enough to get the next few levels.

[Burst Step] had three ranks at the same AP costs as **[Power Strike]**, which meant he could only afford the first rank at the moment. That would be more than enough for his purposes, since the second rank just made it so he could use the skill more often, and the third rank increased the speed boost.

Luke spent 10 AP on rank 1 **[Burst Step]**.

Activating it was a lot like channeling **[Power Strike]** through his body, only without the option of choosing which limb the knot of power would charge through. It had only one option: straight down through his legs. As soon as **[Burst Step]** activated, Luke was propelled forward so fast that only his high perception stat allowed him to see anything at all. His peripheral vision became a complete blur for a fraction of a second, and his focus narrowed down to Ruca's face.

[Power Strike] went through Luke's arm and spread out through his fist, where it was transferred at the point of impact into Ruca's jaw. The bandit was hurled backward to land thirty feet away, flat on his back and a groan of pain on his lips.

Val leaped to her feet, and her blade flashed through the air. Luke slapped it with an open palm, drawing a line of blood across his skin. He hit the blade hard enough that it was knocked out of Val's hand, which didn't slow her down in the slightest. The woman had a half dozen more weapons on her, but before she could go for them, Luke stepped inside her range and hit her with an uppercut that lifted her eight feet into the air.

"Want to grab the money?" Luke asked Zea.

"Sure." She went over and flipped open the box, rifled through it for a minute, and produced a large leather pouch. "Found it."

Luke slipped around Zea to block Ruca, who'd come charging back in with a sword in either hand. The man was fast, almost too fast to keep up with despite Luke having significantly higher agility, but **[Tactical Foresight]** was too good at predicting Ruca's moves. Within three seconds of engaging, Luke smacked an open palm against Ruca's forehead and knocked him on his ass.

"Only take what we need," Luke said. "They've got a legitimate need for the money."

He went over the log, now vacated by the woman he assumed was Val's twin, and kicked Val in the knee as she tried to leap onto it. She howled in pain as she stumbled forward into the fire, and Luke took the opening to shove her out of the flames.

"Stop, drop, and roll," he called out to her when she started frantically patting down her leg.

Zea counted out a bunch of square coins with rounded edges and holes in the center. It took her longer than normal on account of her only having one hand, but Luke was able to hold the two bandits off without too much effort. The trick was keeping them from coordinating with each other, which mostly involved controlling Ruca. Val did not have a level head for fighting and obviously didn't understand her build very well. Luke guessed she'd copied it from Ruca.

"All set," Zea said.

"Start heading down the road," Luke said as he used **[Burst Step]** to intercept Val again. "I'll catch up."

Zea took off running down the road, only stopping to dodge an errant bolt fired by a man in response to Val's infuriated cries to stop the dwifkin. Everyone else just seemed confused about the situation. Luke wasn't taking the fight very seriously, having done nothing but really defend himself after his initial attacks. He hadn't even drawn his weapon.

"Well, this has been fun, but I think it's about time for me to head out," Luke told Ruca. "Best of luck getting all of this sorted out. Maybe have your people stop wasting their ammunition on us and save it for hunting. Can't be expecting Wilby to come up with all the meat, right?"

"You bastard," Ruca spat out. "People are going to starve because of the money you stole."

"I don't really feel like we stole anything," Luke said. "And I'm sure you'll come up with something. We're leaving you most of the money and all the supplies after all."

Ruca and Val managed to come at him at the same time, mostly because Luke had stopped corralling the former and the bandit had managed to sync himself up with his partner. **[Unarmed Martialist]** showed Luke exactly what to do in that situation, and it barely took any effort on his part to twist around Val and shove her into Ruca's path. He was forced to back off or risk skewering her, and Luke used the opportunity to break away from the fight.

"Later!" he called out before using **[Burst Step]** to make it to the road. Luke settled into an easy, ground-eating stride and caught up with Zea a mile or two. The two didn't stop, though Luke didn't hear any pursuit. By the time they took a break, he wanted to be miles and miles away from the camp and any possible danger.

"My arm is fucking killing me," Zea said after a while.

There was that too. Luke needed to ask System how far the closest city was.

Name	Luke Bennet	Zea Stenter
Level	43	35
XP	273559/293811	148551/157276
AP	33	4
Bloodline	SysAdmin III	None
Strength	61	7
Agility	70	30
Stamina	88	27
Perception	55	21
Skills	Burst Step (1)	Arcano Dynamics (2)
	Butchering (4)	Bartering (2)
	Consortium Standard (2)	Bloodline Purification Ritual (2)
	Counter (3)	Cadence (3)
	Deception (1)	Cold Reading (1)
	Detection (2)	Consortium Standard (1)
	Disguise (2)	Cooking (1)
	First Aid (1)	Dagger Mastery (1)
	Leatherworking (2)	Deception (1)
	Life Surge (2)	Disguise (2)
	Mace Mastery (5)	Engraving (4)
	Ostari (1)	First Aid (1)
	Peripheral Awareness (2)	Gem Cutting (1)
	Power Strike (2)	Ghost Script (1)
	Stealth (1)	Goldsmithing (2)
	Survivalist (2)	Keen Instincts (1)
	Sword Mastery (1)	Lock Picking (1)
	Tactical Foresight (2)	Mana Manipulation (3)
	Thalian (2)	Mana Sight (3)
	Torturer (1)	Mending (1)
	Twitch Reflexes (3)	Metallurgy (1)
	Unarmed Martialist (4)	Neyardic (3)
	Wood Carving (1)	Ostari (1)
	Analyze (BL)	Painting (1)
	Remote Access (BL)	Rune Forging (3)
	XP Mask (BL)	Sleight of Hand (1)
		Steady Hands (2)
		Stealth (2)
		Streetwise (2)
		Temperature Acclimation (2)
		Thalian (3)
		Whitesmithing (1)

CHAPTER 15

After about an hour of steady running at a light speed, Luke called for a break. He wasn't at 100 percent following the caravan battle, and he could tell that Zea was hanging on through sheer grit. Her arm was tucked tightly against her stomach and held in place with her good hand, and he could tell each and every step sent a jolt of pain through her.

"You sure we should stop? We're not that far away from those bandits," Zea said.

Luke waved off her concerns. "They're not coming after us. I was watching, and besides, that whole fight was a bit of acting anyway."

"It was?" Zea asked, her eyebrows shooting up. "I recall blades being drawn and stabbings being attempted."

"By Val, yeah. This whole thing was personal for her. Ruca was just putting on a show to keep the peace with her. He could have done much better if he'd tried."

"Maybe he was just tired," Zea suggested. "It's not like any of you were at your best."

"Nah. Val was trying. Ruca wasn't. And Val doesn't know what the fuck she's doing. Her build is almost identical to his, minus a few ranks and stats due to the lower level, and she doesn't know how to use half her skills. He made it look good so she wouldn't be pissed with him after we took the money, but there's no way she's going to abandon her sister to come chase after us."

"Hmm. Well, if you're sure."

"As much as I can be about anything," Luke said. "So, late dinner before it starts getting dark, and maybe we walk through the night to get to the next city?"

"How far away is it anyway?"

"One way to find out. System?"

"Yes, Luke?" the apparition said as it formed out of thin air.

"Got a geography question for you. If we keep going on this road, how far do we need to go to reach a decent-sized town or city where we can find someone with healing magic?"

"I am not able to confirm the location of an individual person, but the closest city south of your current location is three hundred miles away. It is known as Heishin and is the capital of the Beilon Province. It has a population of approximately fifteen thousand people, including both human and aerivesta."

"What's an aerivesta?" Luke and Zea asked at the same time.

"They are a bipedal race capable of flight. You met one when near Tenebrous Valley soon after arriving on Aros."

"Oh, those guys." Luke winced. He could still remember the splitting headache he'd sported after a short telepathic conversation. On the other hand, the enchanted feather he'd received had ended up saving his life, so while he didn't want to have another chat with one, he didn't have any bad feelings about the birdman himself.

"Is it a problem?" Zea asked.

"Nah, nothing like that. They just . . . They're hard to talk to, what with the whole beaks-for-mouths thing. The one I met used telepathy, which apparently gives you a nasty headache."

"It's probably fine here? If they make up a significant portion of the population, I can't imagine having any problems."

"Guess we'll find out when we get there. You want the fast and painful way or the slow and less painful way?" Luke asked.

Zea groaned. "You're going to carry me, aren't you?"

"Up to you. You want that arm fixed or what?"

"Fuuuuck. Fine, let's go as long as I can last and we'll take a walking break." Luke adjusted his pack and scooped Zea up while she huffed and cradled her arm. "You might as well ditch this armor. It's got a dozen holes in it."

"Eh, it's still got good overall coverage, and it's slowed down a lot of attacks, you know? Turned shit that would have gone in one side and out the other into scratches and flesh wounds."

"It's supposed to stop them completely."

Luke shrugged. "Not like I've got anything better after the chain died."

"Well if you want me to make another one, I need both hands working."

"Let's get going then," Luke said, starting in a slow—for him—run. Zea clenched her teeth and held her ruined elbow tighter. It was going to be a long evening for her.

* * *

"You think those people the slavers captured will be okay?" Luke asked four hours later.

Zea just groaned in response.

It had actually been weighing on Luke's mind all evening. He didn't regret keeping some of the money looted out of Torwin's stash, but there'd been a lot of truth to it being difficult to keep that many people fed and clothed. Hopefully someone in that group had some survival-oriented skills, stuff like **[Tracking]**, **[Butchering]**, and maybe **[Leatherworking]**. Most of those people had been basically naked, and it was damn cold at night this far north. Zea had put on her enchanted cloak when they'd stopped for a break an hour ago, and she was still shivering.

"Do you think *you're* okay?" he asked.

"Depends how far away we are from Heishin," she responded weakly.

"Little over halfway, I think. System, can you tell us?"

"You have one hundred sixty miles to go," System said.

"Okay, little less than halfway then. I was close," Luke said.

"Put me down," Zea said. "I need to walk a bit."

"You know, I can make you a sling for your arm," Luke said as he knelt down to let Zea get her feet under her.

"Meh, it's not going to make it hurt any less, and we'll have it fixed up by morning anyway."

"If you say so," Luke said. It was the fourth time he'd offered, and he suspected she was as sick of turning him down as he was of suggesting it. But every time he looked at her, his **[First Aid]** skill went nuts. He'd rarely ever used it, and most wounds healed up well enough on their own, but she didn't have his outrageously high stamina, and while her skin had stretched back over the wound, it was obvious that the joint was, in his professional medical opinion, extremely fucked up.

The sound of people running in unison pulled him away from his examination. A glance down the road showed him a group of people in some sort of armor with swords strapped to their backs and long red scarves trailing behind them running in unison up the road. They were perhaps five miles away, and given the pace they were moving, Luke guessed he'd be seeing them up close in the next ten minutes even if he just stood there and waited.

He counted out eleven people in two rows of five with one leading them, and liberal use of **[Analyze]** put them all in the high 20s except for the one he marked as the leader, who was level 37. A brief perusal of their skills showed a ton of overlap in their builds, with most of the combat-oriented skills revolving around hyper-fast precision strikes with their swords for melee or the use of throwing knives for range. There was also a skill called **[Blade Wall]** that encouraged group tactics by making it easier for them to protect people next to them that every single one of them had. Luke could picture them holding a passage using that skill or fighting in a circle formation against a horde out in the open.

"Got some soldiers coming up the road," Luke said. "I don't think they've got anything to do with us, but maybe we should get out of the way just in case they have issues with random foreigners."

"Nobody else has had a problem with us not being natives," Zea said. She gestured at the countryside and added, "Besides, this is all open plains. Where would we hide that they couldn't see us?"

There was some truth to that. They had at best five minutes before the soldiers spotted them, and there wasn't a tree in sight. The best Luke could come up with was to head out a mile and dig a hole to hide in. Considering the time constraints, it didn't seem like a winning strategy to him.

"That's a lot of guys to take on all at once," Luke said. "What are the chances you could **[Ghost Script]** something up with just one hand?"

Zea gave a short, bitter laugh. "Maybe if it wasn't my right arm that was out of commission and you held stuff in place for me. As it stands, there's no way I'm going to write runes with any sort of accuracy like this."

"Fuck," Luke swore. "Okay, new plan. You can use your whip in your left hand, right?" At Zea's nod, he continued, "If it comes down to a fight, the guy at the front of the line is level 37. I'm going to demolish him as my opener, and you keep your whip moving to give you space. They've got braces of throwing knives across their chests as part of their uniforms, but most of them don't have strength over 35 or agility over 30. Just keep them from getting close until I kill them off."

"You think they'll attack us?" Zea asked.

"I mean . . . No? But it always seems like that's what happens. At this point, I see a potential threat and I start considering the best way to put it down. If they want to talk instead of fight, then fine by me. I just won't expect it until it's happened."

"We're going to find out in a minute. I can see them now too."

The soldiers were running at a decent pace, and since Luke and Zea were still walking too, they met up a minute later. The soldier at the front of the line held up a hand, and his subordinates all stopped. They even ended their run on the same foot, an impressive feat of coordination in Luke's mind.

"Hello," the one Luke had mentally dubbed the captain said in Consortium Standard.

"Hi," Luke said. "Can we help you?"

"Hmm, perhaps. We are Jigon-Sai." The captain looked at Luke expectantly.

"Uh . . ." Luke glanced down at Zea, who shrugged back. "We don't know what that is. We're from the west."

"Of course," the captain said, nodding. "Jigon-Sai are special-operations soldiers from the Imperial Province. We were sent north to investigate rumors that demons have breached the passes between Beilon and Hurang to the east. Have you seen any sign of such creatures?"

"Can't say that I have, no," Luke said.

"And your companion? She can speak?"

"I can," Zea said. "But language skill is only rank 1. Sometimes I don't say what I want to."

"Ah, that is fair. I understand completely. Tell me, where have you been recently so that we can mark that you've seen no demons in that area."

"Uh, just on this road. We got off the boat at Naldrin and have been following the road south."

"I see," the captain said, nodding along as Luke spoke. "And your companion's arm?"

"There was a problem with some bandits farther north. She got shot with a crossbow."

The captain gave Luke a speculative glance. His gaze lingered on the holes in Luke's own armor. "She was not the only one."

Luke shrugged. "My stamina is higher."

"Yes, about that . . . One last question, travelers. You have seen no demons at all in your travels, which have taken you from Naldrin to here but only across the road."

Luke nodded. That wasn't a question.

"You are aware of the demons though, so you have heard the rumors," the captain said. "You know that they are monsters that do not grant XP from the system when killed, nor would you receive a kill notification after dispatching them."

"Right, that's what we heard," Luke said. "Haven't seen anything like that in person."

"Then perhaps you are aware that demons are particularly difficult to hunt down because we are not able to sense their power."

"Ah shit," Zea said softly.

"Tell me, strange travelers," the captain said, his hand going to his sword. "Why can I not sense power from either of you?"

Name	Luke Bennet	Zea Stenter
Level	43	35
XP	273559/293811	148551/157276
AP	33	4
Bloodline	SysAdmin III	None
Strength	61	7
Agility	70	30
Stamina	88	27
Perception	55	21
Skills	Burst Step (1)	Arcano Dynamics (2)
	Butchering (4)	Bartering (2)
	Consortium Standard (2)	Bloodline Purification Ritual (2)
	Counter (3)	Cadence (3)
	Deception (1)	Cold Reading (1)
	Detection (2)	Consortium Standard (1)
	Disguise (2)	Cooking (1)
	First Aid (1)	Dagger Mastery (1)
	Leatherworking (2)	Deception (1)
	Life Surge (2)	Disguise (2)
	Mace Mastery (5)	Engraving (4)
	Ostari (1)	First Aid (1)
	Peripheral Awareness (2)	Gem Cutting (1)
	Power Strike (2)	Ghost Script (1)
	Stealth (1)	Goldsmithing (2)
	Survivalist (2)	Keen Instincts (1)
	Sword Mastery (1)	Lock Picking (1)
	Tactical Foresight (2)	Mana Manipulation (3)
	Thalian (2)	Mana Sight (3)
	Torturer (1)	Mending (1)
	Twitch Reflexes (3)	Metallurgy (1)
	Unarmed Martialist (4)	Neyardic (3)
	Wood Carving (1)	Ostari (1)
	Analyze (BL)	Painting (1)
	Remote Access (BL)	Rune Forging (3)
	XP Mask (BL)	Sleight of Hand (1)
		Steady Hands (2)
		Stealth (2)
		Streetwise (2)
		Temperature Acclimation (2)
		Thalian (3)
		Whitesmithing (1)

CHAPTER 16

Peishan Jo had trained hard to reach level 37. He'd been lucky his talents had been recognized early. That had allowed him to secure a place in the Jigon-Sai, and he was one of the youngest soldiers ever to be promoted to unit captain. Those in charge expected great things from him, but that also put him under greater scrutiny than the other captains.

Whatever else they might say about him, nobody had ever accused Peishan of being stupid. He'd made the connection between these two foreigners having no auras of power and the demons feeling the same immediately. Though there had been no rumors of shape-changing demons who walked and talked as of yet, Imperial Command received new information every day about new types of demons and their strange abilities. It certainly wasn't outside the realm of possibility that some infiltration-type monster would appear and attack his great empire from the inside.

That was why he'd secretly flashed the hand signal to prepare for combat well before his unit had gotten close to the two demons. The worst part of fighting one was how difficult it was to gauge their true power, but it was rare to find a demon Peishan couldn't put down himself. With ten of his companions with him, he didn't expect to have any trouble with this pair, if that's what they truly were.

No one was making any overtly threatening moves, but they were all prepared for combat if it came down to it, and they all knew that the demons were to be captured alive if at all possible. Talking demons could provide valuable information about where the horde had come from, what their purpose was, and most importantly of all, how to send them back.

Of course, the demons weren't content to just be taken. They didn't attack though, which made sense if they were going to display greater intelligence than the average murder machine the empire had been fighting back. They tried to talk their way out of trouble.

"Easy there," the male demon said. "We're not demons. I just have a skill that lets me hide our . . . er . . . power, I think you called it. We call it an XP presence."

"Such a skill does not exist," Peishan said. "There are skills that may reduce it but not eliminate it completely. And does your companion also have such a skill? It would be highly suspicious, as I can think of few reasons a pair of foreigners traveling these lands would have for hiding themselves."

"If we were trying to hide, why would we be walking on the road?" the male demon asked. "And besides, I can turn it off. Here, see?"

Suddenly, power erupted out of both demons. He could feel their strength, and he was no longer quite so certain that his team would be able to capture them. The small female demon was only a few levels behind Peishan himself, and the male demon was far ahead. The female was wounded, but that could just be a trick. He'd personally killed a few demons who'd been able to recover from all but fatal wounds at will.

Perhaps the auras of power surrounding them were also a trick. Peishan knew of no skills that could artificially inflate the amount of power a person projected, but then, no one knew every skill. There were just too many, even for scholars who'd devoted their lives to cataloging them. That wasn't even considering that the demons seemed to somehow exist outside the system. There had been no recorded instances of any demon having an aura of power nor of the system rewarding someone for killing one.

That these two could display such auras was a point in favor of the two not being demons, but Peishan was hesitant to believe the male demon's claim. People had been searching for centuries for a skill such as he claimed, and to have it affect another person besides him? Even if they weren't demons, knowledge of such a skill would be beyond valuable. Peishan could smell a promotion in his future if he returned with the two foreigners. It wasn't the purpose of this mission, but he knew his superiors would be pleased.

Perhaps sensing his story wasn't believed, the male demon said, "Look, I can extend it to you as well. All you have to do is allow it."

"You . . . can?" Peishan hadn't expected that.

"Sure, just . . . like . . . this. There we go."

Gasps sounded from the men behind him, but Peishan barely heard them. He didn't have the words to describe what he'd just experienced. It was like someone had blinded and deafened him. He glanced around, wide-eyed, and saw his men returning his stare.

"Oh, right. I forgot to mention that part," the demon said. "No one can feel your aura of power, but in exchange, you can't feel anyone else's either. Here, you're not looking so good. Let me switch it back for you."

Just like that, everything returned to normal. "Emperor save me," Peishan gasped out. "That was . . . It was terrifying. And you're just walking around half-blind like that?"

The demon shrugged. "You get used to it eventually."

Both demons' auras disappeared again as Peishan exchanged an uneasy glance with his second-in-command. They were both thinking the same thing, that they'd come across something beyond their ability to explain. The best solution was probably to capture the two demons, regardless of whether they actually were demons. If the aura of power around the male was accurate, and especially if he'd devoted his strength to the sublime arts, it would be a rough battle.

The only way to avoid a fight that Peishan could see was to take them at their word, that they weren't demons and that they had some previously undiscovered skill. In that case, all he needed was the name of the skill and a list of prerequisites. If someone in his command could find it in the system's skill store, then Peishan would consider this a fortuitous meeting.

"What is this skill called?" Peishan asked.

"Ah, well. It's called **[XP Mask]**, but . . . it's a bloodline skill." The demon rubbed the back of his head and gave an apologetic smile.

Peishan grimaced. Of course it would be. The worst part was that it made sense. A skill like this being locked to a specific bloodline was the perfect way to hide its existence. No one outside this man's family could ever learn it, and even if it was spread around by a few illegitimate children, within a few generations the bloodline would die out unless they could get access to a ritual master.

That brought Peishan right back to his initial problem. He had no way to confirm this strange power-hiding skill was really a skill or that the two foreigners weren't demons. The only correct move was to capture them for questioning, but he was well aware of the power difference between someone like him and someone with a level in the mid-40s. Just five levels at that range were worth more than the first twenty levels combined.

If they tried to capture these two foreigners, some of his men were going to die. Maybe most of them would die. As the highest-level Jigon-Sai there, he would likely be the first person targeted. If they won, it would be at great cost, and Peishan was by no means certain of victory.

All that was only if he believed the auras he'd felt off the two foreigners were accurate. If they could hide them completely, it stood to reason they might be able to manipulate them in other ways. There were no good answers to be had here, and it might all be for nothing if it turned out that it really was a simple bloodline skill. Getting half of his command killed over something like that would be the end of Peishan's career.

If force was out, perhaps authority would work. Foreigners as a whole were remarkably insusceptible to following the lawful orders of the Imperial Law Enforcement's various organizations, but so far, this pair had been accommodating. Peishan could scarcely imagine it working, but he might try just asking for their cooperation.

"I apologize for the inconvenience, but I will need you to come with me. Understand that it is not imperial policy to detain travelers who've committed no offense, but with demons roaming the lands and your skill mimicking their ability to hide their own power, we'll need to confirm that you aren't demons in disguise before you can leave our custody."

The two demons, or maybe not demons, Peishan honestly couldn't tell at this point, exchanged glances and started talking in rapid-fire sentences using a language he didn't recognize. The male turned back after a few moments of chatter and asked, "Would you have anyone on staff who can fix her arm? We don't mind paying."

"Er . . . Yes. The Jigon-Sai employs healers to keep our soldiers in top shape, though there may be a bit of a wait. With all the demon activity we've been trying to contain, every healer has dozens upon dozens of patients every day."

The two demons said something in that other language again before the male added, "And your healers will work on someone who isn't part of your Jeegon Say?"

"Jigon-Sai," Peishan corrected.

"Right, that's what I said."

"No, you said—never mind, it's not important. Yes, I can request under my authority as a captain-ranked officer to have your friend's injury treated."

Peishan did not add that just because he requested it didn't mean it would happen. There were a lot of injured coming back from the front lines, and a request for healing on a non-life-threatening injury for what would technically be a prisoner was not likely to be a high priority.

"Right," Peishan said. "Lieutenant, select two men to accompany you to the next rendezvous point so you can explain my absence. I will return to Heishin with the foreigners so we can get this whole mess sorted out. With any luck, we'll only be a day behind you."

"Sir," his second said with a salute. He picked out two men, and they set off down the road in a jog.

"Alright, form up and reverse course, half in front and half behind our foreign guests. They are in our care until we return home, and if anything happens to them, I will personally flay the hide off the man who lets an attack through."

Within moments, the unit had reformed into two groups of four with the demons sandwiched between them and started off. Peishan was relieved to see that the two demons kept up without him having to slow the pace. It was one less thing he needed to worry about.

"This is going to blow up in our faces," Zea said.

"They're just doing their jobs. I completely get why the guy thinks we might be demons," Luke told her.

"Small comfort when we end up having to fight our way out of whatever prison cell they try to throw us into."

"Oh, come on. They didn't even try to take our weapons, *and* they sent three of their men off to do go something else. That's a show of trust right there."

Zea rolled her eyes and focused on putting one foot in front of the other. Everyone around her was running in rhythm, but her legs were just a bit too short to keep up if she ran in lockstep with them. The speed was also just a little bit too fast for her to comfortably maintain, but she knew if she said anything about it, Luke would just offer to carry her again. That was humiliating enough when it was just the two of them; no way was she going to let him do it in front of a bunch of other people.

"So, uh, just in case things do go south, you think we should discuss having a plan?" Luke asked.

Name	Luke Bennet	Zea Stenter
Level	43	35
XP	273559/293811	148551/157276
AP	33	4
Bloodline	SysAdmin III	None
Strength	61	7
Agility	70	30
Stamina	88	27
Perception	55	21
Skills	Burst Step (1)	Arcano Dynamics (2)
	Butchering (4)	Bartering (2)
	Consortium Standard (2)	Bloodline Purification Ritual (2)
	Counter (3)	Cadence (3)
	Deception (1)	Cold Reading (1)
	Detection (2)	Consortium Standard (1)
	Disguise (2)	Cooking (1)
	First Aid (1)	Dagger Mastery (1)
	Leatherworking (2)	Deception (1)
	Life Surge (2)	Disguise (2)
	Mace Mastery (5)	Engraving (4)
	Ostari (1)	First Aid (1)
	Peripheral Awareness (2)	Gem Cutting (1)
	Power Strike (2)	Ghost Script (1)
	Stealth (1)	Goldsmithing (2)
	Survivalist (2)	Keen Instincts (1)
	Sword Mastery (1)	Lock Picking (1)
	Tactical Foresight (2)	Mana Manipulation (3)
	Thalian (2)	Mana Sight (3)
	Torturer (1)	Mending (1)
	Twitch Reflexes (3)	Metallurgy (1)
	Unarmed Martialist (4)	Neyardic (3)
	Wood Carving (1)	Ostari (1)
	Analyze (BL)	Painting (1)
	Remote Access (BL)	Rune Forging (3)
	XP Mask (BL)	Sleight of Hand (1)
		Steady Hands (2)
		Stealth (2)
		Streetwise (2)
		Temperature Acclimation (2)
		Thalian (3)
		Whitesmithing (1)

CHAPTER 17

The soldiers moved without stop, which forced Luke and Zea to keep pace with them. That wasn't a problem for either of them in terms of time spent jogging, but Zea's relatively low strength and physically shorter legs made it a bit harder for her to keep up the pace they set. She persevered though, and when Luke asked if she wanted him to carry her for a bit, she turned him down.

A few hours into the run, Luke looked over at Zea and said in Thalian, "System, how far away are we?"

Since no one could see the ghostly blue figure but them, no one would know System was replying. Zea picked up on his plan immediately and replied, "Good idea."

System spoke at the same time. "Another forty-five miles."

"You checked to make sure none of them have [Thalian] on their skill lists?" Zea asked.

"Yep. We're good. One guy does have [Ostari] at rank 1 though, so don't use that. Okay, System, tell me about these guys and their organization. Not the whole history, just what's relevant right now."

"The Jigon-Sai are a branch of the Imperial Law Enforcement division. You might consider them the army of the Empire of the Sun, though there are quite a few differences in how they structure their chain of command and what duties they perform. For example, the Jigon-Sai are one of the most combat-oriented factions of the empire's military, and their field commanders are required to exceed specific levels in order to hold their positions."

"That would leave their upper command in shambles," Zea said. "If this guy is only a captain and he's closing in on level 40, I can't image the people in charge have life expectancies beyond the next decade."

"True. Most of their orders come down from imperial advisors, and the people at the top of the Jigon-Sai's ranks act as field commanders. There is a great degree of fanaticism in their ranks as new recruits are drilled with propaganda about spending their lives for the empire and how their sacrifices allow for prosperity and safety for all."

"Some things are the same everywhere," Luke muttered. "This isn't really telling me anything important. Are they known for any particular fighting style? Do they have a lot of members? If we piss them off, can we expect other branches of their military to help them?"

"Various units within the Jigon-Sai have specific builds their members take in predetermined ratios to form efficient teams designed to tackle a variety of problems, but there is no unifying combat style attributed to the organization as a whole," System explained. "Their numbers are fluctuating right now with many deaths I cannot account for, presumably due to the demons that remain unconnected to the God Machine. And yes, they have enough connections to Imperial Law Enforcement as a whole to be involved with other branches regularly."

"We could have guessed most of this," Zea said. "We should be finding out more about Heishin and their presence in that city."

Before they could continue, one of the soldiers in front said, "Captain, look there!"

The entire group followed the soldier's pointing finger to look east. "What is he pointing at?" Zea asked.

"Smoke," Luke said softly. "Lot of smoke for just a campfire. Still low in the sky too. Whatever's burning just started."

The captain threw a glance at Luke and Zea, ground his teeth, and snapped out an order. "You three, go investigate it. Two of you can stay to assist if needed, but one comes back to report on your findings."

"Sir!" the three chosen soldiers said in unison.

The peeled off from the main group, but before they'd gone even twenty feet, Luke said, "Wait. Look there."

"I don't see anything," the captain said.

"Just over the tree line on the right," Luke told him. "It's hard to see them against the smoke. They look like little people with wings and tails."

He'd spotted five of them so far, though with the smoke so far away, it was hard to make out details. Luke thought they had gray or black skin, were only two feet tall, and had wings as long as their bodies with long, ropelike tails. **[Analyze]** wasn't returning anything so far, but that might have been the distance. Sometimes he had a hard time tagging a target when it was at the very edge of his perception.

It took the soldiers longer to spot what Luke was talking about, but when one of the winged creatures flew up higher and got out from in front of the smoke, they all started swearing. "Demons," the captain said in a grim tone. "We're shorthanded, and we have a job already."

"Perhaps I could help," Luke offered.

Assisting the Jigon-Sai fight off some demons might just build up some goodwill, and even if it didn't, Luke couldn't imagine it would make things worse. Besides, he was curious about these demons. Would **[Analyze]** work on them? If it didn't, what would it say instead? This was his first opportunity to find out, but the soldiers were limiting his options. Luke was sure if he tried to go somewhere without them, it would turn into a fight to keep him in place. Plus there was still the matter of getting Zea's arm fixed up. He wanted to remain on good terms with the Jigon-Sai for as long as possible, especially if it came with perks like that.

"Perhaps," the captain said grudgingly. "Very well. We will investigate these demons and put an end to whatever destruction they are causing. If it becomes needed, you will fight together with me to suppress the enemy."

Luke grinned. "Excellent. This'll be fun."

The captain gave him a look that Luke decided to ignore. Monster hunting was the best part of living on Aros. It was simple, no complications or moral dilemmas. He just walked out somewhere civilization hadn't pacified, and sooner or later something would show up to try to kill him, only to find out that it had bitten off more than it could chew. Luke never worried about if he was doing the right thing or if the monster had a family, or even about having to run away and hide anymore. There were no misunderstandings thanks to a language barrier, no political undercurrents he failed to pick up on.

Simple. That was how he liked it.

As they approached the source of smoke, Luke spotted a few dozen buildings. The fire had been contained to the west side of the village, but there was a lot of it. He was no fireman, but he was betting those houses were done for. If they weren't already, they would be soon. The creatures—demons, supposedly—that had attacked the town where doing their best to keep anyone from getting control of the blaze, so much so that it was mostly the result of the wide space between the west and east sides of town that had prevented the whole thing from going up.

Luke counted at least forty of the demons ducking and weaving through the smoke to dive-bomb villagers armed with pitchforks, shovels, and hoes. Now that he was close enough to pick them out, Luke tried hitting them with **[Analyze]** again, but he still got nothing back. It was just like using the skill on an inanimate object, where it just failed to activate. That had never happened before. Even when he'd fought Lath back in Sicanti's harbor, the skill had returned error messages instead of nothing at all. Luke supposed that verified the claims that the demons were disconnected from the system. His SysAdmin bloodline couldn't pull their statuses from the God Machine simply because the information didn't exist.

A woman with a long sword made of some black iron stood in the center of town, shouting orders and directing the villagers into groups to better defend themselves or protect those who were frantically pulling water from the nearby well. **[Analyze]** tagged her at level 24 with a spread of stats focusing on strength and stamina and a lot of basic skills devoted to farming tasks all under rank 3. The only thing that stuck out to him was a rank 1 **[Leadership]** skill that Luke suspected she'd spontaneously developed in the last hour.

Even as the Jigon-Sai sprinted for the village, three of the gray things descended on a villager who'd strayed too far from his fellows and grabbed hold of him. He didn't even see them coming until they'd already tagged him. They beat their wings in unison and lifted the terrified man off the ground. Luke wasn't sure exactly what the plan was, whether they were just going to drop him from a height or if they were going to carry him into the fire or what, but either way, the woman with the sword was having none of it.

She might have lacked the full suite of combat skills Luke himself had, but raw stats were a power of their own. She leaped twenty feet into the air and brought the blade down on one of the demons, shearing through a wing and an arm. It screeched in agony and released the villager. Without its help, the other two couldn't continue their flight, and the man found himself falling back to the ground. He landed on flexed legs and stumbled forward a step, then scooped up his pitchfork and spun back to face the remaining demons.

For all the village's heroics, they were still slightly outnumbered by the flying demons. Worse, now that Luke was closer, he saw a second type on the ground, ones with big, bulging shoulders, rubbery purple skin, and mouths that opened in four directions, like the straw hole in a lid, except they all had anywhere from three to six long green tongues coming out of them.

"That's gross," Luke said. The tongue demons were taking up the bulk of the defenders' attention since each one had been isolated and surrounded by a dozen people who took turns hacking at it. Their attacks weren't having much of an effect, and the tongues that flailed around were able to gouge thick lines in the ground. Judging by the number of villagers already down, Luke was betting the demons could rip apart people just as easily.

"Gargoyles," the captain said, "and lashers. Too many to fight."

"You think so?" Luke asked. Neither type of demon looked all that tough to him. He was betting he could get in there and crush the tongue fuckers quickly, and with them taken care of, the villagers would be able to get the flying ones, gargoyles apparently, under control.

"Do not be fooled by what you see. The lashers are more dangerous dead than alive."

"How's that?" Luke asked.

"They seem to carry some sort of plant inside their bodies. When slain, the bulb that the tongues are connected to slides out and seeds itself in the ground. Each of those things will have dozens of tongues popping up if the host demon dies."

It was no wonder the villagers weren't killing the demons. Their strategy was just to contain them and keep the problem from getting worse, but Luke wondered what the long-term plan was. Something would have to be done about them eventually.

"How do you kill them then?" Luke asked.

The captain gestured toward the burning houses. "They'll need to be herded in there."

"Wait, what? The demons didn't start the fires?"

"No. This village was well-informed. Look, see there."

Luke followed the captain's gaze and found a group of villagers slowly herding one of the tongue fuckers between the burning buildings. It was strenuously resisting being forced that way, but the group was relentless in stabbing at it with their makeshift weapons.

"Fire, huh? Would there be an issue if they weren't burned one at a time?"

"I don't see why there would be," the captain said with a frown. "What are you thinking?"

"I'm thinking that I could pick one of those up and throw it a good hundred feet," Luke told him. "Want to find out if I'm right?"

Name	Luke Bennet	Zea Stenter
Level	43	35
XP	273559/293811	148551/157276
AP	33	4
Bloodline	SysAdmin III	None
Strength	61	7
Agility	70	30
Stamina	88	27
Perception	55	21
Skills	Burst Step (1)	Arcano Dynamics (2)
	Butchering (4)	Bartering (2)
	Consortium Standard (2)	Bloodline Purification Ritual (2)
	Counter (3)	Cadence (3)
	Deception (1)	Cold Reading (1)
	Detection (2)	Consortium Standard (1)
	Disguise (2)	Cooking (1)
	First Aid (1)	Dagger Mastery (1)
	Leatherworking (2)	Deception (1)
	Life Surge (2)	Disguise (2)
	Mace Mastery (5)	Engraving (4)
	Ostari (1)	First Aid (1)
	Peripheral Awareness (2)	Gem Cutting (1)
	Power Strike (2)	Ghost Script (1)
	Stealth (1)	Goldsmithing (2)
	Survivalist (2)	Keen Instincts (1)
	Sword Mastery (1)	Lock Picking (1)
	Tactical Foresight (2)	Mana Manipulation (3)
	Thalian (2)	Mana Sight (3)
	Torturer (1)	Mending (1)
	Twitch Reflexes (3)	Metallurgy (1)
	Unarmed Martialist (4)	Neyardic (3)
	Wood Carving (1)	Ostari (1)
	Analyze (BL)	Painting (1)
	Remote Access (BL)	Rune Forging (3)
	XP Mask (BL)	Sleight of Hand (1)
		Steady Hands (2)
		Stealth (2)
		Streetwise (2)
		Temperature Acclimation (2)
		Thalian (3)
		Whitesmithing (1)

CHAPTER 18

It turned out the captain did not want to test Luke's claim. Instead he ordered his men to assist with pushing the tongue demons into the flames while he joined the villagers fending off the gargoyles from the sky. The woman with the black sword seemed to recognize the captain, but Luke couldn't follow their rapid-fire conversation.

"Stay close to me," the captain said, switching back to Standard as he turned to face Luke. "You do not need to fight here; this is not your battle, and these are not your people."

"That's cool and all," Luke said. "But I'm not just going to stand around and let people die when I could be helping stop it."

"No, stay here where I can keep you safe," the captain said, but Luke was already scanning for his first victim.

"You good with your whip in your left hand?" he asked Zea while he figured out where to start.

"Yeah, it's all controlled by the enchantment anyway."

"And you're sure it's up to slicing through these demons?"

"Should be fine," Zea told him.

"Do not attack those demons," the captain insisted.

Luke ignored the man and asked Zea, "And if these soldiers try to kill you?"

"I'm not too concerned about any of them besides the captain," Zea told him.

"Alright, stay safe. I'll be back in a minute."

Luke took off at a run that turned into a leap twenty feet into the air, where he brought his mace down in an overhead chop on the first demon. A chunk of its skull broke off, and its head was driven down into its chest cavity. There was no notification ding, but the thing dropped like a rock and hit the ground hard enough to bounce. Luke had to assume it was dead, but if not, at least it'd be an easy kill for someone else to finish off.

If that was as bad as the demons got, Luke had nothing to worry about. Any level 20 with a sharpened piece of metal could kill these things. For Luke, it wasn't even a challenge. The truly hard part of the job was chasing the gargoyles down when they flew into the smoke cloud of the burning buildings. They were practically invisible inside the cloud.

After the first one went down, the rest retreated. Not about to let a threat live, Luke followed them into the smoke. He could easily hold his breath for hours if he needed, so other than stinging his eyes a bit, his only real concern was getting ambushed. He advanced cautiously, eyes straining to sense movement in the smoke, ears trained for the sound of air sliding across gray, fleshy wings.

Other than the surprisingly loud crackle of multiple homes around him going up in flames and the background noise of the villagers still fighting the tongue fuckers, it was silent. Luke peered through the smoke, mostly scanning rooflines for motion. Nothing. He picked out the least burned-out looking house and leaped onto the roof, where the smoke was actually thicker and he could feel the heat coming up from below him.

Extremely aware of the danger of falling through the roof into the burning house, Luke advanced slowly. He almost tripped over the gargoyle before he spotted it in front of him, still as its namesake. It was no wonder he couldn't hear them; they'd completely frozen up, and if he wasn't mistaken, their skin color and texture had changed to perfectly match the smoke. He had to assume some sort of camouflaging ability because they'd definitely been a lighter shade of gray when he'd seen them against the smoky backdrop.

The only reason he'd spotted this one was that the hot hair was carrying the smoke in a contour around its body, kind of like a smoky outline. Even that was difficult to spot, so much so that the gargoyle demon was barely two feet in front of him. It hadn't moved despite his approach, and Luke wondered if it was waiting for him to go by so that it could attack from behind. If he didn't cooperate with that plan, would it just sit there and let him punt it off the roof?

There was only one way to find out. Luke lifted the mace and swung it at the gargoyle's head. Just before it connected, the demon threw itself forward into the air and spread its wings to glide off into the smoke. That was pretty much what Luke had expected to happen, though he was surprised at the speed it had moved.

It was well within his capabilities to match though, and he wasn't afraid of falling twenty or thirty feet anymore. He jumped after it with a **[Burst Step]** to close the distance and clobbered the fleeing gargoyle. Its body went into an uncontrolled spin, and it struck the ground hard. Luke landed nearby and walked over to make sure it wasn't going to get back up.

The demon looked dead, but months of waiting for the kill notification, a lesson only reinforced when he'd had to deal with Lath again after the ants had gotten ahold of him, had made him wary of just assuming things were dead because that's what it looked like.

It had what appeared to be some sort of pasty, wet sludge leaking out of its body and staining the grass. The blow Luke had dealt it had practically torn off one of its wings and pulverized its side where a rib would be on a normal person, but it didn't seem like the gargoyles actually had bones. He was starting to wonder exactly how they reacted to physical damage, and a quick glance toward where he'd left the first body showed him that it was gone.

"Shit, you fuckers know how to play dead, don't you?"

Luke pounced on the downed gargoyle, his mace leading the way. This time, it couldn't just tip itself out into open air, and its last-second attempt to dodge was far too slow. The mace slammed down in the middle of its back and flattened it back to the dirt. Luke didn't let up the pressure. He didn't know where this thing's weak point was, but it obviously wasn't the same as a human's.

More blows rained down on it, targeting limbs, joints, its chest, anywhere he thought there might be something special like that seed he'd once ripped out of a tree elemental. Its skin cracked and tore and more of that heavy sludge rolled out. It reminded Luke of liquid concrete, except a much darker color. After twenty or so strikes, the gargoyle was reduced to a fleshy sac covered in rips in the middle of a puddle of its concrete blood.

If that wasn't enough to kill it, Luke didn't know what would do the job. It was no wonder the villagers were having such a hard time of it defending themselves. Between it taking a dozen of them to prod the tongue fuckers over to the burning buildings so they could torch the bastards and the gargoyles that took forever to kill harassing all the humans, it would be an all-night job for him to clean this up himself.

Fortunately, there were also eight soldiers and one Zea to help the village out. They weren't doing a good job of killing any of the gargoyles, but they'd taken some of the pressure off by freeing up a bunch of villagers when they took over herding two of the tongue fuckers. Now that the clumps of humans were thicker, the gargoyles had less opportunity to snatch people off the ground. It didn't hurt that Luke had chased a lot of them back into the smoke and they had yet to emerge.

"Luke!" Zea yelled. "Could use some help over here!"

He glanced over and saw a crowd of six gargoyles had descended upon the group consisting of Zea, the black-sword woman, and the captain. They weren't doing so hot at fending the demons off, and he could see two more circling around the group to find the right angle of approach.

The ones they were already fighting were covered in scratches and gouges, but that didn't seem to hinder them. Wherever someone had managed to score a hit deep enough to make the demon bleed, its concrete sludge just oozed out of the wound and then hardened to form a rough patch job.

Luke rushed over and scattered the gargoyles when he leaped into the air and crashed through them. One unlucky demon took the brunt of the attack, and he beat it to death just like the last one while the others swirled away on hot currents of air.

"What happened?" Luke asked after the gargoyle was dead. He pointed at the sword-wielding woman and added, "I saw you dismember one of these things on the way in."

She grimaced and held up the weapon for him to see. Its edge was chipped and dulled, in far worse condition than it had been ten minutes ago. "It is like cutting through granite," she said in a heavy accent. "One, two swings, yes. Keep going, and it is impossible."

"It is why I sent my men to help corral the lashers," the captain added. "With this kind of enemy, it is better to capture them in nets, then smash them with heavy weights once they are safely pinned down. They are distractions against the true threats."

"But you don't have any nets," Luke guessed.

"No," the captain agreed. "We were not expecting to find this particular type of demon so far north. They haven't been seen outside the Melthor Province until now. The rumors of demons coming over the mountains from Hurang did not mention the presence of gargoyles."

"They're fucking your plan up," Luke said, noting four of the Jigon-Sai soldiers struggling to deal with the gargoyles near the burning buildings. They had a tongue fucker pointed in more or less the right direction to shove it into the side of the house where it would presumably be burned alive, but a trio of gargoyles were swooping and diving around them, forcing the soldiers to defend themselves from all angles and giving the tongue fucker the chance to escape.

The demons truly were more of a threat than almost anything else Luke had fought. Most of the monsters he'd come across had been animallike in appearance and intelligence. Sure, they had extra spikes or horns and were usually way bigger than they were supposed to be, but they were dumb and usually it only took Luke a minute to tease out the limits of their abilities before he moved in for the kill. There had been the occasional exception, but if Luke had been in danger, it was more because whatever he was fighting was faster or stronger than him.

Demons all seemed to have their own little tricks, like their concrete blood or the supposed tongue-vine eruption that would happen if he killed one of the purple guys. They were also surprisingly individual in their appearances. Every gargoyle's face was different. Some of them had longer or shorter wings or anywhere from three to six claws on each hand. The tongue fuckers were more uniform, but there were still differences in size, musculature, number of tongues, and in some cases, scars on their rubbery skin.

"We need rope to form lassos," the captain said to the village woman. "Nets would be better, but if there aren't any, then there aren't any."

"Not going to find much in the way of rope either," she told him. She nodded at one of the burning houses. "General store's right there. If it hasn't all burned up already, it will soon."

"Too bad your tentacle ball got used up fighting that necromancer," Luke muttered to Zea.

"No kidding. Would have been perfect. Just throw it into the air, turn it on, and watch it go."

"You think anyone's going to risk going into that house for the rope?"

"Not unless they're stupid. Don't you go volunteering for it either," she said.

"I'd rather just kill them the hard way anyway," Luke said.

The conversation was interrupted then by a chorus of screams coming from the north side of the village. Whatever was happening was hidden around the corner of the burning houses, but Luke could hear a snapping and cracking sound, barely audible over the fire and the screaming.

"Probably should go investigate that, huh?" he asked the captain.

Name	Luke Bennet	Zea Stenter
Level	43	35
XP	273559/293811	148551/157276
AP	33	4
Bloodline	SysAdmin III	None
Strength	61	7
Agility	70	30
Stamina	88	27
Perception	55	21
Skills	Burst Step (1)	Arcano Dynamics (2)
	Butchering (4)	Bartering (2)
	Consortium Standard (2)	Bloodline Purification Ritual (2)
	Counter (3)	Cadence (3)
	Deception (1)	Cold Reading (1)
	Detection (2)	Consortium Standard (1)
	Disguise (2)	Cooking (1)
	First Aid (1)	Dagger Mastery (1)
	Leatherworking (2)	Deception (1)
	Life Surge (2)	Disguise (2)
	Mace Mastery (5)	Engraving (4)
	Ostari (1)	First Aid (1)
	Peripheral Awareness (2)	Gem Cutting (1)
	Power Strike (2)	Ghost Script (1)
	Stealth (1)	Goldsmithing (2)
	Survivalist (2)	Keen Instincts (1)
	Sword Mastery (1)	Lock Picking (1)
	Tactical Foresight (2)	Mana Manipulation (3)
	Thalian (2)	Mana Sight (3)
	Torturer (1)	Mending (1)
	Twitch Reflexes (3)	Metallurgy (1)
	Unarmed Martialist (4)	Neyardic (3)
	Wood Carving (1)	Ostari (1)
	Analyze (BL)	Painting (1)
	Remote Access (BL)	Rune Forging (3)
	XP Mask (BL)	Sleight of Hand (1)
		Steady Hands (2)
		Stealth (2)
		Streetwise (2)
		Temperature Acclimation (2)
		Thalian (3)
		Whitesmithing (1)

CHAPTER 19

Y ou need to stay here where I can keep an eye on you," Peishan snapped
at the demon. Or possibly just human, he supposed. There had been
reports of demons attacking one another, so the man's assault on the gargoyles didn't conclusively prove anything, but it was one more piece of evidence in an increasingly large pile that indicated the man had been telling
the truth.

The maybe demon maybe human, Luke, if he'd understood the rambling
foreign tongue the two had been speaking in earlier, shook his head. "I get that
you're trying to do your job, but I'm not going to stand here with my thumb
up my ass while people in front of me get brutally murdered by these things. I
promise I won't leave without talking to you first after the fight's over, but I'm
going to keep getting involved."

Peishan understood that motivation. Teaching a new soldier to not act on
an immediate problem was always a challenge. It was hard to watch something
horrible happen right before their eyes, sometimes barely even a hundred feet
away, to see it in all its vile detail and not help. That was what soldiers were for,
to protect those who couldn't protect themselves.

But sometimes it was a trap, and those victims were just bait or a distraction.
Sometimes the door needed to be guarded, and soldiers had to harden their
hearts against individual suffering to preserve the greater good. It was a difficult notion to instill in good men and women who had joined the Jigon-Sai.

He was just as susceptible as anyone else. That was why they were in this
little flyspeck of a village, after all. Returning to Heishin with two strange foreigners who might or might not be demons was more important than saving a

few dozen people who were irrelevant in the grand scheme of things. He knew that.

His men were here anyway, and not a one of them had argued against the orders. He'd have to justify that to his superiors later. It would probably cost him some political capital to save this village when it could be argued that doing so put his control of two new potential infiltrator-type demons in jeopardy.

In this situation, with the two foreigners being such unknowns, potentially hostile even, the best thing to do was to remove them from the battle. They were variables that only made it more difficult to predict how things would turn out, and Peishan needed to be able to make accurate predictions so that he could have his men in place to prevent problems before they occurred. That was an officer's job, after all.

The problem was that he didn't think he actually had the physical capabilities to stop Luke, especially not after watching the man in action. If he truly wasn't a demon, then he was incredibly strong even for his level. Peishan certainly would not have leaped into literal fires and blinded himself with smoke just for the chance to pursue a demon. There were so many ways that could have ended badly, but Luke had done it without a second thought. And then somehow, he'd come right back out, completely unharmed and still chasing a gargoyle, which he'd proceeded to knock out of the sky and then viciously beat to death despite the demon's insanely high resilience to damage.

His companion was less impressive, though Peishan thought she would fare better against the lashers. Her weapon was some sort of magical whip that left deep grooves in the flesh of any gargoyle that got within range, but it lacked the strength to cut through their dense, stonelike skin. Part of him wanted to put her with a group to pacify lashers, since she'd displayed perfect accuracy and he was sure she could slice off the prehensile tongues that made that type of demon so dangerous in their initial forms.

If he could trust them, that's what he would have done. But they weren't his soldiers, they were his prisoners. For now, they were willing prisoners. As long as he handled them with a light touch, it might stay that way. As soon as they tried to leave, things would get messy. He was very much afraid that outcome was almost inevitable. Luke was already proving that he was not amenable to following orders, probably not even orders whose goals he agreed with if it wasn't how he personally wanted to reach those goals.

In other words, he was a typical lordless wanderer. They had different names in different societies and languages—knight-errant, ronin, adventurer. But they all stood for the same thing: chaos and anarchy.

It wasn't illegal to go around fighting monsters, however, not even if those monsters happened to be demons. As long as the two foreigners didn't attack law-abiding citizens of the empire, they were within their rights.

All that was to say that while Peishan was sure something had gone wrong with shoving one of those lashers into the flames, he absolutely did not want the foreigner over there making it worse. He trusted his men to help the villagers hold back the gargoyles and kill off the lashers one at a time in as safe and controlled a manner as possible.

"Yeah . . . So, I'm going to go check up on that," Luke said.

"No, stay he—and he's gone," Peishan said.

That captain was far too much of a lead-from-the-rear kind of guy for Luke's tastes. He was seriously just going to stand there and watch everyone else risk life and limb while he kept an eye on things, even when something had obviously gone wrong. People were hurt or dying, and the guy just wanted to stand around.

Luke activated **[Burst Step]** and zipped past the houses so fast it might as well have been teleportation. He wasn't sure what he was expecting to find at the north side of the village, but it wasn't three dead bodies that had been dismembered by dozens of vine-like tongues. At least, Luke was pretty sure there were only three. It was hard to tell on account of the fact that each body was in separate pieces, a leg over here, a foot over there, and an arm off to the side. All of them were held up in the air and being whipped back and forth by the frenzied vines.

Near the burning building was the exploded corpse of a tongue fucker. It had black scorch marks on one side, and there were shriveled black vines in the flames. That was only near one limb though, and the rest of its body had been split open from the inside to release a hundred or more of its tongues, which had immediately grabbed hold of the people trying to force it into the fire and ripped them limb from limb.

Two of the soldiers had been caught at the very edge of the tongues' reach and were frantically hacking at the fleshy appendages to free their legs. It was a losing battle though as they were dragged closer and close to the center. As soon as a few of the tongues reached their arms, it would be over for them. Even if they managed to prevent that, the tongues were edged in some way, and both soldiers were bleeding freely from their legs.

Luke only saw two ways he could help. He could go to the soldiers directly and start hacking at the tongues with his knife, but it was a short blade, and while he might do a better job thanks to his higher stats, that would only delay the inevitable. The other option was to go into the burning house itself, grab the corpse from its scorched side where hopefully the heat and open flames would prevent the tongues from attacking him, and haul it fully inside the building. Presumably, as long as the corpse was burning, all of the tongue vines coming out of it would wither up and die. Maybe he might find some spot inside the body itself he could strike to instantly kill the tentacle-monster core.

The obvious problem with that plan was that he had to willingly walk into a burning building that might collapse on him at any moment. Then he stopped to think about it and realized that it didn't really matter. His stamina was so high now that standing on the roof of a different burning house in a cloud of smoke had barely done more than make him mildly uncomfortable and sting his eyes a bit. He'd had worse playing basketball on hot summer days.

How bad could it be? Luke quickly located a window that didn't have flames actively shooting out of it and jumped through. The temperature spiked, and it got harder to see, but his ears pointed him toward the sound of soldiers still screaming. Luke ducked low under the smoke, mostly for better visuals, and made his way toward the back of the house.

It turned out it was far hotter in the house than it had been on the roof, enough that he started sweating immediately, but not so bad that it actually hurt. It felt more like a mild sunburn than anything else. Once he'd grown accustomed to the heat itself, Luke's primary concern was making sure he didn't knock out any walls that might bring the roof down on his head. Though if that happened, he was pretty sure he could dig himself out.

He quickly found the hole that had been knocked in the wall of the house. Two other demon corpses were already in that room, both charred and blackened. They hadn't exploded like the one that was still outside the house. Instead, they'd swollen to three times their normal size until they'd split at the seams and ropy tongue vines had slipped out like entrails.

"Well . . . Ew," Luke said as he kicked one of the bodies off to the side.

His plan seemed to be working, as far as he could tell. None of the tongues were attacking him inside the house at least. He approached the body that had sprouted a killing field, reached down to grab the charred limb, and heaved it into the fire. It didn't make any noises, but his action definitely got the attention of the tongues.

He wondered if they were able to sense him as they started whipping through the superheated air inside the house or if they were just flailing blindly. Outside, the panicked yells of the soldiers increased in volume, but Luke thought that was more from being dragged closer to the flames themselves than from any increased aggression from the demon. If anything, the tongues had gone wild from the flames, and any that weren't already touching the soldiers were ignoring them.

Luke dodged the vines easily enough. **[Twitch Reflexes]** was especially good at getting him out of the way. He wasn't sure how long it would take them to die, but there wasn't much reason to stick around to watch, not when there were other demons in need of killing.

Just before he turned to leave though, Luke paused. The body was sliding across the floor, so slowly that he wouldn't have noticed without his high perception and **[Detection]** to point it out to him. While most of the vines were flailing around, some of them were pushing against the floor and jerking the body back and forth. It looked random, but over a few seconds, the whole thing got a few inches closer to dragging itself out of the fire.

Whether it would make it back out on its own before succumbing to the flames was another matter. Luke wasn't willing to let it try. He hoped those two soldiers were just about done freeing themselves because he snagged a handful of writhing tongues and heaved the entire mass deeper into the house.

Screams laced with renewed fear came from the soldiers. "Whoops," Luke muttered. "Guess they weren't ready after all."

There was no way Luke was leaping over that knot of tongues to help them. That was just asking to get snared and dragged down. He picked the most damaged-looking wall and hoped making a hole big enough for him to walk through wasn't going to bring everything down, then activated **[Burst Step]** and slammed into it.

Name	Luke Bennet	Zea Stenter
Level	43	35
XP	273559/293811	148551/157276
AP	33	4
Bloodline	SysAdmin III	None
Strength	61	7
Agility	70	30
Stamina	88	27
Perception	55	21
Skills	Burst Step (1)	Arcano Dynamics (2)
	Butchering (4)	Bartering (2)
	Consortium Standard (2)	Bloodline Purification Ritual (2)
	Counter (3)	Cadence (3)
	Deception (1)	Cold Reading (1)
	Detection (2)	Consortium Standard (1)
	Disguise (2)	Cooking (1)
	First Aid (1)	Dagger Mastery (1)
	Leatherworking (2)	Deception (1)
	Life Surge (2)	Disguise (2)
	Mace Mastery (5)	Engraving (4)
	Ostari (1)	First Aid (1)
	Peripheral Awareness (2)	Gem Cutting (1)
	Power Strike (2)	Ghost Script (1)
	Stealth (1)	Goldsmithing (2)
	Survivalist (2)	Keen Instincts (1)
	Sword Mastery (1)	Lock Picking (1)
	Tactical Foresight (2)	Mana Manipulation (3)
	Thalian (2)	Mana Sight (3)
	Torturer (1)	Mending (1)
	Twitch Reflexes (3)	Metallurgy (1)
	Unarmed Martialist (4)	Neyardic (3)
	Wood Carving (1)	Ostari (1)
	Analyze (BL)	Painting (1)
	Remote Access (BL)	Rune Forging (3)
	XP Mask (BL)	Sleight of Hand (1)
		Steady Hands (3)
		Stealth (2)
		Streetwise (2)
		Temperature Acclimation (2)
		Thalian (3)
		Whitesmithing (1)

CHAPTER 20

Wood exploded into the open air in a cloud of splinters as Luke bulled his way through the wall. Behind him, the house shuddered, and loose pieces of timber, weakened by the flames, collapsed onto the floor. A chunk of the roof came down right after, exactly what Luke had been afraid would happen.

It buried the writhing mass of tongue vines, but the two soldiers also got caught up in it. One of them was completely hidden by the falling debris, but the other had managed to extract himself enough that his upper half was still exposed. Unlike Luke, however, he didn't have a high enough stamina stat to handle being subjected to the flames like that.

Amid fresh screams of pain, Luke rushed forward and pulled out his knife. With one hand, he lifted the slab of roof that had crashed down on the man, while the other worked his blade to slice any vines he could see still wrapped around the soldier's legs, but for the first time ever, the alchemically treated ever-sharp blade failed to slice through something. It was no wonder the soldiers had been having such a hard time getting free; those tongues were stronger than steel.

If his blade wasn't up to the task, Luke would just have to help another way. He grabbed hold of a tongue vine with both hands and, ignoring the slicing feeling in his palms and fingers, tore it into two pieces. Then he grabbed another, and another, and another. Finally, the soldier was loose. Luke grabbed him with his free hand and shoved him backward, away from the burning house and the deadly, constricting tongue vines.

He threw the chunk of burning roof and timber off to the side and heaved the next piece into the air. The older soldier was on his back underneath it, unconscious and still snarled in tongue vines. His clothing was on fire, and he was covered in burns, but he was still alive. Mercifully, the tongues were not. Sometime in the last few seconds, the demon itself had died, and it was much easier to pull the second soldier out.

"You're not looking so good, buddy," Luke said. **[Analyze]** came back with a 26 for the soldier's stamina, which was comparatively low. Pretty much all of the rest of soldiers where midthirties or higher. "Let's get you back to your boss."

Luke helped the still-conscious soldier to his feet and carried the one who'd been buried to where the captain was arguing with the black-sword woman about something. They fell silent as he approached, at least until Luke set the man down.

"Your recklessness caused the house to collapse," the captain said. "These burns are your fault."

Luke shrugged. "Could have been a lot worse. If I hadn't intervened, they'd have died like everyone else."

Other than that one mishap, things seemed to be going well for the villagers. They were successfully holding back the gargoyles now that the soldiers had started to take over confining the tongue fuckers and herding them into the fires. A number of gargoyles flying around had scars across their skin from being struck, and in three separate spots, a group of farmers were collaborating to kill them. Two villagers armed with pitchforks would pin the gargoyle to the ground while the rest took turns pounding on it with sledgehammers until it eventually deflated and its concrete blood stained the grass.

"That's one way to do it," Luke said, nodding toward the hammer-wielding groups.

"Standard tactic," the sword-wielding woman told him. "Nets are recommended, but I think this way works better."

Before Luke could respond, she rushed off to attack a gargoyle that had managed to separate a woman from the rest of her group and was trying to drag her up into the air. She was small enough that Luke thought the gargoyle might just manage it, but then that black sword struck its wing. It wasn't sharp enough to shear through it anymore, but the impact still forced the demon to drop the woman.

"Looks like things are under control now," Zea said. "Half of those lashers are dead. The gargoyles are being thinned out and aren't causing nearly as many problems as they were ten minutes ago."

The captain grunted but otherwise ignored her while he scanned the village. As far as Luke could tell, Zea was right. There might be some casualties if people made mistakes, but that was always the danger of life-and-death fighting. The captain looked worried. No, scratch that. He looked terrified and like he was barely keeping it under control.

"You know something," Luke said. The man started and looked over at him.

"We should evacuate the village as soon as those lashers are dead," he said.

"We're not evacuating when we're winning," the village woman snapped back. "You've got no proof that more demons are coming."

"It's the smell," the captain said. "That's the real danger of the lashers."

"That burnt-sap stink?" Luke asked.

"Other demons can smell it. It draws them in. If there's anything else in the area, it's heading our way right now."

"Everything in the area is already here, attacking us," the villager said. "If there was anything else, it would have already shown up."

"What kind of demon are you expecting?" Zea asked.

The captain just shrugged. "There will be something. I have to be ready to intercept it. Hopefully there won't be too many."

"Not much we can do about that unless something actually shows up," Luke said. He turned to the sword-wielding village woman and asked, "You have any first aid supplies? This guy's going to have a hell of a time coming back from these injuries if we don't do anything to help."

The woman grimaced and shook her head. "Tried to set up a first aid station an hour ago. The gargoyles swarmed it and killed three people. Tried it again inside a house. They attacked that too."

"Fuck. What have you been doing with the injured?"

"Two guys are carrying them away from the fighting to a farmhouse about a mile out of town. But they can't keep up with how fast people are getting hurt. Maybe we can spare a few more to help now that the Jigon-Sai is here."

"You have your wounded all gathered in one central location? Tell me it's at least guarded," the captain said sharply, his head whipping around to stare at the woman.

The woman shook her head. "Not enough people."

Luke wasn't entirely sure what language the captain started speaking in, but he recognized the tone and assumed the man was reciting a litany of long-winded swearing. He took a moment to compose himself, then called out, "Jigon-Sai!" followed by what Luke assumed were orders. He thought he caught the word for *assemble* or *return* in there.

The village woman said something, questioning what the captain was doing, if Luke understood her correctly. Why did they need so many languages anyway? Things would have been a lot simpler with just one.

"What's going on?" Zea asked Luke.

"Not sure. I think the good captain here is ordering all his troops to pull out of the village. Maybe we're heading for that farm with all the injured on it?"

"Maybe we should just walk away from this whole mess," Zea said. "Not to be heartless, but this isn't our problem, and they've got it under control. Unless you want to spend the next hour fucking around and mopping up the last of the demons, we might as well go."

"Well . . . Maybe. We're probably not going to get a better time to break free of these soldiers without killing them. But we'd be giving up access to their healers if we leave."

"I doubt they were intending to honor that anyway, and we've got enough money to pay for our own."

The Jigon-Sai soldiers had started extracting themselves and were assembling in front of their captain. Of the original eight he'd entered the village with, only six were still standing. One was laid out where Luke had left him, and the other had lost his head to a gargoyle while he was trying to contain a lasher. His body had been left where it had fallen, at least for now.

The captain started snapping out orders while ignoring the screeching rant of the village woman. The rest of the villagers scrambled to fill the holes left behind by the soldiers, but they weren't in a good position to just jump right in, and Luke saw more than a few fresh injuries.

"That's not cool," he said. "Just going to bail on these people like that?"

"We need to get to that medical station immediately," the captain said. "The village can defend itself, but those people are going to die if we don't hurry, and it'll be worse for everyone else."

"Why? What do you think is coming?"

Practically on cue, a tremor shook the ground. It was slight, so small that Luke barely felt it. No one else seemed to notice, but the captain was watching him. "You have a high perception, right? Did you feel the ground moving?"

"Yeah? What does it mean?"

"Go! Now, run!" the captain bellowed. "Blood hunters about to breach a mile that way."

The soldiers all gaped at him, but they quickly got over their surprise and began sprinting out of the village. The sword-wielding woman protested, but her words fell on deaf ears. The soldiers left her behind, and the captain hesitated only long enough to look to Luke and Zea.

"This . . . This is a suicide mission. We go now in hopes of limiting the devastation to come later. The two of you should flee. If you can convince the villagers to go with you, so much the better. I am sorry I was distrustful of you and thought you might be demons in disguise."

The captain ran off without another word, leaving the two of them with the village woman. She'd fallen silent after they left, but she stared at them with tears in her eyes. "I take back any bad things I said about him," she said when she noticed Luke looking at her.

"He seemed pretty certain that he was going to die," Zea said. "What's a blood hunter anyway?"

"Demons that multiply by eating blood. They're individually weak, but their numbers can grow out of control if they're not culled immediately. With all the wounded there . . . I didn't think it would be a problem. There haven't been any demons here before today. They were all in the south and on the other side of the mountains."

"Are you part of their military?" Luke asked. "You seem to know a lot about these."

"No," the woman said with a shake of her head. "My uncle was. He died to the demons a month ago, and I went to fetch his possessions. He had a book detailing the different types of demons we've encountered so far, their tactics and habits, the best ways we've come up with to defeat them."

"That'd be a useful book to have," Zea said. "Could we maybe get a look at it?"

"Doubtful," the village woman said. She pointed at the burning house that Luke had caused to partially collapse. The fire had moved all the way up the exterior walls and was making its way across the roof now. "That was my house."

Luke would have felt bad about it, but honestly, he'd only sped up the total collapse of the building. All the burning houses were destined for the same fate. Their owners had known that when they'd lit the fires to begin with.

Another tremor passed under his feet, this one stronger and lasting far longer. The others felt it this time, and they turned to look out east toward where the Jigon-Sai had run off. Even as Luke watched, something the size of a grain silo burst straight up from the ground and rose a hundred feet into the air. It was a dirty yellow color and had mud caked on its skin, which glistened with some sort of slimy fluid.

The top of the silo split open, and hundreds of dog-sized creatures flew out into the air. They whirled around like some massive swarm of mosquitos and, as one, dove for the nearby farmhouse while the humans inside shouted and screamed.

Six soldiers and a captain weren't going to be enough to stop that, not even close. If the village woman was right about these blood hunters, it was in Luke's best interest to go help them. He glanced down at Zea, who sighed and nodded. She'd obviously come to the same conclusion.

Luke used **[Burst Step]** to throw himself forward and ran as fast as he could.

Name	Luke Bennet	Zea Stenter
Level	43	35
XP	273559/293811	148551/157276
AP	33	4
Bloodline	SysAdmin III	None
Strength	61	7
Agility	70	30
Stamina	88	27
Perception	55	21
Skills	Burst Step (1)	Arcano Dynamics (2)
	Butchering (4)	Bartering (2)
	Consortium Standard (2)	Bloodline Purification Ritual (2)
	Counter (3)	Cadence (3)
	Deception (1)	Cold Reading (1)
	Detection (2)	Consortium Standard (1)
	Disguise (2)	Cooking (1)
	First Aid (1)	Dagger Mastery (1)
	Leatherworking (2)	Deception (1)
	Life Surge (2)	Disguise (2)
	Mace Mastery (5)	Engraving (4)
	Ostari (1)	First Aid (1)
	Peripheral Awareness (2)	Gem Cutting (1)
	Power Strike (2)	Ghost Script (1)
	Stealth (1)	Goldsmithing (2)
	Survivalist (2)	Keen Instincts (1)
	Sword Mastery (1)	Lock Picking (1)
	Tactical Foresight (2)	Mana Manipulation (3)
	Thalian (2)	Mana Sight (3)
	Torturer (1)	Mending (1)
	Twitch Reflexes (3)	Metallurgy (1)
	Unarmed Martialist (4)	Neyardic (3)
	Wood Carving (1)	Ostari (1)
	Analyze (BL)	Painting (1)
	Remote Access (BL)	Rune Forging (3)
	XP Mask (BL)	Sleight of Hand (1)
		Steady Hands (2)
		Stealth (2)
		Streetwise (2)
		Temperature Acclimation (2)
		Thalian (3)
		Whitesmithing (1)

CHAPTER 21

It was a journey of a little over a mile. The Jigon-Sai soldiers were just slightly over halfway there when the silo-shaped thing erupted out of the ground and started spewing mosquitos the size of Labradors into the air. They were moving at a good clip, but they would not reach the farmhouse in time to save the injured villagers from being attacked.

Something about **[Burst Step]** kept it from being constantly on, but Luke could still use it every few seconds. That, combined with strength and agility both close to 70, saw him blurring past the soldiers in seconds. They gaped at him as he sped by, and the captain started to say something, but Luke was well past their group before he got the first word out.

It took him just under a minute to reach the demons, and Luke figured he could maintain that pace for upward of an hour with regular uses of **[Burst Step]** and probably all day long without it. Luke wasn't even breathing hard when he reached the silo-shaped demon, which up close looked more like some sort of giant grub or worm.

He didn't bother trying to navigate the broken earth around the demon. Instead, he turned his forward momentum into a running leap and brought his mace around, at speed and infused with **[Power Strike]**, to slam into the side of the demon. Flesh rippled out from the point of impact and an earsplitting scream filled the air, though it was hidden under the rumble of cracking and breaking ground.

Luke rebounded off the demon and landed thirty feet away, precisely where the tremors were the worst. The entire silo was falling backward, and though it was bending at ground level, more of the yellow flesh that had been hidden underground was forced upward to break free of the dirt. More important to Luke, the point of impact looked like a spot of bad road rash with a big chunk of flesh torn away.

The demon wasn't dead by any means, but Luke had hurt it. If he could hurt it, he could kill it. It would just take time. Unfortunately for the injured, he didn't have that time. The Jigon-Sai would catch up in a minute or so, but until then, someone had to defend the villagers from the giant mosquito demons.

There was a villager on the porch wielding a shovel in both hands, but he was doing little more than keeping a trio of the giant mosquitos, presumably what the captain was referring to when he started yelling about blood hunters, back. That was working for him, except that he hadn't killed any of them and more were entering the house through the windows.

Luke snagged a passing mosquito by one of its back legs and heaved backward to keep it from joining in the attack, but instead of stopping the demon when he pulled, he inadvertently ripped the leg off. The blood hunter let out a loud, angry buzzing sound as it tumbled forward, but it quickly righted itself and fled from Luke. He regarded the multisegmented leg, which dripped a syrupy yellow liquid out one end, then tossed it aside and chased the blood hunter into the house.

It was a big old farmhouse, one of those sprawling things that had been added onto multiple times over its life and that housed three or more generations. Luke landed amid a heap of broken wood, what had once been the shutters before the first blood hunter in had blasted through them. Two men were on the floor on simple blankets, both wrestling with blood hunters to keep from being stabbed by hose-like proboscises that tapered down to sharp points.

The blood hunters weren't strong, but the men they were attacking were already weakened from injuries, and despite their battles being only seconds long, they were losing. Luke brought his mace around in a sideways swipe that slammed one of the blood hunters into the wall, where it splattered as it skidded across the wood and left a long yellow smear behind.

The other injured man still under attack got a foot up under the blood hunter and kicked it into the air, where it wobbled for a second before stabilizing with a flick of its wings and diving back down. Luke intercepted it and killed it with a single blow.

"Get up if you can walk. You've got to get everyone out of here now," Luke told them. "The Jigon-Sai are coming down the road, but they're not here yet. Meet them out there."

Then he was gone before either of the injured villagers could reply. There were plenty of other people in the house, mostly in other bedrooms, and the blood hunters were everywhere looking for them. The demons weren't strong, but they had the numbers to swarm whole towns, and they were still small enough to gang up on the average adult in groups of three or four.

Luke suspected that they wouldn't fare well against a city or really any group of people that was prepared and in good health. There was a reason they'd targeted this farmhouse and not the rest of the village. As he tore through the halls chasing the blood hunters down, he found then focusing on the wounded villagers and only fighting the people caring for them if those people got in the way.

Blood hunters died by the dozens, but there were always more coming in, and too many of the wounded weren't able to get up. That was why they'd been carried out to the farmhouse to begin with. Luke either needed to defend the house in its entirety—something he just couldn't do with so many possible points of entry—or people were going to start dying.

Two of the villagers already had. While Luke did laps as quickly as he could, the caretakers struggled to do more than hold off the blood hunters, and new ones kept appearing and attacking in every room Luke wasn't in. All he was doing was slowing down the inevitable.

Luke arrived in a room to find a shriveled corpse, completely drained of its blood, and the mosquito-like demon that had done the deed had darkened from a brownish-yellow color similar to the earth-piercing silo monster outside to something with reddish tones. It was busy fleeing back out the window, heading back for its . . . mobile hive, Luke supposed. He didn't know what happened when the blood hunter reached home base, but if they wanted it, he opposed it automatically.

He jumped out the window after it, straight up into the air, and swatted the blood hunter like the bug it was. An explosion of stolen blood rained down on the grass below and coated the front side of Luke's body, but at least the demon didn't make it back to its nest. That was probably worth something.

Luke skidded across the ground as he landed, looked up, and saw the soldiers running toward the house. They had swords drawn, and the one in the lead cut down the blood hunters buzzing around the front door, but Luke was afraid it might be too late to save everyone. Even as he glanced over, he saw two more of the demon mosquitos flee out through open windows and head for their hive.

"Kill those!" the captain bellowed at Luke. "If they get the blood back to the carrier worm, more hunters come out."

Luke was happy to comply, but he couldn't fly. Given how high up they were, the only way he had to stop them was to throw the mace. That would, at best, kill one of them, and since he wasn't fucking Thor, the weapon wasn't coming back after he threw it. It could land a mile away.

They flew fast too, faster than he could run if he didn't use **[Burst Step]**. If he did though, Luke thought he could beat them back to the silo-shaped demon, maybe knock it down and block the blood hunters from getting back inside, except that when he looked over, he realized he'd made some incorrect assumptions about how the whole process worked.

A blood hunter he'd missed was already there, and it hadn't flown back inside the big demon. Instead, it had landed on the outside and stabbed its proboscis into the fleshy outer wall. Color drained from the blood hunter and swirled into the carrier demon like food dye being pumped into water. It spread out and grew too thin to make out against the natural yellow of the demon's body over the next few seconds, then the blood hunter fell off the demon and started buzzing away.

Luke wasn't sure what exactly that did, but he had some guesses. Most likely, some of it was consumed as food, and others went to nurturing new blood hunters. He wouldn't have been surprised to learn that he was wrong, but that did seem like the most obvious reason for collecting blood. Even if that wasn't what the demons did with it, he knew better than to let them keep going.

The carrier demon was still tilted at an angle from where Luke had first crashed into it. It would be steep, but he had high stats and plenty of movement abilities. He raced across the open ground to it, leaped onto its side, gave it another hard smack as he landed for good measure, and then used [**Burst Step**] to intercept the next blood hunter just as it was reaching its destination.

Luke smacked it into oblivion, hard enough that the demon's body was ripped in two and its gory cargo left a fresh stain across the grass. A third demon landed at the same time, and even as quickly as Luke had skidded back down the slope of the carrier demon's body, it had already given up half its harvest before he reached it.

He hit it with a flying double kick that not only knocked the blood hunter loose, it broke off its proboscis and left it behind. Three of its legs also snapped off as it tumbled down the length of the fleshy silo, and when it hit the ground, it struggled to right itself so that it could fly away. Luke reached it well before it got to that point and killed it.

It wasn't enough. More and more blood hunters were emerging from the top of the silo, which was still too high off the ground for him to access easily. The carrier demon was also still moving, which wasn't a huge problem for him to handle, but it did add to the difficulty. Worse, as more of the blood hunters poured out, they started actively attacking Luke.

For the first few seconds, it wasn't too bad. He handled them as they came in, and in those moments, he killed more blood hunters than he'd managed the entire time he was in the house. But then the numbers started piling up. Fighting them became a full-body exercise of lashing out with every limb while contorting himself into increasingly improbable positions to avoid being struck.

He didn't know if the blood hunters could pierce his armor, but he wasn't willing to put it to the test.

Then the silo lurched, and Luke was thrown into the air. No amount of **[Twitch Reflexes]** could dodge the demon mosquitos then, and all **[Tactical Foresight]** did was let him know all the ways he was screwed. Luke still fought, of course, and he killed four or five of them before he hit the ground. But he was followed down by another thirty, with more piling on.

As it turned out, steel wasn't strong enough to stop a blood hunter's needle-tipped proboscis. The first blood hunter stabbed his stomach, and he swung through two other ones that were trying to pin down his arm to smack it away. It was quickly replaced by another one, and Luke realized with some horror that they were homing in on his weak points. With the metal plate there already compromised, they were just going to keep coming at him.

Luke flailed and thrashed, but there were so many that he couldn't get free. Even when he managed to climb back to his feet, more just kept coming to pile on top of him. There was really only one thing he could do.

Luke triggered **[Life Surge]**.

Name	Luke Bennet	Zea Stenter
Level	43	35
XP	273559/293811	148551/157276
AP	33	4
Bloodline	SysAdmin III	None
Strength	61	7
Agility	70	30
Stamina	88	27
Perception	55	21
Skills	Burst Step (1)	Arcano Dynamics (2)
	Butchering (4)	Bartering (2)
	Consortium Standard (2)	Bloodline Purification Ritual (2)
	Counter (3)	Cadence (3)
	Deception (1)	Cold Reading (1)
	Detection (2)	Consortium Standard (1)
	Disguise (2)	Cooking (1)
	First Aid (1)	Dagger Mastery (1)
	Leatherworking (2)	Deception (1)
	Life Surge (2)	Disguise (2)
	Mace Mastery (5)	Engraving (4)
	Ostari (1)	First Aid (1)
	Peripheral Awareness (2)	Gem Cutting (1)
	Power Strike (2)	Ghost Script (1)
	Stealth (1)	Goldsmithing (2)
	Survivalist (2)	Keen Instincts (1)
	Sword Mastery (1)	Lock Picking (1)
	Tactical Foresight (2)	Mana Manipulation (3)
	Thalian (2)	Mana Sight (3)
	Torturer (1)	Mending (1)
	Twitch Reflexes (3)	Metallurgy (1)
	Unarmed Martialist (4)	Neyardic (3)
	Wood Carving (1)	Ostari (1)
	Analyze (BL)	Painting (1)
	Remote Access (BL)	Rune Forging (3)
	XP Mask (BL)	Sleight of Hand (1)
		Steady Hands (2)
		Stealth (2)
		Streetwise (2)
		Temperature Acclimation (2)
		Thalian (3)
		Whitesmithing (1)

CHAPTER 22

Peishan knew it was hopeless. He didn't have a tenth of the men he needed to stop a blood-hunter swarm. The carrier demons could spit out thousands of them before they exhausted their reserves. Attacking the carriers directly was a losing strategy since only the strongest fighters could even hope to damage them. Even then, it was usually faster to kill the blood hunters and starve the carrier.

He'd known they weren't likely to stop the outbreak when he'd ordered his men to rush to the farmhouse with all the wounded. They'd all known it. But they'd also all known the alternative was upward of a dozen new blood hunters for each victim they claimed. The whole village was about to be massacred. In hindsight, they could have saved more people by evacuating the fighters from the village proper and telling them to flee.

By the time Peishan had realized that he'd made a tactical error, they were already halfway there. He was just about to order the men to turn back when the foreigner blew past all of them. Cries of surprise went up, his own among them, and then the tall man was gone. A few seconds later, Luke impacted the carrier demon with an incredibly loud crash, made all the worse by the fact that the man actually knocked it back and caused the ground around it to crack and break.

"Gods above," one of his men whispered. "Are we sure he's not a demon too?"

"If he is, we're all fucked," someone else said.

"We're fucked anyway. What difference does it make?"

There was some truth to that. Regardless of either of the two foreigners, they'd stepped into a fight they didn't have the manpower to win. But, for the first time since he'd realized the villagers had accidentally created a blood-hunter bait pile, he wondered if they might make it out alive after all.

By the time they'd caught up with Luke, he was already fighting in the farmhouse to keep the injured villagers safe. He was chasing after a blood hunter that had reaped its harvest and was trying to return to the carrier.

"Kill those!" Peishan yelled to Luke. "If they get the blood back to the carrier worm, more hunters come out."

The foreigner had probably already figured that out for himself, but it was good to make sure. That was the most important tactic for containing an outbreak anyway. If they were going to have any chance of surviving this, protecting the injured villagers and keeping the blood hunters from returning to the carrier with blood were the top priorities, and really, they were the same thing.

Peishan ordered his men into the house, where they put their weapons to good use as they spread out and protected various rooms. Slowly, they managed to relocate everyone to the main living area and start closing off doors to help reinforce the farmhouse. It wasn't foolproof protection by any means since the blood hunters could and would break through wood if they needed to, but the demons also weren't very smart. As long as a few openings were left for them to funnel themselves into, they would.

Things were going . . . Peishan wouldn't say well, but the situation wasn't getting worse. The Jigon-Sai was holding the farmhouse, and the foreigner was attacking the carrier demon. He might even kill the damn thing at the rate he was going, though Peishan didn't think it was likely. At least Luke was killing blood hunters while he worked, and more importantly, his attack on the carrier was causing the smaller demons to focus on him and taking pressure off the farmhouse.

Those hopes were dashed when Luke went down under what had to be a hundred blood hunters piling on him. Peishan knew from personal experience that they could punch through armor, and the stuff the foreigner was wearing had already been battered before this fight had even started. It looked like the man had been shot dozens of times with crossbows, just judging by how many holes it had. Once the blood hunters pinned him down, they'd eat him alive.

At least he'd killed way more than were going to be created using his blood. Peishan had been hoping for more, but it looked like they were all going to die here anyway.

Then the mound shifted, and Luke burst out the side, sending blood hunters flying with mighty sweeps of his mace and vicious kicks as he strode out of the pile. He killed them, seven or eight every second, and the stupid demons just kept rushing in to bury him in numbers. It wasn't that it was a bad tactic; it had probably worked on every single enemy they'd ever encountered, but the demons weren't adapting to the threat of a single person so strong that they couldn't physically hold him down.

That made sense to Peishan. Individuals like that would just survive the swarm, kill their share of blood hunters, and the thousands more that remained would find easier prey to use to replenish their numbers. Except here, they couldn't. This was the kind of place they hit, swarmed over in a matter of minutes, and then retreated to their carrier to be safely transported through the earth to their next target.

Over the next minute, Luke was a blur. It was actually so distracting that Peishan had to shout warnings to his own men when they stopped to stare. Just because most of the blood hunters were focused on the battle around the carrier demon didn't mean some weren't still trying to attack their primary target.

"Hold that damn hallway!" Peishan ordered one of his men, a new recruit whose name escaped him at the moment. "It won't matter if that carrier goes down if the blood hunters get in here and kill us all anyway!"

There was nothing they could do to affect the overall outcome of this battle, but they could stop the blood hunters from getting at the injured humans while that battle was raging outside. If the foreigner won, he would have living people to thank him at the end. If he lost, well, they'd be dead soon after.

Luke had to have killed at least a hundred blood hunters just since he'd triggered **[Life Surge]**. Hell, maybe it was two hundred. He couldn't exactly keep track when they were on him so thick that they blotted out the sky. But for every one he killed, five more took its place.

It had turned into a running battle, him on the move just to get enough space to be able to see and them chasing him down. Every few seconds, the loop he was running took him close enough to the big silo-shaped demon, and he'd smack it with a **[Power Strike]**. Those hits had torn giant chunks of flesh off it, which proved at least that it could be killed.

What he wouldn't give for a few bombs right now. It was too bad Zea had exhausted most of her bag of tricks on that necromancer and his slave caravan. The tentacle ball would have done wonders for cleaning up blood hunters, and Luke was willing to bet if he dropped a bomb down the mouth of that carrier demon, it would fuck that thing right up.

Since he didn't have that, Luke focused on what he could do. Thanks in large part to his latest boost to his stamina, Luke was a **[Power Strike]** machine. He could chain thirty of them in a row and still have the energy to keep fighting, and that was before considering **[Life Surge]**. Of course, factoring **[Burst Step]** into the equation made it a bit harder, since that was a fairly draining move on its own.

His primary concern was that there would still be hundreds of blood hunters in the air when **[Life Surge]** gave out, which even if he devoted himself completely to attacking them was looking like it'd be the case. He wished he knew if the carrier demon would just keep spewing them out indefinitely. One part of him thought that it would have to run out eventually. There was only so much room. The other part reminded him of all the bullshit magic stuff he'd already seen. Maybe it could just keep spewing them out forever. Maybe the only way to win this fight was to destroy the big stationary demon.

That Jigon-Sai guy probably knew. He seemed to know a lot about the demons, which Luke supposed just meant he was good at his job. Unfortunately, the only instruction he'd gotten was to not let the ones who were full of blood make it back to the carrier because that would cause more blood hunters to come out.

From his own observations, Luke knew that some blood hunters were going to come out regardless. They'd just come out faster if the carrier demon got a blood transfusion. That didn't tell him whether they were limitless or not.

What it came down to was he needed to make a choice: kill as many blood hunters as he could or attack the thing that kept coughing them out in hopes that he could destroy it. It was so big that Luke wasn't sure he could actually kill it, and while it was the source of the blood hunters, it wasn't what was actually threatening people.

Luke made his choice and started attacking the demonic mosquitos directly instead of just defending himself from the ones that caught up. His kill rate instantly doubled, then doubled again as he leaped back into the cloud that was chasing him. **[Twitch Reflexes]** went nuts trying to keep up with all the attacks coming from every direction, but **[Unarmed Martialist]** and **[Tactical Foresight]** did a good job of keeping those attacks to a minimum by using blood hunters as shields against other blood hunters.

Over the next minute, he slaughtered hundreds of blood hunters. Every movement killed one or more, every swing swept through them and killed two or three. It didn't stop them. It didn't even slow them down much, except when the corpse piles got so big that they gave Luke a bit of cover.

When **[Life Surge]** ran out, Luke was ready for it. He transitioned into a more defensive stance and kept on fighting, and within another few minutes, he noticed that the numbers were thinning. They were no longer coming at him a dozen at a time and from all angles. In fact, there were only a few hundred left, evenly split between him and the farmhouse.

Luke mopped up his remaining targets and moved to the house to help clean that up too, but when he got there, the Jigon-Sai soldiers had already finished the job. It was strangely quiet now, more the absence of the overwhelmingly loud droning buzz than anything else. Luke could tell he wasn't the only one who felt that way, judging by how nervous some of the soldiers looked when the last blood hunter died.

The captain stepped out the front door, looked around, and nodded. "I can't believe you're still alive," he said. "I can't believe any of us are still alive."

"What about that thing?" Luke asked, gesturing toward the silo-shaped demon. It was almost completely horizontal from all the blows it had taken, but as far as Luke could tell, it wasn't really hurt.

The captain shook his head. "Nothing much we can do, not unless you want to bash it to death. It's no threat unless someone walks into the mouth. It'll retreat back underground as soon as it figures out that none of its bugs are coming back to feed it."

"Does it just . . . die down there? Starve to death?"

"We don't know," the captain told him. "The carriers all look exactly alike. There's no variation in color or size. Maybe there are only a handful of them that just keep coming back. Maybe there are hundreds."

"Seems like we should kill it."

"You can if you want. I'm ordering the rest of my men to return to the village to help finish securing it."

"Oh shit, right," Luke said. "I should get back there too. Just in case."

Zea was probably fine. They'd had things under control when he left. What were the chances of shit going south?

"Yeah, I'm just going to . . . I'll see you there? Right."

Name	Luke Bennet	Zea Stenter
Level	43	35
XP	273559/293811	148551/157276
AP	33	4
Bloodline	SysAdmin III	None
Strength	61	7
Agility	70	30
Stamina	88	27
Perception	55	21
Skills	Burst Step (1)	Arcano Dynamics (2)
	Butchering (4)	Bartering (2)
	Consortium Standard (2)	Bloodline Purification Ritual (2)
	Counter (3)	Cadence (3)
	Deception (1)	Cold Reading (1)
	Detection (2)	Consortium Standard (1)
	Disguise (2)	Cooking (1)
	First Aid (1)	Dagger Mastery (1)
	Leatherworking (2)	Deception (1)
	Life Surge (2)	Disguise (2)
	Mace Mastery (5)	Engraving (4)
	Ostari (1)	First Aid (1)
	Peripheral Awareness (2)	Gem Cutting (1)
	Power Strike (2)	Ghost Script (1)
	Stealth (1)	Goldsmithing (2)
	Survivalist (2)	Keen Instincts (1)
	Sword Mastery (1)	Lock Picking (1)
	Tactical Foresight (2)	Mana Manipulation (3)
	Thalian (2)	Mana Sight (3)
	Torturer (1)	Mending (1)
	Twitch Reflexes (3)	Metallurgy (1)
	Unarmed Martialist (4)	Neyardic (3)
	Wood Carving (1)	Ostari (1)
	Analyze (BL)	Painting (1)
	Remote Access (BL)	Rune Forging (3)
	XP Mask (BL)	Sleight of Hand (1)
		Steady Hands (2)
		Stealth (2)
		Streetwise (2)
		Temperature Acclimation (2)
		Thalian (3)
		Whitesmithing (1)

CHAPTER 23

Luke didn't exactly rush back to the village, but he didn't wait for the soldiers to get organized either. As soon as the captain assured him that no more blood hunters would be spewing out of the carrier, Luke left the farmhouse behind. The entire battle had only taken ten or fifteen minutes, including travel time, but that was plenty of opportunity for things to go wrong.

Normally, he would say that Zea could handle it, but with her one arm practically useless and limiting her ability to use **[Ghost Script]** and many of the weapons she'd built already expended, her ability to defend herself was sharply limited. That wasn't even factoring in how she was light 250 AP from buying ranks in **[Bloodline Purification Ritual]** for him.

She still had her whip, but Luke had seen how little damage that had done to the gargoyles. Of course, no one had an easy time fighting those. That's why it took a whole group of villagers pinning one down and beating on it with sledgehammers to kill it. If something had gone seriously wrong, he'd have seen or heard it. The village proper wasn't that far away.

The village was still standing when Luke got back, though fire had completely claimed four of the houses now. Only two of them were still upright and burning, but that was more than enough to take care of the last three tongue fuckers still fighting. The gargoyles had either all been killed or fled somewhere.

"Huh . . . I was kind of expecting there to be some sort of surprise disaster," Luke said. "But . . . Uh . . . Hmm. Everything looks fine."

He walked over to where Zea was standing near one of the burning houses. She was flicking her whip out in tight arcs to slash at the tongues coming out of one of the demons that had been forced into the flames but not quite far enough to keep it from lashing out.

"How'd it go?" she asked.

"Lost a few people before the soldiers got there. I don't think anyone else died once they were able to secure the house, and I took care of the rest of the demons."

"Not a great day for this village," Zea said. She paused to give her whip another flick that sent its length out to slash through a new tongue vine that was attempting to punch into the ground and drag the bulk of the demon's corpse back out of the flames. The whip sliced through the appendage easily. "I suppose it could have been far, far worse. It's probably lucky for them that we encountered the Jigon-Sai on the road. If they hadn't turned back, they wouldn't have seen this village in trouble and gone to help."

"I'm sure they don't feel lucky," Luke said.

"Luckier than this thing," Zea said, gesturing the tongue demon. Its tongues had stopped thrashing and were instead flopping weakly as its main body was consumed by flames. Luke could see more tongue tentacles moving under its skin, reacting to the heat perhaps. But there was no escape for it.

"No problems while I was gone then?" Luke asked. "I notice all the gargoyles disappeared."

"About ten of them took off south a few minutes ago. There might be more hiding in the smoke, but if so, nobody here can spot them."

Luke took a step back to get a better angle and peered into the smoke-stained sky. If there were any gargoyles, he didn't see them. Considering the condition the houses were in now, he wasn't willing to jump up there and test his weight against the roofs again. Besides, even if there were gargoyles left, they'd be flushed out eventually, and the villagers were well equipped to handle them.

"I think we're probably safe from any aerial attacks, at least unless another batch of blood hunters shows up," Luke said.

"How bad was it?"

"Pretty bad," Luke told her. "They weren't exactly heavy, but there were a lot. Kind of galling that they don't give any XP. I probably would have gained another level or two for wiping them out."

"Another good reason to avoid them in the future," Zea said. "Assuming we can. I was talking to Shenha about it. Apparently the Melthor Province was practically evacuated outside the major fortresses because of how thick the demons are there, and no one's getting through the wall between there and the Imperial Province, which is a problem for us."

"Shenha?" Luke asked. "Oh, the woman with the sword?"

Luke had never been good at remembering names, and with **[Analyze]** allowing him to just look them up whenever he needed, he'd gotten even worse.

He'd seen her name when he'd first checked her out but had immediately for-gotten it and hadn't bothered to fix that.

"That's her. Her uncle was part of the empire's military. He sent her a book he was a part of writing based on all the observations made so far against the demons invading the continent. Apparently, it's been copied thousands of times and distributed all over the empire, so we should be able to find a copy in the next big city. Hopefully it won't be too expensive."

Considering how many tricks every demon they'd met already had at its disposal, Luke was inclined to agree that such knowledge would be an excel-lent investment. He had only a vague understanding of the geography of the eastern continent, a problem he would have made more effort to correct if he couldn't just have System point him in the right direction, but his understand-ing was that they needed to go through several more provinces. If border gates were impassable and the countryside was filled with demons, travel might be impossible.

They could just try to wait it out. There were probably some good grinding spots he could hit to bump up his levels while they let the military fight it out with the demons. Luke wasn't expecting to have any problems with the church, which didn't seem to exist in any form he recognized on this continent, but that didn't mean the Pantheon had given up on killing him. That having been said, leveling up was the perfect response to that, so spending some time hunting monsters, the kind that gave XP, at least, was about the best possible thing he could do besides going straight to the God Machine itself.

Really, it all depended on whether they could find a way to their goal. If the demons themselves were too strong or too numerous, they'd have to wait. Even if they weren't, it might just be impossible to stay there until the native population relaxed their security. Luke supposed that they would just have to make some effort to plan out a more secure route.

"We should get going," he said. "That captain as much as admitted he still suspected us of being demons in disguise. He might have changed his mind, but I don't think the free healing is worth the hassle at this point. I'll turn off **[XP Mask]** as soon as we leave and take the time to grind out some levels and pick up **[Matter Generation]** if we run short on cash."

"Yeah. Having no XP presence at all is too dangerous here," Zea said. "Back home, it was a curiosity, and people just mistook it for being level 1 or 2. Here, they're actively on the lookout because of all the demons that aren't connected to the system."

The demon Zea had been keeping at bay finally finished succumbing to the flames, and the pair walked away. "That's all of them, I guess," Luke said. He frowned when he noticed a crowd of villagers around one particular house. "Or maybe not? What's going on over there?"

"Whatever it is, I'm sure they can handle it."

"Probably," Luke agreed. "Wouldn't hurt to learn a bit more about these demons. Never know what scrap of information is going to save your life."

Zea gave Luke a suspicious look. "That's an unusual attitude coming from you. Maybe you've been replaced and really are a demon after all."

"Hey . . . I think ahead, sometimes."

"You hate studying."

"Sure, math and history. Learning how to effectively kill demons could quite easily be the difference between life and death. These things got tricks. Like, what if I swatted one of those tongue fuckers in the head, then got hentaied by all the tongues that popped out?"

"Got what-ed?" Zea asked.

"Never mind that. You don't want to know."

They came up to the crowd, and Luke peered over their silver-white hair into the house they were all gathered in front of. There was a dead tongue fucker in there, or at least the purple skin suit they wore if he assumed the tongue-tentacle monster was the real demon. The tongues themselves were suspiciously absent, probably in that hole that something had broken through the floor.

"Think it's still alive in the basement?" Luke asked one of the villagers.

"We don't know," the villager told him.

Luke pushed his way through and peered down into the darkness. His perception had long passed the point where a lack of light could hinder him, and he could easily make out the contents of a cellar. It was lined with rough wooden shelves full of glass jars, though two of them had been knocked over and their contents scattered across the floor.

There was loose dirt everywhere and a matching hole to the one that had been made in the ground floor. What there wasn't was a many-limbed tongue-vined demon. "Can those things dig?" Luke asked.

The villagers glanced at one another, and a nervous murmuring started up. People started looking around, and the ones at the edge of the crowd peeled off. One of them went running, and a few moments later, the sword-wielding woman came over. Luke frowned. What was her name again? Zea had just told him. Shay something? No, that wasn't it.

Luke used **[Analyze]** to remind himself. Shenha.

"What did you find?" she asked.

"One of those tongue demons appears to have escaped underground," a villager told her.

"They can dig?" Shenha asked, surprise in her voice.

If she didn't know that, then Luke didn't figure there was much more information to be gained in the village. As long as tongue vines weren't about to erupt out of the ground all around them, he didn't see any reason to stay. It wasn't like he could just hang around forever just in case there was another attack. If anything, that was a job for the Jigon-Sai soldiers.

Luke made his way back through the crowd to Zea. "Guess we're done here," he said. "Let's see about getting to Heishin before it gets dark and getting your arm fixed."

Peishan Jo wasn't thrilled about having to bunk in the village. Enough houses had burned down that everything was crowded, but his men needed time to rest and recover from the attack, and there was still the fear that the single lasher demon that had escaped would come back, perhaps with reinforcements. Day had turned into night, and nothing of the sort had occurred.

The two foreigners were long gone, of course. He'd expected that, encouraged it even. If they were demons, they were the strangest, most cunning ones Peishan had ever seen. But he was convinced he'd been mistaken in his initial impression. The pair was just what they seemed, two foreigners, one of whom had a bloodline skill that accomplished an otherwise impossible feat.

The house he was staying in started to shake, and Peishan was on his feet in an instant. He drew his sword and ran outside to see what was going on, only to find enormous rents being torn through the ground. One after another, until hundreds of them surrounded the entire village, enormous tongues emerged from the dirt. Each one was thicker around than his waist and hundreds of feet long.

Without any further spectacle, the tongues started smashing through walls and grabbing the humans hiding within. Peishan charged, bellowing as he ran for his men to defend the village. His orders were cut short as one of the tentacles smacked into him, turning him into a bloody smear across the ground.

Fleurian wasn't pleased with the results of his attack on the fleshy, weak pink things. There were too few of them to justify coming so far, and the one he really wanted hadn't even been there. Maybe it would have been a different story a few hours ago, but Fleurian hadn't been close enough to respond immediately. This had been a waste of time.

He glanced up and saw one of the stone watchers perched on a tree. A moment's consideration was given to crushing it, if only to snub Ginaxian. Their children often hunted together back home, but they'd been falling out of that habit here in this world.

In the end, the fact that stone watchers weren't good eating saved its pathetic life, and Fleurian sank bank beneath the ground to resume his swim through the earth in pursuit of that most elusive of prey.

Name	Luke Bennet	Zea Stenter
Level	43	35
XP	273559/293811	148551/157276
AP	33	4
Bloodline	SysAdmin III	None
Strength	61	7
Agility	70	30
Stamina	88	27
Perception	55	21
Skills	Burst Step (1)	Arcano Dynamics (2)
	Butchering (4)	Bartering (2)
	Consortium Standard (2)	Bloodline Purification Ritual (2)
	Counter (3)	Cadence (3)
	Deception (1)	Cold Reading (1)
	Detection (2)	Consortium Standard (1)
	Disguise (2)	Cooking (1)
	First Aid (1)	Dagger Mastery (1)
	Leatherworking (2)	Deception (1)
	Life Surge (2)	Disguise (2)
	Mace Mastery (5)	Engraving (4)
	Ostari (1)	First Aid (1)
	Peripheral Awareness (2)	Gem Cutting (1)
	Power Strike (2)	Ghost Script (1)
	Stealth (1)	Goldsmithing (2)
	Survivalist (2)	Keen Instincts (1)
	Sword Mastery (1)	Lock Picking (1)
	Tactical Foresight (2)	Mana Manipulation (3)
	Thalian (2)	Mana Sight (3)
	Torturer (1)	Mending (1)
	Twitch Reflexes (3)	Metallurgy (1)
	Unarmed Martialist (4)	Neyardic (3)
	Wood Carving (1)	Ostari (1)
	Analyze (BL)	Painting (1)
	Remote Access (BL)	Rune Forging (3)
	XP Mask (BL)	Sleight of Hand (1)
		Steady Hands (2)
		Stealth (2)
		Streetwise (2)
		Temperature Acclimation (2)
		Thalian (3)
		Whitesmithing (1)

CHAPTER 24

"Healers are all profiteers and swindlers," Zea announced as soon as they left the clinic.

"I think we'll probably be fine," Luke told her. "It was only twenty gold."

"Only! I could have lived in comfort for a year on twenty gold."

"And now you'll live with the ability to use both your arms."

Zea scowled up at him, but Luke just smiled back. They'd managed to reach Heishin just as the sun was setting and had been directed toward a reputable clinic immediately. The healer himself had been a bland man who'd spent thirty seconds examining the injury before announcing the price to heal it. Zea had balked, but the healer refused to haggle. He'd simply told her that the price was the price, and she could pay it or leave.

Luke suspected that attitude more than the actual amount was what had offended Zea, though she certainly didn't appreciate the price tag. Maybe they could have shopped around and found another healer to do the work cheaper, but now that Luke was on the eastern continent, his appreciation for gold had plummeted. Travel expenses were basically nonexistent as long as monsters continued to throw themselves at them, and while he wouldn't say no to a room at an inn, his stamina was so high that sleeping outdoors, fully exposed to the elements, no longer mattered. Besides, he could go a week without sleeping and be fine anymore.

Well, it didn't matter to him. Zea disagreed with that stance, most strenuously.

"How are we doing for funds?"

"Twenty-two gold, and another six of the local gold," Zea said. She'd used that to pay for the healing session. "If we converted it all into local currency, depending on the fees, maybe forty or forty-five."

"Sounds like we've got plenty," Luke said. "I thought money was tight."

"It *is* tight. This isn't half what I'd need to rebuild my arsenal, let alone resupply for the road. And what about that armor? It's got so many holes in it that we might as well sell it for scrap."

"I guess," Luke said. She wasn't exactly wrong. Steel wasn't really strong enough to stand up to the damage people enhanced by the system could bring to bear. There were plenty of stronger metals available, but getting a full suit of armor made out of them would be . . . problematic. At least, it would unless he did some grinding and picked up some more bloodline skills.

He'd turned off [XP Mask] as planned and was pleasantly surprised to find that there were plenty of people in the low thirties in the city, and someone like him at level 43 wasn't so conspicuous that he drew attention. It probably helped that his rank 2 [Disguise] skill gave him a 15 percent reduction to how much XP people could feel. Even if it only reduced his perceived level by 2 or 3, it brought him closer to the average.

Their appearances were so radically different from the locals with their silvery-white hair and shorter stature, not to mention their clothes were far plainer and utilitarian while the local style seemed to consist of what Luke could only describe as an excessive amount of layers and pointless flowing sleeves and robes. That, far more than their perceived levels, was what drew stares as the pair walked down the street. They weren't the only foreigners, but they were deep into the minority. Every now and then, he'd see someone standing head and shoulders over the natives with brown or black hair but thankfully nobody he recognized.

Luke made sure to use [Analyze] on every foreigner he spotted anyway, just to make sure he didn't encounter another church inquisitor. The overwhelming majority of them were merchants or sailors, though he did spot the occasional warrior, usually employed as a bodyguard for the more richly dressed merchants.

As they made their way deeper into the heart of Heishin, they encountered more and more people packed tighter and tighter together. At some point, it got so bad that the crowd pushed them apart, and Luke spent a long moment parsing through all the overwhelming sights, sounds, and smells to track Zea down. He ignored the annoyed glances he got from a few people as he pushed his way through them to reconnect with her.

"Sure are a lot of people here," Luke said. "You think that's normal?"

"I hope not," she said, chewing her lip. "Maybe they're refugees from other provinces. It might be harder to get a room than I thought."

"Wouldn't be the first time we slept outside," he said with a shrug.

"I hate sleeping outside," she muttered.

"Assuming we can find a place to rent out a room long term, how do you feel about setting up shop in Heishin for a bit?"

"I don't love it," she said immediately. "Too crowded, and why would we anyway?"

"Grinding out levels to get my missing bloodline skills, maybe boost our funds, give you time to enchant some new things."

"Okay, that's not a terrible idea but maybe not in the city," Zea said.

"I don't mind camping out," Luke said. "We could find some place out in the countryside and pitch the tent."

"I was thinking more along the lines of a small village like that one we saved. Some place that doesn't have an extra ten thousand people in it, maybe."

It wasn't a terrible idea. Unless Luke wanted to go on a murdering spree, there wasn't likely to be much XP to be found in the city. They could go down the coast a little ways, maybe find a nice fishing town to stay in, and Zea could set up her portable workshop while he started culling the local wildlife. His only real concern with the plan was running into another group of demons.

"I think we should spend a night in Heishin and see if we can get a handle on what's going on. I thought all those demons were supposed to be farther south, but that obviously wasn't true. We should find out if that was a one-off or if the demons are popping up here too. There's no point in sticking around to grind out XP if the only thing to fight is a horde of demons that don't give any."

"True. And we wanted to get one of those books with all the information the military has already collected on them anyway," Zea said. "Okay, room for the night, errands tomorrow morning, leave in the afternoon."

Luke looked over the sea of silver-white hair surrounding them and shook his head. If all the crowding really was from refugees, he had a suspicion that finding an available room to rent might not be so easy.

"Okay, room for the night, but you have to find it," he said.

"Innkeepers are all profiteers and swindlers," Zea announced as she flounced angrily onto the bed.

"We could have slept outdoors," Luke pointed out.

Zea groaned and flopped over. "Even the beds here suck. And no food! It's highway robbery!"

"We've got supplies left in our bag."

"They won't last forever, and when we have to restock, it'll be three times more expensive than it should be."

"I don't mind cooking whatever I manage to hunt down for you," Luke told her.

Zea made a face. "Gods save me from your cooking. Did you take the first rank in the actual skill yet?"

"I'm not spending AP on that!"

"Just give it up, Luke. If you were going to develop it naturally, you would have now. You are an absolutely terrible cook."

"Hey, my food is edible," Luke defended himself. Zea gave him a flat stare, causing him to sigh and amend his statement. "By a loose definition of the word."

"In all seriousness, everything is way more expensive than I thought it would be. It wasn't like this in Naldrin, and I'm worried the farther south we go, the worse it's going to get. At this rate, even if I don't replace any of the things I enchanted, we'll be out of money in under a month. It's ridiculous; what we've got should last for close to a year of modest living."

"And that's just for supplies, right?" Luke asked.

"Yep. Just food, mostly. This'll probably be the last bed we enjoy for a while unless we come up with a lot of money in a hurry."

"I could take [Matter Generation] first," Luke said. "It would solve all our supply issues, but . . ."

"But [Inflict Status] and [XP Reset] take priority for short-term survival, and [XP Cycle] for long-term," Zea finished for him.

"Really, [XP Cycle] might be even more important if I'm going to grind out more levels. I keep putting off picking it up because it's a solution for a problem that's still a ways down the road, but there's always something else to spend the AP on that's useful now. Sooner or later, I'm going to run out of time," Luke said.

"What's your AP bank look like?"

"33 right now," Luke said. "Maybe I shouldn't have picked up [Burst Step] when I leveled, but it's been pretty useful so far."

"So you need to get to level 46 to get the 125 AP you need for [XP Cycle]," Zea said. "Maybe you should get that first, then skip [Inflict Status] and go straight to [Matter Generation]. If we're going to be running into a lot of demons, you won't be able to use that on them anyway, and if you're grinding levels, hitting monsters with [XP Reset] doesn't really work. They'd just be level 1, and you wouldn't get anything for killing them."

"[Inflict Status] would still be useful for killing monsters, but I don't really need a 200 AP skill to do that. If I ignored it, I'd have enough for [XP Cycle] and [Matter Generation] at level 50 if I don't spend AP on anything else. Well, I'd have 37 AP left over, so I could afford a small thing here or there, or just save it to get [XP Reset] for you."

"What about if . . ."

They discussed possible build orders for another hour, but in the end, it didn't matter unless Luke managed to push his level up high enough to get the AP. There had been remarkably few monsters so far on their journey, demon and necromancer attacks notwithstanding. They didn't know if that was because they'd stuck to a well-traveled road or if the fact that so many people were willing to level up much higher meant that there were just more people out there keeping the wildlife in check.

"System, I know that you can't point out specific monsters or anything, but can you tell us where areas of heavy monster concentrations exist?" Luke asked.

"Certainly. Would you like me to direct you to the closest one?"

"Just a general direction and distance would be fine."

"In that case, the heaviest concentration of monsters is about two miles away, southwest of your current location."

"So close?" Zea asked. "Isn't that inside the city?"

"It is," System confirmed.

"Wait, is the city under attack right now?" Luke asked. "I don't hear any screaming or fighting."

"Oh, gods damn it," Zea swore. "It's a monster arena, isn't it?"

"I cannot offer any information about that."

"What's a monster arena?" Luke asked.

"It's exactly what it sounds like. People fight monsters, other people pay to watch the show and bet on the fights."

Luke thought about that for a moment. "Wouldn't that be perfect for us? I can go kill monsters to get XP, you can bet on the fights to get money."

"Sure, except you're level 43. The odds will be shit for you, and they're not going to just let you kill their entire stock of monsters. We'd make more money working as trappers than gladiators, but you don't get XP for capturing a monster."

"Lots of gambling, huh?" Luke said. "I wonder . . ."

"What are you thinking?" Zea asked.

"That Jigon-Sai guy thought it was a big deal that I could completely hide my XP. If whoever's running this place is also running the gambling, that could be a sweet hustle, right? You think they'd go for it if we pitched the idea to them?"

"The XP will still be shit," Zea said.

"I'll pick up more later. You were worried about money. How much you think we could get if the owners are in on the scam?"

"They might try to double-cross us."

"They might. So, you in or not?"

Zea groaned and nodded her head.

Name	Luke Bennet	Zea Stenter
Level	43	35
XP	273559/293811	148551/157276
AP	33	4
Bloodline	SysAdmin III	None
Strength	61	7
Agility	70	30
Stamina	88	27
Perception	55	21
Skills	Burst Step (1)	Arcano Dynamics (2)
	Butchering (4)	Bartering (2)
	Consortium Standard (2)	Bloodline Purification Ritual (2)
	Counter (3)	Cadence (3)
	Deception (1)	Cold Reading (1)
	Detection (2)	Consortium Standard (1)
	Disguise (2)	Cooking (1)
	First Aid (1)	Dagger Mastery (1)
	Leatherworking (2)	Deception (1)
	Life Surge (2)	Disguise (2)
	Mace Mastery (5)	Engraving (4)
	Ostari (1)	First Aid (1)
	Peripheral Awareness (2)	Gem Cutting (1)
	Power Strike (2)	Ghost Script (1)
	Stealth (1)	Goldsmithing (2)
	Survivalist (2)	Keen Instincts (1)
	Sword Mastery (1)	Lock Picking (1)
	Tactical Foresight (2)	Mana Manipulation (3)
	Thalian (2)	Mana Sight (3)
	Torturer (1)	Mending (1)
	Twitch Reflexes (3)	Metallurgy (1)
	Unarmed Martialist (4)	Neyardic (3)
	Wood Carving (1)	Ostari (1)
	Analyze (BL)	Painting (1)
	Remote Access (BL)	Rune Forging (3)
	XP Mask (BL)	Sleight of Hand (1)
		Steady Hands (2)
		Stealth (2)
		Streetwise (2)
		Temperature Acclimation (2)
		Thalian (3)
		Whitesmithing (1)

CHAPTER 25

System was a constant source of frustration. For all the information he provided, it was always like pulling teeth to get something helpful. He could confirm the concentration of monsters nearby and point in its direction but wouldn't say the name of the business or give actual directions useful for navigating the city. And Luke *knew* System could have told them exactly which streets to take to get there, but no, the best he got was a distance and a direction when he wanted GPS maps.

They eventually ended up in the right district, but finding the monster arena was another matter. They weren't strictly legal, since as a business they specialized in bringing dangerous creatures that would happily slaughter anything that got near them into the middle of a dense urban population center, but Zea took over the search once they got close enough since System wouldn't tell them anything more than that they were in the vicinity of the monster cluster.

"Places like this are open secrets," Zea said. "They have to be in order to make any money. So we're looking for a big business or a warehouse, something with a building five or six times bigger than your average place. Hmm . . . Monster fights though. It might even be bigger than that. It'll need to be ground floor so they have access to an underground area to hold monsters and dig the pits. Closer to the edge of the city is better so that it's easier to transport new monsters in . . ."

She rambled on while explaining the signs she was looking for. Luke dutifully nodded along, though he saw nothing that looked anything like what she was talking about. "There isn't anything remotely like that here," he pointed out.

"It's a big city. There's plenty of places to look still, and if all else fails, we'll find some shady people somewhere and start asking about a place to go for some entertainment and gambling. Someone will point us to the arena eventually."

Soon after that, Luke caught a whiff of something musky and wet. It was a familiar smell out in the forest but not one he expected to find in a city. He put a hand on Zea's shoulder and said, "I smell something."

"There are a lot of smells here," she said.

"No, something that shouldn't be here. Animal stink."

"Can you tell where it's coming from?"

"Probably," he said. "Give me a minute."

Tracking by smell wasn't a precise thing, even with 55 perception. Humans were exceptionally bad at parsing that information even when the smells were strong enough that their noses could pick them up, and making it easier to smell didn't necessarily translate into making it easier to home in on the source of the smell.

For Luke, it was something like hearing dozens of different sounds, all in varying pitches and intensities, all coming from different directions, and trying to lock in on a specific sound to follow it back to its source. It was possible, sure, but he thought it would probably be accomplished more through a lot of persistence than through skill. Even that didn't really describe the scope of the challenge though. It wasn't a few dozen smells; it was hundreds.

They started doing laps around the streets while he determined which direction the smell was strongest in. Half an hour later, they were outside a small shop that sold smoked meats.

"Here," Luke said.

"Are you sure? I'm not doubting, but no one is fighting a monster in this building, let alone drawing in a crowd to bet on them."

"Maybe it's just a front and the entire thing is underground?"

"They'd have to go really far down to dig below the foundations for all the other buildings around it," Zea said. "How would they get rid of the dirt?"

Luke shrugged. "I'm just saying, this is where the smell is coming from."

"Or maybe they do butchering on-site and you're just smelling that?"

"They don't do butchering on-site," Luke said. "I don't even think they do meat processing here. They just sell it."

"Hmm. It would be a good cover, but the location is all wrong."

Luke peered at the store for a moment, then looked around. "Maybe it leads somewhere else? You know, just a tunnel underground that goes to the main arena."

"That's a possibility, but it would still need to go to somewhere nearby."

"The warehouses near the docks are only half a mile away," Luke pointed out.

Zea thought about it for a moment, then shook her head. "System said the monsters were here, not over there."

"Well . . . We could just go in and ask?"

"I don't think this is the place," Zea said. "Too small. Nobody is going in and then not coming out again, so it doesn't lead anywhere else. And, honestly, I don't smell anything. I'm not saying you're wrong about that smell, but it's so faint it needs someone with ridiculously high perception to detect it."

Luke sniffed the air again, then glanced off to the side of the shop. There was a narrow alley separating it from the house nearby. Frowning, he took a step into the alley and looked around. Almost immediately, his eyes lighted on a small crack running along the length of the store. "Found something," he called to Zea.

"A crack in the stone?" she asked as she joined him.

"It's where the smell is coming from. This building is on top of whatever underground holding area they're keeping the monsters in. Maybe it's not the entrance, but it's close. We're definitely in the right area. I think it's time to find some of the clientele and just ask a few questions."

They kept walking around, but stumbling across some seedy-looking Heishin natives squatting in a back alley throwing dice was harder than it sounded, and Luke wasn't really sure what he was looking for anyway. After about half an hour of walking though, Zea stopped and said, "Those three guys right there."

"The ones with the beards?" Luke asked. He studied them, but **[Detection]** didn't point out anything unusual.

"They're gamblers," Zea said.

"How can you tell?"

"One in the front had a tattoo of dice on the palm of his hand. Shitty tattoo, at that. All three of them are carrying money on them, but the bags are too full to be gold. So probably a large amount of copper, maybe some silver mixed in, that they're planning on using to bet on individual hands. The one in the back, see that thing he's doing with his fingers? That's a grip you use for dirty dealing. I bet you if you **[Analyze]** them, you're going to find skills like **[Sleight of Hand]** or **[Oddsmaker]**. Might see **[Cunning Calculation]** if they're any good at what they do, and definitely **[Deception]** or **[Acting]**."

Luke did just that and found all three to be under level 20 with a mix of skills that included everything Zea had predicted, along with some minor fighting skills and a few related to sailing and fishing. "So, what does this mean besides that they like gambling and are cheaters?"

"Means they work together, probably enter a den separately, join a table one at a time, then play off one another to cheat the other people. If they've been doing it long enough, the house will know who they are and be in on it as long as they stick to targeting other patrons. It means they're familiar with places where illegal things happen, which might mean they know where the monster arena is."

Luke nodded along. That all made sense to him, but he still saw one problem. "How do we get them to tell us?"

"Well it's an easy motivation to figure out, isn't it? They like money. We give them some money, they tell us what we want to know."

"And if they lie to us?"

"Then we make them regret it," Zea said, a vicious grin forming on her face.

Zea marched off with Luke following up behind. He wasn't sure what he was expecting her to do, but it wasn't that she would just go right up to them and say, "Hey, can I ask you a question?"

The trio stopped walking and traded glances briefly before one of them said, "Piss off."

Zea flashed a piece of silver at them and said, "You sure?"

"Alright," said the one in the lead. "Hand it over and ask your question."

"Question first. I'm not paying for an 'I don't know' or some crap like that," she insisted.

The man laughed and nodded. Luke caught his hand moving behind his back, signaling something to the other two. They nodded at each other but otherwise didn't move. They couldn't be thinking of jumping Zea, not when she was close to 20 levels higher than any of them and with Luke so obviously standing right there.

"Where do we go to see the fights?" she asked.

"Which ones?" the man responded.

"The ones with the monsters."

The man started laughing. "You'd better have more than some foreign silver in your pockets if you want in on that action. I can tell you where to go, but you're not getting through the door for chump change like that."

Another hand signal. Luke wasn't sure what the trio was up to, but he suspected it was nothing good. Zea kept haggling with the leader of the group while the other two slowly retreated backward until foot traffic started flowing between them and the leader. Luke thought it unlikely that they were abandoning the man.

[Burst Step] worked best when it was providing a speed boost going in a straight line. That was how Luke got the most distance out of each use, but it was a flexible enough skill that it could be used to weave through obstacles too. He'd never tried moving through a crowd with it, but there was a first time for everything.

Luke plotted his route, activated the skill, and appeared behind the two men just as they went to take another step back. Both of them bumped into him, caught a glimpse over their shoulders to see him standing there, and flinched away.

"Hi there," Luke said. "Where are you guys going? Seems rude to just leave your friend behind."

"Er, right, of course. Don't know what we were thinking," one of them said. "Just got in a hurry is all."

"Let's go ahead and just rejoin the group," Luke said as he reached out and clapped his hands down on their shoulders to gently push them back toward where Zea and the third gambler were talking.

The leader had a better poker face than his buddies. He didn't even blink when Luke steered them back over, let alone falter in his conversation. He just kept rattling off directions and answering Zea's clarifying questions. When she was happy with the answer, she handed him the coin.

"Whatever you and your boys were planning, I'd advise you rethink it," she said. Then she looked at Luke and said, "Let's go."

Luke patted one of the trio on the back as he walked by. "Nice meeting you. Have a good one."

They walked away, leaving three confused and somewhat frightened degenerates standing in the street clutching a single silver coin stamped with foreign imagery and shaped in a circle instead of the flattened oval of the local currency. None of them protested their treatment.

"So, what do you think that was about?" Luke asked as they walked away.

"Probably planning to get some of his buddies and mug us," Zea said. "Apparently this place is very expensive to even get into, the kind of place nobles go to waste money on entertainment. If we've got enough money to be asking about it, we've got enough money to be targeted."

"Hmm. Hopefully they gave you good info. All three of them have already run off," Luke said.

"Oh, I imagine we'll see them again, probably with a dozen of their buddies. A few of them might even be higher level, maybe as high as low 30s."

"Not any higher than that, huh?"

"People that strong don't make a living mugging tourists," Zea explained. "If they want to fight, they get jobs as bodyguards for nobles."

Luke thought about that for a second. "That makes sense. Guess if it happens, it happens. In the meantime, where do we go?"

"Right over here," Zea said, pointing down a street. "Should be that big building a few blocks away."

Name	Luke Bennet	Zea Stenter
Level	43	35
XP	273559/293811	148551/157276
AP	33	4
Bloodline	SysAdmin III	None
Strength	61	7
Agility	70	30
Stamina	88	27
Perception	55	21
Skills	Burst Step (1)	Arcano Dynamics (2)
	Butchering (4)	Bartering (2)
	Consortium Standard (2)	Bloodline Purification Ritual (2)
	Counter (3)	Cadence (3)
	Deception (1)	Cold Reading (1)
	Detection (2)	Consortium Standard (1)
	Disguise (2)	Cooking (1)
	First Aid (1)	Dagger Mastery (1)
	Leatherworking (2)	Deception (1)
	Life Surge (2)	Disguise (2)
	Mace Mastery (5)	Engraving (4)
	Ostari (1)	First Aid (1)
	Peripheral Awareness (2)	Gem Cutting (1)
	Power Strike (2)	Ghost Script (1)
	Stealth (1)	Goldsmithing (2)
	Survivalist (2)	Keen Instincts (1)
	Sword Mastery (1)	Lock Picking (1)
	Tactical Foresight (2)	Mana Manipulation (3)
	Thalian (2)	Mana Sight (3)
	Torturer (1)	Mending (1)
	Twitch Reflexes (3)	Metallurgy (1)
	Unarmed Martialist (4)	Neyardic (3)
	Wood Carving (1)	Ostari (1)
	Analyze (BL)	Painting (1)
	Remote Access (BL)	Rune Forging (3)
	XP Mask (BL)	Sleight of Hand (1)
		Steady Hands (2)
		Stealth (2)
		Streetwise (2)
		Temperature Acclimation (2)
		Thalian (3)
		Whitesmithing (1)

CHAPTER 26

The shop was full of display cases, each one showing off various cheeses. There were familiar shades of white, yellow, orange, sometime solid or with holes, and then there were more exotic colors like green and red. A wedge of something like looked like a purple brick took center stage on the counter the shopkeeper stood behind.

"Are you sure this is the place?" Luke asked. "I don't smell anything but . . . well, cheese."

"This is the place our new friend told us to go to," Zea said. "Whether he was lying remains to be seen."

The shopkeeper, an older man whose hair had lost most of its silverly luster and was considerably thinner than average, said something Luke didn't understand, frowned, and said, "Standard?"

"Standard," Luke replied.

"Shoulda known. You don't look like you grew up around here."

"Ha. Yeah, it's weird to think of myself as the strange and exotic one, but here I am anyway."

"I bet all the girls are batting their eyelashes at you," the shopkeeper said.

"No . . . ?"

"Yes, they do," Zea said.

"They—what?"

"You're just too oblivious to notice."

"I am not," Luke objected.

"You are," Zea told him. "It's cute that you don't see it, but a girl basically has to throw herself in your lap and start rooting around under your clothes before you get the message."

"I . . . But, and you said, I was trying to respect, and then . . ."

Luke cut himself off with a heavy sigh, deliberately turned away from Zea to face the now-laughing shopkeeper, and said, "Anyway, I was hoping to get your advice on how to spend some money."

"I recommend buying cheese," the man said, a hint of laughter still in his voice.

"Mmm. Our budget is four gold and six coppers," Luke said, throwing out the number they'd been instructed to use.

"Ah. Big spenders. You could get a lot of cheddar for that much, but maybe you'd like to see some of the expensive stuff I keep in the back?" the shopkeeper asked, his friendly demeanor gone in an instant.

"Yeah, maybe we should," Luke said. "Lead the way?"

"Right through here," the shopkeeper told him.

Luke tossed an **[Analyze]** on the man, just as a matter of habit. Nothing came back suspicious, though the man did have a great deal of skills at rank 3, more than his relatively low level would account for. That wasn't all that unusual for the older people Luke had looked at, though in this case what was unusual was how old the shopkeeper was to begin with. Luke hadn't seen a lot of people over fifty years old on the eastern continent.

Or maybe he had, and they all just aged really gracefully. It wouldn't be the weirdest thing he'd ever seen.

The storeroom had very little in the way of actual product in it, which made sense to Luke when he considered how primitive Aros's ideas on refrigeration were. Most of the space was taken up by a small office in one corner, some storage racks in another, and a set of cellar doors in the back. A drop bar prevented them from being opened from below, but it wasn't locked into place, and the shopkeeper lifted it out of the way.

"Head down the stairs, follow the tunnel until you get to the main arena. Don't try to start shit or the guards will put you down," he said, all traces of pleasantness now gone from him. "Don't come back up this way. This is an entrance only. Exits are elsewhere. Understand?"

"Got it," Luke said. Zea just nodded.

They started down the stairs, and the door closed behind them. There were no lights of any kind, which wasn't a problem for Luke but made him wonder how people who didn't have high perception were supposed to navigate. Even if the tunnel went in a straight line, it would still be awkward to grope his way along blindly.

The sound of the drop bar falling into place came from behind him, causing Luke to snort. "As if that dinky little piece of wood could stop me," he muttered.

He felt the presence of XP well before he saw it, and not a small amount either. There were dozens of sources ahead, maybe as many as a hundred. Most of them were relatively weak, as low as level 10 in one particular case, but there were a handful above level 30. "Time to turn **[XP Mask]** back on," Luke said.

"Hopefully these people aren't as observant as that Jigon-Sai captain," Zea said.

Their plan was simple, but it relied on people not knowing Luke's level. Most people didn't pay close enough attention to see that Luke didn't present any XP at all while using his skill and just assumed he was extremely weak. Every now and then he got a weird look when someone made a connection between his age and apparent lack of XP, but it had never been a big deal prior to reaching the eastern continent.

It probably wouldn't matter now either, except that the demons had taught people to be wary. Their hope was that a bunch of people gambling on monster fights wouldn't have any firsthand experience with dealing with a levelless demon. The disguise only needed to hold long enough to locate whomever owned the arena and arrange a meeting.

They rounded a bend in the tunnel and found a well-lit cavern in front of them. Two guards flanked the entrance, both above level 30 and with stat spreads and skill selections that told Luke if it came to a fight, both would go in for an immediate grapple and try to keep him pinned down. They looked close enough in appearance and age that Luke had them pegged as siblings, possibly even fraternal twins.

They turned to look at Luke and Zea in unison. "New money," one said.

"Looks like it," the other agreed.

"Better tell them the rules."

"No fighting outside the pits. All bets are final. What happens down here stays down here. If you recognize someone you met at the arena out in the city, no, you didn't. Don't approach them or give any indication that you know that person. Understand?"

"Yes," Zea said.

Luke nodded but said nothing. They'd already agreed that when they got to the monster arena itself, she'd take the lead. Despite Luke having a stronger grasp on the language, they both knew that Zea would do a better job hammering out a deal with the arena master. Anything and everything they did now could influence how that negotiation played out, so his job was to stand close by and be quiet.

"Go on in," the left guard said.

"Where do I go to talk to someone about signing up to fight?" Zea asked as she stepped into the cavern.

Luke followed along behind her and got his first good look at the cavern. It was illuminated by lanterns strung up on chains, about twenty of them or so spaced evenly apart. Upon closer inspection, the light wasn't great, but anyone with a perception over 7 or 8 would be able to see just fine. Since that was most people, it made sense not to waste the extra effort on brightening the place even further.

The center of the cavern held an enormous pit about two hundred feet wide and thirty feet deep. Concentric rings of bleachers had been carved into the stone around it, except for the north and south ends, where metal gates of some sort had been installed. Those had some sort of private boxes over top either side. The whole thing reminded Luke a lot of a coliseum, except without the sand.

The rest of the cavern was full of interesting sights as well. What looked like street-vendor stands lined one wall with a scattering of tables in front of them. Luke had to stop himself from laughing out loud when he realized it was essentially a miniature food court. Past that was an unattended cage attached to the stone that had its sole window shuttered. The only way in or out of the cage was through a door carved into the wall.

The cavern wasn't particularly crowded, but it wasn't empty either. Considering there was no fight scheduled for another two hours, at least according to the giant painted sign near what Luke assumed was the betting cage, it kind of surprised him just how many people were there. It wasn't just guards either; there were plenty of low-level people who'd apparently shown up for no other reason than to spend some money. Perhaps they had some meetings about other illicit businesses and the arena was a good place to avoid the prying eyes of legitimate authorities.

"Hey, quit staring and let's go," Zea said. She grabbed his arm and guided him toward the north wall.

There was a door-shaped hole carved into the stone with what looked like the bars from a prison cell fitted into it and a woman standing on the far side. She looked Luke and Zea over as they approached, then asked, "What do you want?"

"Looking to sign up for a fight or two," Zea said.

"Both of you together? You sure? Your boyfriend would get turned to paste."

"Can we speak to whoever organizes that?" Zea asked, ignoring the woman's commentary.

She shrugged and said, "Wait here," before disappearing down the tunnel.

"You think they'll go for it?" Luke asked after a minute of silence.

"Probably. It'll be good money for them. Good for us too."

A few minutes later, the woman showed back up with an incredibly fat man in tow. "Which one?" he asked.

"They didn't say," the woman told him.

"Hnngh. Girl's alright, probably draw a decent crowd for being nonhuman. Guy's a loser. Not interested."

"Could we speak somewhere private?" Zea asked. "We've got a proposition for you. I think it'll make both of us a lot of money."

"I fucking doubt it, but sure. Let 'em through."

The woman opened the bars, and Luke took a second to **[Analyze]** her before stepping through. Level 32, well-rounded stats and a focus on bare-knuckle brawling and cats, for some reason. She had three different skills devoted to cats, including one really weird one called **[Cat Milker]** that Luke was almost afraid to look up in the skill store. He immediately regretted it.

"What's wrong?" Zea asked, noting the look on his face.

"She's got a skill for, uh . . . collecting fluids from cats for breeding purposes."

Through some monumental effort of will, Zea stopped herself from turning to look at the woman walking behind them now. "She doesn't speak Thalian, right?"

"Nobody here speaks Thalian," Luke told her.

"Well, just ignore it then. Not our business what she does on her nights off. What about the big guy? Tell me he doesn't have anything better than **[Barter-ing]** rank 1."

"Rank 2 and also **[Swindler]** at rank 3."

"Going to be a hard round of negotiations," Zea said, looking perversely pleased by the prospect. "What's his name?"

"Gotayi."

"Everyone's got weird fucking names here."

"Hey, whatever you two are mumbling in that barbaric excuse for a lan-guage, knock it off," Gotayi said. "Speak a civilized tongue or stay silent."

"Oh, and he's kind of a prick, huh?" Zea added.

Luke just nodded.

Gotayi led them about a hundred feet down the tunnel before stopping at a door and opening it with a key. "Alright, come on in. Tell me what scam you want to pull here and I'll tell you if it's worth the time."

"How do you know it's a scam?" Zea asked.

"Your boy there obviously isn't level 1, and you think you're going to make a lot of money somehow, so, go on, tell me the play."

Zea took a breath and said, "Well, you're not wrong, but let's go inside first? Don't want to risk anyone overhearing it."

Name	Luke Bennet	Zea Stenter
Level	43	35
XP	273559/293811	148551/157276
AP	33	4
Bloodline	SysAdmin III	None
Strength	61	7
Agility	70	30
Stamina	88	27
Perception	55	21
Skills	Burst Step (1)	Arcano Dynamics (2)
	Butchering (4)	Bartering (2)
	Consortium Standard (2)	Bloodline Purification Ritual (2)
	Counter (3)	Cadence (3)
	Deception (1)	Cold Reading (1)
	Detection (2)	Consortium Standard (1)
	Disguise (2)	Cooking (1)
	First Aid (1)	Dagger Mastery (1)
	Leatherworking (2)	Deception (1)
	Life Surge (2)	Disguise (2)
	Mace Mastery (5)	Engraving (4)
	Ostari (1)	First Aid (1)
	Peripheral Awareness (2)	Gem Cutting (1)
	Power Strike (2)	Ghost Script (1)
	Stealth (1)	Goldsmithing (2)
	Survivalist (2)	Keen Instincts (1)
	Sword Mastery (1)	Lock Picking (1)
	Tactical Foresight (2)	Mana Manipulation (3)
	Thalian (2)	Mana Sight (3)
	Torturer (1)	Mending (1)
	Twitch Reflexes (3)	Metallurgy (1)
	Unarmed Martialist (4)	Neyardic (3)
	Wood Carving (1)	Ostari (1)
	Analyze (BL)	Painting (1)
	Remote Access (BL)	Rune Forging (3)
	XP Mask (BL)	Sleight of Hand (1)
		Steady Hands (2)
		Stealth (2)
		Streetwise (2)
		Temperature Acclimation (2)
		Thalian (3)
		Whitesmithing (1)

CHAPTER 27

Gotayi let Luke and Zea into the office, which was lit by a pair of candles set into holders on the wall. It was in most other respects a plain, normal office except for what was obviously a safe tall enough for Luke to climb into sitting in one corner. The metal wasn't normal steel either but some sort of pale, lustrous blue thing that caught the reflected light of the candles to make it dazzle.

Gotayi saw Luke looking at it and said, "Gets annoying after a while actually. Sure it's pretty, but sometimes I don't need a giant twinkling box in the corner distracting me."

He crossed the room, pulled down some sort of sheet that had been piled on top of the safe, and covered it. Then he spun in place, leaned against the side of his desk, and crossed his arms. "Okay. Wow me."

"It's a pretty simple concept," Zea said. "You know he's not a level 1."

Gotayi nodded and eyed Luke up. "So what?"

"So, what level is he?"

The fat man froze for just an instant before a grin spread across his face. "I don't know. And neither will the audience. The betting will be wild."

"You control the odds, right? So here's a wild card fighter. Maybe he loses to a level 5 monster, maybe he kills a level 30 monster easily."

"Can he play the fool in the arena? It doesn't matter if no one knows his true level if he puts down every monster in one hit."

"I've got a rank in **[Deception]**," Luke said. "And 2 two ranks in **[Disguise]**."

"Not as good as **[Acting]**," Gotayi said, "but we can probably make it work. You'll need to drag the early fights out, make it look like a fluke that you won. What's your weapon skill at?"

"Rank 5."

"No shit?" Gotayi's eyebrows shot up. "You any good at resisting your skills when they try to force you to do something you don't want to?"

"Decent at it."

The pit manager gave a noncommittal hum and sized Luke up. "Mace is no good anyway," he said with a look of disgust. "Don't know why anyone would use such a barbaric weapon. How's your **[Sword Mastery]**?"

"Rank 1," Luke told him.

"Perfect," Gotayi said. "You won't even have to fake being incompetent with it then. That's barely good enough to avoid stabbing yourself in the foot."

Luke wasn't thrilled about the idea of using a sword. He'd done that once with the pair he'd stolen from some goblins, though they'd admittedly been too small for him to comfortably hold. Either way, he'd always found his mace to be more than sufficient to meet his needs. Well, except for that one time he'd broken his original on a giant's skull after his strength stat had gotten too high.

"Perhaps for the early fights, but then he can switch later," Zea said. She opened her mouth, frowned, and looked over at Luke. "What is the word for *misdirection* in Consortium Standard?"

After Luke told her, Gotayi started nodding along. "Yes, a bluff. That is a fine idea. But right now this is all hypothetical. It assumed your man here can actually fight. What level is he really?"

Luke toggled **[XP Mask]** off, just for a second, and met Gotayi's eyes. Then he turned it back on again. The pit manager looked surprised and suddenly nervous, no doubt just finally realizing that he had a monster in his office. That bodyguard who'd followed them was far below Luke in strength and wouldn't be able to do much of anything to save Gotayi if Luke decided to kill him.

"Relax," Luke said. "We follow the plan. Everyone benefits. I don't need to crack your skull and bust open your pretty little safe."

"Ha, as if you could," Gotayi said. "Blue coralite is practically indestructible. You'd need to max out **[Blacksmithing]** and then take another skill specifically for working with the metal just to shape it."

"That so?" Luke asked with interest. He glanced over at the safe, covered in the sheet so that only the bottom inch or so was visible. "They make weapons out of that stuff?"

"They do," Gotayi said. "And, my friend, if this goes as well as we hope it will, you might just be able to afford one. Maybe a nice sword to replace that savage monstrosity strapped to your back right now."

"Uh, yeah . . . I'll think about it."

"Okay, I think we can make this work. We'll need to hammer out the specifics, but before that, there's one more thing to test," Gotayi said. "We got to make sure you can put on a good show."

The fat man gestured for them all to exit the room and then proceeded to lead them farther away from the arena. Luke knew for a fact that his underground navigation skills were utter shit, but he was almost positive they were getting closer to that meat shop he'd gotten hung up on when he started smelling the monsters.

The tunnel curved all the way around the arena, sloping down as it went, until they came to a giant holding area with dozens of enclosures. All sorts of monsters were stuck in the pens, everything from a level 5 steel-fang wolf to a level 30 steam surger. That one was trapped in some sort of glass box that was half-full of water.

"How do you put that in the arena to fight someone?" Luke asked.

"I don't," Gotayi said. "I use it to clean up the blood stains."

"Ah . . ."

Someone Luke hadn't seen yet must have some sort of skill for monster taming or controlling. Luke couldn't see any other way to make a creature that seemed to be made of nothing more than a cloud of hot water that was constantly condensing on the glass and reforming behave. He wondered how he could even fight such a creature. He could imagine his mace going straight through it without doing anything more than making the mist swish around.

"This guy right here," Gotayi said, stopping near a pit that had some sort of big lizard with a frill going down its spine in it. Luke quickly threw an [**Analyze**] out to see what he was dealing with.

[**Name: Sunspot Monitor**]
[**Level: 8**]
[**XP: 1722/2059**]
[**AP: 0**]
[**Strength: 3**]
[**Agility: 9**]
[**Stamina: 5**]
[**Perception: 8**]
[**Skills:**]
[**Solar Fin (3)**]
[**Blinding Flash (1)**]
[**Venomous Bite (2)**]

That was a long way away from being a threat. "What about him?" Luke asked.

"These are a local monster. Not too hard to find, not too hard to catch. They're good warm-up fights for new challengers. Now I'm sure you could drop in there and kill it in a second, but that's not a good show. If this scam is going to work, I need to know if you can let it chase you around for twenty minutes and make it look realistic. Can you kill it in a convincing way to make it look like a fluke so people will bet against you in the next round too?"

Luke wasn't worried about its bite. With a strength that low, it wouldn't be able to puncture his skin. Unless it could also spit the venom into his eyes or something, he was probably safe. He wasn't sure what the deal with that fin was though. **[Blinding Flash]** sounded obvious enough, but Luke was well past the point of relying solely on his eyes, especially against such an inferior opponent.

"You want me to fight it now?" Luke asked.

"I want you to put on a good show. Hop in there and make me believe that you're really a level 1 with no aura of power about you."

Luke was about to hop into the enclosure when the fat man added, "And leave that weapon behind. Use a sword, like a real warrior."

With a sigh, Luke pulled his mace off the harness and held it out to Zea. She took it from him, then nearly dropped it in surprise. "Fuck, that's heavy!" she swore as the head clanked against the stone.

"I keep telling you to put more points in strength," Luke said. Then he switched back to Standard and asked, "Any other requests before I go in?"

"I'd prefer you don't kill it. No big loss if you have to, but it's a waste of money. Just survive."

The monitor lizard looked up from where it was lying when Luke dropped into its pen. A tongue flicked out from between its teeth, and it lumbered to its feet. "Looks hungry," Luke muttered to himself.

Perhaps they'd been starving it, or maybe it was just territorial and aggressive, but either way, the lizard charged at him with no hesitation at all. Luke slipped to one side as it rushed past, easily dodging snapping teeth. He resisted the urge **[Unarmed Martialist]** gave him to lash out with a foot and break the knee on the lizard's back leg.

"No good," Gotiya said. "Looked too easy. Cut it closer and look more desperate, like you're having a hard time keeping up with it."

Easier said than done. Luke had no problem cutting it so close that the monitor's snout touched him before dodging out of the way, but it took a lot more work to make it look anything other than deliberate. It was a conscious effort to force himself to slow down, to put himself in positions where he'd be off-balance and have to scramble—slowly—out of the way.

"Better," the pit manager called down to him. "Maybe let it nip you a bit. Not too much, just to get a bit of blood on the floor. It'll poison you if you let it, so be careful."

"That's a bad idea," Luke told him. He blurred back over the railing to stand next to Zea and handed her one of his gauntlets. "Here, hold this."

With his arm bare up to his elbow, Luke jumped back in and wagged it around to get the lizard's attention. It lunged for Luke immediately and sunk its teeth into the exposed flesh, only for exactly what Luke had expected to happen. It could chew, but it couldn't puncture through.

"Oh, yeah. That's no good. We could probably get you some blood packets to crush and make it look like you're wounded, but you'll have to be careful about palming them. You got any ranks in **[Sleight of Hand]**?" Gotiya said.

"I do not, no," Luke said.

The pit manager didn't look happy about it, but he nodded. "Not a deal-breaker," he told Zea. "Maybe we can get him rank 1 with a bit of practice. He's got enough agility for it. Gods above, look at him go."

Luke pried the monitor lizard's jaw open, then blinked his eyes rapidly when a bright light started shining from its frill. He shoved the lizard away and leaped back, but at the last second made it look like a stumble. He could hear the lizard's claws ticking against the stone as it scrambled back in to attack him.

"Watch out," Zea called down.

"Oh, I'm fine," Luke said. "Figured I should practice reacting to this, right?"

He sidestepped the rush with a long, deliberate dodge that took him much farther out of harm's way than he needed to, and it was so poorly timed that the lizard had the space to readjust its course. As it closed in, Luke hopped over it and said, "You want me to keep going?"

Gotiya considered it for a second, then said, "No, I think we're good. Let's head back to my office and we'll discuss the hard numbers. I'm thinking five or so easy fights, nothing over level 15, just to get people interested and betting. Once they realize you're not a pushover, we'll start bringing the bigger monsters out in a succession of increasingly difficult fights."

"Sounds like there's a lot of money to be made in the bets on that," Zea said, her grin predatory.

Gotiya matched it easily. "Yes, yes there is."

"Great. I can't wait to talk about how big our cut is going to be."

Name	Luke Bennet	Zea Stenter
Level	43	35
XP	273559/293811	148551/157276
AP	33	4
Bloodline	SysAdmin III	None
Strength	61	7
Agility	70	30
Stamina	88	27
Perception	55	21
Skills	Burst Step (1)	Arcano Dynamics (2)
	Butchering (4)	Bartering (2)
	Consortium Standard (2)	Bloodline Purification Ritual (2)
	Counter (3)	Cadence (3)
	Deception (1)	Cold Reading (1)
	Detection (2)	Consortium Standard (1)
	Disguise (2)	Cooking (1)
	First Aid (1)	Dagger Mastery (1)
	Leatherworking (2)	Deception (1)
	Life Surge (2)	Disguise (2)
	Mace Mastery (5)	Engraving (4)
	Ostari (1)	First Aid (1)
	Peripheral Awareness (2)	Gem Cutting (1)
	Power Strike (2)	Ghost Script (1)
	Stealth (1)	Goldsmithing (2)
	Survivalist (2)	Keen Instincts (1)
	Sword Mastery (1)	Lock Picking (1)
	Tactical Foresight (2)	Mana Manipulation (3)
	Thalian (2)	Mana Sight (3)
	Torturer (1)	Mending (1)
	Twitch Reflexes (3)	Metallurgy (1)
	Unarmed Martialist (4)	Neyardic (3)
	Wood Carving (1)	Ostari (1)
	Analyze (BL)	Painting (1)
	Remote Access (BL)	Rune Forging (3)
	XP Mask (BL)	Sleight of Hand (1)
		Steady Hands (2)
		Stealth (2)
		Streetwise (2)
		Temperature Acclimation (2)
		Thalian (3)
		Whitesmithing (1)

CHAPTER 28

The sword was a garbage weapon. Sure, it could cut through stuff, but that was the only thing it did better than the mace. When using one, Luke had to worry about things like the angle of impact or dulling the edge, plus it was so light and flimsy he was afraid it would just snap in half if he hit something too hard.

It was fine for the show, but he couldn't imagine trying to actually fight someone strong with it. Rationally, he knew it was the fact that rank 1 **[Sword Mastery]** couldn't hold a candle to rank 5 **[Mace Mastery]**, but he just couldn't get on board with trying to hold a sword properly. It seemed like a lot of needless complications to the fine art of beating monsters to death with a heavy piece of metal.

He made a conscious effort to remind himself that this wasn't a real battle, that he'd just be fighting one of those monitor lizards. The real difficulty was in making the fight look close, and the sword was honestly irrelevant to that. He could crush its skull with a single punch quicker than it could hope to react.

At the moment, he was sitting in a waiting room just behind the west-side portcullis leading into the arena. A different enforcer was standing next to the doorway, this one level 37. Luke had given him a once-over and was confident that even without a weapon, he could win if it came to a fight. He suspected the enforcer was also confident in his own abilities, but he suffered from the same flaw almost everyone had. Too much AP had gone into things that had nothing to do with fighting.

Luke wasn't immune to that problem himself, not when he considered some of his more ill-informed purchases like **[First Aid]** or **[Stealth]**, but with over 1000

AP worth of skills and only 100 or so having been spent on noncombat skills, he was heavily specialized. Probably the only person he'd ever met, at least since Luke had gained access to **[Analyze]**, who was as tightly focused on combat as him was Adrevald Lath. And that man had been a monster, literally at the end.

The door opened, and a petite, short woman of about five feet stepped through. Her hair had been done in some sort of elaborate braid and piled on top of her head, so thick that Luke thought it would affect his balance to have that much weight there. If that was the case for the woman, she was well used to it and moved without any hesitation.

"Luke?" she asked, not quite stumbling over the unfamiliar name. When he nodded, she added, "I'm Suisung. I'll be your coordinator for tonight's fights."

"How many are we doing?" Luke asked.

"Just two for now. The boss had three sunspot monitors brought in to fight, one juvenile and two adults. The adults are for the second round."

Luke realized he actually didn't know if the one he'd played with earlier was full-grown. It wouldn't make a huge difference, but maybe if they got significantly bigger, he could add weaving through their legs and attacking their underbellies into the routine.

"How big are the adults?" Luke asked.

"About this tall," Suisung said, holding her hand up just over her waist. "Twice as long with the tail."

There went that idea. That was fine, it just meant the one he'd already seen was mostly grown. He'd just stick to the moves he'd already worked out. They'd left his armor and mace back at the inn with the idea that Luke could put on a decent performance if he used only the loaner sword.

"Since this is your first appearance, we're not expecting much in the way of crowds. Most people don't want to pay to see a fight against something this weak," Suisung told him. She paused, and then said, "You . . . Ah, you're sure you can handle this?"

Luke had to laugh. Gotayi hadn't even told the other employees about the scam, by the looks of it. Maybe he was paranoid they'd get in on the betting and take too much money out of the arena's coffers. The whole scam would fall apart if too many people found out about it, after all, and there had to be some canny gamblers watching for specific people to place bets.

"I think I'll be alright. Word of advice, put a little money on my victory."

"We're not allowed to bet on the fights," Suisung said immediately.

"Like that ever stopped anyone," Luke said. "You do what you want, but the pit manager wouldn't be setting this whole thing up if he thought I was going to die in the first fight."

"Yes, well . . . I have a few things to go over with you before the fight starts in half an hour."

"What kind of things?" Luke asked. He couldn't imagine what other details needed to be stated.

"All sorts of stuff," she began enthusiastically. "There's your contractual obligations for fight length, an in-the-event-of-your-death disclaimer, fines that might affect your pay in the event that the corpse of the monster is too damaged to be harvested for resources—"

"I thought Zea took care of that already."

"Is that your partner? She did most of the contract paperwork, but there's still a few things left to go over with you."

Luke groaned and leaned back to look up at the stone ceiling. "This was not part of the plan," he said.

The fight, when he finally got to it, went about as well as could be expected. Someone positioned on top of the wall on the north side of the arena did a running commentary to keep the crowd stirred up that included some rather harsh critiques of Luke's form and reaction time. He mostly just tuned them out and focused on making it look realistic while he played with the juvenile monitor lizard. It was a bit smaller than the one he'd practiced on, but he made it work.

The sword sucked, no doubt about that. He deliberately let the lizard knock it out of his hands as it rushed at him while he scrambled to get clear. Honestly, the whole act was easier without **[Sword Mastery]** whining in his head about proper grip and lining up the edge of the weapon. Luke didn't remember the skill being so annoying back when he'd first gotten it, but he'd admittedly only used a sword for a day or so before discarding his sword for his first mace.

After he lured the lizard off to one side of the arena and made a sprint around it to recover his dropped sword, Luke let it push him to the ground and, just before its jaws could descend on his face, rammed the sword into its open mouth and up into its brain. There was a small mental ding to confirm the death while he kicked the body off of him.

[You have slain Sunspot Monitor (level 6). 36 XP awarded.]

"Unbelievable!" the commentator shouted. "I thought for sure our newest challenger was done after a single match, but the son of a bitch pulled it off!"

There was some scattered applause, but everyone knew exactly how weak the giant lizards were. That was why this had just been a warm-up show before the main events. In an hour or two, he'd be back out there fighting two full-grown lizards at the same time.

The whole scheme had better net them a nice chunk of gold because the XP benefits were practically nonexistent.

The crowd was a bit bigger when Luke fought two of the monitors at once, and then the next night they put him up against a level 20 blood-bite flea, and it turned out fleas were absolutely fucking hideous when blown up to the size of fat raccoons. They also had to hang up a net of metal chains just to keep the thing inside the arena.

That fight became mostly a game of dodging around as it leaped in the air and tried to fall on him. The only real challenge was how fast it moved, deceptively so for something that only had 40 agility, but Luke attributed that to a skill it had called **[Spring Legs]**. If he'd had his mace, he would have swatted it across the arena to splatter against the wall, something he was sure the crowd would have loved. Well, the ones who weren't sitting by that wall would have loved it, at least.

He ended up leaning into **[Unarmed Martialist]** to punt it across the arena instead, then finishing it off with his borrowed sword once it broke one of its legs. That earned a much healthier set of cheers and even some foot pounding on the ground while the commentator yelled out, "No way this guy is level 1! But what is his real level? How many more fights can he win before he bites off more than he can chew? And how much money are the lucky betters going to win on that fight?"

Fleurian paused and felt the vibrations coming through the stone. He was in his most compact traveling form, that of a single, long serpentine tendril that wormed its way through the earth and stone. Unlike his smaller children, he was far too massive to ever manipulate a crawler. The simple act of inserting even one of his limbs into the stupid demons would shred it from the inside.

He'd been crawling under this bastion of mortality for days, trying to locate his prey. But there were just so many targets, and they all looked so similar. It was impossible to narrow it down, and he'd worried that if he just burst up in a random place, he'd get a satiating meal and nothing else. That would come later, after he found the one he sought, but for now, the hunt continued.

Until he felt the vibrations, at least. That was . . . unusual, if for no other reason than they were much deeper underground than the surface dwellers usually went and in reasonably high volume. There were a lot of prey all gathered together in one place.

Fleurian changed direction. Even if his chosen prey wasn't there, he could use a good snack anyway. If the meal was kind enough to package itself up in an underground box, he wasn't going to refuse to eat. It was such a small, enclosed area anyway that he could strike and be gone, hopefully with a few hundred humans to consume.

Then the vibrations died down. Fleurian continued his swim anyway and circled underneath where he'd felt them, but they were gone. There was barely any prey left above him now, certainly not enough to satiate him. Perhaps they'd be back. If so, Fleurian would reach them much, much faster now that he'd created a path to their underground snack box.

Somewhat disappointed, he wriggled away.

"How're we doing?" Luke asked Zea.

"Good, good. We're up forty gold from our share of the bets."

"Really? Damn, way more than I expected."

"Just don't ask how much Gotayi has made. You might have played it up a little too good in those first few fights. The odds are still against you, but they're rising, and people are starting to bet on you to win."

"Well, that's what I'm here for," Luke told her.

"Hmm. Yeah. Why do I get the feeling this guy's going to try to screw us on the big jackpot at the end though?"

"Because you're paranoid," Luke told her. "But usually right. What do you want to do about it?"

"Nothing yet," Zea said. "But keep an eye on how much security he has tomorrow. If he starts bringing in a bunch of extra people, like way more than the crowds would dictate, that's probably a good indicator he's going to try to cheat us."

"Let's hope it doesn't come to that," Luke said. "How many more fights in the contract?"

"Three, all in a row tomorrow."

"One more day and we're out of here then."

Perfect. What could go wrong in just a single day?

Name	Luke Bennet	Zea Stenter
Level	43	35
XP	274177/293811	148551/157276
AP	33	4
Bloodline	SysAdmin III	None
Strength	61	7
Agility	70	30
Stamina	88	27
Perception	55	21
Skills	Burst Step (1)	Arcano Dynamics (2)
	Butchering (4)	Bartering (2)
	Consortium Standard (2)	Bloodline Purification Ritual (2)
	Counter (3)	Cadence (3)
	Deception (1)	Cold Reading (1)
	Detection (2)	Consortium Standard (1)
	Disguise (2)	Cooking (1)
	First Aid (1)	Dagger Mastery (1)
	Leatherworking (2)	Deception (1)
	Life Surge (2)	Disguise (2)
	Mace Mastery (5)	Engraving (4)
	Ostari (1)	First Aid (1)
	Peripheral Awareness (2)	Gem Cutting (1)
	Power Strike (2)	Ghost Script (1)
	Stealth (1)	Goldsmithing (2)
	Survivalist (2)	Keen Instincts (1)
	Sword Mastery (1)	Lock Picking (1)
	Tactical Foresight (2)	Mana Manipulation (3)
	Thalian (2)	Mana Sight (3)
	Torturer (1)	Mending (1)
	Twitch Reflexes (3)	Metallurgy (1)
	Unarmed Martialist (4)	Neyardic (3)
	Wood Carving (1)	Ostari (1)
	Analyze (BL)	Painting (1)
	Remote Access (BL)	Rune Forging (3)
	XP Mask (BL)	Sleight of Hand (1)
		Steady Hands (2)
		Stealth (2)
		Streetwise (2)
		Temperature Acclimation (2)
		Thalian (3)
		Whitesmithing (1)

CHAPTER 29

With a muttered warning about using some other entrances occasionally, the cheese-shop owner let Luke and Zea through his cellar access to the arena. Zea smiled and promised they would, but if everything went well, they'd never be back after tonight anyway. The shopkeeper gave them a grumpy scowl in response. Luke just kept his mouth shut and took the lead down the tunnel.

If there was anything he didn't like about this plan, it was leaving his weapon behind. He could and had fought unarmed, plenty of times even, but he felt safer when he had his mace, especially since if Gotayi was going to cheat them, tonight was the night. Leaving the armor behind . . . Well, he hadn't given up on it yet, but the guy they'd had look at it for repairs had quoted a price tag that was far beyond their means. Just banging out all the metal that had been dented in from being shot a few dozen times had cost them a handful of gold. Luke suspected his armor was on its last leg, that one more good fight would be the end of it.

That fight wouldn't be tonight though, since it had been left in their room with his mace. When he fought monsters in the arena, he did it wearing a set of clothes in the local fashion and a stupid flimsy sword. It worked, and he supposed the handicap made for a better show, but Luke constantly had three different skills reminding him of how inefficiently he was fighting. It was incredibly annoying.

This was the last night of their little scam. After the first two performances, everybody knew he wasn't level 1, and though a few people had tried to stalk Luke after he left, he'd been able to spot them and shake them loose easily enough. Whatever information they were hoping to gain, they'd failed. He couldn't imagine it helping them anyway. He maintained his **[XP Mask]** skill the entire time, and he didn't do any fighting anywhere else, so honestly, what was there to find out?

"Place seem kind of busy to you?" Zea asked as they got close.

"Little bit, but a big crowd is a good thing, right?"

"I suppose."

They rounded the corner and saw hundreds of people already in the arena. "Oh, damn," Zea said, stopping near the enforcers. "That's . . . *a lot.*"

"Spectacle's here tonight," one of them told her.

"What's that mean?" Luke asked.

"He's a gladiator, like you. Except he only does random appearances whenever he feels like it, and they're all spur-of-the-moment. Boss hates dealing with him, says he fucks the whole schedule up, but the crowd loves Spectacle, so . . ."

"This is going to be a problem for us, isn't it?" Zea asked.

"Looks like it," the enforcer told her.

"Well, I guess let's go talk to Gotayi and find out if you're still on the schedule for tonight," Zea said, looking over at Luke. He gave her a nod, and the enforcers let them through. Everywhere they looked, the place was packed with people. Every seat at their food court area was taken, with dozens more eating while standing up against the wall. The stands around the pit were about three-quarters full, and some of the arena's employees were setting up some temporary bleachers on the north and south sides of the pit to accommodate the crowd.

Even the betting cage had a line that wound back and forth a hundred people long. Whoever Spectacle was, he must put on a hell of a show considering how little notice he'd given. The energy of the crowd reminding Luke of when he'd been young, back before his mother had died. They'd gone to the county fair, one that was packed so full it was hard just to even get around. Luke had some vague memories of being jostled around and his hand slipping out of his father's as traffic tore them apart.

That was what it was like walking through the arena, like if he didn't pay attention, he'd turn around and find Zea had been carried off in some other direction. That didn't happen, of course. Her strength was on the low end of average, but her agility was significantly higher than most of the other spectators'. Besides, even if they did get separated, it wasn't like they didn't know where they were going. They'd just meet back up at that jail-cell-looking door.

They were halfway there when Luke spotted Gotayi coming out onto the main floor. He had a ferocious scowl on his face as he snapped orders to people and stomped around. Luke would have thought he'd be ecstatic about the crowd, but it looked like the opposite was true.

"Gotayi!" Zea called out.

He spun in place, jowls swinging wildly the whole way, and gave them a glare. "Of course, and there's you two. Look, it's not going to happen tonight. Fucking Spectacle wants to perform. Everybody bend over, grab your cheeks, and spread 'em. Who gives a fuck if we don't have half the staff we need and are running out of food an hour before the show even starts."

"We have a contract," Zea said, as calmly as she could while still shouting to be heard over the crowd.

"I know! It even has a Spectacle clause in it because this dick's contract takes precedence over everyone else's. The former owner negotiated it with him, and we're stuck with it."

"What are you talking about?" Zea demanded. "I read that thing front to back, and—"

"It's part of the compensation-if-your-slot-gets-bumped section," Gotayi said, interrupting her. "Look, I really don't have time for this right now. If you want to come back in six hours, we can discuss it, otherwise just show up at the normal time tomorrow and I'll have you rescheduled. Now either go buy some food, place a bet, or get lost."

Without waiting for a response, the fat man trundled off. He was immediately yelling at the woman standing in the betting cage to work faster. She gave him an obscene gesture and otherwise ignored him, much to Gotayi's annoyance.

The pair retreated to the south side of the arena where there was less going on and they didn't need to shout to hear each other. Other than a steady stream of people coming in from a nearby entrance, they were more or less alone. At least, they were in the sense that nobody was standing within thirty feet of them. The enforcers were too busy collecting coins from each new spectator entering the cavern to pay any attention to them, and the customers were eager to get over to either place their own bets or just claim seats in the rapidly filling stands.

"Hey, how come we never paid to get in?" Luke asked as he watched the scene.

"Probably because we came at a time with no entertainment lined up the first time, and now we're a fighter and his manager, so we're here to work, not relax."

"And so we've come full circle," he said.

Zea laughed a bit and shook her head. "It's not really the same." Then she got quiet for a moment before adding, "I hope not. The Bloody Harbor is gone because of us. I mean, because of the church, but they destroyed it and killed everyone while looking for us. It would really suck to have another place reduced to rubble just because we were associated with it."

* * *

Fleurian had been swimming ever-widening lazy circles underneath the city, waiting for something to catch his attention. Patience was not one of his strengths, and he was becoming frustrated with the area. If his prey was there, he couldn't tell, and the idea of breaching the surface for a quick meal before moving on with the hunt was becoming more appealing by the hour.

He was just considering where he might find the greatest volume of food to snatch up in one single go when his route took him near the giant pocket of empty space in the ground. The vibrations weren't nearly as strong as those from the surface, but they were considerably stronger than usual. Perhaps there was a meal to be had there first.

He altered the arc of his circling pattern to bring him closer to the buffet. He wanted a better look before making a decision.

"You want to catch the show?" Luke asked.

"Eh, we can if you want," Zea said. "I'm not super interested. I've had enough front-row battles to a man killing random monsters to last me a lifetime."

"I'm kind of just curious about who this Spectacle person is. What makes him so important that he gets to come in and do whatever he wants, whenever he wants?"

"Eh, he's probably related to the owner or something. This whole thing reeks of privilege. If it's not that, it's because of a lot of fucking money being spent by someone who's got too much spare time on their hands."

"Easy way to find out, I guess," Luke said. He took a few steps over to the enforcers and asked, "Who is this Spectacle person, anyway?"

"That's the big question, isn't it?" the enforcer told him as he collected a single silver coin from a man walking by. "Nobody knows. Comes in covered from head to toe in black. Can't see an inch of his skin. Brings his own monsters to fight, and not weak ones either. We're talking stuff that's up to level 50, puts on his show, and leaves. But everything is on his terms, always last-minute, and while it makes the arena a lot of money, it's hell on the employees."

"Well that explains why Gotayi hates the guy," Zea said.

"Why? Does he hate money?"

"Probably not worth it to him," she explained. "He's not the owner, so whatever cut he's getting as a commission for setting up and running the fights isn't worth the headache."

Luke thought about that for a second, then shrugged. "So, you're saying nobody knows who Spectacle really is?"

"Maybe the owner of the place but definitely nobody else," the enforcer said absently. He reached out to grab a small woman who'd been attempting to sneak by in the middle of a group. "Three silver for you."

"What?! That's triple what everyone else is paying!" the woman protested.

"Fine, get the fuck out then."

The woman sullenly pulled out a purse and paid triple admission price to get in. The enforcer waved her through, put one coin in the box, one in his pocket, and flipped the third to his partner.

"Interesting," Luke said.

"What are you thinking?" Zea asked.

"I think we should see the show. Maybe we'll recognize Spectacle's style."

"Why would we—ah. I see. Yeah, that's not a bad idea." Zea turned to the enforcers, who'd only been half paying attention to answer a question anyway, and said, "Thanks for explaining."

"No problem. Sorry your fight got bumped," the enforcer told Luke.

"Shit happens. Have a good night, fellas."

"Was supposed to be on a date with my girl," the other enforcer muttered.

"Yeah, but just think of how much extra coin you're gonna have for your next date instead."

"Won't be a next date if I keep having to cancel at the last minute to pick up shifts."

"Invite her to a fight," the enforcer told his luckless friend.

Luke and Zea headed toward the stands, and he quickly lost track of that particular conversation once they were in the middle of the crowd. "So no need to see the whole thing," Luke said, pitching his voice. "I just want to get a look at the guy, see what he can do, and then we can bail."

"The sooner, the better," Zea yelled back.

There were no seats left at this point, but they found a place standing on the outside edge of the arena and waited for the show to start. It was only a couple minutes before the rumble of the arena gates being lifted shook the stone under their feet.

"Here we go," Luke muttered. "Let's see who you really are."

Name	Luke Bennet	Zea Stenter
Level	43	35
XP	274177/293811	148551/157276
AP	33	4
Bloodline	SysAdmin III	None
Strength	61	7
Agility	70	30
Stamina	88	27
Perception	55	21
Skills	Burst Step (1)	Arcano Dynamics (2)
	Butchering (4)	Bartering (2)
	Consortium Standard (2)	Bloodline Purification Ritual (2)
	Counter (3)	Cadence (3)
	Deception (1)	Cold Reading (1)
	Detection (2)	Consortium Standard (1)
	Disguise (2)	Cooking (1)
	First Aid (1)	Dagger Mastery (1)
	Leatherworking (2)	Deception (1)
	Life Surge (2)	Disguise (2)
	Mace Mastery (5)	Engraving (4)
	Ostari (1)	First Aid (1)
	Peripheral Awareness (2)	Gem Cutting (1)
	Power Strike (2)	Ghost Script (1)
	Stealth (1)	Goldsmithing (2)
	Survivalist (2)	Keen Instincts (1)
	Sword Mastery (1)	Lock Picking (1)
	Tactical Foresight (2)	Mana Manipulation (3)
	Thalian (2)	Mana Sight (3)
	Torturer (1)	Mending (1)
	Twitch Reflexes (3)	Metallurgy (1)
	Unarmed Martialist (4)	Neyardic (3)
	Wood Carving (1)	Ostari (1)
	Analyze (BL)	Painting (1)
	Remote Access (BL)	Rune Forging (3)
	XP Mask (BL)	Sleight of Hand (1)
		Steady Hands (2)
		Stealth (2)
		Streetwise (2)
		Temperature Acclimation (2)
		Thalian (3)
		Whitesmithing (1)

CHAPTER 30

The east gate, the monster gate, opened first. The thing that slithered out looked like the result of a jellyfish, a grizzly bear, and a python having an ecstasy-fueled orgy in a pool full of green Jell-O. It was huge, probably twenty feet long from the tip of its snout down to the tentacle-laden tip of its tail. Its skin was a mottled blue-and-green pattern and hung loose on its frame, so loose in fact that great folds of it hung draped off its shoulders. It walked on six legs, each one with more tentacles on the backside and ending in great razor-tipped claws.

Its neck was easily six feet of its length, and the creature waved it around slowly as it surveyed the humans gathered overhead. The tentacles hanging off its face were three feet long, longer by far than the six-inchers on its legs or the foot-longs hanging from its chest. They stirred in agitation as the noise increased and started lashing back and forth like an angry cat's tail.

"Well, that is pretty fucking ugly," Zea said, though Luke could barely hear her over the fervor of the crowd.

[Analyze] told him it was a venomous gleesing constrictor at an impressive level 40. Its stats were all in the low 30s, except for its stamina at 51, and most of its skills seemed to revolve around either some sort of awareness the tentacles hanging all over its body granted or one of half a dozen different poisons its touch could inflict. It also sported a random skill or two that enhanced its teeth and claws, but it looked to Luke like the monster's primary method of attack was to close the distance, engulf its prey in the flabby folds of its body, and poison it to death.

If it were him fighting, Luke expected he'd have a lot of difficulties with this one. The monster's longer tentacles gave it a better range than Luke would have even with his mace, and its relatively low perception was balanced by the insane number of tentacles reading changes in the air around it giving it a full view in every direction, possibly at a limited range.

Melee fights definitely favored the monster, and a good strategy would revolve around finding some way to disable or destroy the tentacles hanging all over its body. Or, in Luke's case, a **[Burst Step]** followed by a **[Power Strike]** right to its face to bring it down in one blow would likely be the optimal strategy. He'd rely on his overwhelmingly high stamina to resist any poisons he was struck with and recover from any damage. **[Life Surge]** would be his backup for the possibility that he couldn't kill it in a single hit and started to get overwhelmed by the tentacles stinging him.

He was more curious how the mysterious Spectacle planned on handling it, though. The west gate had finished rising, and he heard footsteps coming from inside it.

Spectacle appeared across from the gleesing constrictor. He, and it was definitely a he, was wearing a skintight body suit that had to be enchanted in some way. There were no ties or buttons on it, and as far as he could tell, nobody in Aros knew what a zipper was. Spandex was another unknown concept to them, and Luke couldn't see another way to stuff a human body into something that tight without resorting to magic.

The suit covered his entire body, right up to the crown of his head. The man's face was the only part of his body that the suit didn't cling to every contour. There was just enough extra material that everything between the nose and the chin appeared as one smooth plane. The eyebrows to the cheekbones were similarly flat. Luke almost wondered if there was some kind of mask built into the inside of the suit causing the effect, considering that he could count the man's abs and had a pretty good estimate of the size of his dick.

Spectacle held a curved longsword in one hand, almost a katana but with a regular cross guard instead of one of those all-the-way-around guards the ninjas and samurai in TV shows always had. It was unsheathed, a black blade that looked like it was carved from one solid length of obsidian with electric-green veins running down its side.

[Name: Hakiro Shansaron]
[Level: 48]
[XP: 400872/411260]
[AP: 0]
[Strength: 51]
[Agility: 77]
[Stamina: 64]
[Perception: 59]
[Skills:]

[Blade Master (5)]
[Archery (4)]
[One Sword, One Mind (5)]
[Tapestry of the World (5)]
[Unbreakable Will (5)]
[Executioner (3)]
[Shining Strike (3)]
[Spirit Tap (3)]
[Ignite (2)]
[Bone Sunder (2)]
[Aura Flare (3)]
[Quick Shot (2)]
[Deadly Reach (2)]
[Empower Arrow (2)]
[War Leader (4)]
[Wind Seeker (2)]
[Eledarn (3)]
[Consortium Standard (3)]
[Animal Husbandry (3)]
[Sewing (1)]
[Carpentry (2)]
[Dancing (4)]
[Calligraphy (4)]
[Cartography (2)]
[Blacksmithing (1)]
[Hunting (3)]

"Jesus fucking Christ," Luke breathed out. His words were drowned in the cheering of the spectators, but Zea saw the look on her face.

"What is it?" she yelled.

He shook his head. There was no way they could hold a conversation right now, not while the crowd was losing their shit over this guy. Luke was pretty sure Spectacle was even stronger than Lath, but unless someone was regularly purging him of XP madness, he was a ticking time bomb. And a lot of those combat skills were advanced skills made by merging other base skills together, then ranked up to max again. **[Tapestry of the World]**, for example, was something Luke himself might one day pick up, since it combined a lot of sensory abilities into one package, merged it with an analogue of his own **[Tactical Foresight]** skill, and then kicked the prediction power up to max.

This guy was literally seeing the future, at least a second or two ahead, and that was just *one* of his advanced skills. **[Wind Seeker]** put Luke's own **[Burst Step]** to shame with its ability to go in any direction, make instant turns, and weave through obstacles, and Luke was willing to bet it was faster both on its own and due to Hakiro's higher agility. Strength also played a large part in maximum speed, but Luke wouldn't bet on himself in a race.

He got more and more nervous as he pored over the skill store and identified each ability. If Hakiro decided to kill every single person in the arena right now, there was nothing Luke or anyone else could do to stop him. It really drove home exactly what the difference was between someone like Luke who'd picked up all his skills through AP and someone who'd actually devoted their life to mastering those skills. Luke was only 5 levels behind, but he'd need probably 1000 AP to catch up to Hakiro.

It also drove home exactly how powerful his bloodline was. **[Inflict Status]** for 200 AP and **[XP Reset]** for another 50 were all Luke needed to crush Hakiro instantly, without any sort of difficulty whatsoever. Nobody would be able to stand up to that in a straight fight. Nobody besides a demon anyway.

They spent the next five minutes watching Spectacle live up to his namesake. He tumbled like an acrobat and subjected the gleesing constrictor to a death by a thousand cuts. Tentacles were lopped off one at a time as Spectacle expertly danced around the edge of the monster's range. It really was a dance too, with the man leading the monster in a game of give-and-take, their positions looping around each other in a dizzying display of coordination.

Spectacle knew this monster inside and out. He knew how it thought, how it would react, and how far he could push it. He led it around by the nose, and by the time he was ready to go in for the kill, Luke was over the whole show. It was flashy as all hell, but while Spectacle might take half an hour to kill the monster, Hakiro could have done the deed with a single blow delivered so fast it would take a high-speed camera to measure the microseconds the attack took.

The fans ate it up, and Luke could see why. **[Analyze]** returned most of them between level 15 and 20, with only a few of the stronger ones reaching 30. The strongest person, besides Spectacle, Zea, and him, was an enforcer at level 34 on the other side of the pit near the betting cage. To them, the whole thing was probably a dazzling show.

The noise steadily grew more deafening as the fans cheered and started pounding their heels on the stone. It was so loud, in fact, that none of them noticed the sound of the stone cracking, not until the first screams cut through the cheering at least. Things started to fall apart almost immediately as huge, writhing flat tentacles a foot wide broke through the floor all over the arena. A dozen of them shot straight up through the crowd and started flailing around wildly.

A hundred people died in those first few seconds. Each tentacle was over twenty feet tall, and all of them swept the crowds around them. People who were hit somehow stuck to the green tentacles and were dragged across the stone or slammed into the next person. Explosive showers of blood erupted all throughout the stands.

Luke recognized them immediately. Those were the tongues of one of those tongue-fucker demons blown up to mammoth proportions. Each one was twenty or thirty times thicker than it was supposed to be, and there were so many of them already wreaking havoc in the cavern. More kept erupting from the stone and blindly flailing around. Anyone who got caught died in seconds.

"Time to go!" Luke yelled over the screaming. He grabbed hold of Zea, held her tight, and leaped over the heads of the panicked audience as they jostled one another in an attempt to break free of the crowd.

The tongues continued their bloody harvest, but Luke got far away before any new ones could surface near him. He managed to touch down in an empty spot near the outer edge of the crowd, but it was only empty because a new tongue was rising up there. Before it could begin its attack, he activated [Burst Step] and lunged for one of the exit tunnels.

An enforcer was there, struggling to help his partner get free from a tongue tentacle's grasp. Whether it was some function of the slimy coating that glistened on its surface, a weird skill, or just plain magic, Luke didn't know, but somehow anything the tongues touched just stuck to them. Worse, as they started flailing, people just turned into shivering cuts of meat that fell apart into bloody piles.

The good news was that, as strong as the tongues were, they weren't insurmountable. The free enforcer was managing to hold the tongue still from flailing via the grip he had on his partner, though Luke could tell just from the expression on the man's face that it was a painful experience.

Luke set a stunned Zea down and turned toward the tongue. She staggered a step, caught her balance, and muttered, "I think I'm going to throw up."

"Not now," Luke said. "Get down the tunnel. I'll follow you out as soon as I take care of this."

[Power Strike] surged down his arm, and Luke blurred forward to strike the tongue at a spot about four feet off the ground. Chunks of . . . not meat, but something wet and gloppy that Luke didn't have a word for blew out the side of the tongue, and it curled up on itself.

The enforcer got his friend free, and Luke shoved the two of them toward the exit, but all three froze at the same time. Zea was standing about ten feet from the mouth of the tunnel, staring in horror as six new tongues broke through the stone and shot straight up to pierce the ceiling, then flailed in place. Chunks of stone came crashing down, and Zea scrambled backward with a shriek.

"Oh fuck," Luke said. "That's not good."

They were trapped.

Name	Luke Bennet	Zea Stenter
Level	43	35
XP	274177/293811	148551/157276
AP	33	4
Bloodline	SysAdmin III	None
Strength	61	7
Agility	70	30
Stamina	88	27
Perception	55	21
Skills	Burst Step (1)	Arcano Dynamics (2)
	Butchering (4)	Bartering (2)
	Consortium Standard (2)	Bloodline Purification Ritual (2)
	Counter (3)	Cadence (3)
	Deception (1)	Cold Reading (1)
	Detection (2)	Consortium Standard (1)
	Disguise (2)	Cooking (1)
	First Aid (1)	Dagger Mastery (1)
	Leatherworking (2)	Deception (1)
	Life Surge (2)	Disguise (2)
	Mace Mastery (5)	Engraving (4)
	Ostari (1)	First Aid (1)
	Peripheral Awareness (2)	Gem Cutting (1)
	Power Strike (2)	Ghost Script (1)
	Stealth (1)	Goldsmithing (2)
	Survivalist (2)	Keen Instincts (1)
	Sword Mastery (1)	Lock Picking (1)
	Tactical Foresight (2)	Mana Manipulation (3)
	Thalian (2)	Mana Sight (3)
	Torturer (1)	Mending (1)
	Twitch Reflexes (3)	Metallurgy (1)
	Unarmed Martialist (4)	Neyardic (3)
	Wood Carving (1)	Ostari (1)
	Analyze (BL)	Painting (1)
	Remote Access (BL)	Rune Forging (3)
	XP Mask (BL)	Sleight of Hand (1)
		Steady Hands (2)
		Stealth (2)
		Streetwise (2)
		Temperature Acclimation (2)
		Thalian (3)
		Whitesmithing (1)

CHAPTER 31

It took the tentacles seconds to bring the roof of the tunnel down and bury it. Behind them, the tentacle he'd stunned with a **[Power Strike]** was already moving again. Both enforcers turned to face it, but Luke was far faster than either of them.

He pulled Zea back from the reach of the tentacle that the enforcers were struggling with, then pivoted and dashed forward to strike the base of the offending limb with a kick. For something that was able to bore through stone, it was surprisingly malleable. The tentacle buckled under the kick but didn't tear or otherwise show any visible signs that it had been injured. Luke didn't even want to think how tough it must be that he couldn't do any appreciable damage to it without resorting to **[Power Strike]**.

What it did do was start vibrating in place, so fast that its outline blurred and little chunks of stone came loose around its base. When it lashed out again, Luke jumped straight over its side swipe. The enforcers were not so lucky. One of them went low, just under the tentacle's bulk, but the other was struck in the chest. That guy blew apart in a shower of blood and gore, like he had been struck with a foot-wide chain saw blade.

"Holy fuck," Luke swore.

The blur disappeared, leaving a standard tentacle again, but Luke was hesitant to approach it. He didn't know the limits of this skill, if that was even what it was, but he had a very clear mental image of trying to punch the thing, only for his hand to disappear in a cloud of bloody mist while chunks of bone splattered across the front of his shirt.

The enforcers were armed with clubs, which under normal circumstances would be more than enough. They had a decent range, would leave bruises, and if necessary, could break bones. That was all it took to keep a crowd of somewhat intoxicated fight fans in check most days. Against an invasion of giant tongue-shaped tentacles, it was worthless.

The enforcer that was still alive broke his club against the springy tentacle with an inarticulate cry of rage. A second later, he was flying through the air to smash heavily into the stone wall. His corpse flopped onto the floor, leaving behind a streak of blood that ended in a slowly growing pool.

"I regret leaving my mace at home," Luke told Zea. "Don't know if it would do anything, but I'd feel better having it."

Zea pulled out her whip, charged the enchantment with a flick of her wrist that caused the pieces of antler to spread out and form its length, then sliced it across the tentacle. It bit in deep, deep enough to tear out a chunk of fibrous, mushy plant material but not enough to cut all the way through it. Undeterred, she worked the whip to arc out and back in several more times. By the fourth cut, she managed to slice completely through the tentacle.

A twenty-foot length of it crashed down to the floor, far too late to do either enforcer any good. It also didn't stop the stump from writhing around, though Luke wasn't quite sure if that was from any sort of pain or just its regular motions. It didn't bleed or drip ichor or anything like that either. Mostly, it looked kind of like cutting a vine.

"Now what?" Zea asked. They were safe for the moment, but both enforcers were dead, and their way out was buried under thousands of pounds of loose stone. It would take hours to dig through that, even as physically empowered by the system as he was.

"Find a different exit, I guess," Luke said, but he had his doubts about the viability of that plan. There were eight different tunnels leading in or out of the arena, and every one of them was either clogged with people fleeing the attack or already collapsed. Whatever the creatures doing this were, they were coordinated enough to corral their victims in. Even as he watched, a trio of tentacle vines burst out of one of the remaining open tunnels in a shower of red gore, killing a few dozen people in under a second.

There was only one spot that was clear of tentacles. Inside the arena itself, Spectacle had put his blade to good work. In the thirty seconds or so that the attack had been going on, he'd severed no less than sixteen tentacles that had broken into the pit. Even as Luke watched, he activated one of his skills and blurred forward too fast to track. Two more tentacles collapsed to the ground behind him as he returned to normal speed on the other side of the pit.

Plenty of people had noticed that Spectacle was hacking apart any tentacle that was near him and had fled into the pit hoping to shelter under the protection of his sword. Spectacle did not appear amused by this, not that Luke could blame him. Having a surging crowd chasing after him made it much harder to move freely.

Much to Luke's annoyance, he found himself almost missing that stupid sword he'd waved around during his own performances. A mace would be better, of course, but something to cut through the tentacles would be an acceptable substitute. Spectacle certainly made it look easy.

Perhaps the gladiator would save the day. He was well equipped to dart about, hacking down tentacles, but at the same time, more and more kept coming up. It would take two or three Spectacles to stay on top of the tongue tentacles, and there didn't seem to be a limit to how many burst through the stone.

Luke and Zea surveyed the arena for a few seconds. New tentacles appeared faster than they could be destroyed. Quivering piles of meat, bones, and blood coated the floor. All but one exit had been caved in, and that one went down even as Luke started to point it out. The only man successfully resisting the attack was being handicapped by the press of people trying to stay close to him.

"We're fucked, aren't we?" Zea asked in a quiet voice.

"Let's circle around to the north wall," Luke said. "We'll bust down that gate leading into the offices. There are no tentacles in there."

"What if some pop up and drop the ceiling on us?" she pointed out.

A new tongue tentacle broke out of the stone between them. It shot directly at Luke, who let **[Unarmed Martialist]** guide his limbs into a flurry of punches and kicks that battered the tentacle but failed to actually destroy it. Zea's whip flashed left, then right, then back again, and the tentacle plopped onto the stone while the stump continued to wiggle about.

"We don't have any better options that I'm seeing," Luke said. "We need to get down to the weapons lockers if nothing else. I'm doing fuck all to help right now. If we're lucky, the back way out will still be there."

Together, they edged around the arena. Luke ran interference on tentacles that got in their way, even though he couldn't put them down. They didn't have time for Zea to hack the tentacles apart, not as fast as new ones were still coming up a minute after the attack had started. The worst parts were when they encountered pockets of other people trying to fight back. Most of them were just regular people wielding nothing but belt knives. Luke scooped one up off a corpse, but it broke immediately upon being stabbed into a tentacle, which hardly seemed to notice.

He should have brought his ever-sharp knife with him, though he was well aware that ever sharp was not the same as ever durable. Chances were it would have broken just as quickly as the cheap one he'd scavenged off the corpse. Stolen weapons were not doing much good though, not even as much as his own fists. Every time Luke hit one of the tentacles, he was reminded of the first one's blurred outline as it shredded a human being in under a second.

When they made it to the cage door, Luke ripped it right out of the wall and ushered Zea in. They needed to move quickly, not in the least because if any tentacles found them in the hallway, there was very little room to dodge and a very low ceiling. The odds of that happening were only going to increase as other people followed them through the new exit, and he could only hope that if and when the demons attacking the arena dropped the tunnel, Luke and Zea would already be out the other side.

Luck was with them for once, and they fled down the tunnel to the storage area, where he grabbed three different swords and slung them over his shoulder. "Overkill?" Zea asked.

"Probably not. They're not great quality," he said. "I'll have to be gentle just to keep them from bending or breaking."

"Where to now?" she asked.

"The monster-holding area," he said. "There's a tunnel that goes all the way out of the city. I think they use it to bring in new monsters."

"That's going to be miles long," Zea said.

"If you've got a better idea . . ."

"Fuck. No. Okay, let's do it."

The duo rushed off again. It was weirdly quiet now, with the screams mostly gone and the rumbling as tentacles broke through stone absent. As they ran the length of the service tunnels circling around the arena, Zea asked, "Do you think there's anybody alive back there?"

"I don't know. I hope so," Luke said. He didn't think it was likely there'd be any survivors, not by the time it was over. The only question was whether the demons would fully emerge from underground to attack the city or if they'd be content just killing a few hundred people in the arena.

"Look, blood," he said as they turned a corner. The wall had been blown out, and a single mangled corpse was lying there, but a trail of blood led deeper down the tunnel. Someone had escaped the demon's tongue tentacle, though not without great cost.

"Nothing we can do about it," Zea said.

"No. I just hope the blood doesn't lead other demons this way. We don't really know how these things sense the world around them."

They reached the holding area for the monsters and paused. It was in ruins, with great portions of the ceiling collapsed and all the monsters dead. Thankfully, there were no tentacles there at the moment, but for all Luke knew, they could come rushing back out of the holes they'd left behind. He charted a path that avoided them as much as possible and led Zea toward the back of the cavern.

"How did you even know about this?" she asked.

"Saw it when we were first negotiating."

"I didn't see anything," she muttered.

"Wait," Luke said, freezing in place. "There's . . . something . . . I can't tell what it is. A person, maybe?"

Luke advanced cautiously, Zea right behind him. They didn't go twenty feet before Luke figured it out. "Gotayi," he said.

The fat pit manager had dragged himself almost a hundred feet down the tunnel before he'd succumbed to his wounds. Clutched to his chest was an iron box, locked. Luke picked it up and felt the weight shift inside. A single shake was enough to confirm his suspicions. "Looks like he tried to grab whatever money he could get away with and made a break for it. Maybe he'd have made it if he'd left it behind."

"No point in leaving it with him," Zea said.

"I suppose not. It's not like he can use it—wait. Do you hear that?"

"No?"

Luke peered through the darkness, and his hand clenched on the hilt of the stolen sword. Again, he wished he had his mace. "Take the box," he said harshly. "Run for the exit. I'll catch up when I can. There's something behind us."

Name	Luke Bennet	Zea Stenter
Level	43	35
XP	274177/293811	148551/157276
AP	33	4
Bloodline	SysAdmin III	None
Strength	61	7
Agility	70	30
Stamina	88	27
Perception	55	21
Skills	Burst Step (1)	Arcano Dynamics (2)
	Butchering (4)	Bartering (2)
	Consortium Standard (2)	Bloodline Purification Ritual (2)
	Counter (3)	Cadence (3)
	Deception (1)	Cold Reading (1)
	Detection (2)	Consortium Standard (1)
	Disguise (2)	Cooking (1)
	First Aid (1)	Dagger Mastery (1)
	Leatherworking (2)	Deception (1)
	Life Surge (2)	Disguise (2)
	Mace Mastery (5)	Engraving (4)
	Ostari (1)	First Aid (1)
	Peripheral Awareness (2)	Gem Cutting (1)
	Power Strike (2)	Ghost Script (1)
	Stealth (1)	Goldsmithing (2)
	Survivalist (2)	Keen Instincts (1)
	Sword Mastery (1)	Lock Picking (1)
	Tactical Foresight (2)	Mana Manipulation (3)
	Thalian (2)	Mana Sight (3)
	Torturer (1)	Mending (1)
	Twitch Reflexes (3)	Metallurgy (1)
	Unarmed Martialist (4)	Neyardic (3)
	Wood Carving (1)	Ostari (1)
	Analyze (BL)	Painting (1)
	Remote Access (BL)	Rune Forging (3)
	XP Mask (BL)	Sleight of Hand (1)
		Steady Hands (2)
		Stealth (2)
		Streetwise (2)
		Temperature Acclimation (2)
		Thalian (3)
		Whitesmithing (1)

CHAPTER 32

Tension built in Luke's neck as he stared back down the tunnel. There was something there, but he couldn't find it. And that didn't happen to him, not anymore. Not even Lath had been able to sneak up on him, and the inquisitor had had a skill specifically to help him be quiet and unobtrusive. Admittedly, he hadn't used it much in his hunt for Luke and Zea.

[Detection] saved Luke's life. It drew his eyes to a streak in the darkness, something there and gone in an instant, and the only reason Luke kept his head on his shoulders was his immediate reaction. He dove to floor of the tunnel and rolled past Gotayi's corpse as something streaked through the air overhead and skidded to a stop thirty feet past Luke's position.

It rebounded instantly, but this time Luke saw its approach. He timed it, slid to the side as it was going by, and smacked a hand out to catch it by the face. His attacker contorted in the air and tumbled to a stop, untouched. Before it could throw itself at him again, Luke said, "Spectacle, stop."

"Why? Are you different from all the other demons?"

"I'm not a demon," Luke said, annoyance in his voice. **[XP Mask]** was starting to become more of a problem than it was worth. "I'm just a guy with a bloodline skill that lets me hide my XP."

Luke turned off the skill and let his XP presence slip out. Spectacle froze in place, his head cocked to the side. "Impossible," he uttered.

"No, seriously, it's for real. I already had this conversation with those Jigon-Sai guys."

"No, not that," Spectacle said. "You have the SysAdmin bloodline."

"You . . . You know what my bloodline is?" Luke asked.

"Only from the stories."

"What fucking stories?!"

Spectacle glanced behind him, shook his head, and said, "Later. That demon is going to bring this whole arena down in a few minutes. It's only slowed down because it killed almost everyone and seems to be making some sort of effort to fling the bodies into a mouth that came up through the floor in the pit."

"Shit. Everyone's dead?"

Spectacle nodded once and walked past Luke. "Come with me. We've got a lot to talk about if you really are a descendant of William Bennet."

"That's my dad," Luke said. "He went missing from my world nine months ago. I guess time works differently here, and it's been centuries since he died."

"I don't know," Spectacle said. "You should talk to my aunt. She knows more about this than anyone else in the family."

Spectacle kept walking, and Luke fell into place behind him. "My friend is farther ahead," Luke said. "We should catch up to her in a bit."

"The dwifkin you were standing with during my show?" Spectacle asked.

"Yes."

"She's a thousand feet in front of us, not moving."

"How the hell . . . Oh, your **[Tapestry of the World]** skill?" Luke asked.

Spectacle paused, then nodded. "You can see my status," he said. "That's . . . weirdly violating."

"Sorry."

It hadn't escaped Luke's notice that Spectacle hadn't put away that black-metal sword yet, nor had he removed the mask covering his face. Maybe that was just a sensible precaution in case any more giant demon tongues attacked them, or maybe he was protecting himself from Luke. It had only been thirty seconds ago that Spectacle had tried to kill him, and despite the man's apparent knowledge of Luke's family and bloodline, Luke had precious little reason to trust Spectacle.

Perhaps more important was the question of why Zea had stopped. Luke had assumed the tunnel would hit the surface somewhere outside the city, that way new monsters could be smuggled in unnoticed, but maybe he'd been wrong about that. Maybe it spilled out into some guarded warehouse or just ended at a locked door Zea couldn't get past. He couldn't imagine why it would terminate well short of the city limits, but he also couldn't think of a reason Zea would stop if she had room to keep moving forward.

"Do you know what those demons were?" Spectacle asked.

"Uh, maybe. They kind of looked like these purple things that had tongue-shaped tentacles coming out of their mouths. But I think the bodies were just kind of like clothes they wore to move around, and the actual demon is just a mass of tentacles. Only, the ones I fought had tongues that were a few inches wide, not a foot or more, and only ten or fifteen feet long, not fifty."

"The lashers, yes. I thought they bore a resemblance myself," Spectacle said. "But I've never seen them traveling outside of their flesh carriers, nor have I seen any that approach that size. It concerns me. What if . . ."

"What if what?" Luke prompted.

Spectacle shook his head. "I'm probably wrong. And it's complicated. I guess in broad strokes, there's supposed to be different tiers of demons, and the higher up you go, the bigger they get."

"That's interesting. How do you know all this stuff?"

"Also complicated," Spectacle said. "This isn't the first time we've had demons on Aros. There are records."

"Doesn't sound that complicated."

Spectacle ignored him and said, "Your friend is just ahead."

The tunnel curved to the left, then abruptly ended at an immense underground canyon. It was a hundred feet wide and filled with loose stone. Zea stood at the edge, peering off into the darkness. She glanced over her shoulder as Luke and Spectacle came into view, paused, and gave Luke a questioning glance. He just shrugged in reply.

Spectacle brushed past Zea and looked down into the canyon. "Something dug this out. Something big."

"One thing or many things," Luke said.

"We already know the tongue demons can burrow through stone," Zea said. She looked over at Spectacle and added, "Making new friends?"

"I wouldn't go that far," Luke told her. "But he's certainly interesting. Seems to know a lot about my family and demons in general."

"That's suspicious," Zea said. She looked over at Spectacle and said, "Anything you want to add to the conversation?"

"Not really," he said. "I don't care if you believe me. Right now my concern is escaping from the demon or demons, and for everybody's sake, I hope it's *demons* plural and not one massive lasher."

"What if it is just a single huge demon?" Luke asked.

"If the history books are to be believed, then it would take someone over level 60 to kill it."

"Fuuuuuuuuck," Luke said.

"Well put," Spectacle told him dryly.

"Fuck all that," Zea said. "Focus on what's important right now. Can we get across this?"

"I can," Spectacle said.

Luke considered the canyon of open air separating him from the tunnel they'd been following. He could see the opening directly across from them, fifty or sixty feet away. If he got a running start and used **[Burst Step]** at just the right moment, he thought he could make it. Besides, even if he failed, it wasn't like he couldn't climb back out. He doubted the fall would hurt.

"Probably," Luke said.

The black-clad man took a few steps back, then sprinted forward and leaped out into the canyon. He made the jump with grace and landed on the far side a second later. "Guess he wasn't lying," Luke said. "I'm going to assume I'm carrying you."

"Unless you've got a lot of rope for me to climb down and then back up the other side," Zea told him.

"I do not. Hey, what'd you do with that cashbox?"

"Dumped the box into this hole. The money's in my pack."

That was probably for the best. It saved him having to lift the weight, not that ten or twenty pounds was much to him these days. Every bit helped though, especially when he was making such a long jump. Luke considered using **[Life Surge]** for the jump, but on the off chance that Spectacle betrayed them, he wanted to save that.

"Okay, let's do this," he said. He took a few steps back, beckoned for Zea to jump up into his arms, and got himself into position.

"You sure you can make this jump?" she asked.

"Nope."

"What do you mean, 'Nope'?" she said, alarm in her voice.

"Means maybe I will, maybe not."

Zea started struggling to get free, but Luke held her tightly. "You put me down right this instant!" she demanded.

"Hold on tight," Luke said, pushing off the stone while Zea screamed.

Hakiro was well accustomed to perceiving the world around him without using his eyes. They hadn't worked right since he was a child anyway, showing him mostly blurs of movement and washed-out colors, especially in bright lights. When he'd gained his first level, he'd immediately put his AP into perception, and that trend had continued until he'd reached 20.

It hadn't fixed his eyes. He'd given up at that point and turned to skills. That had been time-consuming to the extreme. As he understood it, most people perceived the system as words they could read, but Hakiro was forced to listen to endless lists of options. It was simply maddening listening to a dry repetition of lists of skills over and over again. It was a minor miracle he'd managed to find anything of use at all.

That was long ago. Now he *saw* everything, for lack of better term. There were no blind spots in his **[Tapestry of the World]**, just an endless sea of information that got fuzzier the farther away from him it was. He clearly saw the stranger across the chasm, heard him argue with his partner, and perceived the pressure the man exerted against the stone when he pushed himself into a jump.

It was because of his skills and his perception that he knew the instant things went wrong. The demon had found them, and it was coming. Tremors shook the stone, just as they had back in the arena. The demon burrowed through it with incredible speed, faster than an average man could run on flat ground. It must have been some demonic magic that allowed it to move like it did, though the chasm it had cut through the earth probably helped speed it on its way.

Before Hakiro could so much as call out a warning, the demon burst out of the darkness, its huge central maw hanging in the air at a level with the two strangers while a hundred tentacles lanced out to catch them and block all possibility of escape.

The stranger saw the demon coming a second after Hakiro did, and he reacted admirably. With his last instant of freedom, he twisted in the air like a cat and hurled his diminutive partner toward Hakiro.

"Catch!" he bellowed as the woman went flying straight at Hakiro.

"Luke!" she all but screamed. Then the tentacles flashed through the darkness and engulfed the stranger.

Hakiro caught the dwifkin with one arm, spun in a circle to diffuse the momentum, and set her down on her feet. "Run," he ordered. "Do not let his sacrifice be in vain."

"We can't leave him," she said, pulling out that strange whip he'd seen her wield back at the arena.

"We cannot fight this creature. It is a paragon, an elder demon, one of the primordial progenitors of their kind."

"I won't leave him."

Her voice was cold. The whip flowed out, shards of bone running its length, and she hacked down at the tentacles. If the demon even noticed, it paid her no mind. That did nothing to stop her; if anything, it drove her into an even greater fury.

Hakiro made to grab her and pull her away, but then he noticed something that made him freeze in place. The stranger, Luke, had been buried under tons of demon flesh, should have been crushed to a lump of meat and his remains tossed into the demon's maw.

Except, somehow, he had resisted the incredible pressure. Somehow, and Hakiro couldn't imagine how, he was still alive.

Name	Luke Bennet	Zea Stenter
Level	43	35
XP	274177/293811	148551/157276
AP	33	4
Bloodline	SysAdmin III	None
Strength	61	7
Agility	70	30
Stamina	88	27
Perception	55	21
Skills	Burst Step (1)	Arcano Dynamics (2)
	Butchering (4)	Bartering (2)
	Consortium Standard (2)	Bloodline Purification Ritual (2)
	Counter (3)	Cadence (3)
	Deception (1)	Cold Reading (1)
	Detection (2)	Consortium Standard (1)
	Disguise (2)	Cooking (1)
	First Aid (1)	Dagger Mastery (1)
	Leatherworking (2)	Deception (1)
	Life Surge (2)	Disguise (2)
	Mace Mastery (5)	Engraving (4)
	Ostari (1)	First Aid (1)
	Peripheral Awareness (2)	Gem Cutting (1)
	Power Strike (2)	Ghost Script (1)
	Stealth (1)	Goldsmithing (2)
	Survivalist (2)	Keen Instincts (1)
	Sword Mastery (1)	Lock Picking (1)
	Tactical Foresight (2)	Mana Manipulation (3)
	Thalian (2)	Mana Sight (3)
	Torturer (1)	Mending (1)
	Twitch Reflexes (3)	Metallurgy (1)
	Unarmed Martialist (4)	Neyardic (3)
	Wood Carving (1)	Ostari (1)
	Analyze (BL)	Painting (1)
	Remote Access (BL)	Rune Forging (3)
	XP Mask (BL)	Sleight of Hand (1)
		Steady Hands (3)
		Stealth (2)
		Streetwise (2)
		Temperature Acclimation (2)
		Thalian (3)
		Whitesmithing (1)

CHAPTER 33

For all the shit Luke had endured since he'd been taken to Aros, nothing compared to the pain of those dozens of tentacles crushing him. It wasn't just the pressure either; no, they had texture to them like a particularly rough and slimy piece of sandpaper. Even if Luke had been wearing his armor, he didn't think it would stand up to this kind of punishment. His clothes were immediately shredded, and the tentacles rasped across his body.

The first few seconds of contact were a series of disorientating shoves in random directions and a burning sensation as his skin was abraded. It wasn't until he activated **[Life Surge]** that Luke had enough strength to begin fighting back. He hooked an arm around the tentacle pressing against his stomach and squeezed.

Other tentacles rushed across his body, but with **[Life Surge]** pushing his strength and stamina higher, Luke held himself stationary. His free arm pushed a tentacle aside so that he could grab the hilt of one of the swords strapped behind his shoulder, and he ripped it free while channeling a **[Power Strike]** down his arm. The blade severed a tentacle cleanly, which did little to give him more room, but it was a start.

He passed the sword to his other hand and drew a second one. Then he got to work. The blades weren't made to stand up to this kind of pressure, but Luke didn't care. He didn't need them to survive the fight, just to give him some room to move. **[Power Strike]** after **[Power Strike]** drove them through fibrous plant flesh as he chopped through the knot of tentacles he was caught in.

Abruptly, there was nothing underneath him. Luke fell twenty feet to the floor of the underground canyon. He had two full seconds to get a good look at the demon, to see the hundreds of tongues extending out of an impossibly big mouth in every direction, and to get a look at the number of severed tentacles littering the canyon around him before the demon realized he'd escaped. Instantly, its remaining tongues descended on him again.

This time Luke was ready. He wasn't midleap with a passenger in his arms, and the demon no longer had the element of surprise. As the tongue-shaped appendages slammed down around him, Luke dodged around them. **[Burst Step]** helped keep him from being hit when too many came at him at once, and **[Tactical Foresight]** worked hard to keep him out of that situation in the first place, and he wasn't shy about using his stolen swords.

Those were rapidly turning into worthless scrap metal, their edges dulled and blunted and the steel itself getting just a little bit thinner with each pass through a tentacle. Sometimes the length of a fleshy green pillar would blur, and Luke did his best to dodge those when he could. Perhaps inevitably, a wall of demon tongue slammed down on one side, and a vibrating tentacle swept across the only open space Luke had to work in.

His only option was to parry the blur. Anything else would take too much time. If he'd had even an instant to think about it, he wouldn't have tried. He knew the swords hadn't been up to the task even when they were in good shape, let alone now. Even with **[Power Strike]** surging down both arms and into the blades, he knew as soon as he made contact with the tentacle that it wasn't going to be enough.

He swept both blades up in parallel arcs. The one in his right hand shattered immediately. The one in his left bit in an inch or two at most, then snapped. Then the tentacle slammed into him, pinning him between the wall of tongues and its own blurred length. Fresh pain flared across his stomach, chest, and the underside of his arms where the tentacle pushed up against them.

There was a flash of black, and the tentacle dropped to the ground. "I must be crazy to be doing this," Spectacle said.

"Fight or run?" Luke asked.

"There's no running."

Spectacle cut through three more tentacles closing in on them, and Luke had to admit the other man put him to shame when it came to using a sword. It wasn't just that his weapon was made up of something that could actually stand up to the demon. It was the way he moved, flowing, elegant even. Each motion led smoothly into the next, like Spectacle was dancing with the tentacles. By comparison, Luke felt brutish and slow.

Then again, he'd been hit dozens of times in this fight and was still on his feet. Could Spectacle stand back up after even a single blow? Somehow, Luke doubted it. Somewhat mollified that he had his own areas where he excelled,

Luke pulled the last of his three stolen swords off his back. "What I wouldn't give for a good mace right now," he muttered.

"Ugh. You have no class at all," Spectacle told him. "You might as well beat on things with a club."

"Clubs would also be fine," Luke said.

"Risking my life for this," Spectacle muttered to himself. "I'll try to keep as many of these tentacles off you as possible. Your friend said she was making something using one of her skills that you'd want. Something to feed to that mouth over there."

Luke grinned. It practically had to be an explosion. Zea's first resort was always to blow a threat up. **[Ghost Script]** was good at making quick and dirty bombs too. While he wasn't sure exactly how she was planning on getting that bomb to him, or even why she needed to, it was good to have a clear direction.

"Where is she?" Luke asked as he leaped over a tentacle that skimmed across the ground behind him. His sword flashed, and he severed the offending limb before landing on top of it.

"Still up in the tunnel."

That could be a problem. Luke could barely keep up with the demon when he had solid ground under his feet, let alone while scaling fifty or sixty feet of sheer cliffs to reach Zea. There was no way he could get up to her, and it was way too dangerous for her to come to him. If anything, she should be running away as fast as she could.

Running away never seemed to be an option Zea considered. She'd gotten herself into trouble more than once by staying to fight with Luke in battles she had no business being in, but she'd also saved his ass a few times as well. He trusted her judgment, but he wasn't sure exactly how he was supposed to link back up with her prior to killing the demon.

Luke had a bit over a minute left before **[Life Surge]** dropped and, if at all possible, he wanted to avoid needing to use it back-to-back again. That extra thirty seconds was not worth the after-effects unless it was literally life-or-death. The problem was that Luke didn't have a strategy. He'd needed the power boost just to survive being crushed inside the ball of tentacles, and he had no idea how to kill the demon.

The fact that all the tentacles had even come from one single entity was mind-boggling to him. Some of them were hundreds of feet long, and all of them could push through stone easily. This thing would have ripped apart tanks without any apparent effort and completely ignored any sort of small arms fire. Luke was strong enough to split steel like it was Styrofoam now, and he couldn't get through one of those tentacles barehanded without a **[Power Strike]** to reinforce his attack.

With no way to get to Zea and no idea how much time she'd need to finish drawing the runes on whatever she was using, Luke didn't see a good way to incorporate her into any plan he came up with. He'd just have to trust that she'd find an opening and make herself useful. In the meantime, the obvious weak spot was the mouth all the tongues originated from.

That thing was creepy in and of itself. It wasn't a whole face, just a kind of seed-shaped ball of green flesh split open on one side. It had ridges of a sort along that opening that resembled lips, but there were no other features. Perhaps the worst part of it was that those lips were easily twenty feet wide, and they were parted a solid fifteen feet.

Luke was no expert at physics or math, but he was pretty sure it wasn't possible for all the tentacles filling the canyon to fit inside that seed. There was definitely some kind of bullshittery happening there, though perhaps not the system-induced sort. A quick glance around showed Luke all the severed tongue tentacles, which far, far outsized the seed pod. Luke wondered what would happen if he broke the pod open. Would it kill the demon, or would it just release all the hidden tongues it still held in reserve all at once?

Spectacle had firmly proven that cutting through random tentacles wasn't going to do any good. If they wanted this demon dead, the only way Luke knew was with fire. Unfortunately, he didn't have any on hand. Failing that, his fallback option was to hit things until they stopped moving. He just needed to get there first.

"New plan," Luke said. "I'll keep tentacles off you, and you go fuck up that demon's day."

Spectacle dodged between four different tentacles coming at him from different angles using some sort of move that involved him jumping into the air, turning sideways, and spinning to keep his limbs clear. It looked like something someone taking up breakdancing might have done, only done at speeds faster than a normal human was capable of seeing, let alone moving.

"How exactly are you going to do that?" the black-shrouded man asked.

Luke sent a **[Power Strike]** through his remaining sword and severed a tentacle coming their way. "Like that. But only if you hurry."

[Power Strike] was both draining and not meant to be used with a bladed weapon. He knew he was going to break the sword quicker this way but only if the demon didn't do it first. One way or another, the fight was going to be over in the next minute or two, so he figured he might as well go all in on the plan with the best chance of succeeding.

Spectacle darted around Luke, putting himself closer to the wall. "Keep it busy," he commanded, and the pair leaped forward together.

Luke couldn't match Spectacle's sheer speed or coordination, but he had the other man completely outclassed in terms of raw strength. Not every tentacle needed to be cut apart either. In fact, sometimes it was better to redirect one into the way of another one. The tentacles didn't seem to care if they got tangled up with one another, and whatever slime coating they had on them was enough lubricant to pull themselves back apart.

But for a few seconds here and there, Luke could take two or three out of action and use them as shields to block new tongues from reaching them. In a fight like this one, where everyone was moving a hundred miles an hour, a few seconds was a lot. He flanked Spectacle's advance and blocked the majority of the tentacles that tried to snag them, and together the two of them rushed the seed pod.

It loomed overhead, anchored in midair by at least eight different tentacles that had bored into the stone above their heads. There was no convenient way to reach it, not unless they wanted to brave the tangled mess coming directly out of its mouth. Luke had already been caught in that once, and he wasn't eager to repeat the experience. Fortunately for him, he had a better idea.

He cupped his hands in front of him, looked at Spectacle, and said, "Want a lift up?"

Name	Luke Bennet	Zea Stenter
Level	43	35
XP	274177/293811	148551/157276
AP	33	4
Bloodline	SysAdmin III	None
Strength	61	7
Agility	70	30
Stamina	88	27
Perception	55	21
Skills	Burst Step (1)	Arcano Dynamics (2)
	Butchering (4)	Bartering (2)
	Consortium Standard (2)	Bloodline Purification Ritual (2)
	Counter (3)	Cadence (3)
	Deception (1)	Cold Reading (1)
	Detection (2)	Consortium Standard (1)
	Disguise (2)	Cooking (1)
	First Aid (1)	Dagger Mastery (1)
	Leatherworking (2)	Deception (1)
	Life Surge (2)	Disguise (2)
	Mace Mastery (5)	Engraving (4)
	Ostari (1)	First Aid (1)
	Peripheral Awareness (2)	Gem Cutting (1)
	Power Strike (2)	Ghost Script (1)
	Stealth (1)	Goldsmithing (2)
	Survivalist (2)	Keen Instincts (1)
	Sword Mastery (1)	Lock Picking (1)
	Tactical Foresight (2)	Mana Manipulation (3)
	Thalian (2)	Mana Sight (3)
	Torturer (1)	Mending (1)
	Twitch Reflexes (3)	Metallurgy (1)
	Unarmed Martialist (4)	Neyardic (3)
	Wood Carving (1)	Ostari (1)
	Analyze (BL)	Painting (1)
	Remote Access (BL)	Rune Forging (3)
	XP Mask (BL)	Sleight of Hand (1)
		Steady Hands (2)
		Stealth (2)
		Streetwise (2)
		Temperature Acclimation (2)
		Thalian (3)
		Whitesmithing (1)

CHAPTER 34

[**Burst Step**] wasn't really supposed to be used for upward momentum. It wouldn't be all that effective that way, probably not enough to justify the expenditure of Luke's stamina in a normal situation, but Luke did not think he could jump forty or fifty feet straight up on his own. Twenty feet was well within his capabilities, but he needed an extra boost for this.

"Jumping in two, one, now," Luke said as he activated the skill and rocketed upward.

Spectacle kept his balance easily and cleared the remaining distance once gravity took hold of Luke around the halfway mark. With his sword leading, he came up level with the seed pod and stabbed at the demon. The blade skittered across the curve of the seed and failed to penetrate, but Spectacle was undeterred and switched targets to the mouth.

He tried to, at least. It turned out not even his agility and skills were good enough to dodge the demon's tentacles from that close. Within a second of his first attack on the seed, a dozen tentacles slapped down on itself, like some sort of giant hand swatting at a mosquito. Spectacle somehow managed to spin his momentum in a new direction and slip between those tentacles without being touched, but he lost access to the demon's seed core in the process.

Luke needed to get up there and help, but he didn't know how. The canyon walls weren't something he could just casually climb, and there was no way he was going to wriggle through the mass of tentacles flailing malevolently through the air. Maybe if they were just moving randomly, he'd have considered it. But they weren't. In reality, they were guided by an intelligent mind and were actively chasing down threats. When they didn't need to burrow through the ground to reach their targets, they were insanely fast too.

For all that Luke had become accustomed to his superhuman feats of athleticism, he had a hard time shifting his thinking to include his capabilities. Moving faster and hitting harder was one thing, but he could do so much more if he only took the time to consider exactly how unlimited his options were compared to what they'd been back on Earth.

No, he couldn't jump fifty feet straight up, but he didn't need to. Luke from Earth would take an hour to climb that wall if he could manage it at all. He'd go carefully, looking for handholds, terrified of falling and splitting his skull on the rocks below. Hell, if he was honest with himself, he probably wouldn't even make an attempt unless there were no other options.

Luke, resident of the world called Aros, was strong enough to rip through stone with his fingers and make his own handholds. His legs had enough power to kick the walls and create spots for him to stand, and he could jump high enough that he'd only have to do it once or twice. The hardest part of climbing the wall would be fending off the demon trying to kill him.

He took an instant to dodge around a trio of tentacles coming for him, dragged his blade through one with a **[Power Strike]** infused into the swing to ensure it severed the tentacle fully, and then he launched himself at the wall.

Luke hit the stone about twenty feet off the ground hard enough that he drove his free hand and both feet into the stone. It buckled with thunderous cracks, but Luke didn't take the time to stop and inspect just how solid his holds were. He threw himself straight up, mostly using the strength in his arm since his legs didn't exactly have room to flex. That was more than enough power to launch him ten feet farther up the side of the canyon, and this time he grabbed hold of a convenient spur of rock and rested his feet against the vertical stone surface.

It was practically a Spider-Man pose, except that if he let go, he'd fall to his . . . well, not death, but maybe a bruise or two if he landed badly. Of far more danger was the tongue-shaped tentacle swooping down on him from above. Luke shoved off from the wall and threw himself another fifteen feet higher, just a bit too short to make it to his target.

He was going to land in the slime-covered knot of tentacles below it unless he did something, and that was exactly where he didn't want to be. Fortunately, he still had that junk sword, and there was a stationary tentacle the seed was using to keep itself stable up in the air nearby. Luke drove the sword in as he passed by, used his momentum to dodge around the edge of the tentacle, and braced himself for a final leap.

His feet slipped despite the rough surface of the tongue tentacle, but that wouldn't have been an issue on its own. No, the real problem was that cheap fucking steel couldn't handle anywhere close to the pressure he was putting on it even when it was in good condition. The blade snapped inside the tentacle, leaving Luke holding a handle with about four inches of sanded-down steel sticking out, and he was all of a sudden falling back down to the floor of the canyon.

[Power Strike] worked better when channeled through a mace, but a punch could still get the job done. In this case, it was more of an openhanded swipe, but Luke had the force behind it to tear into the tentacle and rip out a handful of its fibrous innards. His arm was up to the elbow inside the demon, but he'd stopped falling.

"What are you doing?" Spectacle demanded as he slipped by on his way down. Somehow, despite being in a free fall, the man still managed to twist and spin to keep himself safe using nothing but that length of slender black metal. He kicked off a tentacle that came at him from below, intent on smacking him between two other tentacles. It didn't even look like the man was trying, but he was still avoiding every attack.

"Breaking open that thing," Luke said. He lunged upward, half dragging the tentacle with him before he twisted it to block another tentacle and released his grip. Luke landed on the demon's mouth, one foot wedged between two tentacles near the lip and the other pressed against the smooth, rubbery green skin.

And then he hammered it with his fists. Over and over again, a dozen times in a second. He sent **[Power Strike]** after **[Power Strike]** through his arms and into the seed. For the first time ever, the demon reacted to being injured. A basso scream erupted out of its mouth, setting all the tentacles to trembling and causing chunks of rock to shake themselves loose from the ceiling and fall.

Something cracked, and a chunk of flesh slipped loose to splatter against the ground. Luke took that as a good sign and focused his efforts there, at least until **[Twitch Reflexes]** started screaming at him. Before he could react, a tentacle grabbed hold of him and flung him out into the canyon. Pain flashed through Luke's body for a second before **[Life Surge]** took care of it.

He climbed back to his feet, took two steps, and staggered as **[Life Surge]** gave out. "Good timing," Luke said. No less than six tentacles filled his vision, all coming at him from different angles. "Maybe not."

The bad news was that Luke wasn't durable enough to survive being hit by those tentacles without **[Life Surge]** fortifying him. Oh, he wouldn't die on the first or second hit, probably not even the tenth, but they would wear him down soon enough. More bad news, he didn't think he was agile enough to dodge them, even with all his skills helping.

The good news was that the injury he'd dealt the demon counted for something. Many of the tentacles were just flailing around blindly now, with only a handful actively pursuing him. Luke lurched left as one rushed past him like a speeding train, then hopped over another that tried to loop around and strike him from the side. The next two came from directly above, and both punched deep into the stone as he used **[Burst Step]** to get out from beneath him.

An explosion ripped through the canyon, impossibly loud as it echoed across the stone. It was followed immediately by the deafening thunder of dozens and dozens of tentacles smacking against the ground. There were so many, in fact, that Luke couldn't even find the seed pod anymore. A few ragged and tattered tentacles hung limply from the stone overhead, but the central seed had been buried in the pile of wet, slimy tentacles.

"Like a meatball hiding in a plate of spaghetti," Luke said to himself. "Goddamn I love that woman. Blowing shit up should be a national pastime."

Luke hurried over to the pile to join Spectacle, who was watching it warily while his hand tightened on the hilt of his sword. He didn't turn to look at Luke as he approached. "I hate not knowing if it's dead."

"Where'd the bomb go?"

"Right into that opening you made when you were pounding on it," Spectacle told him.

"Ha, nice."

"You alright?" Spectacle asked.

Luke wasn't really feeling too steady on his feet, but that was an expected side effect of using **[Life Surge]**. "As long as that demon doesn't start moving again, I'm fine."

As if summoned by his words, something burst out of the pile of tongue tentacles and hurled itself at the two men. Luke had a brief impression of a sphere of spongy green-and-purple flesh with hundreds of hairlike strands coming off it in every direction, except that they were only proportionately hairlike. In actuality, each strand was an inch or two thick, and he'd be willing to bet they looked like tongues.

It was hard to say because as soon as the demon's core appeared and attacked, Spectacle activated one of his skills. His sword's black surface started glowing gold, and some sort of pressure started rolling off him, forcing Luke's feet to slide back several inches across the stone. Then Spectacle disappeared from next to Luke.

A sound not unlike the tearing of a wet piece of cardboard, only a hundred times louder, filled the air. The fleshy orb split in half, and chunks of loose tentacle hair went flying in every direction. A moment later, both halves burst into flames. Spectacle stood on the far side, his sword now black again.

"I believe it is truly dead now," he said. "Come, we should rejoin your friend and get out of here before anything else shows up."

"Uh . . . Yeah." Luke eyed the two flaming pieces of demon corpse. "Shit, I need to pick up some skills like that."

They climbed back up to where Zea was waiting. She eyed Spectacle as he walked past, then turned to Luke and asked, "You alright?"

"I'll be fine. Nothing a good night's sleep can't fix."

"You don't look fine."

"I'm not fine, but let's not show any more weakness in front of our new friend than we have to. I'm pretty sure this fight took a lot more out of me than it did out of him, and I don't know how friendly he's going to be once we're out of here."

"As long as he doesn't attack us . . . Do you think he will?"

"I don't think so, but he knows something about my dad. I need to find out more."

"Tomorrow," Zea said. "You need to get some rest and some new equipment. We've got a nice war chest now, thanks to Gotayi."

"You two coming?" Spectacle asked from farther down the tunnel.

"You're sure he doesn't speak Thalian?" Zea asked.

"It's not on his status," Luke told her.

Somehow, she didn't seem very reassured.

Name	Luke Bennet	Zea Stenter
Level	43	35
XP	274177/293811	148551/157276
AP	33	4
Bloodline	SysAdmin III	None
Strength	61	7
Agility	70	30
Stamina	88	27
Perception	55	21
Skills	Burst Step (1)	Arcano Dynamics (2)
	Butchering (4)	Bartering (2)
	Consortium Standard (2)	Bloodline Purification Ritual (2)
	Counter (3)	Cadence (3)
	Deception (1)	Cold Reading (1)
	Detection (2)	Consortium Standard (1)
	Disguise (2)	Cooking (1)
	First Aid (1)	Dagger Mastery (1)
	Leatherworking (2)	Deception (1)
	Life Surge (2)	Disguise (2)
	Mace Mastery (5)	Engraving (4)
	Ostari (1)	First Aid (1)
	Peripheral Awareness (2)	Gem Cutting (1)
	Power Strike (2)	Ghost Script (1)
	Stealth (1)	Goldsmithing (2)
	Survivalist (2)	Keen Instincts (1)
	Sword Mastery (1)	Lock Picking (1)
	Tactical Foresight (2)	Mana Manipulation (3)
	Thalian (2)	Mana Sight (3)
	Torturer (1)	Mending (1)
	Twitch Reflexes (3)	Metallurgy (1)
	Unarmed Martialist (4)	Neyardic (3)
	Wood Carving (1)	Ostari (1)
	Analyze (BL)	Painting (1)
	Remote Access (BL)	Rune Forging (3)
	XP Mask (BL)	Sleight of Hand (1)
		Steady Hands (2)
		Stealth (2)
		Streetwise (2)
		Temperature Acclimation (2)
		Thalian (3)
		Whitesmithing (1)

CHAPTER 35

The tunnel dumped them out in a barn just outside the city. Luke wasn't sure exactly how many miles it ran, but it must have been an enormous expenditure to dig it. He'd be the first to admit he didn't know much about farming, but the barn looked weird to him too. There was something like a set of stables on one wall but with steel cages instead of wooden stalls. Maybe that was standard practice on Aros, but he kind of doubted it.

"There's nobody here," Spectacle said. "Hmm. I need a change of clothes, and so do you."

The swordsman wasn't exactly wrong. The collar of Luke's shirt was still intact, but not much else. His pants looked more like a loincloth now, except a bit breezier. Luke sighed and nodded glumly. "These were supposed to last, too."

"They're growing back," Zea said. "Half an hour ago, none of this material was here."

"Huh, how about that. I didn't think the magic would survive with this little bit left," Luke said. "How long will it take to grow back all the way?"

"Day or two," she said. "Eh, maybe three. There's not a lot left, so it'll take a bit to really get going."

"So I need clothes," Luke said. "Don't suppose there's a convenient clothes-line anywhere nearby."

"No," Spectacle said. "This farm is a front. Nobody lives here. Take a look outside and you can see what condition the house is in."

Luke pushed open the barn doors to find a dilapidated old house surrounded by overgrown weeds. The front door hung crooked in its frame, and the shutters had been torn from the windows. The roof was, surprisingly, still in one piece, for what it was worth.

The barn was in much better condition, though from the outside, it was easy to mistake it for a matched set with the house. It was in desperate need of a fresh coat of paint, and there were more than a few rotting boards. The interior was solid, at least. Whatever group of smugglers was using the place was at least taking good enough care of the barn that it wasn't likely to fall down anytime soon.

Of course, they weren't going to have much use for it now that the arena had been destroyed. Luke couldn't imagine it would be hosting any fights in the near future, and the smugglers would need to bridge the canyon the demon had carved across their tunnel anyway. If they hadn't gotten away with a considerable chunk of money, Luke would have been annoyed at all the wasted time down there.

"You two are about the same size, right?" Zea asked.

Luke glanced over at Spectacle. They had similar builds, but Spectacle was at least three inches shorter. Maybe it looked different from her angle. "Uh, no, no, we're not," Luke told her.

"Hey, I'm not looking for a hassle here. If I buy two shirts and two trousers in the same size, will that be good enough?"

"If you bought them in my size, I guess," Luke said. "They'd be a bit big on him. If you bought them in his size, they wouldn't fit me."

Zea gave them both a dirty look and said, "Wait here. You'll get whatever I give you."

Then she stomped off toward the city, leaving the two men to stand outside an old barn. They watched her leave in silence, neither moving until she was a mile away.

"Your friend is quite decisive," Spectacle said.

"Some days," Luke agreed. "Uh, listen . . . I don't want to pry into your personal life or whatever. I mean, you're wearing a mask for a reason, right? But your family knew my dad?"

"We did, centuries ago. You must understand that this was generations and generations back, thirty or more. We have stories and legends, not facts. Some of those legends are true, I'm sure, but I don't know if I can tell you what you want to know."

"Whatever you can tell me," Luke said.

"Hmm. Alright. Let me think. William Bennet was an off-worlder who appeared almost a thousand years ago. He was known as William Wyrmsbane at the time of his death in the fourth century. Supposedly, he had perfect mastery of the system itself. It was within his power to change anything and everything about your status, even to the point of taking away skills and giving you new ones. For that reason, he was able to adapt himself to every individual dragon he fought so that he could exploit their weaknesses."

"Hold up. Are you telling me that my old man used to hunt dragons?"

"Quite successfully, if the stories are to be believed. He's directly credited with the deaths of at least three of the dragon emperors as well as being the primary reason what eventually became the Hurang Province was pacified. Prior to his intervention, the area was supposed to have been infested with thousands of lesser wyrms."

Luke tried to picture his father fighting a dragon, but he couldn't make his own mental image line up with that reality. Really, he couldn't picture his dad fighting anything. When he thought of his father, he pictured a broken man with a swelling beer gut who spent all his time either working or shit-faced, sometimes both at the same time. Bill Bennet hadn't been one to hold down a job for more than six months.

Even when he thought back to before his mom's death, he couldn't remember his dad doing anything noteworthy or exciting. He was just a normal guy whose life had taken a bad turn and who hadn't been very good at dealing with it. Luke could picture the man beating a marmot to death with a crowbar, grunting and swearing the whole time, but to go up against something with real power . . . No.

"We still have some of the weapons your father supposedly used kept in places of honor in the archival vault," Spectacle said. "It would be my great-uncle's decision whether to release them, but if there was ever anyone who deserved to hold them, it would be his descendant."

"I already have a weapon," Luke said absently. He was still trying to picture his dad leaping through the air with a sword or axe and smiting the ever-loving shit out of giant lizard.

"Is that so?"

"Left it back at the inn we were staying at. It wasn't part of my gladiator disguise," Luke explained.

Spectacle laughed. "That's fair. I don't normally walk around covered from head to toe in an assassin's garb."

"Probably for the best. I can see, like, all your business right now." Luke made a vague gesture at Spectacle's waist.

"There's supposed to be a coat that goes over this."

"You should have worn it," Luke told him.

"Yes, well, it wasn't my choice to leave it behind. But that's neither here nor there. We're talking about the legend of William Wyrmsbane."

"I honestly don't even know what else to ask," Luke said. "Just . . . All the questions I can think of, you won't be able to answer. He's been dead for centuries. I'm sure you don't know what he was like."

"We have some accounts left behind back at our family's home," Spectacle said. "Maybe the information you're looking for is there."

"Maybe. It's hard to picture my dad being some big hero. He couldn't even get his own life together the last time I saw him. Every night was a race to the bottom of the bottle. Then he'd get up, still buzzed, and go to work in the morning. He always said he had to work hard at the beginning of the day because the hangover would kick in halfway through. Doesn't sound much like a legendary dragon-fighting hero, does it?"

"William was not without his demons," Spectacle said. "Perhaps that is what led to his death. It was always assumed that he finally succumbed to XP madness somewhere alone out in the wilderness. With his level as high as it was, it was practically inevitable, no matter how great his mastery of the system. Some fates cannot be avoided."

"Eh, I already fixed that," Luke said. "Just need another 82 AP."

"I'm sorry, I must have misheard you," Spectacle said slowly. "I'm sure you didn't just say you know of a skill that lets you overcome XP madness."

"Well it didn't exist until a few months ago. I made it with the system's help."

"A bloodline skill then. Does . . ." Spectacle hesitated, then steeled himself. "Does it only work on you?"

"Supposed to work on anyone, but it only delays the onset. I have to keep using it over and over."

Spectacle let out a shaky breath. "You would be able to purchase this skill with a few more levels?"

"Yup," Luke said.

"Would you be willing to use it on someone for me? My older brother, you see, he's . . . He's on the edge. He's in seclusion now, but soon he will be called on to perform his role as the sacrifice in the Rite of the New Generation."

Luke thought back to that thing he'd seen when he'd first reached the eastern continent, that line of men at high levels lined up to be murdered, one by one, by a guy who was half their level. That had had the air of something military, but Luke could imagine a similar, more private ceremony for long-established families.

For that matter, Spectacle wasn't that far away from being on the shanking end of one of those events. He was already level 48, and a good round of [XP Cycle] could easily add a few years to his life. To his credit, the man hadn't asked for himself. It wouldn't cost Luke anything extra to hit everyone he could see with the skill though. He just needed to gain a few levels and actually pick it up first.

Perhaps mistaking Luke's silence for hesitation, Spectacle pressed on. "I'm sure we could compensate you somehow, even beyond access to the artifacts your father left behind."

Luke shook his head. "It's not that. I was just thinking of something I saw when I first got here, a public event where a bunch of high-level people were killed one at a time by someone who was in his mid-20s, level wise. This system is such shit that this kind of stuff happens."

Who'd ever heard of a game that punished people for leveling too high? The Pantheon was a bunch of shitheads for building a system like that. He got that it was the little chunks of divine essence that were responsible, but they could have built XP cycling into the base system when they designed the God Machine. But no, the skill hadn't even existed until he'd asked System to create it for him.

"I'll help if I can, but I need to put on a few more levels first, and demons aren't exactly good XP. I don't know how long I can afford to just stick around this area either. The worse this demon-invasion thing gets, the harder it's going to be to keep traveling. If we don't get moving again soon, it might delay us by months or even years."

"That should not be a problem," Spectacle said. "I'm sure our patriarch will allow you use of the family's leveling grounds once he learns that you're of the SysAdmin bloodline."

"Oh, well, in that case, I guess it'll be pretty easy then? How long could it take to get 50000 or so XP?"

"Well . . . It'll be faster than if you just go roaming the wilderness looking for random monsters. I can't say for sure how many weeks that will take."

Luke blew out a sigh. "Nothing's ever easy, is it? Well, it's worth exploring, you know, once I have pants again. Zea's probably still going to be an hour or two before she gets back. So, what else can you tell me about my dad?"

Name	Luke Bennet	Zea Stenter
Level	43	35
XP	274177/293811	148551/157276
AP	33	4
Bloodline	SysAdmin III	None
Strength	61	7
Agility	70	30
Stamina	88	27
Perception	55	21
Skills	Burst Step (1)	Arcano Dynamics (2)
	Butchering (4)	Bartering (2)
	Consortium Standard (2)	Bloodline Purification Ritual (2)
	Counter (3)	Cadence (3)
	Deception (1)	Cold Reading (1)
	Detection (2)	Consortium Standard (1)
	Disguise (2)	Cooking (1)
	First Aid (1)	Dagger Mastery (1)
	Leatherworking (2)	Deception (1)
	Life Surge (2)	Disguise (2)
	Mace Mastery (5)	Engraving (4)
	Ostari (1)	First Aid (1)
	Peripheral Awareness (2)	Gem Cutting (1)
	Power Strike (2)	Ghost Script (1)
	Stealth (1)	Goldsmithing (2)
	Survivalist (2)	Keen Instincts (1)
	Sword Mastery (1)	Lock Picking (1)
	Tactical Foresight (2)	Mana Manipulation (3)
	Thalian (2)	Mana Sight (3)
	Torturer (1)	Mending (1)
	Twitch Reflexes (3)	Metallurgy (1)
	Unarmed Martialist (4)	Neyardic (3)
	Wood Carving (1)	Ostari (1)
	Analyze (BL)	Painting (1)
	Remote Access (BL)	Rune Forging (3)
	XP Mask (BL)	Sleight of Hand (1)
		Steady Hands (2)
		Stealth (2)
		Streetwise (2)
		Temperature Acclimation (2)
		Thalian (3)
		Whitesmithing (1)

CHAPTER 36

It turned out Zea was an incredibly bad judge of clothing sizes. Luke's fit, more or less. Spectacle, on the other hand, got pants that were too short by about six inches and a shirt that strained across his shoulders and chest. He put it on and twisted once, and the fabric split at the seam.

"Oops," he said.

"How important is it that you cover up your gimp suit?" Luke asked him.

"My what? You mean the assassin's garb? Well, it would be a bad idea to walk around town wearing it," Spectacle told him. "I'm not really an assassin, of course. It's just a costume for the performance, but my actual clothes are buried under tons and tons of rubble."

"Let me rephrase the question. Is it going to be a problem?"

Spectacle sighed and shook his head. "I think it will be fine. My family's home is on the edge of the city anyway. As long as I remove the mask and gloves, I suspect we'll reach it without issue."

"Why would we be going to your family's home?" Zea asked.

Luke took a minute to get Zea caught up to speed on the conversation they'd had while she was in the city, mostly focusing on finding out about his father and using whatever hunting ground they had to buff his level so he could finally start buying the bloodline skills he needed to combat XP madness.

"Well, there is one issue," Zea said. "Our stuff is still back at that inn, including your weapon."

"Right," Luke said. "Uh . . . Head there first?"

Spectacle, who was in the middle of peeling off the skintight gloves that Luke had assumed were all one piece with the suit, paused and said, "The other way around would be better. If necessary, we can send a servant to fetch your belongings."

Spectacle pulled the mask off the top of his head, revealing a short shock of pale silvery-white hair and another mask underneath it. This one was a thin piece of white ceramic that covered his eyes and nose, like one of those fancy masquerade masks rich people wore in the movies when they went to parties with live orchestras playing the music. The biggest difference Luke could see was that it didn't have eyeholes to see through.

It seemed like an unnecessary handicap to Luke, but Spectacle had been wearing it plus a layer of black cloth over it the entire time, so he obviously knew what he was doing. He tucked the mask and gloves inside his pockets and said, "Let's be off if you're ready?"

Luke glanced at Zea, who nodded. "Whoever you send should probably have at least 10 or 12 in strength. That mace is fucking heavy."

"A mace? You weren't making a joke earlier?" Disappointment filled Spectacle's voice. "I suppose it explains your lack of proficiency with a blade."

"Man, what is it with everyone in the city shitting on my choice of weapon?" Luke asked. "Honestly, this whole country. Everyone wants to use a sword and nothing else. What's so great about a sword?"

"It is the noblest of weapons," Spectacle said. "Learning its use is akin to learning the tools of an artist's trade. A swordsman's work is poetry in motion."

"Oh. Uh, okay. I guess." Luke didn't get it, but he wasn't going to argue about it. "I'm just going to keep using what I've got now, and people can think I'm an uncultured barbarian or whatever."

Spectacle didn't quite sniff in disdain, but Luke got the impression he wanted to. It was an active effort for Luke not to roll his eyes, but somehow, he managed. "Come on, let's get going."

Hakiro didn't know what to make of the strangers. For the son of a legendary figure, Luke seemed like a normal person. There were eccentricities, sure, but they were mostly little culture shocks that any foreigner would go through, nothing Hakiro hadn't seen before.

It was disappointing, in a way. William Bennet was the sole reason his family existed, his ancestors having been rescued from the Dragon of the Setting Sun when the Alliance of Flames had collapsed, and Hakiro meant that literally. His many-times-removed great-grandfather had been part of that battle, and his personal accounts described the Dragon Emperor as a terrifying creature, supposedly level 40, which was practically unheard of for the long-lived monsters.

A level 5 drake was more than a match for a level 20 warrior. Make it a dragon, and it would fight a level 40 warrior to a standstill. The Dragon of the

Setting Sun had supposedly been even more powerful than the Dragon of the Rising Dawn, according to Hakiro's ancestor, despite many historical accounts claiming they were on par with each other. When the forces of humanity had rebelled and moved to kill the Third Dragon Emperor, they'd brought forces equal to what had taken the field against the First Emperor, only to find themselves sorely outmatched.

William Bennet had turned that fight around single-handedly. He'd been a force of nature, one capable of pinning even an elder wyrm to the ground and sealing its jaws shut. In a very real sense, every living human on the eastern continent owed their freedom to William Bennet. Without his intervention, the rebellion would have failed, Hakiro's family line would have been extinguished, and the Third Emperor would have swiftly moved to consolidate the territories left behind by his counterparts.

The dragons had been driven back, their elders murdered in their golden palaces, and the wyrmlings left to fend for themselves in the wilderness. Man ruled the land, and William Wyrmsbane became a legend, a figure so mythical there was serious debate among scholars as to whether he had ever even existed.

And here was his son, supposedly, just an ordinary man, and barely one at that. He couldn't be more than twenty or twenty-one. Luke was strong enough, physically stronger than Hakiro even, but he was remarkably inexperienced and a touch naive. Then again, the man could see other people's statuses. It had to be pretty easy to be trusting when he knew someone else's stats and skills. Luke would know whom he could handle in the event of betrayal and whom to keep a wary eye on.

Great-Uncle Fujoka would handle negotiations with Luke Bennet, as was his right as the patriarch of the main branch of the family. Given his attitude toward the family's historical collection, Hakiro doubted the patriarch would be inclined to go easy on the off-worlder. Maybe if Hakiro introduced him to Aunt Valera first, she might sway the negotiations a bit.

Hakiro didn't honestly care, as long as they reached an agreement that included curing his brother's XP madness. Naghan had sacrificed everything for the family and was on track to die at the age of thirty-one. Now, Hakiro had a chance to bring him back from the brink, and he wasn't going to let it go. He'd pay whatever price Luke asked himself, if that was what it took.

He was probably worrying over nothing. Great-Uncle would see the value of pushing back XP madness if for no other reason than getting a few more years of use out of the family's most powerful warriors, especially considering the demons were starting to show up in numbers in the Beilon Province now.

Since the demons didn't grant XP upon dying, a group of mentally stable warriors leveled up into the 40s and 50s was the perfect defense force. If they could get enough people out of the house and onto the battlefield they might even make a fortune hiring out their services. If there was anything that motivated Hakiro's patriarch, it was the thought of profits.

They just needed to get Luke to the estate and convince Hakiro's great-uncle of all of this.

Though the east gate was closer to the barn they'd come out of, Hakiro decided to lead them around the city to the north gate instead. It was closer to his family's home, and they could move far faster out in the farmlands surrounding the city than they could through streets crowded with refugees, even at a vastly reduced speed that allowed Zea to keep up with them.

The gate guards gave Hakiro wary glances, perhaps recognizing the tight black underclothes visible thanks to the torn shirt he was wearing, but they let the group through without incident. After that, Hakiro led them a quarter mile into the city itself and ended their journey at a pair of red-painted gates surrounded by stone walls fifteen feet high and topped with ornate metal spikes.

A solitary guard stood in front of the gate, level 28 according to **[Analyze]**, and he recognized Hakiro immediately. The guy practically tripped over his own feet scrambling to get the gate open when he noticed the group approaching. "Sir!" he said. "I'm glad to see that you're safe."

"Why wouldn't I be safe?" Hakiro asked.

"The . . . uh, the incident, sir?"

Luke exchanged glances with Zea but kept quiet and let Hakiro do the talking. He'd advised them to allow him to make the introductions and get them to the right people who could make decisions since both had confessed they weren't familiar at all with the local customs and were likely to inadvertently step on some toes, which was mostly just a nice way to say that they were uncultured rubes not fit to mingle with high society.

Hakiro let his lips curl down into just a hint of a frown. "What incident is this now?"

"With the giant sinkhole, sir? I've heard it encompassed something like twenty blocks in the southeast corner of the city."

"Why would I be in those slums?" Hakiro demanded.

"Oh, of course not, sir. How foolish of me," the gate guard stammered.

Without another word, Hakiro brushed past them. He gestured for Luke and Zea to follow, and the poor guard jumped ✦ to get out of their way. Once they were inside and the gates were closed, the tension dropped out of Hakiro's shoulders.

"It's so tiring playing this game," he told Luke. "Sometimes, I wish I could just walk away from it all. Go where I want. Do what I want. Act how I want. You understand?"

"Not really," Luke said.

Hakiro snorted. "You do all of that already, don't you?"

"Yeah, pretty much. Why should I care what some snotty rich family thinks of me?"

"You'd best care what this one thinks," Hakiro advised him. "At least until you get what you want. Come on, I want to introduce you to Aunt Valera before my great-uncle finds out you're here. Things will go better if she's advocating on your behalf, and she's obsessed with history. Meeting the living descendant of William Wyrmsbane will be the highlight of her year."

Hakiro led them through a manicured courtyard, filled with far too many flowers and sculpted trees. A stone footpath wound through it all and even had a little bridge to take them over a creek no more than two feet wide. Even a child could have easily hopped over it, but Luke supposed that wouldn't be proper decorum.

"It's just over here," Hakiro said, pointing toward something that reminded Luke of a picturesque cottage, despite looking nothing like one. It was probably the location, what with the whole garden-style courtyard that looked like it needed a dozen full-time landscapers to tend to it.

They'd barely set foot on the trail when a person wearing what had to be a uniform of black and gold appeared as if out of nowhere. It was a loose pair of pants cinched at the ankles with a gold stripe running down the front of the left leg and a white shirt with way too much material in the sleeves. They were wearing a mask similar to Hakiro's, except it covered their entire face, leaving nothing but medium-length hair showing. They appeared so fast Luke barely had a second to notice them coming before they dropped down from the sky to land in front of Hakiro.

"Master Hakiro," the person said. Luke couldn't tell their gender through their loose clothing, and their voice resonated strangely in the air. "Welcome home, sir. The patriarch wishes for your presence immediately."

Hakiro's face went blank, completely expressionless. "Very well, I'll attend to him right now." He turned to Luke and Zea. "Just follow the trail and knock on the door. My aunt is the one with the golden hair pins holding up what has to be five pounds of hair."

"Your pardon, Master Hakiro. The patriarch wishes for *all* your presences."

Name	Luke Bennet	Zea Stenter
Level	43	35
XP	274177/293811	148551/157276
AP	33	4
Bloodline	SysAdmin III	None
Strength	61	7
Agility	70	30
Stamina	88	27
Perception	55	21
Skills	Burst Step (1)	Arcano Dynamics (2)
	Butchering (4)	Bartering (2)
	Consortium Standard (2)	Bloodline Purification Ritual (2)
	Counter (3)	Cadence (3)
	Deception (1)	Cold Reading (1)
	Detection (2)	Consortium Standard (1)
	Disguise (2)	Cooking (1)
	First Aid (1)	Dagger Mastery (1)
	Leatherworking (2)	Deception (1)
	Life Surge (2)	Disguise (2)
	Mace Mastery (5)	Engraving (4)
	Ostari (1)	First Aid (1)
	Peripheral Awareness (2)	Gem Cutting (1)
	Power Strike (2)	Ghost Script (1)
	Stealth (1)	Goldsmithing (2)
	Survivalist (2)	Keen Instincts (1)
	Sword Mastery (1)	Lock Picking (1)
	Tactical Foresight (2)	Mana Manipulation (3)
	Thalian (2)	Mana Sight (3)
	Torturer (1)	Mending (1)
	Twitch Reflexes (3)	Metallurgy (1)
	Unarmed Martialist (4)	Neyardic (3)
	Wood Carving (1)	Ostari (1)
	Analyze (BL)	Painting (1)
	Remote Access (BL)	Rune Forging (3)
	XP Mask (BL)	Sleight of Hand (1)
		Steady Hands (2)
		Stealth (2)
		Streetwise (2)
		Temperature Acclimation (2)
		Thalian (3)
		Whitesmithing (1)

CHAPTER 37

Fujoka Shansakun, patriarch of the Shansakun family, was probably compensating for something. His office had a disgusting amount of decorations made from precious metals and gemstones, everything from a mask made of beaten gold with rubies for eyes on the wall to a small jade statue of something that looked like an elephant to Luke, at least if an elephant had a trunk long enough to scratch its own ass. A set of pens cast in silver sat on one side of his desk next to an inkpot made of some type of crystal. Even the desk itself was made of some deep-brown wood sanded, varnished, and polished to a shine.

In contrast, Fujoka himself was maybe five two, almost completely bald, and so thin and scrawny that Luke honestly wondered if he'd been afflicted by some wasting disease that had eaten away his health. He had liver spots on his head and skin textured like paper. His clothes, thick robes richly dyed in shades of crimson, dark purple, and gold, hung heavily off his frame, as though they'd been made for a man twice his size.

Only his eyes showed any form of vitality, and in them Luke saw a shrewd, calculating man, one who had clear priorities and a willingness to sacrifice anyone and anything on the altar of those goals. Luke knew he wasn't the best at reading people, but Fujoka made him feel entirely like a piece of meat being weighed for its value.

"Take that mask off," Fujoka snapped at Hakiro. "I've told you a thousand times not to wear that in my presence."

"Apologies, sir."

Hakiro removed the mask and moved to put it in a pocket, only to remember that he was wearing the too-small clothes Zea had picked up for him. He let his hand fall to his side, the mask still held in it. Luke saw with some surprise that the other man's eyes were both foggy and unfocused, almost like he wasn't using them to see, like he couldn't use them at all.

That explained how Hakiro had developed his **[Tapestry of the World]** skill so high. That skill was a combination of three lesser sensory-enhancement skills for hearing, smell, and touch, all of which would have taken over 500 AP to max out before they could be merged into an advanced skill. It would have taken the first 35 levels' worth of gains to buy it all outright, and even then, that would only have put **[Tapestry of the World]** at rank 1. Hakiro had it at rank 5.

Fujoka gave his great-nephew a sniff that practically dripped with disdain. "Who are these people you've invited into my home? More scholars for my niece to question?"

"No, Patriarch," Hakiro said. He glanced at Luke, then added, "This man claims to have the SysAdmin bloodline."

"Impossible," Fujoka said flatly.

"I believe him, Patriarch."

"I don't care what an idiot like you believes. Just because he managed to trick some branch line battle fodder doesn't mean I'm going to let him run whatever scam he's trying to pull."

"Wow, so you're kind of a dick, huh?" Luke said.

Fujoka just gave him a withering look before switching from Consortium Standard to what Luke assumed was Eledarn. It was coming up often enough that he was starting to consider it a worthwhile investment to pick up the language.

"You're such a smooth talker," Zea whispered to Luke. "Maybe let the other guy do the negotiating before you get us killed."

The two easterners were speaking rapidly, or rather, Fujoka was scolding him and Hakiro was taking the abuse with a series of, "Yes, sir," and, "No, sir," responses. Considering anyone in the room, even Zea, could have reached out and snapped Fujoka like a twig, it was particularly galling.

"Level 26," Luke said loudly, interrupting Fujoka midtirade.

"What?"

"59826 XP. 6 unspent AP. Strength at 5, agility at 7, stamina at 14, perception at 20."

Fujoka's face paled, then flushed an angry red. "What do you think you're doing?" he demanded.

"You said it was impossible for me to have the SysAdmin bloodline," Luke told him. "I'm proving you wrong."

"Preposterous. I don't know where you got your information from, but it's not from some fictional bloodline some foreigner supposedly had centuries ago."

"Oooh, don't let Aunt Valera hear you say that," Hakiro said.

"Enough out of you," Fujoka snapped. "The day I need my niece's opinion on how to run my family is the day I pass the title on to my son."

"Is that a fact?" a new voice said from outside the room. The door opened to reveal a woman in her late forties whose hair was piled up into a bun just as large as her head and held in place with at least a dozen golden pins. Despite that, the whole bun swayed dangerously, threatening to spill out with each step she took as she entered Fujoka's office.

"If I wanted your opinion on these foreigners, I would have sent someone for you," Fujoka told her. "I would appreciate if you didn't barge in here like you own the place. You don't. I do."

"And I would appreciate if you didn't try to cut me out on matters that so obviously concern me," she snapped back. "Just because you don't care about our family's history doesn't mean everyone else feels the same. Don't think I won't report you to the Council of Elders if you try to pull this on me again."

"This would only concern you if this kid actually was the descendant of William Wyrmsbane, and since he's a myth anyway, it's impossible. Even if he does have the SysAdmin bloodline, that's not proof of any connection."

"I think the Council might disagree," Valera told him. "Why don't we schedule an emergency meeting and find out?"

"There's no need to bother them with something this trivial."

"It doesn't seem trivial to me. Or are you going to tell me it's a coincidence that this young man was able to rattle off your numbers."

"Information can be bought. Any decent con man knows that."

"Can you do it again?" Valera asked, turning to Luke.

"Read someone's status? I can read everyone's status," Luke told her.

"A claim we should be able to easily verify," Valera said. "We'll just pick a handful of people, verify some information beforehand, and have you confirm it. What else can you do?"

"I can turn off the XP presence people have. I think you call it an aura here? I can do it for anyone, as long as they let me."

"Fascinating," Valera said. "Do it to me."

With a shrug, Luke used **[Remote Access]** to connect to Valera's system and then toggled her XP presence with **[XP Mask]**. She gasped and looked around in shock. After a few seconds, Luke used **[XP Mask]** a second time to reset her back to normal.

"Sorry, I should have mentioned that it also prevents you from feeling anyone else's XP," he told her.

"Yes, it's . . . It was a bit of a surprise. Quite alright though."

Hakiro said, "He says he has a bloodline skill that will let him reset XP madness. He needs a few more levels to build up the AP to take the skill, but he's willing to use it for our family if we let him see his father's stuff and help him gain the levels he needs."

Fujoka wasn't good at hiding his feelings, something Luke thought the guy running a large family probably should have been able to do. There had to be a lot of politics involved in it, especially if there were a bunch of other old people who could countermand his orders. Plus there would no doubt be interactions with the city itself. The family obviously had a lot of money and Luke was guessing all the land, as their compound encompassed within the city walls could not have come cheap.

It was easy to tell what was going through his mind at that moment. Luke didn't know the particulars, but the man was obviously in the throes of pure, unadulterated greed. Something about that proposal had sparked an idea in Fujoka, and he couldn't have been more obvious if he started rubbing his hands together and laughing manically.

"Fine," he said. "Let's say I believe you about your bloodline. How long will you need before you can restore some of our less-stable-minded warriors to fighting condition?"

"However long it takes me to get from level 43 to 46," Luke said.

"That's a lot of XP," Fujoka told him. "I'd have to get out the charts, but if I recall correctly, somewhere in the neighborhood of 60,000."

Luke shrugged. "125 AP. That's what it takes to get there. If you want me to reset anyone back to level 1, that's another 50 AP and they have to agree to it."

He decided to leave unsaid that for another 200 AP, he could add [Inflict Status] to the mix and forcefully reset people to level 1. Fujoka struck him at the kind of person who would be unscrupulous about abusing something like that. It was better for everyone if it didn't become general knowledge that it was even an option in the first place.

"Would it cost you anything to use this skill once you acquire it?" Fujoka asked.

"Not as far as I know. None of my other bloodline skills have any restrictions like that."

"And you could use it as many times as you want?"

"Yeah."

The patriarch of the Shansakun family grinned wickedly and said, "I think we can come to an agreement."

"Fantastic," Luke said. "In that case, let me introduce you to my manager. She handles all negotiations on behalf."

Zea stepped forward, a grin of her own to match the old man's on her lips.

Luke might have felt bad for Fujoka by the time everything was over if the man hadn't been such a colossal dickbag about things at the beginning. Since they were trading a unique, priceless service, Zea had hammered him with that fact repeatedly.

She wanted supplies, workshops, maps, language lessons, lodging for both of them, and the services of an armorer, a woodworker, and a blacksmith. It wasn't that any individual thing was all that great of a demand, but she had a lot of them. Luke just sat back and smiled while she extracted concession after concession from Patriarch Fujoka.

By the time negotiations were over, he was in a nasty mood, but Zea had gotten nearly everything she'd demanded. Valera had long since gotten bored with the process and left partway through, only stopping to mutter something to Hakiro on her way out. Luke shot him a questioning glance, but he just shook his head and said, "Later."

Once they were back out into the garden courtyard, Hakiro let out a low laugh and said, "You're vicious. I don't think I've seen Patriarch Shansakun raked over the coals that hard in my entire life."

"Thanks," Zea said, taking Hakiro's words as a compliment.

"Someone should be back with your belongings in the next hour or so," Hakiro said. "In the meantime, you have another appointment."

"Let me guess, Valera?" Luke said.

"As you might imagine, she's excited to meet you. She's always loved the old stories."

"Might as well head there next," Luke said. "But after that, I'd like a bath and a bed."

"It's a bit early for that."

Luke shrugged. "Killing giant man-eating hentai demons takes it out of me."

"What does this word mean?" Hakiro asked.

"Never mind. Something from my world that doesn't need to become well-known here. It's just something that's associated with monsters that have lots of tentacles."

Hakiro blinked at that. "You . . . You have enough problems with tentacled monsters that they have their own terminology?"

"Just . . . No, never mind. Come on, which way are we going?"

Name	Luke Bennet	Zea Stenter
Level	43	35
XP	274177/293811	148801/157276
AP	33	4
Bloodline	SysAdmin III	None
Strength	61	7
Agility	70	30
Stamina	88	27
Perception	55	21
Skills	Burst Step (1)	Arcano Dynamics (2)
	Butchering (4)	Bartering (2)
	Consortium Standard (2)	Bloodline Purification Ritual (2)
	Counter (3)	Cadence (3)
	Deception (1)	Cold Reading (1)
	Detection (2)	Consortium Standard (1)
	Disguise (2)	Cooking (1)
	First Aid (1)	Dagger Mastery (1)
	Leatherworking (2)	Deception (1)
	Life Surge (2)	Disguise (2)
	Mace Mastery (5)	Engraving (4)
	Ostari (1)	First Aid (1)
	Peripheral Awareness (2)	Gem Cutting (1)
	Power Strike (2)	Ghost Script (1)
	Stealth (1)	Goldsmithing (2)
	Survivalist (2)	Keen Instincts (1)
	Sword Mastery (1)	Lock Picking (1)
	Tactical Foresight (2)	Mana Manipulation (3)
	Thalian (2)	Mana Sight (3)
	Torturer (1)	Mending (1)
	Twitch Reflexes (3)	Metallurgy (1)
	Unarmed Martialist (4)	Neyardic (3)
	Wood Carving (1)	Ostari (1)
	Analyze (BL)	Painting (1)
	Remote Access (BL)	Rune Forging (3)
	XP Mask (BL)	Sleight of Hand (1)
		Steady Hands (2)
		Stealth (2)
		Streetwise (2)
		Temperature Acclimation (2)
		Thalian (3)
		Whitesmithing (1)

CHAPTER 38

L ady, I don't want you to take this the wrong way, but you are creeping me out."

Valera ignored Luke as she circled around him again. Off to the side, Zea looked about ready to attack the woman, and Hakiro just shifted in place, clearly uncomfortable. Luke stood in the middle of the room, still dressed in the clothes Zea had bought him that didn't fit all that well, while Valera sized him up.

After her fifth rotation, she announced, "I can see the resemblance. You really could be the descendant of William Wyrmsbane."

Luke rolled his eyes. "I can't believe anybody called my dad that. More like Bill Beersbane."

To Luke's surprise, Valera started laughing. "He was well-known for the astonishing amount of alcohol he consumed."

Luke gave her a sour grunt. His father had been a low-functioning alcoholic who bounced from job to job, completely incapable of taking care of his three children after his wife died. It was one of the reasons Luke rarely drank himself. When his friends in high school had managed to get a case of beer, Luke always caught shit for not wanting to have more than one or two if any at all. It had almost gotten him kicked off the baseball team when he'd gotten into a fistfight with Kenny Brown over it in the eleventh grade.

If his dad had prioritized stamina in his build, Luke could easily picture the man downing entire kegs in one marathon drinking session that lasted from sunup to sundown, then doing it again the next day. There were drinks created to cater to high-stamina individuals—Luke had accidentally gotten blackout drunk off a single beer once when he'd first arrived on Aros—but he doubted there was anything that would work on him like that now that his stamina was up to 88.

They'd gone over what Valera was referring to as temporal acceleration in regard to their two worlds, and she seemed to accept the idea at face value. Luke knew nothing about it beyond what System had told him, that his brother had died almost a century ago despite being missing for barely a month and that his father had died about eight hundred and fifty years ago. He'd disappeared eight or nine months prior to Luke's own abduction, and the idea that their worlds moved at different speeds through time was the only reasonable explanation any of them could come up with.

With that all out of the way, Valera started asking him questions about his dad. So many questions. Luke didn't have answers at first since her curiosity was focused on the life of William Wyrmsbane on Aros. In that regard, she knew far more than Luke did.

Around the fifth time she mentioned some feat of glory he was known for, Luke cut her off and said, "Look, it's cool that you think this guy was just the greatest thing to ever walk the planet, but I don't know him. My dad didn't do any of this stuff before he disappeared. All I'm going to tell you are stories about a man who didn't have enough energy left to raise his kids after he got home from work. He worked, he drank, he slept. He repeated. Every now and then we'd move somewhere new when he ran out of places to put in applications around where we were living."

"Those can't be your only memories of him," Valera said.

"When I was six, he used to help me with my math homework," Luke said. "Then Mom got sick, and everyone was focused on that until she died. And then it was booze. Cheap beer. Cheap vodka. Cheap whiskey. I remember him coming home pissed off because he got fired again for drinking on the job when I was thirteen. I remember him giving my sister fifty bucks to take my brother and me clothes shopping at the thrift store for a new school year. I remember him selling our kitchen table and our TV for a hundred bucks to pay rent one month."

Luke looked around at this shrine thing they were standing in. There were wall scrolls with ink paintings of a man that could have been Luke's father if he were twenty years younger and a hundred and fifty pounds lighter and had never started drinking. The only one that really captured Will Bennet's personality was one where he was about to lay a beatdown on some sort of bipedal bear-looking thing that had four arms and a shark's mouth full of teeth. Luke's father had had that exact look on his face one day when he'd come flying out of the bedroom right around noon with a hand raised and ready to administer a whupping to both boys for being too loud and waking him up when he was trying to sleep through his hangover.

Seeing his father finally get his shit together, acting like a hero, loved and adored, it made Luke's blood boil. It wasn't fair. Half of Luke's life had been spent dealing with a drunk who had no interest in his kids and honestly seemed to resent them for existing, and here was the same man with a fucking shrine dedicated to how great he was. If it hadn't been part of the contract Zea had hashed out to let Valera pester him with all the questions she could think of, Luke would have turned around and walked out right there.

And to think, not twelve hours ago he'd been eager to visit this place and find out about his father's life on Aros. Luke honestly didn't know what he'd expected, but it wasn't this.

There were good memories too, but the older Luke got, the more they became few and far between. Lizzie basically took over raising Curt and Luke when she turned eighteen. If Valera had been interested, Luke could have told her lots of stories of spending time with his siblings, of them helping him with homework or school projects, of going to the park to play basketball, of Lizzie handing him the money to buy sports gear so he could practice during the summer months and telling him not to ask where she'd gotten it.

The tour moved into the next room. If the first room was all artwork with attached stories painted on canvases, the next room was completely different. For one, the door had a lock on it, and Zea's eyebrows shot up in surprise when she got close to it. "This is pretty heavily enchanted," she remarked.

"It's not that I think anyone in the family would try to steal from here, but the artifacts inside are some of the only remaining remnants of William Wyrmsbane's legacy," Valera told her. "The whole room is enchanted, not just the door."

"Hmm, do you mind if I . . . ?"

"Take a look?" Valera finished for her. "Go ahead. I'm told a great deal of effort was spent protecting them from casual examination, so please, if you do find some weakness in the enchantments, let me know so I can arrange to have it fixed."

She opened the door then, pausing with her hand on the handle long enough for the entire thing to flash with a faint blue glow for a second. It faded away, and Valera turned the handle to let them into the new room.

The first thing that caught Luke's eye was a huge, two-handed sword mounted on the wall opposite of the door. The blade was five feet long and six inches wide, mostly black but edged in white. Veins of blue, red, and yellow ran through the white portion of the sword, all originating from a rock set in the pommel that had the three colors banded through it over and over.

"Fancy sword," Luke said.

"One of William's many weapons," Valera explained. "It's made from a core of dragon bone with a dream stone edge powered by tetracite filigree."

"Yeah, I don't know what any of that means."

"Dragon bone is practically indestructible," Zea said. "You need rank 5 in blacksmithing, alchemy, and enchanting just to work with it, and the tools and materials required to shape it are beyond expensive. That sword is probably worth ten thousand gold, more than the rest of this estate combined."

"I don't know about it being worth more than the whole estate," Valera said, "but yes, it's the single most valuable artifact your father left behind before embarking on what we believe was his final journey. He had a whole set of custom weapons crafted of those materials, but the spear was never found after he disappeared."

"Not my style," Luke commented. He glanced over at some of the other weapons mounted on the wall around it, all of them made in the same materials. Immediately to its left was a half-moon battle-axe, and past that was some sort of glaive. To the right was a morning star, a flail, and finally, a mace. Luke's eyes lit up at the sight of it. "Now that, that is something I'd use."

Much like the sword, the haft of the mace was black with a striped stone capping the bottom of it. Veins of red, blue, and yellow ran up its length, and the entire head was crisp white metal that had a grain to it. It reminded him somewhat of granite but smoother.

"Ah, yes. Your father didn't find much use for that unless he planned on fighting heavily armored foes, but he wasn't one to let propriety get in the way of effectively defeating his enemies. When the mace was the best weapon for the job, he used it," Valeria told him.

She gestured away from the display of weapons toward a glass case with several books lying inside of it. "This is what I wanted you to see," she told Luke. "The real reason I believe you are who you say you are isn't because of your bloodline skills or what you look like. Here, let me show you."

Valera touched the corners of the case with both hands, and the glass vanished in a shimmer of light. Delicately, she reached in to pull out one of the books and flipped through the pages. "This is one of William Wyrmsbane's personal journals. He often mentioned things from his own world, including his family."

She held the book up for Luke to read. He was somewhat thrown to see it written in English and spent a second using **[Analyze]** on Valera to see if she had a skill for the language. Nothing showed, but she did have rank 3 **[Deciphering]**, which he supposed could be used to translate a foreign language. Luke didn't have a skill for his native language either, now that he thought about it. He supposed that made sense for the system not to recognize a language that wasn't spoken on the planet it governed.

Luke peered at the words, written in his father's tight, angular script.

For all the nightmares this world has given me, I have to credit it for my returned health. I feel half my age, no, better. Stamina combined with Tracia's healing magic has me feeling better than I have since Heather died. My own cancer is completely gone, so far as Tracia can tell at least. It certainly feels like it's gone.

I've been spending a lot of time thinking of my children, of all the ways I failed them. Lizzie really stepped up to the plate for me, but she shouldn't have had to. She was the only one old enough to really remember exactly what Heather went through, and I think she realized I was sick too. As far as I know, she never told her brothers. She just quietly started doing more and more until soon she was running the whole house.

There was no beating it, not according to the doctor. If I hadn't been chucked headfirst into Aros, I'd be dead by now. I know that, in my head, it's a good thing that I'm here. One way or another, I was going to disappear soon, but I still feel like a failure as a parent. I know Luke resents me. It's hard to blame him. I was so caught up in my own miserable life that I neglected all of them. If he ever sees me again, I'm sure the first thing he'll want to do is punch me in the face. And I'd deserve it. I just wish I'd figured this all out back on Earth.

The only thing I can do now is close that Goddamn door for good, so none of them end up here. This place has already claimed my sister and my nephew. I won't let System take my kids too.

Luke blinked rapidly and cleared his throat. "That's . . . Could I read the rest of this?"

Name	Luke Bennet	Zea Stenter
Level	43	35
XP	274177/293811	148551/157276
AP	33	4
Bloodline	SysAdmin III	None
Strength	61	7
Agility	70	30
Stamina	88	27
Perception	55	21
Skills	Burst Step (1)	Arcano Dynamics (2)
	Butchering (4)	Bartering (2)
	Consortium Standard (2)	Bloodline Purification Ritual (2)
	Counter (3)	Cadence (3)
	Deception (1)	Cold Reading (1)
	Detection (2)	Consortium Standard (2)
	Disguise (2)	Cooking (1)
	First Aid (1)	Dagger Mastery (1)
	Leatherworking (2)	Deception (1)
	Life Surge (2)	Disguise (2)
	Mace Mastery (5)	Engraving (4)
	Ostari (1)	First Aid (1)
	Peripheral Awareness (2)	Gem Cutting (1)
	Power Strike (2)	Ghost Script (1)
	Stealth (1)	Goldsmithing (2)
	Survivalist (2)	Keen Instincts (1)
	Sword Mastery (1)	Lock Picking (1)
	Tactical Foresight (2)	Mana Manipulation (3)
	Thalian (2)	Mana Sight (3)
	Torturer (1)	Mending (1)
	Twitch Reflexes (3)	Metallurgy (1)
	Unarmed Martialist (4)	Neyardic (3)
	Wood Carving (1)	Ostari (1)
	Analyze (BL)	Painting (1)
	Remote Access (BL)	Rune Forging (3)
	XP Mask (BL)	Sleight of Hand (1)
		Steady Hands (2)
		Stealth (2)
		Streetwise (2)
		Temperature Acclimation (2)
		Thalian (3)
		Whitesmithing (1)

CHAPTER 39

Luke was not allowed to take the journals out of the enchanted shrine, not because Valera didn't trust him, but because the books were old as dirt and outside of the confines of the room, they were afraid that the paper would crumble away to dust.

And probably they didn't trust him either. Supposedly, those journals were worth quite a bit of money. Luke wasn't willing to press any sort of claim of ownership on his father's writings. If he was honest with himself, he didn't recognize the man those journals portrayed anyway. There were obviously some secrets his father had kept. The fact that he'd been dying of cancer just like Luke's mom but hadn't bothered to tell any of his children was a big one.

Fucking asshole. Luke *was* going to punch his dad in the face the next time he saw him.

The entries that related to William's life on Earth were few and far between. Valera pointed them all out for Luke to read, and then he mostly skipped toward the end to look for clues about what to expect besides the big-ass dragon apparently squatting on top of the God Machine. That had been close to a thousand years ago, but Luke doubted he was lucky enough that it had died of old age. He wasn't even sure dragons did that.

No one else seemed to know either, but Luke was betting he could get some general facts out of System as soon as he had some privacy. Speaking of System, it appeared that Luke's father and his brother were in agreement that trusting the apparition was a bad idea. It wasn't so much that William had caught him lying about anything, just that System was spectacularly uncooperative with releasing information at the best of times, and whatever rules that determined what he was and was not able to share were a mystery.

William had suspected System was not quite as rule bound as he tried to come off as, that there was an actual intelligence behind that translucent blue facade that was picking and choosing when to be helpful and when not to. William had tested this and determined that System was most helpful in regard to anything that involved getting William closer to the God Machine and least helpful involving everything else.

Maybe that was why Luke hadn't ever noticed anything suspicious. He hadn't really deviated much from his own goal of reviving his family and getting everyone back home, and System had been consistent about what kind of help he could offer, with behavior changes only coming when Luke managed a bloodline purification.

Or maybe Luke just wasn't smart enough to catch on.

There was one other thing Luke found in the journal that surprised him. His dad wanted to bring his mom back from the dead too. He was convinced there had to be a way to do it, despite System repeatedly telling him it was impossible. She hadn't died on Aros, and the system had no record of her. The closest it could get to reviving her was to create some sort of homunculus based off of William's memories.

"No way that could turn out bad," Luke muttered to himself when he read that part.

Their belongings arrived from the inn at some point while Luke was going through his father's writing, but Luke wanted to get everything done in one go. They had a busy schedule to keep if they wanted to meet Fujoka's imposed deadlines. First thing in the morning, Luke would be escorted to the family's private training grounds, though he would only be given access to the monster-ranch portion of it. Training up his current skills wasn't a prerequisite to obtaining **[XP Cycle]** and **[XP Reset]**, so Fujoka was adamant that Luke didn't need access to those resources.

If he'd wanted it badly enough, he probably could have gotten it as a concession anyway, but he'd told Zea he didn't care, and she'd used that loss of access as a bargaining chip to secure other resources instead. Luke wasn't entirely sure which particular thing they'd traded away that access for; he just knew that Fujoka looked harried, and Zea looked like a cat that had gotten into the cream by the time that meeting had ended.

Sometimes, having high stamina was a curse. Luke returned to the room he'd been given for the night, separate from Zea for whatever reason, got a bath, and changed into clean clothes that actually fit. His enchanted clothes were starting to regenerate, but at the moment they looked like a crop top and hot pants, so he was happy to leave them in his backpack for another day or two.

Once he was settled in for the night, Luke found that he couldn't sleep. Mentally, he was exhausted. Between the hentai demon and the emotional scabs he'd torn open in relation to his father, he was ready to just drop face-first into the bed and hopefully dream about nothing. Physically speaking, however, he was pretty sure he could run four or five laps around the city before he even started to get tired.

Back on Earth, he'd known how to solve this problem. A good run would tire him out, or sometimes a lap around the weight room if his buddy who worked at the local gym was doing the night shift and would let him in for free. Luke would work up a good sweat, get a quick shower, and collapse. That wasn't a solution anymore. By the time he got tired, the sun would be coming back up again.

So he spent the first half of the night stewing over everything before giving up and walking out of his room. A guard stationed in the hallway, one who wore a mask like so many of the staff did, looked up immediately and said, "Is there anything I can help you with, sir?"

"Can't sleep," Luke told him. "Is there somewhere I can go to burn off some energy?"

"Of course, sir."

Luke thought there was some hesitation in the man's voice, but it was hard to judge with the mask hiding everything except his eyes. Either way, the guard beckoned for Luke to follow and led him outside the building, where he was handed off to another person, this time with a mask that only covered two-thirds of her face. She led Luke the long way around the garden and down a stone path set into the grass.

"So what's with the mask thing?" Luke asked as they walked.

"It denotes how far we are from the main branch of the family," she said. "I would be considered a third cousin to the current heir."

"I see. So the smaller the mask is, the closer the person is? What about the ones who have full masks?"

"Those people are employed by the family but not a part of it," the woman told him.

Luke wasn't really sure what to think about such an odd tradition, but lots of things were done differently here, and he wrote it off as just one more case of culture shock. Nobody else seemed to care about it anyway.

As they walked, Luke started hearing the sound of flesh smacking against wood. All he could picture was a guy beating on a wooden training dummy, but he knew that wasn't right. That would be more of a cracking sound, and it would be faster paced. Instead, it was kind of a hollow drumming sound that had a few different tones.

The woman led the way to what appeared to be a giant wooden obstacle course a few hundred feet long. It curled around, following the curve of the outer wall, and there were three people in the middle of it while two more watched. The only one Luke recognized was Hakiro. He'd placed his unique masquerade mask with no eyeholes back on his face. There were no straps to hold it in place, so Luke assumed it had been enchanted in some way.

The people running the course were hopping through like ninjas, bouncing off posts and sprinting across balance beams barely an inch wide that wobbled with every step, then scaling a forty-foot-high wall that only had a handhold once every ten feet, and only a single handhold at that.

Even as Luke watched, one of them came to a rope bridge that had no planks and took a flying leap over the edge. The guy caught the rope about thirty feet out and started crossing hand over hand. He was making good progress until one of the other participants reached the beginning of the bridge. Instead of leaping after him, the second guy seized the rope and gave it a hard shake. It whipped wildly back and forth, so much so that the man crossing it lost his grip with one hand and had to perform some acrobatics to swing around and catch his ankles on the rope he was hanging from.

"Huh. Yeah, that'd be good for burning off some energy," Luke said. "Thanks for showing me where to go."

"It was my pleasure," the guard told him. She smiled and added, "Good luck."

Luke made a beeline to Hakiro, who stood there staring up at the third person. She'd gotten stuck on the wall with almost no handholds and was trying to position herself like some sort of awkward spider with her hand and her foot on the same nub.

"Come on, you know that's not going to work," Hakiro called out. "Sando and Asher have been fighting each other the whole way, and they're both still ahead of you."

The girl let her foot swing free, braced herself with both hands on the nubby handhold, and threw herself up as far as she could. She fell two feet short of grabbing onto the next handhold and scrambled against the bare wood as she fell back down. There was no saving her, and she landed heavily on the ground at the base of the wall, fully twenty feet below where she'd started.

"Oof," Luke said when she hit the ground. "That sounded like it hurt."

Hakiro glanced over and shook his head. "Working through the pain is a good lesson too," he said before raising his voice again. "Start back over from the front."

"You mind if I give it a go?" Luke asked.

"If you want. Give me a minute to let them get to the end and you can take a turn," Hakiro told him. He turned to face Luke fully. "Let me guess, couldn't sleep?"

"Not even a little bit," Luke confirmed.

"Yes, that happens to the warriors here a lot. Once your stamina gets high enough, your body stops needing it but your mind still does. That's why we have stuff like this in use all night."

Luke watched the two men struggle to throw each other off a series of rope swings that were nothing more than wooden discs with holes in the centers that rope was threaded through and knotted on the bottom, then move on to a spinning platform that started moving right before they got to it as an operator standing below got the signal. The operator ran around the base pillar, pushing it with a handle to make the whole thing rotate.

One of the men was knocked off shortly after landing, having failed to compensate for the spin properly and being sabotaged by his opponent before he could regain his balance. The lone man cleared the remaining obstacles in under thirty seconds, and the girl at the front failed again when she reached the wall.

"Your turn," Hakiro said, gesturing toward the starting position.

Luke headed over, looked at Hakiro for permission to start, and took off like a rocket as soon as the man's hand went down.

Name	Luke Bennet	Zea Stenter
Level	43	35
XP	274177/293811	148551/157276
AP	33	4
Bloodline	SysAdmin III	None
Strength	61	7
Agility	70	30
Stamina	88	27
Perception	55	21
Skills	Burst Step (1)	Arcano Dynamics (2)
	Butchering (4)	Bartering (2)
	Consortium Standard (2)	Bloodline Purification Ritual (2)
	Counter (3)	Cadence (3)
	Deception (1)	Cold Reading (1)
	Detection (2)	Consortium Standard (2)
	Disguise (2)	Cooking (1)
	First Aid (1)	Dagger Mastery (1)
	Leatherworking (2)	Deception (1)
	Life Surge (2)	Disguise (2)
	Mace Mastery (5)	Engraving (4)
	Ostari (1)	First Aid (1)
	Peripheral Awareness (2)	Gem Cutting (1)
	Power Strike (2)	Ghost Script (1)
	Stealth (1)	Goldsmithing (2)
	Survivalist (2)	Keen Instincts (1)
	Sword Mastery (1)	Lock Picking (1)
	Tactical Foresight (2)	Mana Manipulation (3)
	Thalian (2)	Mana Sight (2)
	Torturer (1)	Mending (1)
	Twitch Reflexes (3)	Metallurgy (1)
	Unarmed Martialist (4)	Neyardic (3)
	Wood Carving (1)	Ostari (1)
	Analyze (BL)	Painting (1)
	Remote Access (BL)	Rune Forging (3)
	XP Mask (BL)	Sleight of Hand (1)
		Steady Hands (2)
		Stealth (2)
		Streetwise (2)
		Temperature Acclimation (2)
		Thalian (3)
		Whitesmithing (1)

CHAPTER 40

The truth was that the obstacle course wasn't designed for someone of Luke's level. The first section, for example, was comprised of platforms that had obstructions hanging between them. Challengers were supposed to go around by leaping to the left or right and using the poles rising up out of the ground as walls to bounce off of. They would follow a zigzag pattern as they went back and forth.

Luke noted that the obstructions were simple sheets of wood hung off a rope strung up overhead, and that the rope was only ten feet above the small platforms he was supposed to land on. He jumped straight up over top of them, landed on the rope, and ran forward in three great bounding strides that took him to the far end of the first obstacle.

The second obstacle was a twenty-foot-wide pit with a rope hanging in front of it. Luke was supposed to climb the rope and use the handholds provided at the top to cross, kind of like crossing the monkey bars as a kid. Instead, he took a running start as he came down from the first section and leaped the entire pit in one go.

The entire course went like that. It wasn't hard enough to challenge him. The wall with the single nubby handhold slowed him for a second as he landed on the second peg from the top, balanced on one foot, and launched himself straight up and over it. Many of the lesser obstacles he avoided altogether by either jumping through empty space or leaping up to the framework overhead and using it to help him cross.

From front to finish, it took him about two minutes to complete.

Then he ran it again, and again, each time shaving a few seconds off his time. After his fourth lap, Hakiro flagged him down and said, "I think this course might be a bit too easy for you. Besides, we should let the people who are actually supposed to be training get back to it, don't you think?"

"Oh, right. Sorry about that," Luke said.

"It's fine. They've had enough of a break." Hakiro paused and regarded him. "Maybe something a bit more exhausting? By the time you run yourself out of energy on this one, the sun'll be up anyway."

"What did you have in mind?" Luke asked, peering around. He didn't see a second obstacle course anywhere.

"Sparring ring will tire you right out," Hakiro said. "I'll be your partner."

"If you're sure," Luke said. He didn't want to hurt the man, but the truth was Hakiro was a higher level than him and fairly strongly combat oriented.

"Don't worry about holding back. We've got plenty of on-staff healers. And by plenty, I mean three. That's more than enough to fix any sparring injuries."

Hakiro led Luke to a dirt circle lined with rocks and a simple wooden railing. It was a hundred feet wide and had a little tool-shed-looking thing at one end. Hakiro went inside, then came back out with a set of padded jackets, metal vambraces, and a pair of dull swords. "Here, put these on," he told Luke, passing him the jacket and the vambraces.

"Oh damn, these are pretty heavy," Luke said as he fastened the metal to his forearms.

"Help wear you out faster," Hakiro said. "And I know the sword isn't your weapon of choice, but it is mine. You'll be on offense, and this'll help keep me safe."

That all made sense to Luke. He put on the protective gear—the padded jacket was also lined with some sort of heavy metal strips—and gave the sword a few test swings. "What is this all made out of?" Luke asked. He was pretty sure he had better than four hundred pounds of metal on him.

"Some sort of steel-and-pyre-gold alloy, I believe. Bit softer than a standard weapon and a hell of a lot heavier, so it's useful for training purposes. It'll still hurt to get hit with it, of course, but at the level we're working at, the sword will bend before we do."

"And pain's an excellent motivator to learn not to repeat mistakes," Luke said, thinking back to some of his initial fights when he had first arrived on Aros. Even with his new stats making him stronger and more resilient, he'd gotten his ass kicked more than once. He hadn't always learned his lesson the first time, but he'd damn well done his best.

Hakiro took his place about twenty feet away from Luke in the center of the ring and raised his sword. Luke's own weapon felt awkward in his hands, like it was poorly weighted and balanced even though he knew it wasn't. He was used to all the heft being at the end; swords just weren't built that way. It didn't help that he was going from a rank 5 **[Mace Mastery]** to a rank 1 **[Sword Mastery]** skill.

"Come at me whenever you're ready," Hakiro said.

Luke took a few practice swings to get a feel for the sword. He had no idea what pyre gold was, but it was certainly heavy. If the sword weighed less than fifty pounds, he'd be surprised. Between that and the vambraces on his arms, his attacks were going to have a lot of inertia behind them. They'd hit hard, but changing direction or reacting to counters was going to be difficult.

He couldn't decide if this was a lesson about thinking ahead before committing to an attack or if it was just weight training to build up strength and stamina. Probably both, and maybe a few other reasons he hadn't thought of besides. For Luke though, it meant tiring him out faster, which was exactly what he was here for.

"Here I come," he said, then blurred across the distance in an instant with **[Burst Step]**.

Luke's opening attack was a straightforward lunge. It relied on the power of his movement skill to cover the distance before Hakiro could react to it, but he would have honestly been surprised if it had worked. Hakiro wasn't caught off guard. Far from it, he was moving a fraction of an instant before Luke even started his attack, and by the time they met, Hakiro had already sidestepped and had his blade up perpendicular to the ground to block Luke from turning his lunge into a horizontal slash.

He also kicked out at Luke's ankles in an effort to break Luke's footwork. That at least was something that translated over regardless of which weapon Luke was using, and **[Unarmed Martialist]** served him well there. Luke backed up a step, then attacked again. Each slash or lunge was intercepted or blocked, and though Luke had a definite strength advantage, Hakiro's technique was far, far superior.

They went round in circles for about five minutes, Luke pushing relentlessly in an attempt to wear down his opponent and force him to make a mistake and Hakiro thwarting every attack with ease. He made it look effortless too, like he was battling with a kindergartner.

[Burst Step] was less useful when engaged in a one-on-one duel in melee range since it didn't work great for anything other than straight-line movements. He hesitated to use **[Power Strike]** in a sparring match, mostly because he knew he was stronger than Hakiro and the skill would do nothing but cause damage. That wasn't the goal here, so Luke held himself back from using it.

That having been said, **[Life Surge]** was always good for tiring him out a bit, and Luke was nothing if not competitive. He knew Hakiro could kick his ass in a sword fight, but he also knew that playing fair was for chumps. He activated the buff skill just as Hakiro moved to slip out of the way of an attack. The man had a measure of Luke's speed now. He knew exactly when to move and how far, until all of a sudden he didn't.

Luke landed his first blow against Hakiro, though even that was a glancing thing, barely clipping his opponent's arm. He got in one more good strike before Hakiro adjusted, and soon the two were moving in what might have appeared to a casual observer to be a wild and uncontrolled brawl.

"So you're a cheater, are you?!" Hakiro said with a laugh. "Very well, let's see how you do when I fight back."

Then something happened with the XP Luke could feel inside his opponent, something that washed over Luke and beat down on him, that demanded he drop his weapon and surrender. To call Hakiro's XP presence intimidating would be doing it a disservice, but whatever it was, Luke knew the solution. He activated **[XP Mask]**, and the pressure disappeared instantly.

Luke's sword flashed by his eyes, so fast that the blinded man had no choice but to drop to his knees to dodge it. His own blade glowed brightly for a moment as he slashed upward, striking Luke's parry and throwing the weapon out wide. Luke stumbled back two steps, giving Hakiro more than enough space to get back to his feet.

"Trickster," Hakiro said.

"If you're not cheating, you're not trying hard enough."

Luke struck again, only to be foiled by Hakiro, and then he heard a soft ding in his head. Frowning, he stepped back and held a hand up.

[Congratulations! Sword Mastery has reached rank 2. 250 XP awarded.]

"Huh, how about that," Luke said. "Got a rank-up in **[Sword Mastery]**."

"You must have been close already if a single sparring session was all it took," Hakiro said.

"Not . . . really?" Luke tried to recall all the times he'd used a sword. Other than in the monster arena for a few fights, he hadn't touched one since he'd first arrived, back when he'd been scrambling to find any sort of weapon to defend himself with. He'd spent more time fighting against people with swords than he'd spent wielding one himself.

Maybe that had helped too. Knowing how to defend against a swordsman was an important part of knowing how to wield a sword. There was a decent amount of overlap there. Or maybe it was just the fact that he was fighting against a guy with some sort of advanced sword-using skill that was maxed out at speeds that would be a blur to a normal person. That was probably good for an insanely fast development speed too.

Luke wasn't particularly excited about the new rank. The XP was a drop in the bucket, and he had no real interest in learning to use a sword properly anyway. The distraction had only served to break the rhythm of battle, so he supposed it was better to get it out of the way now rather than when he was fighting something as strong as Hakiro for real.

[Life Surge] gave out then, and Luke's shoulders sagged. "I think I'm done for the night," he said. "Thanks for the help."

"It was no problem at all. If you ever reconsider learning the sublime art of swordsmanship, I would be happy to instruct you."

"I'll keep that in mind," Luke said, as diplomatically as possible. He was going to be working with Hakiro for the next few weeks, and these people from the eastern continent all seemed to be touchy about their belief in the almighty sharpened metal stick being the superior instrument of violence.

Luke made his goodbyes, walked back to his room, and took a moment to rinse himself off with a bowl of water that someone had left there after he'd first gone out. He assumed one of the guards had done it, or at least passed the request onto a servant. These people really were quite familiar with the peculiarities of high-stamina people.

Clean, worn out in a good way, and with his mind finally quieting down, Luke dropped face-first into his bed and slept.

Name	Luke Bennet	Zea Stenter
Level	43	35
XP	274427/293811	148551/157276
AP	33	4
Bloodline	SysAdmin III	None
Strength	61	7
Agility	70	30
Stamina	88	27
Perception	55	21
Skills	Burst Step (1)	Arcano Dynamics (2)
	Butchering (4)	Bartering (2)
	Consortium Standard (2)	Bloodline Purification Ritual (2)
	Counter (3)	Cadence (3)
	Deception (1)	Cold Reading (1)
	Detection (2)	Consortium Standard (2)
	Disguise (2)	Cooking (1)
	First Aid (1)	Dagger Mastery (1)
	Leatherworking (2)	Deception (1)
	Life Surge (2)	Disguise (2)
	Mace Mastery (5)	Engraving (4)
	Ostari (1)	First Aid (1)
	Peripheral Awareness (2)	Gem Cutting (1)
	Power Strike (2)	Ghost Script (1)
	Stealth (1)	Goldsmithing (2)
	Survivalist (2)	Keen Instincts (1)
	Sword Mastery (2)	Lock Picking (1)
	Tactical Foresight (2)	Mana Manipulation (3)
	Thalian (2)	Mana Sight (3)
	Torturer (1)	Mending (1)
	Twitch Reflexes (3)	Metallurgy (1)
	Unarmed Martialist (4)	Neyardic (3)
	Wood Carving (1)	Ostari (1)
	Analyze (BL)	Painting (1)
	Remote Access (BL)	Rune Forging (3)
	XP Mask (BL)	Sleight of Hand (1)
		Steady Hands (2)
		Stealth (2)
		Streetwise (2)
		Temperature Acclimation (2)
		Thalian (3)
		Whitesmithing (1)

CHAPTER 41

The Shansakun training grounds were about one hundred and fifty miles east of the city. The family owned a huge swath of forested land, one that was rough with hills and valleys, ravines and gullies, and had more than its fair share of monsters. Specifically, it was home to several massive colonies of giant spiders that had invaded at some point. Efforts to exterminate them had been largely unsuccessful; no matter how thorough the humans were, the spiders just kept coming back.

Short of burning down thousands of acres of old wood, most of which the Shansakun family had no claim to, there were really only three choices. They could sell the land, but it wasn't worth a fraction of what they'd paid for it once the spiders took over. They could hire professional hunters with specific builds designed to search out spider colonies and destroy them, which would no doubt cost a fortune and take years to do the entire forest, even if they could get the families who owned other slices of it to agree.

Or they could do what they'd done. They bought up huge sections of it on the cheap from other families who wanted nothing to do with it now that it was so much harder to extract resources from it and turned it into a giant XP farm. The spiders could get upward of level 20 when they were full-grown, mostly from fighting and killing other spiders from different colonies, and more importantly, there were hundreds of thousands of them, maybe even millions of them.

They were a group of ten, including Luke and Zea. Hakiro was there, as were the two men who'd been running the obstacle course last night, Sando and Asher. Their own trainer had accompanied the group, as well as two servants, a chef, and a single healer. The servants and trainees all had huge, heavy packs full of supplies. Rich noble families were not accustomed to roughing it, even on expeditions to hunt giant spiders.

When Hakiro had told them that they were heading to a hunting lodge, Luke had pictured something between a shack in the woods and a log cabin. When he'd seen how many people were coming along, he'd mentally upgraded the log cabin to have at least five or six bedrooms.

The reality was both more and less than Luke had expected. There were four buildings arranged in a square with a thirty-foot wall surrounding them. Mounted above that in a dome that barely rose over the roofs was an extremely fine mesh made of pencil-thin cables. As soon as Zea spotted it, her gaze sharpened, and she said, "That's enchanted."

"To keep the spiders out," Hakiro said. "The big ones can't fit, and the smaller ones are killed by the magic. You can hear it crackling and buzzing at night, like a swarm of angry hornets guarding your rest."

Luke couldn't help but snicker at the thought. They'd be sleeping under a magic bug-zapping mosquito curtain. He wondered if Zea could make something similar, like a cape or cloak he could swing around that would shock the shit out of any spiders it touched.

The group stopped at the sole gate in the walls and waited while Hakiro's partner produced a key to unlock it. Once they were inside, Luke saw a well in the center of the four houses. Hakiro pointed to the building in the northeast corner, moving in a clockwise direction and said, "Kitchen and mess hall, supply storage, trainee barracks and med station, and trainer rooms."

"So, where do we rate?" Luke asked, glancing back and forth between the trainee building and the trainer building.

"Normally, we come out with fifteen to twenty trainees and a half dozen instructors. We're a bit light this trip, however. Asher and Sando will have plenty of space in the barracks, the servants have their own quarters in their buildings, and the four of us will each claim a room," the other trainer said.

Luke tossed a quick **[Analyze]** his way, just to get his name, which was Jalet. It was kind of a weird name, considering everyone else's, but so was Asher, now that he thought about it. The two were both paler skinned than everyone else, not including Luke, and while they had the standard silver-white hair the rest of the natives did, their features were decidedly not native.

There was no doubt some immigration story in there, and Luke suspected the two were related, but it wasn't really his business, and he couldn't see it making much of a difference to what he was here to do. Both Jalet and Asher seemed to be well acquainted with the Shansakun household. Luke was not anticipating any drama there.

That cook, on the other hand, had been grumbling under his breath since they left. Luke got the impression that the man would rather be anywhere but here and appeared to have drawn the short straw in some sort of lottery among the staff. If not for the fact that Luke still hadn't managed to achieve even rank 1 **[Cooking]** somehow, he would have strongly considered eating his own cooking. There was liable to be less spit in it that way.

The group split up, with the cook and servants heading to the east side of the camp while the healer and trainees walked into the barracks. That left Luke, Zea, Hakiro, and Jalet to enter the final building. Luke wanted to say he was surprised at how luxurious it was, but when he compared it to the main compound, he couldn't really find the heart.

"It's a bit rustic, I know," Hakiro said, misinterpreting the look on Luke's face.

"Please. He'd sleep under a bush if I let him," Zea said.

"Wrong," Luke shot back. "I wouldn't sleep."

"Okay, true. You'd push yourself for a week straight, then sleep for three hours under a bush, and then you'd be up and moving again."

That was a fairly accurate assessment of how Luke's sleep cycle worked these days. He tried to sleep for a few hours every night, but he wasn't always successful. Mostly he just acted as a giant body pillow for Zea to snuggle while his mind drifted. It was kind of like dozing but still being aware of the world around him, and it had more or less replaced actual sleep except for a few hours a week.

"There will be no sleeping under bushes here," Hakiro said. "Go claim a room and then meet back outside. We're going to do our first walk around the area so I can go over what dangers to look out for, what flavors of monster you can expect to find, and what areas to stay away from."

"Alright, this is pretty straightforward," Jalet said.

Sando muttered something, but not in Consortium Standard. Jalet paused, shot him a look, and said, "Because it's rude to our guests. Get used to speaking the trade language around foreigners. Most people outside the Beilon Province don't speak Eledarn."

They were a few miles outside the hunting lodge, as Hakiro called it. Luke would have said it was more like a small fortress. The trail they walked circled around their base with regular intersections. They stood at one such T junction, and Jalet pointed deeper into the woods. "Each of these junctions leads off to a different colony of spiders. For the most part, they're pretty similar. There's some variety in size, and the blue-shell lurkers are significantly more durable than any other breed, but a giant spider is a giant spider. Most of them are going to die from a single good hit.

"The thing to remember is to watch out above and behind you. These aren't going to be duels. They won't wait for you to kill one before another moves forward to challenge you. Mobility and reaction speed are going to be your key defenses as you fight dozens of spiders at once. We'll avoid the venomous varieties while we're here—they're not worth the risk—but we're still going to go over them so if you do end up facing one down, you'll know what you're up against."

Zea had stayed behind in their room. When Luke left, she was already unpacking some of the raw materials she'd coerced out of Fujoka and plotting out her next creation. It was too bad she didn't want to gain XP anymore. This was feeling more and more like an express route to higher levels. If the strongest monsters were only level 20, it was almost risk free too.

They started down the trail, with Hakiro in the front and Jalet bringing up the rear while Luke and the two trainees took the middle. Jalet made sure to stress that they weren't safe there, as spiders rarely felt the need to follow trails to begin with. Sando and Asher were both pretty jumpy, but considering they were only level 25, Luke supposed he couldn't blame them too much.

He considered saying something, but before he could, **[Peripheral Awareness]** pinged to a threat, and **[Unarmed Martialist]** had him moving before he'd even fully registered it. A spider the size of his fist leaped down from overhead on a silk dragline, fangs gleaming and legs ending in wickedly sharp points.

Luke caught it in his bare hand and squeezed. There was a brief popping sound, and some yellowish ichor seeped out of the crushed body. A ding sounded in his mind.

[You have slain Weeping Spinner (level 14). 201 XP awarded.]
[This creature has slain 521 other creatures.]
[Total kills for this type of creature: 1.]
[Highest-level kill: 14.]

"Hmm. Neat. A weeping spinner," Luke said.

"It seems the lessons must be put on hold," Jalet announced. "That breed creates large mobile colonies. The rest will be on us in moments. Prepare yourself."

"Gods above, protect us," Asher said, his voice breaking and his hands trembling.

"How did you get to level 25 if you're afraid to fight?" Luke asked him.

Before he could get his answer, another spider launched itself at the group. Hakiro skewered it with his blade, but in the second it took him to intercept and kill it, another six were in the air. After that, it was like spiders were raining from the sky, and it was all Luke could do to catch and kill them as they poured down on him.

"Okay. Fuck spiders," Luke said five minutes later.

[You have slain 142 creatures between levels 11 and 17. 26530 XP awarded.]

[Congratulations! You have reached level 44. 44 AP awarded for use.]

"That was an unusual number of fully grown weeping spinners to be migrating," Hakiro said. "I wonder if something has happened to upset the balance of the colonies."

"How many did you kill?" Jalet said to his two trainees.

"Twenty-two," Sando said.

"N-nine," Asher added.

Luke's eyebrows shot up. He hadn't paid a lot of attention to the other two trainees, but he would have expected them to do better than that. With a mental shrug, he dismissed them. That spider swarm had enough XP in it to boost him up a full level. If he was lucky, he'd score a few extra before he had to go back to the city and fulfill his half of the bargain.

After that, well . . . Luke might just sneak into the woods again and do a little XP grinding on his own. Once he had **[XP Cycle]** up and running, it wouldn't matter if he leveled up to 60 or 70. Hell, if his dad's journals were to be believed, he might need those levels to beat this dragon that was supposedly guarding the God Machine.

"I think that will be enough for today," Jalet said, sharing a glance with Hakiro. "Until we know what caused this aberrant behavior, it's too risky to delve any deeper."

"Better to be safe," Hakiro agreed.

Well, there was always tomorrow. If every day went like this, he'd be good to go inside a week. In a way, this method was even better than the anthills he'd been using. As far as he could tell, the spiders didn't spray him with pheromones and chase him around by smell. Even if they did, he was staying in a place with antispider enchantments.

As they trudged back, Luke did his best to temper his expectations. The experts on this little trip seemed to think that encounter was weird, so he probably shouldn't be planning his future as if that was going to be a typical run in. Still, it would be nice to get the level grind done and over with.

Name	Luke Bennet	Zea Stenter
Level	44	35
XP	301158/315159	148551/157276
AP	77	4
Bloodline	SysAdmin III	None
Strength	61	7
Agility	70	30
Stamina	88	27
Perception	55	21
Skills	Burst Step (1)	Arcano Dynamics (2)
	Butchering (4)	Bartering (2)
	Consortium Standard (2)	Bloodline Purification Ritual (2)
	Counter (3)	Cadence (3)
	Deception (1)	Cold Reading (1)
	Detection (2)	Consortium Standard (2)
	Disguise (2)	Cooking (1)
	First Aid (1)	Dagger Mastery (1)
	Leatherworking (2)	Deception (1)
	Life Surge (2)	Disguise (2)
	Mace Mastery (5)	Engraving (4)
	Ostari (1)	First Aid (1)
	Peripheral Awareness (2)	Gem Cutting (1)
	Power Strike (2)	Ghost Script (1)
	Stealth (1)	Goldsmithing (2)
	Survivalist (2)	Keen Instincts (1)
	Sword Mastery (2)	Lock Picking (1)
	Tactical Foresight (2)	Mana Manipulation (3)
	Thalian (2)	Mana Sight (3)
	Torturer (1)	Mending (1)
	Twitch Reflexes (3)	Metallurgy (1)
	Unarmed Martialist (4)	Neyardic (3)
	Wood Carving (1)	Ostari (1)
	Analyze (BL)	Painting (1)
	Remote Access (BL)	Rune Forging (3)
	XP Mask (BL)	Sleight of Hand (1)
		Steady Hands (2)
		Stealth (2)
		Streetwise (2)
		Temperature Acclimation (2)
		Thalian (3)
		Whitesmithing (1)

CHAPTER 42

One thing that Luke really, really liked about the spider forest was the trees. More specifically, he liked how much space there was between the trees. It was far more open than the almost junglelike density he'd pushed through in other forests on the western continent, even if those openings were clogged with thick spiderwebs. Since killing spiders was what he was here for, Luke just took the webs as a sign he was going in the right direction.

After their first near-disastrous trip, at least from everyone else's point of view, Jalet and Hakiro had taken a few hours to walk the trails near their hunting camp. They'd come back with the conclusion that whatever might be happening, it was far enough away that the local populations were feeling at most a ripple effect from it and that the different colonies were still placed in the same formation they'd always been in. Individual borders might have shifted a bit, but it was nothing for the human hunters to worry about.

That had led to Luke's first hunt in the trees themselves instead of just being assaulted on the trails. Most of the forest was spacious enough to pass between trees without issue, and the underbrush was thin enough that it more suggested a path than demanded it. The real problem was the abundance of spiderwebs with lines as thick as his pinkie. Often, they were as much as ten or fifteen feet wide and just as tall, if not more so. Worse, there was a ceiling of webbing overhead that the spiders used to get around without ever descending to ground level.

Come to think of it, all that extra webbing blocked out enough sunlight that it probably had something to do with why there was so little vegetation on the ground. More importantly to Luke, it was also the staging point where most spiders liked to ambush their prey, which meant he spent just as much time looking up as he did forward.

It turned out that the group that had fallen on them the first day had been some sort of raiding party or something and that most spiders were closer to level 5 than they were to 15. Luke killed a few hundred the next day, but he only got a fraction of what he needed for the next level. When he grumbled about it, Hakiro told him that was far more typical than their first encounter, that if they'd been out with a normal group of trainees, they would almost certainly have lost a few of them.

That was all well and good, but now that Luke was finally gaining XP again, he was eager to get on with the process. The next time something like the hentai demon popped up, he wanted to be able to put it down quickly and easily.

The days started blending together, and he quickly grew sick of spiders, but Luke put in the work anyway. It wasn't like someone else could do it for him.

At the beginning of the second week, Luke finally took a night off to sleep. He and Zea were sharing a room, a fact which seemed to be upsetting Sando to no end. Luke only knew because he'd overheard the trainee out in the courtyard talking to Hakiro about it while he was eating dinner. Sando had been told in no uncertain terms that it was none of his business and to keep his mouth shut, lest he offend Luke or Zea.

Luke chuckled, shook his head, and went back to his meal. It wouldn't be the first time someone who disapproved of interspecies relationships made some noise about it.

When he got back to the room, Zea was sitting on the floor with her portable worktable in front of her. "What are you making today?" Luke asked.

"Just playing around with some runes I haven't used before," she told him. "I'm trying to integrate them into some ideas I had back on the ship, but the mana keeps cascading through the enchantment and breaking things apart. I think I can fix it with a set of regulation runes at the fourth axis, but that takes up space I need for the dispersion runes, and if I move them back any farther than the sixth axis, I have to add even *more* regulators."

Luke nodded along while she ramped up her explanation. He understood almost nothing she was saying, but it was obviously important to her, so he listened without complaint. There wasn't much he could do to help besides offering moral support, but he liked to think he did that like a pro. About five minutes into her minirant, she stopped suddenly and glanced over at the rock she'd been working on.

"Thought of something?" Luke asked.

"Maybe . . . I think . . . It might work. I need to test it," she said absently.

"Quack, quack," Luke muttered.

"What?"

"Nothing," he told her. "You go ahead and see if your idea works."

Thanks to the time he'd spent reading his dad's journals, Luke was spending a lot more time thinking about his family lately. And he had plenty of memories of listening to Curt drone on and on about a problem he was trying to solve, only to cut himself off in the middle of his rambling explanation about why it was a problem and why a certain solution wouldn't work. Then he'd call Luke his favorite rubber duck and run off to implement whatever solution he'd invented.

Luke missed Curt. He hadn't been perfect, but he'd been a hell of a good brother.

"I'm going to take a nap," he told Zea, who waved him off while she examined the rock she had placed in the middle of her worktable.

Luke found the XP grind went much faster when he went out on his own. Both Hakiro and Jalet objected to that at first, but after the fifth day straight that he came back unharmed, they eventually stopped bitching at him to stay with the group.

Without having to slow down or split the XP, Luke killed well over a thousand spiders in that time. Some were as small as the ones back home. Some looked like they'd crawled straight out of Australia and were the size of his face. And then some looked like they came out of an RPG video game. Of the bigger varieties, most came up to his knee, some reached waist height, and a few could look him eye to eye to eye to eye to eye. Luke did not like those ones.

But finally, after a week of work, he heard that ding in his mind and checked his notifications.

[You have slain Wolf-Spine Recluse (level 9). 82 XP awarded.]

[This creature has slain 116 other creatures.]

[Total kills for this type of creature: 47.]

[Highest-level kill: 12.]

[Congratulations! You have reached level 45. 45 AP awarded for use.]

"One more to go," Luke muttered, eyeing up his new total of 122 AP. If only he hadn't wasted 3 AP, he'd have enough now, but that wasn't how it had worked out. If he could take his AP back from his neglected **[First Aid]** or **[Stealth]** skills, he would in a heartbeat. The system didn't allow for that though, so he'd just have to gain one more level. That was probably for the best anyway, since it'd give him a bank of 43 AP to use in case of emergencies.

It was still a good milestone to stop at for the day. He'd been out hunting spiders for six hours straight, and it had been overcast and raining all morning.

What had started as a light misting had slowly turned into a cold drizzle. When Luke turned to head back to the trail, however, he blinked in surprise.

One of the bad things about having such high perception was that he noticed a lot of little details, and the dark didn't hide much from him these days. There had to be about a thousand spiders in the trees looking at him. They weren't making any aggressive moves, but every time he took a step, they shifted in place. He was not by any means an expert on spiders, but if Hakiro and Jalet were to be believed, wolf-spine recluses were territorial and there should be barely any other spiders nearby.

Luke took a moment to use **[Analyze]** on a few dozen spiders and confirmed they were all crystal-fang widow-makers, which shouldn't be anywhere near where he was in the woods. Worse, crystal fangs were among the smartest species in the forest. They weren't gathered for no reason, and while he'd been carving his way deeper into recluse territory, they'd apparently been trailing along behind him and stringing their own crystalline webs, ones that were razor edged and required a great deal of care to navigate unless he wanted to show back up at the base camp looking like he'd lost a fight with a weed whacker.

The trainers had both been insistent that Luke not fuck with crystal-fang widow-makers, despite his assurances that he could handle the poison they injected when they bit. It was supposed to harden internal organs into calcified lumps, and while he was confident that **[Life Surge]** could burn it away before it could do any real damage, he was happy to forego the experience. Besides, there were plenty of other spiders that weren't venomous, able to shoot razor wire out of their asses, and smart enough to work in cooperative packs.

"Okay, guys, I'll tell you what. You're all set up over there already, so I'll just go around this way," Luke said. "And you all have a good time taking over this territory, okay? You don't fuck with me, I won't fuck with you. Everybody wins except those wolf-spine spiders, and who cares about those guys, right?"

The spiders, predictably, remained silent as their thousands of eyes stared at him.

"Right, good talk. I'm just gonna . . . Yeah."

The creepiest part of that was that so many of them had snuck up on him. That was not supposed to happen, but the widow-makers were completely silent and damn near see-through with their crystal needle hairs. Luke glanced back frequently to see the spiders slowly filling the area he'd left behind, spinning their webs and claiming new acreage in the name of the crystal-fang widow-maker colony.

It took Luke about twenty minutes to get back onto the main trails and away from the widow-makers. They had apparently been following him for quite a while, slowly moving in and taking over more and more new territory without him noticing. Maybe it was the rain helping hide them. Whatever the reason, he had to circle through a new stretch of woods instead of backtracking, which resulted in him killing a few dozen more spiders that tried to attack him as he walked.

Luke made it back to the gate and slipped inside with a wary eye behind him. Their camp was the only spider free part of the entire forest, thanks entirely to the enchantments powering the wall and the mesh canopy overhead. The only way for spiders to get in was when someone entered or left. Even burrowing spiders couldn't get underneath the wall.

He didn't expect any of the widow-makers to follow him, and he'd already checked to make sure none were hitching a ride on his clothes, but he was still cautious. That whole scene had creeped him right the fuck out. As soon as he was through the gate and closed it behind him, he went looking for Hakiro.

"You're not going to believe what I ran into," Luke said. "About a thousand crystal-fang widow-makers deep into wolf-spine territory. The damn things were stalking me, spinning new webs after I killed the local spiders and moved on."

"There have been too many instances of aberrant behavior lately," Hakiro said with a frown. "I am tempted to end this expedition early. Tell me, how close are you to obtaining the AP needed for your new skill?"

"About 20000 short still," Luke said after consulting his status.

"At least another few days then, even with you going out alone. Be careful, something is amiss in the forest."

"You can say that again," Luke said, shuddering as he recalled thousands of eyes all staring at him intently.

Name	Luke Bennet	Zea Stenter
Level	45	35
XP	317194/337550	149301/157276
AP	122	4
Bloodline	SysAdmin III	None
Strength	61	7
Agility	70	30
Stamina	88	27
Perception	55	21
Skills	Burst Step (1)	Arcano Dynamics (2)
	Butchering (4)	Bartering (2)
	Consortium Standard (2)	Bloodline Purification Ritual (2)
	Counter (3)	Cadence (3)
	Deception (1)	Cold Reading (1)
	Detection (2)	Consortium Standard (2)
	Disguise (2)	Cooking (1)
	First Aid (1)	Dagger Mastery (1)
	Leatherworking (2)	Deception (1)
	Life Surge (2)	Disguise (2)
	Mace Mastery (5)	Engraving (4)
	Ostari (1)	First Aid (1)
	Peripheral Awareness (2)	Gem Cutting (1)
	Power Strike (2)	Ghost Script (1)
	Stealth (1)	Goldsmithing (2)
	Survivalist (2)	Keen Instincts (1)
	Sword Mastery (2)	Lock Picking (1)
	Tactical Foresight (2)	Mana Manipulation (3)
	Thalian (2)	Mana Sight (3)
	Torturer (1)	Mending (1)
	Twitch Reflexes (3)	Metallurgy (1)
	Unarmed Martialist (4)	Neyardic (3)
	Wood Carving (1)	Ostari (1)
	Analyze (BL)	Painting (1)
	Remote Access (BL)	Rune Forging (3)
	XP Mask (BL)	Sleight of Hand (1)
		Steady Hands (2)
		Stealth (2)
		Streetwise (2)
		Temperature Acclimation (2)
		Thalian (3)
		Whitesmithing (2)

CHAPTER 43

After the incident with the crystal-fang widow-makers, Luke started paying a lot more attention to what was going on behind him. He'd been a sloppy idiot for his first week when he thought there were no dangers to someone with his level in the forest. A hundred spiders, or even a thousand, couldn't actually hurt him, so he hadn't been too worried about getting surrounded.

Seeing all those widow-makers sitting there staring at him had changed his mind. Most spiders were about as dumb as he'd expect an Earth spider to be. Those guys weren't, and he found that scared him just a little bit. There was no telling what they might have cooked up to capture him if they decided they wanted to, and the idea of being webbed up in a cocoon of razor-edged ass wire didn't strike him as a good time.

That didn't stop him from going out, of course. The whole point of being in the forest was to gain enough levels to afford **[XP Cycle]** and, if possible, **[XP Reset]**. As much as he would have liked to round the set out with **[Inflict Status]**, Luke couldn't see spending an extra month or so in the forest. The contract they'd made with the Shansakun family was only to get four or five levels, not ten.

As Luke closed in on level 46, he started having to explore farther and farther away from the lodge. It continued to rain incessantly, so much so that many of the spiders Luke was supposed to be hunting disappeared into various hiding places and holes to get out of the weather. The ground turned to mud, and eventually, the whole group decided to just take a break for a few days in hopes that the storm clouds would move on and leave the forest to dry out.

* * *

Luke was sparring with the two trainees in the courtyard between the four buildings, though in his mind it was less sparring and more being a mobile training dummy for them. They weren't fast enough to overwhelm him, even working together, and they lacked the raw damage output to push through his blocks. He could see frustration mounting on their faces as they tried and failed to hit him over and over again.

So much for their sublime art of swordsmanship.

He let himself get worked into a position where they were flanking him, forcing him to react to attacks from either side simultaneously. The simple solution was to use **[Burst Step]** to reposition himself, but it was funnier to see them getting more and more worked up because they were using every trick they knew and they still couldn't touch him.

If he hadn't heard quite so many muttered comments about him being an uncultured barbarian lacking in any form of manners or grace or seen all the sneers and dismissive looks on their faces when they saw him using a mace instead of a sword, he probably would have been less of a dick about it. But he *had* heard the digs and seen the looks, so Luke was letting himself have fun with it.

[Congratulations! Peripheral Awareness has reached rank 3. 1000 XP awarded.]

That was unexpected. He'd just had a skill rank up on its own a few weeks ago, and to get another one so soon, and one at rank 3 even, was a nice little perk. It was a bit of a surprise, but unlike his spar with Hakiro, the trainees weren't pushing him hard enough that he had to pause the fight to process the change.

[Skill synergy detected between Counter, Peripheral Awareness, and Twitch Reflexes. Merge these skills together into new skill: Area Denial?]

Luke came to a full stop so unexpectedly that Asher's sword smacked off his hip and Sando barely managed to pull his attack in time. Luke didn't react to either attack, barely even felt them, really. He read the notification a second time, then opened his skill shop to look at **[Area Denial]**.

[Area Denial: React to attacks coming from practically any direction, even if you can't see them, and punish attackers within range. This skill can function against multiple attacks at the same time.]

[Prerequisites: Counter (rank 3), Peripheral Awareness (rank 3), Twitch Reflexes (rank 3), agility: 50, perception: 50.]

"Are you alright?" Jalet asked as he moved closer. "Luke?"

Luke blinked and said, "Oh, sorry. Just got a rank-up, and it triggered a skill-synergy notification."

"Congratulations," Jalet said with a smile. "That is an excellent milestone to reach. I hope it was something good."

"Sounds like it," Luke said. "The prereqs are certainly steep enough. Guess I'll find out here in a minute."

He mentally prodded the yes option to the prompt asking him if he wanted to merge the skills together. For a second, nothing changed, and then a new awareness snapped into place in his brain. A minute ago, he'd known where Asher and Sando were and had been keeping track of their movements out of the corners of both eyes while he deflected their attacks.

Now, he could practically predict how they were going to move before they even started. He was aware of the squelching of the mud beneath Asher's heel as he subtly adjusted his balance, of Sando's hand shifting on the hilt of his sword to angle the blade away from his leg as his arm dropped down to his side, even of Jalet's unmoving stillness, if for no other reason than the rain pelting down on him.

"Holy shit, that's trippy," Luke said. He didn't quite stagger backward, but it was an effort of will to hold himself upright while his brain got used to all the new sensory information coming in.

Jalet must have sensed something because he moved forward and placed a steadying hand on Luke's shoulder. "Just give it a minute. Sensory skill?"

"Yeah. Kind of. It's complicated."

"Advanced skills always are."

[Area Denial] wasn't seeing any of them as a threat right now, at least. The skill was making Luke very, very aware of Jalet's hand on him and what steps he'd need to take to grab hold of the offending arm, put it in a locking hold, and drive the man face down into the mud to pin him. It also had some suggestions for attacking the man's exposed ribs, but unlike some other skills, the knowledge wasn't intrusive. Luke could act on it, and the skill would guide him through the motions if he chose to, but it wasn't screaming at him to move.

Before he could say anything, the sound of footsteps coming down the trail from outside the lodge reached him. They were muffled by the rain but not so much that Luke couldn't pick it out. "It sounds like we've got a visitor," he said, turning to look at the gate.

Hakiro was already walking out of the building they were sharing and heading to the gate, presumably having felt whomever it was that was approaching with his own skills. The two trainees exchanged questioning glances, and Asher asked, "Is that normal?"

Jalet shrugged. "Probably just a messenger from the main compound. We'll see what the family wants here in a moment."

A kid, maybe fifteen years old and only level 14, slipped through the gate and followed Hakiro to the kitchen hall. He was wearing the same uniform the house servants had, except it was stained with soot and torn in places. His mask covered his whole face, judging by his tan lines, but the boy wasn't wearing it now. Instead, he had a burn mark traveling up his neck onto his cheek.

"Uh, are there any fire-breathing spiders in the forest I should know about?" Luke asked.

"Not that I'm aware of," Jalet told him, a frown on his face.

"Also, that kid seems kind of weak to be sent into this place on his own. Is that normal? I would have figured any messenger they sent in on a solo mission would have been at least level 30, maybe even with a specialized build."

"No, no it's not."

That was a bad sign to Luke. Whatever was going on was outside of normal and expected circumstances, which probably meant an emergency, which on Aros pretty much always meant somebody somewhere was using extreme violence as a lever to get whatever it was they wanted.

"I think I'm going to go pull Zea out of whatever project she's working on," Luke said. "I'll meet you guys in there?"

They parted ways, a troubled Jalet leading his two trainees into the building Hakiro and the messenger had disappeared into, and Luke dashing into the trainer house. He spared a moment to scrape the mud off his boots before heading toward the room he shared with Zea; there was no point in making the work any harder for the servants.

"Hey," he said, poking his head in. "Are you doing anything that you can't pause right now?"

Zea glanced up from her worktable, where she had the adjustable arm clutching what appeared to be a length of fine silver chain. The other end was tied to a loop across the table, and she was etching something so tiny he wouldn't have been able to sort out the individual lines without his high perception.

"No, it's nothing I can't walk away from. Why, what's going on?"

"I don't know yet. Some messenger just showed up. He's just a kid, way too low a level to be in here, and he's beat to hell. But, like, not from the trip through the forest. Hakiro is talking to him now or maybe just getting some food in him. Not sure, but either way, I'm guessing it's going to be bad news and that it'll probably be relevant to us."

"One second," Zea said. She etched a few more lines into the chain, set the tool down, and scooted backward to get her legs out from under the table. Luke would have entered the room fully and held out a hand to help her up, not that she needed it, but he hadn't been successful in cleaning all the mud off his boots, and the less he tracked across the floor, the easier it would be to clean up.

The pair stepped out into the rain together, with Zea pulling the hood up on her cloak before she left the house and Luke just ignoring it. He was already soaked through anyway. A few more seconds wasn't going to make a difference. They hustled across the yard into the kitchen hall, where four different tables were set up with a dozen chairs around each of them. The group was filling up half of the one in the back-right corner while a servant was busy hustling back and forth between the kitchen to bring out food.

There was an open tube sitting in the middle of the table, the kind that would have a scroll stored in it, and Jalet was frowning as he read from said scroll. Hakiro sat next to him, silent and still. Luke spared a moment to wonder if **[Tapestry of the World]** even allowed for Hakiro to read. It almost seemed like it had to, but when Luke thought about it, he realized there wasn't a lot of mandatory reading on Aros, and for occasions like this, there were others who could read messages for Hakiro.

Or maybe he'd just already read it and had passed it on to his colleague. That was also a valid possibility.

"So, what's going on?" Zea asked.

"One moment," Jalet said as he finished reading through the message.

The messenger himself was guzzling down water and trying to eat his own body weight in cold food, mostly in the form of sandwiches. Luke's stomach gave an involuntary gurgle at the sight of the food, causing everyone to pause what they were doing and look over at him.

"I'm not apologizing for being hungry," he told them flatly. Then he turned to the guy running more food from the kitchen to the table and asked, "Think I could get some of those sandwiches too?"

"Of course, sir," the man said. He deposited a plate at the far end of the table and scurried back off for the next load.

"It's bad news, I'm afraid," Jalet said as he put the scroll down.

"No shit. Did anyone think it wouldn't be?" Luke asked.

"We're leaving in the morning. We need to get back to the city as soon as possible. Hakiro is going ahead tonight."

"Oooh, shit. That is bad," Luke said. "But I haven't finished gaining the last level I need."

"No choice. Demons attacked the city. Twice. Scouts report they're gathering up numbers for a third assault. We'll be fighting in just under twenty-four hours."

Name	Luke Bennet	Zea Stenter
Level	45	35
XP	326521/337550	149301/157276
AP	122	4
Bloodline	SysAdmin III	None
Strength	61	7
Agility	70	30
Stamina	88	27
Perception	55	21
Skills	Area Denial (1)	Arcano Dynamics (2)
	Burst Step (1)	Bartering (2)
	Butchering (4)	Bloodline Purification Ritual (2)
	Consortium Standard (2)	Cadence (3)
	Deception (1)	Cold Reading (1)
	Detection (2)	Consortium Standard (2)
	Disguise (2)	Cooking (1)
	First Aid (1)	Dagger Mastery (1)
	Leatherworking (2)	Deception (1)
	Life Surge (2)	Disguise (2)
	Mace Mastery (5)	Engraving (4)
	Ostari (1)	First Aid (1)
	Power Strike (2)	Gem Cutting (1)
	Stealth (1)	Ghost Script (1)
	Survivalist (2)	Goldsmithing (2)
	Sword Mastery (2)	Keen Instincts (1)
	Tactical Foresight (2)	Lock Picking (1)
	Thalian (2)	Mana Manipulation (3)
	Torturer (1)	Mana Sight (3)
	Unarmed Martialist (4)	Mending (1)
	Wood Carving (1)	Metallurgy (1)
	Analyze (BL)	Neyardic (3)
	Remote Access (BL)	Ostari (1)
	XP Mask (BL)	Painting (1)
		Rune Forging (3)
		Sleight of Hand (1)
		Steady Hands (2)
		Stealth (2)
		Streetwise (2)
		Temperature Acclimation (2)
		Thalian (3)
		Whitesmithing (2)

CHAPTER 44

With about ten hours on the clock until they departed, Luke didn't think he could scrape together the last 11000 XP he needed to level up one more time, not unless he got lucky with another cluster of high-level spiders attacking all at once. He was almost eager for that to happen, just so he could test out his new **[Area Denial]** skill properly.

"Everyone get some rest," Hakiro said. "You'll be traveling all through tomorrow, and it's likely you'll be fighting within a few hours of getting home."

The two trainers moved off to a different table to have their own whispered discussion while Luke started working on the plates of food that were coming out from the kitchen. At the far end of the table, the messenger who'd brought the news was also eating, albeit at a much more sedate pace. The boy looked ready to topple over at any moment, and Luke had his suspicions that the reason they weren't leaving right away was that someone would have to literally carry the messenger back out of the forest if they tried.

Then again, the trainees weren't in much better shape. Luke had been sparring with them for hours, and while he was merely ready for a good meal, their stamina was much lower. If they were pushed, the trainees would probably make it back to Heishin with just enough energy to stagger to their rooms before they dropped.

"One warrior isn't going to make a difference to the city," Jalet hissed, drawing Luke's attention. "But it could be life and death to these boys."

"I know." Hakiro's voice sounded pained. "I do, believe me, but I have my own oaths. I can't delay my departure now that I know."

"I don't know if I can protect them all by myself. I can't be in two places at once," Jalet said.

"Ask Luke to help you. He's looking to snag more XP anyway."

"I would feel more comfortable if you were here instead."

Luke snorted softly as he took another bite of his sandwich. It was only a few miles to the edge of the forest. Chances were that they wouldn't be attacked by anything, and even if they were, they had enough fighters to keep the servants, healer, and cook safe in the middle of the group. If Hakiro wanted to run ahead early, that was his business.

"What are you going to do?" Zea asked, drawing Luke's attention back from his eavesdropping.

Luke shrugged and finished chewing. "Kill some spiders, I guess. Probably won't get enough of them to get the last level I need before we leave."

"You want to go with them?"

"I guess? I doubt our contract says anything about me defending them from demonic attack, but it's going to be hard for them to pay up their end of it if they're all dead."

"We actually got most of our side from them already," Zea said. "There were a few hard-to-find materials they didn't have on hand, but we're doing pretty well there. The biggest thing is getting you enough levels to buy **[XP Reset]** and **[XP Cycle]**. Do you think they'll let us stay behind so you can finish?"

"Probably not," Luke said. "I guess it wouldn't hurt to ask."

He got up and crossed the dining area to join Hakiro and Jalet at their table. They fell silent at his approach, and as Luke went to sit down, Hakiro said, "We're having a private discussion right now."

"Not really," Luke said. "But it seemed less rude to participate if I sat over here rather than just yelling across the room."

"You . . . heard us?" Hakiro asked.

"You weren't being that quiet."

"The enchantments in the table are supposed to prevent sound from carrying," Jalet said. "They aren't scheduled for maintenance for another two years. I wonder if someone damaged them."

Luke hadn't ever noticed anything like that, but then again, usually everyone sat at the same table when they ate anyway. They didn't have near enough people to fill up the all the available seats. All the enchantments he knew about seemed to be working correctly, or at least he hadn't heard Zea grumbling about anything being broken.

Now that Luke thought about it, he wondered if Zea had something to do with the noise enchantments failing. He glanced over and saw her stealing food off his abandoned plate. She looked innocent, but he didn't know if he believed her.

"That's a problem for another time," Hakiro said firmly. "You've heard our plans then. I will be leaving in the next hour, and the rest of you will follow in the morning. We'll be relying on you to keep our people safe from any attacks that come from the rear while Jalet holds the front. Sando and Asher will have to hold the sides."

"About that. I've got no problems escorting everyone out of the forest, but I think I'm going to need a few days to get another level. Maybe even a week. Is it going to be an issue if we stay here without you all?"

"In a word, yes. The enchantments are keyed to our family," Hakiro said. "You won't be able to access the hunting lodge without Jalet or me here. There's also the fact that we could use another strong warrior on the front lines back at the city. It's . . . There was a lot of damage from the previous attacks. Supposedly an elder demon joined the attacking demons, some sort of giant woman made of metal who leaves flaming footprints as she walks."

"I get that, but wouldn't it be better for me to grind out this last level so that when I come back, I can get twenty other people back into the fight?"

Hakiro didn't turn to look at Luke as he spoke. He didn't need to. "If we were defending against barbarian raiders or some sort of monster outbreak, I'd agree with you. But demons are unique. We don't get XP from killing them, so I'm sure all the older warriors are out there fighting already. Please, have some patience. We'll come back to finish your training once things are safe, I promise. It's in my family's own best interest to see that we do."

"Besides all that, there's something weird going on with the spider colonies right now. I've never seen anything like it, and I've been training new warriors here for twenty years," Jalet added. "Until that gets sorted, it's far more dangerous than usual to be here. We were already planning on cutting this trip short as soon as you gained your next level."

It looked like they were both set on their decisions. If Luke wanted to keep hunting here, he'd be doing it under his own power with his own resources. He expected they'd object to that as well since he had yet to fulfill his half of the contract. It just made sense that they'd want to keep their eyes on him until then.

If this had all happened even a week later, it would have been a nonissue. All he could do now was make the most of the last few hours available to him. If he went deeper into the forest, it would be more dangerous, but that was kind of the point. The more monsters he found, the faster he'd gain XP. It was hard to picture any one monster that could actually threaten him, and as long as he was careful, they shouldn't be able to swarm him.

"I'm going to get as much XP as I can before we leave in the morning," Luke said.

"You should get some rest so you're at your best tomorrow," Jalet objected.

"Nah, I'm fine. I don't need to sleep for a few more days at least. I know I won't push through to the next level before morning, but every little bit helps. Maybe I'll get lucky and run into another one of those swarms like we did on the first day."

"Only you would think that was good luck," Hakiro told him.

Luke shrugged and said, "I'll go let Zea know so she can prepare, and we'll be ready to leave when the sun comes up."

The cold didn't bother him, even if the rain was a bit annoying. The mud was the worst of it, but **[Area Denial]** was quickly showing Luke the difference between a basic skill, even one at max rank, and an advanced skill. Spiders he didn't even realize were there were dying when his mace swept through them and blasted them off of whatever branch they were lurking on. Nothing within five feet of him snuck up on him.

Luke had to revise exactly how aware of the world around him he thought he was. Yes, he noticed far more than he had back on Earth, and skills like **[Detection]** enhanced that even further, but he hadn't really given a lot of consideration to how other creatures would also have ranks in **[Stealth]** or, in the case of some spiders, **[Stalker]** and how, even at rank 2 or 3, that would help counteract his high base perception.

[Area Denial] did not give a single solitary fuck about **[Stealth]** or **[Stalker]**. If something got within a few feet of him and tried to sneak attack him, Luke was reacting before he even knew what it was. And the farther away from the hunting lodge he got, the more spiders there were. At some point, he was forced to abandon any ideas he had about which kind of spider was supposed to be where. Either the maps were completely wrong outside of the mile or two around the base, or everything had changed in the last few days.

The XP was also coming remarkably quickly. He was easily clearing more than 1000 an hour, and as long as that didn't slow down, he thought he just might pull that final level in time for their departure. The only downside there was that he had to keep going deeper and deeper to find spiders in the quantities he needed, and it turned out that the bigger, tougher ones all liked to congregate in the deep woods.

The bigger spiders tended to be ambush predators rather than trappers, which actually worked out in Luke's favor. It was far easier to smash them with his mace than to try to tear through the webs, not that there weren't tons of spider silk strung up through the trees by the smaller monsters anyway. But on the rare occasions that a big one decided they did want to do some interior decorating, their webs proved significantly harder to break.

"Look," Luke told the spider sitting at the top of the web thirty feet over his head. "We both know if you come down here, I'm going to bash your guts out. You're level 24, and that's great and all by spider standards, but it's not going to save you from me. So, I'm going to make myself an exit right over here, and if you're smart, you'll stay the hell away from me."

The spider watched him silently. It was the size of a compact car, with fangs as long as his damn arm. He really didn't want to have to kill it for a very simple reason. It was going to be a giant mess, and he hated fighting next to the webs. They weren't strong enough to hold him, but it was like having one of those roided-out gym bros back home who got all aggressive and wanted to prove they could shove whomever they wanted around grabbing at him while he fought.

Luke reached up to the web and tore it from its anchor point on the tree. The spider shifted in the branches overhead, no doubt preparing itself to skitter down and attack him. "I'm serious," Luke called up as he tore another anchor point free. "I do not have time to play with you, and you're not worth the effort for how little XP you give. Just keep your happy ass up there and we won't have a problem."

The third anchor point popped loose, and the spider descended down its web.

Name	Luke Bennet	Zea Stenter
Level	45	35
XP	329784/337550	148551/157276
AP	122	4
Bloodline	SysAdmin III	None
Strength	61	7
Agility	70	30
Stamina	88	27
Perception	55	21
Skills	Area Denial (1)	Arcano Dynamics (2)
	Burst Step (1)	Bartering (2)
	Butchering (4)	Bloodline Purification Ritual (2)
	Consortium Standard (2)	Cadence (3)
	Deception (1)	Cold Reading (1)
	Detection (2)	Consortium Standard (2)
	Disguise (2)	Cooking (1)
	First Aid (1)	Dagger Mastery (1)
	Leatherworking (2)	Deception (1)
	Life Surge (2)	Disguise (2)
	Mace Mastery (5)	Engraving (4)
	Ostari (1)	First Aid (1)
	Power Strike (2)	Gem Cutting (1)
	Stealth (1)	Ghost Script (1)
	Survivalist (2)	Goldsmithing (2)
	Sword Mastery (2)	Keen Instincts (1)
	Tactical Foresight (2)	Lock Picking (1)
	Thalian (2)	Mana Manipulation (3)
	Torturer (1)	Mana Sight (3)
	Unarmed Martialist (4)	Mending (1)
	Wood Carving (1)	Metallurgy (1)
	Analyze (BL)	Neyardic (3)
	Remote Access (BL)	Ostari (1)
	XP Mask (BL)	Painting (1)
		Rune Forging (3)
		Sleight of Hand (1)
		Steady Hands (2)
		Stealth (2)
		Streetwise (2)
		Temperature Acclimation (2)
		Thalian (3)
		Whitesmithing (2)

CHAPTER 45

Luke had an hour left until sunrise, and he still needed 3000 XP. That was pretty much a nonstarter by itself, but he also needed to backtrack to the hunting lodge to leave with everyone else, which meant he had about twenty minutes before he was out of time. Unless he got extraordinarily lucky, his push to level up to 46 was a bust.

He'd been trying to find the main nest of the whisper-silk crawlers for the last two hours. That was the XP mother lode right there, and he'd targeted them specifically because he'd tested the strength of their threads and found them to be far too weak to seriously threaten him. Unless he went to sleep and let hundreds of them restrain him, there was no conceivable way they'd be able to stop him.

It was too bad they were among the stealthiest of the colonies. Luke had found plenty of evidence of their work but very few of the spiders themselves. Looking back on it, he'd made the wrong call deciding to go after this particular breed instead of something more aggressive. Unfortunately, aggressive almost always paired with solitary and territorial, and he just didn't have the hours left in his night to hunt down a bunch of level 10 spiders one at a time.

Luke stopped walking and looked around. There was a smell in the air, something faint and hidden under the rain but still lingering. He couldn't quite place what it was, but he knew he should recognize it. Curious and no longer bothering to try to find the main nest since he was basically out of time anyway, Luke sniffed again and turned to follow the scent.

Tracking by nose was difficult, no matter how high his perception got. Human brains just didn't seem to be wired to do it properly. In this case though, it was pretty easy to figure it out. The smell was burnt wood, and within a minute, he stepped into a hole in the forest filled with nothing but the scorched and charred remains of trees. Nothing higher than Luke's knee still stood in the field of soot.

As he took a step forward, his foot crunched down on something. Luke glanced down and saw a crusty black spider, curled up from the heat and cooked to death. Once he knew to look, he found dozens more scattered around, half buried in muddy soot.

"Man, what the fuck is this?" he asked out loud. It had been raining for days, sometimes a drizzle and sometimes a real downpour, but never really enough to storm. There was no way a random lightning strike had started a wildfire that had contained itself perfectly to this small area.

[Area Denial] activated itself, and Luke's leg kicked out before he'd even recognized the sound of movement behind him. Something small and lightweight went flying away. It was only a foot tall, not counting a long, thin tail, but it was durable enough that when Luke launched it backward, it rolled with the blow and landed upright twenty feet away.

Dozens more creatures rose up from underneath the blanket of soot and ash covering the clearing, and Luke noticed wickedly hooked stingers on the ends of their tails. His first thought was that maybe he'd get lucky and pull that last level after all, but when **[Analyze]** refused to trigger on them, he groaned.

"Fucking demons. Of course you are," he said with a sigh. There'd be no XP here.

Without being able to tell exactly what he was fighting, Luke opted to take a cautious approach to the battle. He started backing toward the edge of the clearing in an attempt to keep the demons from coming at him from every angle. The demons watched him with their coal-black eyes and chittered to one another quietly with voices that sounded like rats running across an attic floor.

Luke thought he had his identification narrowed down to two or three types of demons, but he couldn't be sure. Though he'd made the effort to pick Hakiro's brain about the demonic invasions, the swordsman hadn't known a lot, and nobody else seemed to either. Luke had gotten some information but nothing definitive. Supposedly, there'd be one of those books with all the information the army had gathered about demons waiting for Luke when he got back to the city. Fat lot of good it did him right now.

But if he had to guess, his money was on imps. It was either that or gremlins, but he was pretty sure gremlins had big, floppy ears and no tails. Gremlins probably would have been better since imps were one of those monster types that just kind of came in an endless wave, a wave that was on fire.

These imps, if that's what they were, had soot-colored skin stretched taut over tiny frames and short, bony limbs. They were proportioned like humans, except their whole bodies were literally nothing but skin and bones, and they stood no taller than Luke's knee.

On some unknown signal, the imps all launched themselves at Luke at the same time. Their mouths opened to reveal little jagged triangles of rock for teeth that were backlit by flickering flames coming up from their throats, and Luke could feel the heat radiating out of them well before they got close enough to bite.

His mace whipped around him, driven by rank 5 **[Mace Mastery]** and rank 2 **[Tactical Foresight]**. Imp after imp exploded into clouds of glowing charcoal dust as they swarmed across the clearing. Only once the horde got coordinated enough to start coming at him from every direction did **[Area Denial]** kick in.

Luke had never gotten that multitarget offensive skill he wanted, but this particular combination was working pretty well. He was basically spinning like a top while adjusting the position of his weapon to blast through dozens of imps. In fact, he was going so fast he was starting to tear a hole in the ground where he stood. Rather than risk hitting a buried rock and throwing his footwork off, Luke shifted a step to the left every few seconds.

Everything seemed to be going fine, but the thing about imps was that they didn't really run out of numbers. They had a weird and somewhat disgusting ability to unhinge their jaws completely and hack up what looked like lumps of used-up charcoal that would quickly unfold into brand-new imps. If the sizes didn't quite line up, well, Luke chalked that up to a quirk of demon magic.

So while he'd killed probably a hundred imps in the opening minute of the fight, the clearing was quickly filling up with so many new imps that he thought he might actually be behind where he'd started. If Luke wanted this fight to end anytime soon, he needed to go on the offensive. He burst through a cloud of soot and ash and dashed forward, mace lashing out to smite any imps he ran past.

The ones at the far end of the burned-out clearing were busy barfing up reinforcements instead of paying attention when Luke crashed into them. Imps died at a rate of four or five a second, but even as Luke worked through that group, the ones who'd been chasing him reversed and started their own summons. By the time Luke had fully killed off the reinforcements, he had a new crop on the other side of the clearing to deal with.

"This is fucking ridiculous," he growled as he activated **[Burst Step]**.

On the bright side, he was pushing the imps so hard that most of them had stopped trying to kill him. It had become a game of stamina, where Luke rushed to kill them faster than new ones could be created, and if there was one thing he was confident in, it was that he'd keep going for hours after anyone else had run out of steam.

It was going to make him late coming back if he didn't figure out a way to speed this up though. It hadn't escaped his notice that as more and more imps formed, the amount of loose ash on the ground was slowly going down, and he suspected that was making up the difference in mass between a full-size imp and the lump they barfed up onto the ground when they were summoning a new one. But just by eyeballing the clearing, he could tell that wasn't going to be a quick solution. There was enough raw material to make hundreds more imps that would keep him occupied for the next hour.

He could always just run away. The imps weren't that fast individually, and he had miles of woodland to lose them in. It wasn't like he was gaining any XP from them either. All he was doing was clearing out a pocket of demons that seemed to reproduce endlessly anyway. If the imps did follow him back somehow, there'd be other people to help kill them.

Luke made a concentrated effort to kill the spawners near the south side of the clearing so that all the imps would be clustered as far away as possible, then he broke away from the fight and darted into the woods. A high-pitched screeching like metal on metal went up behind him, but he didn't look back or stop to fight. Any imp that got close to him received a mace moving at high speeds, and within a minute, the cries had faded away, and Luke was alone in the forest again.

Well, relatively alone. A random spider launched itself off a branch at face height in an attempt to go for Luke's eyes, and he swatted it out of the air to splatter against the trunk of a nearby tree. Ignoring the ding in his head, Luke kept running. He was going to be late, but he figured they'd probably forgive him when he told the group about the imps.

The rain had let up sometime while Luke was fighting, but it wasn't until he stepped out onto a wide trail that he recognized there was smoke mixed in with the overcast clouds. It wasn't just a single plume either. He climbed up a tree and took a quick look around to count no fewer than sixteen more columns of smoke drifting up into the sky.

Luke would have thought it was something he'd done, but he didn't see how that was possible. It likely meant there were more clusters of imps in the forest, and perhaps they'd just become active with the dawn or with the change in weather. Demons that burned things down and spawned more of themselves from the ashes were probably sensitive to fluctuating weather.

All that mattered to Luke was getting back and getting everyone out of the woods sooner rather than later. If the weather starting to clear up had been what kept the imps dormant, then Luke was willing to bet the remaining spider colonies would be going nuts as soon as the imps burned down their homes.

He jumped down from the tree and took off down the trail at a jog, try-ing to remember exactly where he was and which bisecting trails he needed to follow. Thankfully, his **[Survivalist]** skill helped with navigation, and he soon found himself back on the main trail that circled around the hunting lodge. Luke picked up his pace, not liking the columns of smoke he was seeing popping up closer and closer.

The lodge came into view, and he froze in shock. The timber walls were smoking, and the enchanted mesh dome across the top was sagging under the weight of hundreds of imps as they tore at it. The sounds of his companions yelling to one another as they fought filled the air, and the doorway that allowed Luke to enter and exit the lodge had been ripped out of the wall and left discarded in the weeds nearby.

The glow of fire lit the interior, and without a second's hesitation, Luke rushed through the open doorway.

Name	Luke Bennet	Zea Stenter
Level	45	35
XP	334827/337550	148551/157276
AP	122	4
Bloodline	SysAdmin III	None
Strength	61	7
Agility	70	30
Stamina	88	27
Perception	55	21
Skills	Area Denial (1)	Arcano Dynamics (2)
	Burst Step (1)	Bartering (2)
	Butchering (4)	Bloodline Purification Ritual (2)
	Consortium Standard (2)	Cadence (3)
	Deception (1)	Cold Reading (1)
	Detection (2)	Consortium Standard (2)
	Disguise (2)	Cooking (1)
	First Aid (1)	Dagger Mastery (1)
	Leatherworking (2)	Deception (1)
	Life Surge (2)	Disguise (2)
	Mace Mastery (5)	Engraving (4)
	Ostari (1)	First Aid (1)
	Power Strike (2)	Gem Cutting (1)
	Stealth (1)	Ghost Script (1)
	Survivalist (2)	Goldsmithing (2)
	Sword Mastery (2)	Keen Instincts (1)
	Tactical Foresight (2)	Lock Picking (1)
	Thalian (2)	Mana Manipulation (3)
	Torturer (1)	Mana Sight (3)
	Unarmed Martialist (4)	Mending (1)
	Wood Carving (1)	Metallurgy (1)
	Analyze (BL)	Neyardic (3)
	Remote Access (BL)	Ostari (1)
	XP Mask (BL)	Painting (1)
		Rune Forging (3)
		Sleight of Hand (1)
		Steady Hands (2)
		Stealth (2)
		Streetwise (2)
		Temperature Acclimation (2)
		Thalian (3)
		Whitesmithing (2)

CHAPTER 46

Electric-blue sparks rained down overhead as imps tore up the enchanted antispider mesh. They provided the only light since the imps had blotted out the morning sun, and in those flickering sparks, Luke saw the trainees struggling against a hundred imps. They were arranged in a triangle with the noncombatants in the middle, but only Jalet was successfully fending off the imps. Sando was getting slowly overwhelmed, and the only reason Asher wasn't in the same boat was that Zea was focusing most of her support on him.

Smoke was curling up through the roofs of all four buildings and coming out through slats on the inside, and the overall temperature inside the ring of buildings was at least fifteen degrees hotter than out in the forest. More imps kept pouring out through the open doors, with the heaviest concentration coming from the building that held the kitchen.

It was an all-too-familiar scenario, except the spawners were hidden away inside the buildings, and the numbers were so high that even with four people fighting them, they couldn't make any headway. Maybe if Hakiro hadn't left early, it would have been a different story.

Luke smashed through the first imp to get inside his range without slowing down. He blew past the knot of people struggling to keep themselves from being overwhelmed and barreled into the dining area, where he put **[Area Denial]** to good use as he forced his way deeper into the building. A steady stream of imps was coming out from the kitchen, probably using the built-up ash from a week's worth of preparing food on a woodstove.

As weak as each individual imp was, Luke couldn't just ignore them. Between the never-ending stream of bodies, the thick smoke that hung in the air from the fires the demons had started, and the dancing shadows from the fiery lights in the backs of their throats when they opened their mouths, Luke was starting to find his high perception to be a liability.

He didn't need to kill every imp in the dining area. He just needed to get past them to the kitchen. Luke swatted away a trio of imps trying to jump on his back as he ghosted past one of the tables that was burning around the edges, then pivoted to dodge an imp that had been crawling across the ceiling to drop on his head.

He was close enough now to use **[Burst Step]**, even if the way wasn't exactly free of obstructions. He body-slammed through at least twenty imps as he blurred forward and clipped dozens more, but when he came out of the skill, he was inside the kitchen. The imps he'd hit when he was moving fell away, most of them dead or close enough to it that all they could do was twitch. The few that were still lucid enough to fight tried to bite down on him, but Luke grabbed hold of them and hurled them away.

Then he laid into the imps that were hurling up chunks of charcoal-colored stone, killing them so fast that they didn't have time to barf up a single new demon after he got started. He even scattered the ash from the fireplaces. If he was right, without it all piled up together, they wouldn't be able to produce new imps so quickly.

With that mission accomplished, Luke turned to leave and realized he had a whole new problem. If he didn't defend the kitchen, it would just fill with new imps. They weren't exactly smart or even all that coordinated, but enough of them would flood in behind him that they'd just start the spawning operation back up again.

Just like in that clearing in the forest, there was no good solution. Eventually, he supposed the imps would run out of ash, but since they were also actively burning down the buildings, it became a question of whether they could refresh their supply faster than they used it.

The forest really was the worst possible place to fight a demon like this. The only thing that was effectively keeping them contained was the constant rain, and while Luke was sure it would be starting back up again within a few hours, that didn't help now. It especially didn't help since the demons had somehow managed to get inside the buildings, where they were protected from the rain.

The only solution Luke saw was to run, but they had people below level 15 with them. It would have to be a fighting retreat, and with so many imps coming at them, Luke didn't think it was possible to protect them all while on the move. Nothing he had in his tool kit was going to help him in this situation.

It took Luke three minutes to finish clearing out the dining area. Without access to huge piles of soot and ash, the imps couldn't spawn new demons as quickly, though nothing Luke could do seemed capable of stopping them completely. The coal rocks just took longer to unfold into imps outside of the kitchen. Maybe they were pulling ash particles from the air or something. There was certainly enough of it, given that every imp Luke killed seemed to burst apart into a cloud of the stuff.

He fought his way back out into the yard and moved to take the pressure off Sando. With no more imps coming from the kitchen, at least for the moment, the defense had stabilized itself somewhat, though Luke could already see new imps sneaking around the outskirts of the lodge toward the building. The door was gone, and other than standing in the doorway to physically guard it, there was no way to keep the imps from getting inside.

Maybe that was exactly what they should do. Luke and Zea could work on breaking a hole through the wall so the group could escape into the woods while Jalet and his trainees used the door as a choke point. The building was slightly on fire, but Luke was confident he could bust out long before that became a problem.

Just as he opened his mouth to call for the retreat, a glob of molten metal dripped down from overhead to splatter against his shoulder. Luke glanced up and saw the imps had finally succeeded in chewing a hole in the mesh and were now busy widening it. "Fuck," he yelled as he tore the sleeve off his shirt and flung it away. Most of the metal went with it, and what didn't he flicked off with his fingers, leaving an angry red welt on his skin.

It was painful but not enough to stop Luke from fighting. "Back up to the kitchen," Luke yelled. "I've got it cleared out for now!"

"We need to get out through the gates," Jalet yelled back. "If we stay trapped in here, they're going to wear us down with sheer numbers."

"We'll go through the wall," Luke said, rushing forward to grab one of the servants just before another chunk of metal landed on him. That section was at least still solid and didn't splash when it landed.

"You can't go through the wall. It's enchanted."

"I bet I can break it anyway," Luke said. "And if I can't, we have an enchanter right here who can."

Zea was busy directing her whip through an insane display of precision that killed imps coming in from three different directions, but she said, "I can't do shit if I'm fighting like this. Get me somewhere with some cover and I'll work on it."

"See?" Luke demanded. "Let's go."

The argument was interrupted by a sharp crack overhead. Something gave in the mesh, and a huge piece of it slammed down, taking thirty or forty imps along for the ride. It broke the group's defensive formation as Asher was caught underneath it, and the imps immediately swarmed over him. The intact part of the mesh might have protected him from being bitten or clawed at, but it was glowing with heat, and he immediately started screaming.

His screams were intermingled with those of the cook, who'd been holding a butcher's cleaver in one hand and a frying pan in the other. The cleaver went into the skull of the first imp to approach him, and he bashed another with the frying pan just by swinging it wildly. Then six more imps all leaped on him at once and started tearing him apart.

It happened so fast that by the time anyone could react, the cook was already dead. Maybe if there hadn't been other imps taking up Luke's attention, he could have gotten there in time. Maybe not. It didn't matter now because more chunks of the mesh were coming down on top of them, and no one had time to spare to help anyone else. Luke grabbed Zea and one of the servants and used **[Burst Step]** to get them into the kitchen just before the mesh hit the ground.

It glowed molten yellow where it hadn't liquified completely around the edges. Jalet managed to cut himself free, though not before he was burnt all over. Back on Earth, Luke would have said that would be it for the man, that he'd be dead from his injuries almost immediately. On Aros, things were different. Despite the horrific burns, Jalet stood tall and laid into the imps around him with his sword.

The rest of the staff was not so lucky. Both trainees were under there as well. There were a lot of screams for a few seconds, and then things were silent except for the sound of Jalet's ragged breathing as he fought.

That brief lull was enough for Luke to say, "Clear out any imps left in here. See if you can get us through the wall and out of the lodge."

Zea nodded and ran deeper into the smoke-filled dining area while Luke planted himself in the doorway and smashed down any imps that came at him. He tried getting Jalet's attention, but the man ignored him and kept trying to fight his way through the mesh to where his two trainees were buried under it.

Then the imps did something strange. One of them puked up a charcoal stone onto the liquid metal of the mesh. Then another did the same thing. And another. Soon, there were thirty imps all dry heaving as they ejected spawning stones from their mouths. Things got worse as the stones started to soak up the liquid metal like a sponge and glowing bright brownish orange.

The stones themselves became liquid, and soon the glops of it were clumping together. Over the span of no more than ten seconds, almost the entire mesh liquified and congealed into one giant bronze-colored blob of molten metal.

Then an arm sprouted out of the side.

"Oooooh shit, that's not good," Luke whispered.

The blob started to lift itself into the air on a pair of long, thick, muscular legs. A second arm appeared opposite the first, and an amorphous sphere stretched out of the top. It had no facial features at first, but that quickly resolved into a pair of eyes and a nose and cruel, smiling lips. The metal person kept getting bigger and bigger until she was fully formed.

Standing almost twice as tall as Luke and wearing some sort of toga-looking thing, except it went up to both shoulders instead of leaving one bare, was a woman made entirely of what appeared to be molten bronze. She had an Amazonian build, her limbs thick with muscle. Luke could have easily pictured her in some sort of Greek art gallery at a museum if she wasn't alive and moving.

A malevolent presence filled the area, and the woman held up one hand. Molten bronze surged down her arm and into her open hand, where it formed into a bar that resolved itself into the shape of a jewel-capped scepter.

From start to finish, the demon's formation took less than three seconds. Then she leaned down, swung the scepter, and dashed Jalet's brains out across the ground in a single blow.

Name	Luke Bennet	Zea Stenter
Level	45	35
XP	334827/337550	148551/157276
AP	122	4
Bloodline	SysAdmin III	None
Strength	61	7
Agility	70	30
Stamina	88	27
Perception	55	21
Skills	Area Denial (1)	Arcano Dynamics (2)
	Burst Step (1)	Bartering (2)
	Butchering (4)	Bloodline Purification Ritual (2)
	Consortium Standard (2)	Cadence (3)
	Deception (1)	Cold Reading (1)
	Detection (2)	Consortium Standard (2)
	Disguise (2)	Cooking (1)
	First Aid (1)	Dagger Mastery (1)
	Leatherworking (2)	Deception (1)
	Life Surge (2)	Disguise (2)
	Mace Mastery (5)	Engraving (4)
	Ostari (1)	First Aid (1)
	Power Strike (2)	Gem Cutting (1)
	Stealth (1)	Ghost Script (1)
	Survivalist (2)	Goldsmithing (2)
	Sword Mastery (2)	Keen Instincts (1)
	Tactical Foresight (2)	Lock Picking (1)
	Thalian (2)	Mana Manipulation (3)
	Torturer (1)	Mana Sight (3)
	Unarmed Martialist (4)	Mending (1)
	Wood Carving (1)	Metallurgy (1)
	Analyze (BL)	Neyardic (3)
	Remote Access (BL)	Ostari (1)
	XP Mask (BL)	Painting (1)
		Rune Forging (3)
		Sleight of Hand (1)
		Steady Hands (2)
		Stealth (2)
		Streetwise (2)
		Temperature Acclimation (2)
		Thalian (3)
		Whitesmithing (1)

CHAPTER 47

Lacking any better way to measure a demon's strength, seeing her kill a powerful human of level 39 without any apparent effort was a good way to get a feel for what Luke was dealing with. He was uncomfortably reminded of just how overpoweringly strong the hentai tentacle demon had been, how it had taken Hakiro and Luke working together just to create openings to damage the seed bulb all its tongues had sprouted from, and how Zea had thrown in one of her magical explosions to stun it so that Hakiro could finish it off.

Hakiro was not here now, and Zea was going to be too busy to assist. Luke had gained a few levels since the battle with the hentai demon, but he hadn't spent any of the AP. He supposed the silver lining was that he had 122 AP he was sitting on right now that was supposed to be banked for **[XP Cycle]**, but he had a very real fear that even that wouldn't be enough. Hakiro had said something like a warrior of at least level 60 was needed to successfully fight an elder demon single-handedly.

Luke hoped to fuck that the molten giant in front of him wasn't an elder demon.

At the metal demon's appearance, all the imps went nuts with their chittering cries, and the demon responded by opening her mouth and unleashing an unholy screech that reminded Luke of some of those digitized Pokémon cries that had come out of Curt's battered old secondhand Game Boy when they were kids, only cranked up to jet-engine decibels and causing the malevolent aura to pulsate in time with the undulating scream.

"What the fuck is going on out there?" Zea yelled from deeper in the kitchen.

"New demon," Luke yelled back, his eyes not leaving the molten-bronze woman for an instant. "I don't think I can beat her, so, uh, the quicker you can make an exit, the better."

"Sir," the servant said in a tiny voice, barely more than a whisper. "I think that is the demon that was mentioned in the message."

"No shit," Luke said. "She's pretty distinctive, huh?"

The giant woman turned her attention from the bloody smear on her scepter as it finished burning away to stare at Luke. There was an intensity in that, like all of a sudden that evilness floating in the area around them got focused and slammed straight into Luke's brain.

[You have been afflicted by the following condition: Curse—Dream of Despair (12s).]

She took a step forward, just one single step, but it cleared six feet easily. Luke knew that he needed to move, that if he just stood there, he'd be dealt with the exact same way Jalet had been. But then, what did it matter? Even at his best, he couldn't compete with a demon that powerful. Why bother struggling just to live an extra few seconds?

A second step brought the Amazonian giant close enough to strike him. She brought one arm up, her scepter in line with his skull. This was it. For all the pain, all the desperation, every foe overcome and obstacle broken through, it was all for nothing. Here, now, he'd finally met something so implacable that even attempting to resist it was pointless.

"—uke! Luke!" a voice screamed from somewhere behind him. Luke knew that voice. He focused on the sound and searched around inside his brain for a moment until he recalled who it was.

Zea.

The scepter started coming down, and the largest part of Luke wanted to just let it. It would only hurt for a moment, one last scrap of pain on the way out. Then all the struggles would be over. Maybe there would be some kind of afterlife where he could finally rest.

But what about Zea? That small core inside him insisted that if he just let himself be killed, she'd be next, and she didn't deserve that. She was only here because of him. All the dangers she'd been through, everything she'd suffered, that was all because of him. It would be a betrayal to just give up and die when he hadn't even begun to repay her for all the help she'd given him.

[Condition: Dream of Despair (10s)]

Part of him woke up there. It pulled itself out of the black depths of his own mind and realized that there was still a reason to keep fighting, still someone he cared about in danger. If he died, she would follow soon after. But it was a small part.

That was enough to reconnect Luke to the rest of his emotions though. And at that moment, the primary emotion he was feeling was sheer, unadulterated rage. This demon was in his head, fucking with him. She thought she could make him lay down and die. No fucking way was he going to let her get away with that.

[Life Surge] sang through his veins, and **[Power Strike]** filled his arms as he channeled the skill into his mace. It arced overhead, striking the scepter a foot away from his skull, so close that he could feel the blistering heat coming off it. The weapon was batted aside, and a shower of molten metal drops splattered across the imps off to the side. Their chittering screams turned agonized as the metal melted through their bodies, the heat apparently enough that they started to combust into clouds of ash.

The demon woman's mouth formed into an *O* of surprise for just a moment before Luke's mace whipped back around the other way and struck her across the cheek. He had to stretch to his maximum height to reach her, right up to standing on his toes to strike her solidly instead of skipping the head of his mace across her chin, but he did it.

Instead of her head snapping to one side from the force of the blow, the weapon ripped through her cheek and took more blobs of metal with it. Luke stepped to the side to avoid being touched by them as they flew through the air and watched closely to see if the demon showed any sort of reaction to the hit. He wasn't terribly surprised when metal dribbled down her face to fill in the gouge he'd carved out.

Her retaliatory kick also wasn't a big surprise. Luke slid to one side and smacked his mace against her knee. She didn't react other than to shift around some more of her molten body to fill in the new dent he'd made. It wasn't the first time Luke had fought something that was human shaped but didn't feel pain, but he didn't have a lot of hope that he'd find some easily exploited vulnerability to take her out.

Then the imps got involved.

It wasn't that Luke had forgotten they were there, but he'd kind of expected the molten-bronze Amazon would fight him solo for some reason. He wasn't sure why exactly he was surprised to have them descend on him, but he reacted quickly anyway. **[Area Denial]** was perfect for this kind of combat, and between that skill and **[Tactical Foresight]**, he was able to hold the door to the kitchen area for the next few seconds.

More and more ash filled the air, so much that Luke had to stop breathing and found it harder and harder to see. Against just the imps that might have been fine, but the molten-bronze demon wasn't content to stand back and watch. She also didn't care if she killed the imps while she wildly swung her scepter about.

Luke dodged around it, extremely aware that he was wasting time. **[Life Surge]** was not a good choice for a battle of attrition, which was essentially what fighting a horde of imps was, but he'd needed it to save his life after snapping out of the curse the demon had used on him. Now that it was running, he was on a clock to shift something in his favor before it ran out and left him in an even worse position than he'd started.

Holding the door against the imps was a delaying action. It limited his mobility, kept him locked in one place and fighting on the defensive. Worse, the longer he fought in one area, the harder it got to keep fighting. Zea and the sole surviving servant were back in the kitchen where the building met the outer wall, trying to figure out how to cut through the enchantments so they could escape, and they needed all the time Luke could give them.

If he retreated into the dining area, he could escape the cloud of ash, but the molten demon would probably rip the front of the building off to get at him. Unlike the outer wall circling the lodge, it had no special reinforcements that Luke was aware of, and considering how much of the building was already on fire, he was confident that there weren't any.

If the top of the building got destroyed, it would make a hole too wide for him to defend. The imps would get past him, and that would be the end of their escape attempt. Maybe if he bypassed the dining hall and made a stand at the kitchen, that might work. The dining hall was big enough for the molten demon to move in, and she seemed focused entirely on Luke. It could work.

The decision was taken from him when the roof behind him collapsed from the fire, exposing a huge chunk of the dining hall. "Shit," Luke swore as he backpedaled to avoid the demon's scepter screaming down. Flecks of metal jumped off when it impacted the ground, forcing Luke to dart to the side to avoid them.

He leaped up from the ground in front of the kitchen to perch on the top of the now-roofless wall for a second, made eye contact with the demon, and shoved himself backward into the burning debris filling the dining hall as she reached out to grab him. Her fingers missed his boot by inches, so close that he could feel the heat through the leather and it started to blacken near the toes.

"How are we doing back there?" Luke yelled to Zea as he scrambled to fend off the imps that were slipping past him to the kitchen. **[Burst Step]** didn't like it when he used it to get around so much clutter, but he managed to angle slightly off to the side of the doorway, then jump into place when he fell out of the skill.

"It's not working," Zea said. "Everything I try just gets bounced back. We need to find another way out."

"What if I just break it? If I hit it hard enough, the wall would give, right?"

"Maybe. It would definitely blow up. Not sure how big that explosion would be."

The front wall of the building shattered as the bronze demon kicked it. Luke warded off shards of loose stone with a hand raised in front of his face, then coughed when he inadvertently inhaled a bit of ash from a pair of nearby imps that had gotten riddled with shrapnel.

"Figure something out!" Luke yelled.

They didn't have another fallback point, and Luke knew he only had twenty or thirty seconds left on **[Life Surge]**. For all the times he'd hit the molten-bronze demon, it hadn't done much of anything. Maybe it was slightly smaller from lost mass, judging from all the rapidly cooling metal splatter all over the ground, but he'd need to get a lot more aggressive if he was going to make any headway, and he had some real concerns that if he took enough metal out of her body, she might just reabsorb everything and leave him right back where he started.

Maybe they could go up and over. The mesh that had capped the lodge was gone. Thirty feet was a hell of a jump, but if he did it with **[Life Surge]** running and used **[Burst Step]**, he might pull it off. The trick would be extracting Zea and the servant from the kitchen and taking them with him.

He sent another **[Power Strike]** into his mace to parry a downward smash of the demon's scepter and sent her strike off to the side, where it dusted an imp that was coming his way. For one, the demon seemed to anticipate the action, and her leg came up to kick Luke while he was still off-balance.

Luke went flying, his side raw and his clothes smoldering as he tumbled through the air. Imps descended on him, already racing to reach him even before he landed, but even more imps poured into the suddenly undefended kitchen. The servant started screaming.

And the ten-foot-tall molten statue of an Amazonian woman moved into place between Luke and Zea, cutting him off from saving her.

Name	Luke Bennet	Zea Stenter
Level	45	35
XP	334827/337550	148551/157276
AP	122	4
Bloodline	SysAdmin III	None
Strength	61	7
Agility	70	30
Stamina	88	27
Perception	55	21
Skills	Area Denial (1)	Arcano Dynamics (2)
	Burst Step (1)	Bartering (2)
	Butchering (4)	Bloodline Purification Ritual (2)
	Consortium Standard (2)	Cadence (3)
	Deception (1)	Cold Reading (1)
	Detection (2)	Consortium Standard (2)
	Disguise (2)	Cooking (1)
	First Aid (1)	Dagger Mastery (1)
	Leatherworking (2)	Deception (1)
	Life Surge (2)	Disguise (2)
	Mace Mastery (5)	Engraving (4)
	Ostari (1)	First Aid (1)
	Power Strike (2)	Gem Cutting (1)
	Stealth (1)	Ghost Script (1)
	Survivalist (2)	Goldsmithing (2)
	Sword Mastery (2)	Keen Instincts (1)
	Tactical Foresight (2)	Lock Picking (1)
	Thalian (2)	Mana Manipulation (3)
	Torturer (1)	Mana Sight (3)
	Unarmed Martialist (4)	Mending (1)
	Wood Carving (1)	Metallurgy (1)
	Analyze (BL)	Neyardic (3)
	Remote Access (BL)	Ostari (1)
	XP Mask (BL)	Painting (1)
		Rune Forging (3)
		Sleight of Hand (1)
		Steady Hands (2)
		Stealth (2)
		Streetwise (2)
		Temperature Acclimation (2)
		Thalian (3)
		Whitesmithing (1)

CHAPTER 48

The more the demon made of molten metal that somehow held its shape like a solid object moved around, the more fires she started. Outside, it hadn't been as bad. The ground was wet, and after the grass had been burnt, the fires had died out. If anything, she'd helped dry out the mud into crisp, blackened dirt.

Inside the ruin of what had been their dining hall, things were dry. The floor was wood, the tables were wood, and the debris from the ceiling was, for the most part, wood. Fires sprouted up with every step the demon took, and they began spreading rapidly. The demon didn't even notice, and the imps didn't seem to care. They were just clumps of ash pressed into a shape and given life anyway. Even if the fires did hurt them, new imps just sprouted out of their remains as soon as another imp showed up to barf a lump of charcoal into the pile.

Luke's feet kicked up clouds of ash and soot as he desperately fought off attacks coming from all sides. **[Area Denial]** was a lifesaver, far more useful than its component skills had ever been, but even the merged skill wasn't enough to stop hundreds of imps and a giant molten statue at the same time. The only good part of the whole situation was that the metal demon seemed to be focused exclusively on Luke.

He'd given up on keeping the imps out of the kitchen. Zea would have to defend herself, which meant they needed a new strategy. If he could lure the molten woman back out of the wreckage and into the open courtyard in the center of the lodge, he thought he could keep her occupied. Zea would need to fight a running battle while she escaped, hopefully with the one remaining servant still alive. Once she was gone, Luke could flee as well.

Fortunately, the demons didn't seem to be that smart. They were vicious and aggressive, but their tactics had been relatively straightforward and simple. The imps were especially dumb with their whole strategy of rushing right into the meat grinder and relying on their superior numbers and the ability to end-lessly continue spawning more of themselves.

Then again, it was kind of working for them. Luke had killed hundreds, maybe thousands of them in the last hour, and there was no shortage of new imps to take their places. His side, on the other hand, was down to just him, Zea, and a servant whose name he couldn't recall. Technically, Hakiro was probably still alive, but he'd left hours ago before the rains had let up. It sure seemed like the demons were winning when Luke considered how many people were dead.

"I need to lure this big demon away," Luke yelled to Zea. "You'll have to fight through the imps and get out the front gate if you can't get through the wall. I'll catch up with you later, but if we don't get out of this fire, we're going to die."

Without waiting for a response, and knowing she was too busy anyway since he could hear the sounds of fighting from the kitchen, Luke started moving back toward the courtyard. The imps kept coming, mostly in an effort to drive him back toward the molten demon, but **[Area Denial]** kept Luke safe from them. They did slow him down and forced him to go directly through areas that were actively on fire more than once.

All the while, the Amazonian giant chased after him, spreading more fire in her wake and destroying things with every brutal swing of her scepter. She was fast, but her attacks were clumsy, easy to predict. If he'd had a good way to hurt her, he would have said he could win this fight. Maybe if she didn't have all the imps backing her up, he could have come up with something.

Since his strategies mostly consisted of hitting things with a heavy metal stick until they stopped moving and that wasn't really working all that well, it was entirely possible he was just in an unwinnable confrontation. That was why he was focused so heavily on finding a way out. He knew that as soon as he got outside, **[Burst Step]** would be all he needed to escape. All he had to do was keep the demon busy until Zea and the servant were clear.

Luke broke free of the imps long enough to slip through the shattered wall and out under the open sky. The molten demon followed him immediately, of course, her scepter leading the way in a downward strike that cratered the ground Luke had been standing on. He dodged to one side and smacked her wrist with his mace.

He hadn't expected it to work since she hadn't reacted to any other attacks he'd made like a normal person would have, but in his mind, he'd hoped that the impact would force her to drop the weapon. Instead, all he got was a glob of hot metal stuck to his mace until he whipped it to the side and threw it clear.

The gouge he'd left in the demon's wrist instantly filled as orange glowing liquid metal rolled into it.

There had to be something he could do to slow her down. He swung his mace underhanded and kicked up a giant chunk of dirt at her, hoping it would help cool her down a bit. The dirt broke apart and blackened on her skin until it burned away to nothing, and the demon kept swinging her scepter at him like she hadn't even noticed.

Out of the corner of his eye, Luke saw Zea emerge from the kitchen. She was covered in ash and had burns on her arms, but she was still in the fight. The servant trailed along behind her, armed now with a broom held in both hands. A knife was stuck through her belt. Both weapons were useless against the demons, and it looked like the servant knew it. She practically cowered behind Zea, which would have been laughable given the difference in height, but the pile of charred corpses not thirty feet away ruined the mood.

Luke wanted to help clear out the imps, but that was the moment **[Life Surge]** gave out. All of a sudden, the demon's wild swings seemed to be moving a lot faster. Luke scrambled to stay ahead of her and succeeded mostly through liberal use of **[Burst Step]** to keep out of her range. Even that had its drawbacks though, since every time he used it, he landed in another pile of imps that were more than happy to take a break from vomiting up charcoal-colored rocks to attack him.

The giant bronze demon struck at him again, and this time when Luke tried to parry the swing, she threw him to the ground. Perhaps sensing weakness, her malevolent aura sharpened, and Luke felt dread worm its way through his guts.

[You have been afflicted by the following condition: Curse—Dream of Despair (8s).]

It was easier to cut through it this time, but it still slowed Luke down. The amount of effort it took to force himself to keep fighting was insane, and Luke honestly wasn't sure how much of his will to go on came from his urge to protect Zea and how much was sheer unbridled spite at this demon who was fucking with his head.

Just the knowledge that she was screwing with him, that this was temporary and he could break through it, was enough to keep him in the fight. Seconds ticked by while Luke struggled against both the demons and the magically inspired doubts plaguing his mind, but if the goal was just to survive for eight seconds, he could do that.

Pain flared across the side of his face as the molten demon backhanded him. Luke's feet left the ground, and the world spun around him until he crashed through a wall, and the desire to just lie there and give up was practically overwhelming. A few seconds later, his head cleared, and Luke leaped to his feet just as the first imp reached him.

Something was wrong. The molten demon had never hesitated to chase Luke down, and she was more than fast enough to catch up to him. By all rights, he should have been killed while he lay on his back with his head spinning. Instead, he had a nasty burn across the side of his face from where the molten metal had touched him, a crick in his neck, and a hell of a lot of bruising along his shoulders and back. Thankfully, he hadn't smashed into the wall with his head.

Through the haze of ash floating around the interior of the lodge, Luke saw Zea's arm swing forward and her whip cut through the air. It scored a line across the molten demon's face, but if that bothered the Amazonian woman at all, she didn't show it. The demon casually advanced two steps and swung her scepter down at Zea, who had already begun retreating as soon as her whip made contact.

She wasn't going to make it in time, not with her strength so low. She lacked the explosive speed a high strength stat could give her, and while her agility no doubt let her plot the exact course that scepter would take as it slammed down on her, she was helpless to do anything to stop it.

Luke needed **[Burst Step]** to give him more than it ever had. More speed. More distance. He *needed* to get between Zea and that scepter. The skill pushed through him and hurled his body forward, but it wouldn't cover half the distance, and Luke couldn't wait for it to be ready again, not even for a second. He pulled at it, demanded that it activate a second time.

He was fifteen feet away, flinging his body forward with a second use of **[Life Surge]** pushing him to his maximum speeds. The scepter came down, the feet between its molten shape and Zea's fragile body disappearing almost in slow motion to Luke's enhanced senses. He roared, hoping the sound would distract the demon, that she wouldn't follow through with her swing.

He was ten feet away, desperate to activate **[Burst Step]** again, desperate to intercept the strike. Zea started to turn, her own body slow to react to what she saw, nowhere near fast enough to escape the demon's reach. It wouldn't be enough.

He was five feet away, so close that he could smack the demon's weapon aside with a single step forward. All the momentum he had going for him would easily overpower the molten demon's strength. She was strong, but not so strong that she could resist him. But Luke needed to take that last step still.

The orange-glowing bronze metal connected with Zea's body and smashed her into the ground so hard that she bounced five feet back into the air and landed twenty feet away. In between her hitting the ground and her shooting back up, Luke's mace tore the demon's hand off at the wrist. The huge chunk of liquid metal lost its cohesion as it flew through the air and struck the outer wall of the lodge, right between kitchen and the trainers' rooms.

The enchantments sparked, trying to resist the damage, and started to fail. Luke noted that only distantly, the same way he saw the servant go down as dozens of imps descended on her. Those were distractions though because the only thing he cared about right now was seeing Zea standing back up.

Her body landed, bloody and broken, and flopped limply. Where her face had been was nothing but torn bone and cartilage and spilled-out brain matter. She was twenty feet away, and Luke, whose eyes could pick out a facial expression on someone half a mile from him, saw in perfect clarity.

Zea was dead.

Name	Luke Bennet	Zea Stenter
Level	45	35
XP	334827/337550	149301/157276
AP	122	4
Bloodline	SysAdmin III	None
Strength	61	7
Agility	70	30
Stamina	88	27
Perception	55	21
Skills	Area Denial (1)	Arcano Dynamics (2)
	Burst Step (1)	Bartering (2)
	Butchering (4)	Bloodline Purification Ritual (2)
	Consortium Standard (2)	Cadence (3)
	Deception (1)	Cold Reading (1)
	Detection (2)	Consortium Standard (2)
	Disguise (2)	Cooking (1)
	First Aid (1)	Dagger Mastery (1)
	Leatherworking (2)	Deception (1)
	Life Surge (2)	Disguise (2)
	Mace Mastery (5)	Engraving (4)
	Ostari (1)	First Aid (1)
	Power Strike (2)	Gem Cutting (1)
	Stealth (1)	Ghost Script (1)
	Survivalist (2)	Goldsmithing (2)
	Sword Mastery (2)	Keen Instincts (1)
	Tactical Foresight (2)	Lock Picking (1)
	Thalian (2)	Mana Manipulation (3)
	Torturer (1)	Mana Sight (3)
	Unarmed Martialist (4)	Mending (1)
	Wood Carving (1)	Metallurgy (1)
	Analyze (BL)	Neyardic (3)
	Remote Access (BL)	Ostari (1)
	XP Mask (BL)	Painting (1)
		Rune Forging (3)
		Sleight of Hand (1)
		Steady Hands (2)
		Stealth (2)
		Streetwise (2)
		Temperature Acclimation (2)
		Thalian (3)
		Whitesmithing (1)

CHAPTER 49

There was a single instant of perfectly crystallized and frozen time where Luke absorbed every last detail, everything from the crooked angle of Zea's neck to the scorched flesh across her torso. He could smell the stink of a torn-open body and taste the blood in the air, somehow sharper now even though there was just one more corpse among many.

Part of Luke wanted to scream, to deny it, to beg the gods to take it back. That part wanted to rush to Zea, to dump all his AP into healing magic right now and fix this. He didn't know if he had enough, but he had to try.

That part of him didn't care that there were hundreds of imps still in the lodge, all either attacking him, creating new imps, or burning down the wooden buildings. It didn't care that a demon in the shape of a ten-foot-tall statue of an Amazonian woman made of molten bronze stood behind him, already reforming her lost hand and scepter. It didn't even care about any of the other bodies in the courtyard.

As much as Luke wanted to fix this, to somehow bring Zea back, that wasn't his skill set. He wasn't a creator. He didn't mend broken things. Luke was a destroyer, good for violence and not much else. And he sure as hell had a good target to unleash his rage on now.

[Life Surge] still pushed his body to its peak. Luke could hear his heartbeat pounding in his ears now, so fast and so loud that it drowned out everything else. Slowly, at least it seemed to him, he turned around to face the demon who'd killed his best friend, a woman he loved even if he'd never said it out loud. Her face was as expressionless as always, uncaring about what she'd done.

And Luke stopped thinking rationally. He stopped trying to plan, and he stopped trying to strategize. He didn't care if he got hurt. He didn't care if he made it out alive. He had one goal and one goal only.

He was going to kill that fucking bitch of a demon.

With a roar, Luke leaped at her and brought his mace down in a two-handed **[Power Strike]**. It tore through her chest, ripping out a chunk of living metal flesh to splash against his legs. Distantly, he felt the burning pinpricks of heat strike his skin as it burned through the cloth of his pants. Luke didn't care about that. What he did care about was that the attack hadn't gone as deep as he wanted.

He had a fix for that though. It was probably long overdue anyway. Luke dumped 30 AP into his strength, bringing it up to 91. For a split second, his entire body flashed through with pain, like a head-to-toe muscle spasm. Once upon a time, that would have been enough to leave him on the ground weeping. That day wasn't today.

Luke whipped the mace around in a full circle as **[Area Denial]** triggered to blast apart two imps coming at him from behind, then ended his spin to hammer the mace into the Amazonian demon again. This time, he struck her knee hard enough to tear off a leg. The demon fell down onto the stump, but she lunged out with her hand and wrapped it around Luke's arm.

It was big enough to cover him from shoulder to elbow, and his shirt immediately flashed into flames. An instant later, the material burned away, revealing bubbling red flesh between the demon's fingers. Luke brought his mace around one-handed and smacked it down on her wrist. The impact vibrated through the liquid metal and sent a fresh round of pain into him, but it didn't loosen the demon's grip.

So Luke did it again, only this time with **[Power Strike]** backing the swing up. He stumbled backward as the demon's hand was torn free and reverted to liquid metal. It splashed down to the ground near his feet except for the bits that clung to his arm. Those pieces burned down into his skin, in some spots all the way to the bone, but **[Life Surge]** was already working to repair the arm enough to make it functional. Until then, Luke would fight one-handed.

Luke wasn't the only one able to recover from an injury though. The demon had grown a new leg and was even now generating a new hand, but she was also noticeably shorter now. It wasn't by a lot, only half a foot, and some distant corner in the back of Luke's mind recognized it as a path to victory, but all he cared about at the moment was hitting her again.

So that was what he did. **[Power Strike]** after **[Power Strike]** rained down on the demon from every angle. He used **[Burst Step]** when he needed to slip around her or when too many imps started trying to pile up on him, and one hammer blow at a time, he ripped away the metal that made up her body. Soon, the entire courtyard was coated in rapidly cooling droplets of bronze.

The demon kept reshaping her body to regain her lost shape as more and more mass disappeared. If Luke could have kept it up, he would have beaten her into nothing more than specks of metal on the ground. But **[Life Surge]** ran out well before he reached that point, with the demon still solidly over eight feet in height, and he stumbled to a stop. His mace, now warped and beaten from the abuse he'd put it through, glowed hot and blistered the skin on his palm.

"No," he growled. "I'm not done with you."

20 more AP went into stamina. The pain receded slightly, and the weight of his mace was light in his hands again. He rushed forward as the demon screeched and met his charge. Her scepter smacked down across his bare back at the same time his **[Power Strike]** slammed into her hip. He didn't quite rip entirely through her pelvis, but Luke tore out a chunk of metal big enough to sever her entire leg.

The demon didn't even try to retain her balance. She just tipped herself forward, arms outspread to keep him from escaping, and dropped down directly on top of Luke. The body slam brought him to his knees, and his entire body screamed in agony as liquid metal held in shape only through demonic magic pressed down on him.

It was too much. The weight. The heat. The pain. The exhaustion. That dark presence that hung in the air urged him to give up, to take the easy way out, to just lay down and die. Luke's lips formed into a snarl as the image of Zea's broken body flashed through his mind, and he triggered **[Life Surge]** again.

The strain of three uses in less than five minutes threatened to tear him apart. The skill danced through his body like lightning, burning through him just like the demon attacking his flesh, but Luke held on against it and heaved upward. The demon rose an inch, then two, then shot two feet straight up, her body folded around Luke's outstretched arm as he rose to his feet and threw her to the side.

Vicious burns covered his face, shoulders, arms, chest, and back. More burns showed across his thighs and feet. In fact, the only part of him that wasn't red or black was his shins and his lower stomach where they'd been protected by the rest of his body being on top of them. He didn't care.

With one hand, he scooped up the rod of red-and-gray intertwined metal that used to be his mace. The head had been completely melted away, and the haft itself was bent in three different spots. The end was nothing more than strips of ragged metal, and for all its self-healing properties, Luke didn't think it was going to come back from this fight. It couldn't handle his new strength, and the nature of its opponent pouring more and more heat into it only compounded that issue. Luke didn't care about that either.

He brought the rod of metal up into the air, then slammed it down on the demon's skull. Then he did it again, and again, and again. An imp leaped at his face, but Luke caught it with his free hand. Without interrupting the rhythm of his strikes, Luke crushed its skull in his hand and cast the body aside where it burst into a cloud of ash as it hit the ground.

Luke was so focused on his task that he didn't realize what was happening at first, not until the molten demon's malevolent aura sharpened and spiked into his brain again. Luke tore through it in a second, but that was all the time the demon needed to get away from him. She was fully reformed now except for her head, and also only about six feet tall. Close to half her body was scattered across the lodge.

She stood across from him, not twenty feet away, while the imps all rushed toward her. They climbed over top of one another to get there, where they collapsed into ash that swirled around until it formed a huge circle in the air. The interior was pitch-black, and as soon as it solidified, she took a step backward into it.

"No!" Luke screamed.

[**Burst Step**] propelled him across the courtyard. The broken haft of his mace came down as he slashed the air where the demon had been, but there was nothing there now, just a cloud of ash drifting through the air and fat raindrops that he hadn't even realized were coming down until now.

Everything was quiet.

Luke swayed on his feet as [**Life Surge**] gave out again. "No," he repeated, his voice a whisper. "No, you won't . . . You won't get away. I won't let you. Not . . ."

He fell face-first to the ground, and everything went dark.

It was the pain that woke him. Without the heady mixture of pure adrenaline and [**Life Surge**] to insulate him from it, Luke could feel every injury. The burns still covered his body, a long way from being healed. He was running on nothing but fumes after burning through his stored calories with a triple [**Life Surge**], and his mind was a wrung-out dishrag.

Cataloging all of that took a second, then his eyes snapped open. "Zea," he said, forcing himself upright.

The rain had doused the fires and pushed all the ash in the air down to the ground, where it had mixed in to turn the mud gray. Luke sloshed through it, barely upright, until he found Zea's body. It was just as he remembered it except her clothes were soaked through now.

Luke fell to his knees in front of her corpse and stared at it dully. He hadn't protected her, hadn't even avenged her. The demon who'd killed Zea had escaped, and Luke had no way to track her down. All that was left was a cold body that didn't go up past the nose.

"System," Luke said.

"Yes?" System asked as he appeared.

"Do I need to do something special to preserve her body for when I revive her?"

His family was all long gone, and while Luke hadn't given much thought to it, he supposed the system would create new bodies for them. Zea already had a body, and if she was going to come back in it, he felt he should probably do his best to keep it in good shape.

"You cannot resurrect her," System told her.

Luke shot the apparition a sharp look. "What do you mean? Why wouldn't I be able to? The whole point of this journey was to bring a bunch of dead people back to life."

"Your family is not native to Aros, and the Pantheon holds no dominion over your souls," System said. "Zea is. Her soul is with Zixin, the goddess of death. Unless she agrees to release Zea's soul back into the world, true resurrection is impossible. The closest you could achieve is a homunculus of her."

Luke stared down at Zea's body silently. That was it then. She was really gone. After everything they'd gone through, this was the end for her, and there was nothing he could do to change that.

Tears mingled with the rain running down his face as he sat there. His body ached, especially his left arm where the demon had grabbed him, but Luke ignored it. Slowly, like a machine struggling to get moving, he rose to his feet and picked a spot to dig Zea's grave.

Name	Luke Bennet
Level	45
XP	334827/337550
AP	72
Bloodline	SysAdmin III
Strength	91
Agility	70
Stamina	108
Perception	55
Skills	Area Denial (1)
	Burst Step (1)
	Butchering (4)
	Consortium Standard (2)
	Deception (1)
	Detection (2)
	Disguise (2)
	First Aid (1)
	Leatherworking (2)
	Life Surge (2)
	Mace Mastery (5)
	Ostari (1)
	Power Strike (2)
	Stealth (1)
	Survivalist (2)
	Sword Mastery (2)
	Tactical Foresight (2)
	Thalian (2)
	Torturer (1)
	Unarmed Martialist (4)
	Wood Carving (1)
	Analyze (BL)
	Remote Access (BL)
	XP Mask (BL)

CHAPTER 50

The only good thing about the demon attack was that a lot of imps showed up and killed a lot of spiders, so many in fact that Luke barely saw one the entire time he was at the ruined lodge. With the overhead mesh gone, the fact that the walls were intact no longer mattered. Spiders began to show up but not in large numbers, and most of them were only level 3 or 4 at most.

That gave Luke some time that he desperately needed, both to recover and to get his own affairs in order. The burns were healing but slowly, and Luke had completely cleaned out the bag with all their food. There were no other supplies at the lodge, mostly because the initial attack had struck just as everyone was getting ready to leave. All the luggage was piled up in the yard between buildings and had been destroyed in the fighting. Zea had been carrying the travel bags she and Luke used, and they'd been the only thing to survive.

So Luke had one meal's worth of food, and not even a full one after his ill-advised use of **[Life Surge]**. He was sorely tempted to use the skill again, just to try to speed up the healing on his ruined body, but without another source of food, he didn't want to risk it. It was too bad there really wasn't much of anything but various bugs in the forest.

Luke dug one grave with his bare hands at the base of an old oak tree not too far from the lodge. Lacking anything remotely resembling a shovel, he scooped great handfuls of dirt out of the ground until the grave was deeper than he was tall. Only then did he place Zea's body in it. He had no coffin or box of any sort, but he supposed it didn't much matter at this point.

After he finished burying her, Luke drove the remains of his mace into the ground as a sort of headstone. "I guess this is it," he said softly as he sat next to the fresh-turned earth of Zea's grave and tried to ignore the itchy sensation of raw flesh scabbing over. "I'm going to miss you. I . . . Doing this without you just feels wrong, you know?"

He patted the bag with all her enchanting supplies and equipment in it. "I don't even know what to do with this. Do I keep it? Do I sell it? Is that disrespectful? I can't use it myself, and I don't know what any of it's worth. How mad would you be if I let someone swindle me on selling it?"

Luke held up her whip and shook it. "Hell, this thing is already finished. I've watched you use it a hundred times. No idea how to turn it on, and I'd probably end up cutting my toes off if I managed to do it accidentally."

There were other things in the bag, some engraving equipment, a set of what looked to him like fine-tipped paintbrushes, the foldout worktable she used so often, and copious amounts of notes that looked like Zea had written them herself. There were also various rocks, teeth, bits of wood, leather, and rolled-up blank scrolls made of flexible paper that was about ten times thicker than normal paper.

At the bottom of the bag was a white stone, perfectly round and about the size of a robin's egg. It was flecked with red dots and hung from a silver chain that had been woven into a sort of net. Luke vaguely recognized it as the last thing he'd seen her working on, though it didn't look like she'd managed to finish it. The chain itself had tiny runes on it, but the stone was untouched.

With a heavy sigh, Luke hung it around his neck. "Something to remind me of you," he told the grave.

He should have bought **[XP Reset]** and left her back on the western continent where she was safe, except of course that she wasn't, not with the inquisitors and the church looking for him. He could have put her on a different ship, one heading back south. That could have worked if Lath hadn't interfered.

It was too late for regrets and what-ifs now. She was gone, and unlike his own family, he couldn't bring her back without the permission of a goddess who, presumably, wanted him destroyed. Most of Luke's dealings to date had been with the worshippers of Hestoc or Dar, but he had no reason to think any of the rest of the Pantheon would be better predisposed toward him.

The only thing Luke could do now was avenge Zea's death. He needed a new weapon, but he had a good idea where to find one. Whether the Shansakun family would cooperate was debatable, but considering he'd be using it to help defend the city, he hoped they'd at least loan him the weapon.

If he was really lucky, the metal demon would be there too. He'd like to kill her as quickly as possible. This time he wasn't going to let her get away. Depending on how cooperative the Shansakuns were, he had his eye on some skill upgrades to help him make sure he finished the demon off.

It was hard to make himself move, both because of the burns that still covered his entire body and because he just wasn't ready to leave Zea's grave yet. Then the first spider showed up. It was one of those crystal-fang widow-makers, and while it made no move to attack him, Luke soon spotted three more joining it.

Slowly, he stood up and hefted the one bag he was taking with him. It was all but empty except for his magical clothes that would regrow themselves, the remainder of their money, and some camping equipment. The bag with the rest of Zea's enchanting supplies went back to the lodge to the room they'd shared. The spiders could guard it from looters.

Once he was done, he followed the trail west back toward Heishin. The spiders, perhaps sensing somehow that he was leaving, let him go in peace.

If Luke had been in good condition, he would have run all the way to Heishin and been there within four hours. As he currently was, that was hardly an option. What he really needed more than anything else was food to feed to **[Life Surge]**.

Nothing presented itself during his first day of travel, but on the second day, Luke felt a spark of XP a few hundred feet off the side of the road. He dutifully turned to follow it after determining it had come from some type of warren in a small copse of trees surrounded by what looked like abandoned farmland. After crossing a few hundred feet of fallow fields, he found a hole in the ground under a mess of roots that was a foot in diameter.

Whatever was in there was in no mood to come out, perhaps because it could sense Luke's XP as well and knew it was outclassed. He judged it to be around level 20 anyway, hardly strong enough to be a threat under normal circumstances. With no weapon and still badly injured, Luke suspected it would be a different story.

He technically still had a knife, but after he'd destroyed his mace, he was hesitant to use it in a fight. 91 strength was a lot of force to bear on a thin piece of steel, even if it had been alchemically treated. If that snapped, a lot of things would get a lot harder unless he could find a good replacement.

Luke felt like he needed a break anyway, so he sat down right over top of the warren, turned on **[XP Mask]**, and hoped the animal nearby would be stupid enough to come out and attack him now that he felt so weak. If that didn't work, he supposed he could go in after it. He didn't exactly love the idea, but he needed something to eat.

An hour went by, and he was starting to feel pretty dumb about the whole idea, at least until he heard the sound of claws scraping against dirt and saw a whiskered snout stick out of the hole. Luke froze in place and waited to see if the rest of the animal would appear. After a few exploratory sniffs, the head appeared, followed swiftly by a long body. **[Analyze]** told him that it was a cinder-fur weasel, notable only for the fact that its coat was the red of dying embers and that it could shake its body to release a swarm of painfully hot sparks.

It wasn't an enemy Luke was eager to face given his own burns. Nothing made a burn hurt worse than more heat. But there was a simple solution to that problem.

Luke activated **[Burst Step]** to close the distance and kicked the weasel in the head hard enough to shatter its skull. It dropped straight down to the ground, and he hauled the rest of the body out with one hand wrapped around its paw.

"Come on, let's get you skinned and carved up," Luke told the body.

[Butchering] and **[Leatherworking]** had plenty to say about how Luke handled the dead weasel, and after he'd gotten it prepped, he lit a small fire using some loose bark and sticks as tinder. Luke pulled out all the pans, sighed, and said, "Fine, you win. I fought it as long as I could, but I give up. This is for you."

Luke spent 1 AP on rank 1 **[Cooking]** before he made his meal. It was perhaps the first time he'd made something edible, though the meat was too hot, too dry, and too tough. It was, at the very least, not burnt. That was a small improvement, but it was a step in the right direction.

After Luke had eaten his fill, he triggered **[Life Surge]** and just spent a moment enjoying the lessening of pain. The burns scabbed over thicker, and various fluids of indeterminate viscosity pushed their way out, staining his clothes from the inside and making Luke scowl in annoyance. Everything got crusty, but by the time the skill ran out, he was feeling better.

That wasn't to say that the pain was gone or that he was fully healed. Even with his stamina now in the triple digits, his injuries were so bad that it wasn't going to be an overnight process getting back into fighting shape. All his traveling wasn't helping matters, but Luke couldn't afford to sit around doing nothing right now.

He ate more of the weasel he'd killed and wished Zea had been there to share it with him. Then he found a stream to clean himself up in and hung his clothes to dry. After a few hours of rest, he packed up as much of the meat as he could wrap in his shirt and started walking again. He had a long way to go to get back to Heishin, and he was eager to finish the trip.

He walked all through the night, stopped twice for a break, and used **[Life Surge]** again the next morning. Even that wasn't enough to get him back up to 100 percent, though the scabs started flaking and falling off. The scars left behind were . . . impressive, though not in a good way. They'd cover almost his entire body once he was healed, and Luke had some concerns about a loss of flexibility.

If that happened, he supposed he had enough gold to see a healer about it. For now, his goal was to move faster. The sun had just risen, and he ate his leftovers as he walked. Once they were all gone, he started to jog. He had every intention of reaching the city by noon.

Name	Luke Bennet
Level	45
XP	335286/337550
AP	71
Bloodline	SysAdmin III
Strength	91
Agility	70
Stamina	108
Perception	55
Skills	Area Denial (1)
	Burst Step (1)
	Butchering (4)
	Consortium Standard (2)
	Cooking (1)
	Deception (1)
	Detection (2)
	Disguise (2)
	First Aid (1)
	Leatherworking (2)
	Life Surge (2)
	Mace Mastery (5)
	Ostari (1)
	Power Strike (2)
	Stealth (1)
	Survivalist (2)
	Sword Mastery (2)
	Tactical Foresight (2)
	Thalian (2)
	Torturer (1)
	Unarmed Martialist (4)
	Wood Carving (1)
	Analyze (BL)
	Remote Access (BL)
	XP Mask (BL)

CHAPTER 51

Luke had never seen an entire city burn, but there had been some truly massive wildfires back on Earth that left the air smoky miles and miles away. The only question in Luke's mind once he started smelling the smoke was whether any part of the city still stood. He could easily picture tens of thousands of imps descending on the city, their numbers growing at an exponential rate as more and more of it burned down until there was nothing left but ashes and demons.

That wasn't the state of Heishin, fortunately. The city's walls were in bad shape, at least on the east side, but they still stood. Luke got through without any sort of incident, though he could clearly see the looks people gave him behind his back. If he hadn't been so tired, he might have made some effort to find a mirror so he could see just how bad the scars were, but he was almost afraid to look. Being able to feel them all over his face was bad enough.

If the skin on his head looked anything like his arms and legs, it was no wonder people were cringing at the sight of him. Then he got into the city itself and found he wasn't the only one recovering from massive burns. There were plenty of people working on clearing away the husks of burned-down homes who had their own networks of webbed scars visible.

For all the holes Luke had had poked into him over the last year or so, he didn't have much in the way of scars. He wondered if burns were different or if his other injuries had healed so fast that they just hadn't left anything. Maybe in a few days, the scars would start to smooth out too.

The east and north sides of the city seemed to have the worst of the damage, though Luke didn't take the time to wander around. The streets were choked with debris, and nobody seemed to want to clean it up. Perhaps everyone who'd lived in that district of the city had died in one of the attacks. Even then, Luke was surprised that the city was just left in that condition. It was a prime breeding ground for more imps, if nothing else.

The Shansakun family compound was still standing, but huge chunks of its wall were missing, and Luke could see that quite a few of the buildings had burned down. Unlike most of the rest of the district, there were at least thirty people working diligently to clear away the mess.

"Stop right there," someone said. Luke looked over at a man in his early twenties wearing armor covered in scorch marks and holding a two-handed sword in front of him. A quick use of **[Analyze]** revealed the man to only be level 24, which made him either extraordinarily brave or incredibly stupid to get in Luke's way.

"What do you want?" Luke asked.

"No one is allowed into the estate right now," the man said.

Luke's brow furled as he looked the man over. He wasn't wearing one of the servant masks, and his armor looked nothing like anything Luke had seen from anyone else during his initial visit. "Do you . . . You know . . . Do you work here?" he asked.

"I've been contracted to guard this area, yes. I can't allow you to loiter around here."

The man was a mercenary. That made sense. The Shansakuns were low on man power now, but they still had plenty of money. Luke could go right through him, but since he was planning on borrowing one of their sacred relics, he felt like a bit of diplomacy might be the better course.

"They're expecting me," Luke said. "My name is Luke Bennet. I was part of a group that went to the Shansakun training grounds. A messenger was dispatched to summon us all back. Hakiro should have already arrived."

"I don't know anything about that," the man said, but he sounded less sure of himself now.

"That's fine. Can you just escort me to someone who can make a decision? Whoever is in charge of coordinating the security, maybe?"

The temp waffled a bit before eventually realizing that Luke was trying to help and agreeing to take him to someone higher up the chain. He took Luke down the street to where the main gate used to sit. It was nothing more than some scorched hinges and splinters of black wood sticking out of the frame now.

Luke got handed off to another set of mercenary guards, both around level 30 this time, who took him to a pavilion that had been erected at some point after the fighting had ended, judging by how clean it was compared to everything else. It didn't even have that smoky stink embedded in the cloth.

He was forced to wait there while someone went to the main house, still standing somehow despite so many other buildings being nothing but piles of blackened timber. About ten minutes later, Hakiro came to meet him.

"Where's everyone else?" he asked softly, probably already knowing the answer but dreading having to hear it confirmed.

"Demons attacked the lodge right around dawn, as soon as the rain let up. No one . . ." Luke's voice hitched there. "No one else made it."

"Come with me," Hakiro said as he started back toward the main house. "Everyone is going to want to know what happened."

It turned out Fujoka had died in the first attack, and rather than replacing him directly, the family Council of Elders were trying to rule by committee. They'd divvied up responsibilities among themselves through some method that Luke couldn't figure out. Each one was obviously trying to interfere with decisions that in reality had little to do with their own areas but that they tried to justify anyway.

That was the impression Luke got, at least. Mentally, he stamped the word *politician* on each of their foreheads and then did his best to ignore them while they bickered. A very large part of him wanted to walk out right now. Their posturing while they tried to negotiate with one another was of no interest to him. The only thing that kept him in his seat was that he hadn't gotten a chance to ask for his favor yet, and pissing them off was a surefire way to make sure they said no.

The longer the meeting went on, the more Luke started to think asking was a bad idea. If he asked for his father's mace, they would probably say no. And then when he took it anyway, they'd know he'd done it. They might even make it harder to steal it if they knew he wanted it. About the only thing Luke was certain of after an hour of sitting there while the elders of the Shansakun family argued with one another about the best course of action was that there wasn't a single person there who wouldn't try to squeeze some sort of concession from Luke in exchange for letting him get his hands on his father's mace.

Luke thought that talking to Valera directly about her collection might result in a better outcome. She'd either be more inclined to help because of who he was, or she would be the person most strongly against it because of how much she treasured those relics. Luke wasn't sure which way she'd lean, but he figured he had better odds with her than he did with the council.

After another half an hour, during which time Luke grew progressively more and more annoyed, the council meeting finally ended. Free at last, Luke and Hakiro beat a hasty retreat out of the building and into the smoke-stained sunlight of the courtyard.

"Is it always like that with those guys?" Luke asked.

"Where you give a three-minute report and then have to sit there for an hour just in case they want to ask a follow-up question, but they inevitably move on to other topics that have nothing to do with you and still won't let you leave? Yep, that's normal. Never thought I'd miss Great-Uncle Fujoka, but the council sure proved me wrong. I really wish they'd hurry up and figure out who's going to take over the day-to-day stuff."

They kept walking while they talked, though Luke wasn't sure exactly where they were going. "I'm sorry about your friends at the lodge," Luke said. "The big metal demon . . . I couldn't protect them."

"I have no idea how you're even alive right now," Hakiro told him. "That demon has killed hundreds of defenders between levels 35 and 45 already. Each time it's retreated, it took a group of level 50s working to push it back."

"I spent a bunch of AP on strength and stamina," Luke admitted. "Sorry, looks like I need two levels now instead of one before I can get [XP Cycle]."

Hakiro shrugged. "Barely out of reach and well out of reach both mean the same thing in the end."

"Do you think that demon will come back?" Luke asked.

She'd taken several runs at Heishin, according to the message they'd received, but the city was still standing. Luke hoped that meant she would try again and that with the dragon-bone-and-whatever mace his father had left behind in his hands, Luke could kill her next time they met.

"If we're lucky, no. But . . . Probably, yes. At this point I don't think anyone is expecting the demons to just give up. From what I understand, the only reason Heishin wasn't razed to the ground was the weather. Something about the rain . . . I don't know. It doesn't seem like it should be enough to do more than inconvenience them, does it?"

"Maybe they can't make new imps out of wet ash," Luke said.

"Maybe. Either way, I just hope the demons stay away long enough for the Imperial reinforcements to reach the city."

"I didn't know we were getting reinforcements," Luke said. He wondered if they'd make much of a difference. Anything that increased his odds of killing the demon woman made of molten bronze was a welcome change in his mind. He'd prefer to kill the demon himself, but he'd still be fine with it if someone else finished her off. The important part was that she was dead.

Luke looked around and asked, "By the way, where are we going?"

"There aren't enough rooms for everybody, so we've got some tents set up at the training grounds," Hakiro explained. "We'll get one assigned to you to use, and hopefully I'll be able to tell you how the family wants to proceed with our deal by tomorrow."

"About that," Luke said. "I actually don't need any of that stuff anymore. Most of it was for . . . It was for Zea. And she's . . ."

Luke trailed off, unable to make himself say it out loud. Hakiro seemed to understand. "What do you want to do now?" the swordsman asked.

"I want to kill that demon," Luke said immediately. "After that, I guess get a few more levels, do the thing for your brother and whoever else needs it, and then I'll leave. I need to keep going south."

"There will be more demons there," Hakiro warned. "You don't even seem to have a weapon anymore."

"Well, about that," Luke began. "I kind of destroyed my old mace fighting a demon made of superheated metal. It was supposed to repair itself, but there wasn't really much left of it after the fight was over."

"I imagine not," Hakiro said. "We should be able to source a replacement, though I can't promise it'll be as strong as the one you lost."

"Thing is, my strength it up to 91 now," Luke said. "I was hoping you'd let me borrow my father's mace."

Name	Luke Bennet
Level	45
XP	335286/337550
AP	71
Bloodline	SysAdmin III
Strength	91
Agility	70
Stamina	108
Perception	55
Skills	Area Denial (1)
	Burst Step (1)
	Butchering (4)
	Consortium Standard (2)
	Cooking (1)
	Deception (1)
	Detection (2)
	Disguise (2)
	First Aid (1)
	Leatherworking (2)
	Life Surge (2)
	Mace Mastery (5)
	Ostari (1)
	Power Strike (2)
	Stealth (1)
	Survivalist (2)
	Sword Mastery (2)
	Tactical Foresight (2)
	Thalian (2)
	Torturer (1)
	Unarmed Martialist (4)
	Wood Carving (1)
	Analyze (BL)
	Remote Access (BL)
	XP Mask (BL)

CHAPTER 52

Hakiro stopped walking and asked, "You're serious?"

"Yup," Luke said.

"I can't see any circumstance in which that would happen. I am having trouble picturing a scenario where you're even allowed to touch one of those artifacts, let alone given possession of it to use in actual battle."

"Hmm. Well, the way I see things is that half of this city has already been burned down, and it's just a matter of time until the next attack. The rain is already slowing down, so I'm thinking sometime later today, yeah?"

"Probably," Hakiro agreed. "But that's not going to be enough to convince anyone."

Luke shrugged. "Okay, well, if that's how you feel, then I guess I'll go buy the best I can afford and just keep on heading south. I've got other stuff to do anyway."

Luke had no plans on leaving Heishin until he got a crack at that demon again. As long as the city was still standing and the imps kept showing up, he'd be in the area. There was no reason for Hakiro or anyone else associated with his family to know that, however. Luke might not have learned much about negotiations from Zea, but he knew that much.

"I'm sure we can find something for you that you can use effectively at your current level of strength without handing out one of my family's most valuable possessions," Hakiro said.

"Mmm. Well, I guess let's see what you come up with," Luke said. It wasn't that he doubted such weapons existed, but given this country's weird obsession with all things sword and the apparent cultural disdain for maces in particular,

Luke would bet that even if half the city hadn't been destroyed, it would have been a tall order to find someone who would be persuaded to make a mace strong enough for him to effectively use. He doubted there was one already crafted and ready to purchase at any weapon shop within a hundred miles.

"I'll put in a requisition to our quartermaster as soon as we get you settled in," Hakrio promised. "Uh . . . Maybe get you on the list to see a healer too."

"I wouldn't say no, but I don't know what they could do at this point. It's mostly just scars," Luke said. He'd avoided looking in too many windows on his way through the city, not that there were many left by this point.

"A bit of healing can smooth that out. It might not go away completely, but you're going to have some reduced flexibility the way you are now. Best to get it fixed as soon as possible."

Hakiro led Luke to a training yard that had been overtaken by row upon row of tents. There were at least a hundred, though not all were occupied. They found the end of the line, and Luke claimed that empty space as his own. Considering how little he had in the way of worldly possessions, there wasn't much to do but hang the little placard that declared the tent occupied and then get out of the rain.

Once he was left on his own, Luke checked the progress of his regenerating clothes. They were about halfway toward being a full shirt and pants again, meaning they were nowhere near ready, and he was stuck in his current outfit.

It was too bad the estate was in shambles. The closest to luxury Luke was getting right now was the tent to keep the rain off him and a cauldron set up under a square of canvas for people to fetch a meal from nearby. From what he could tell, they were bringing their own bowls and spoons.

He had something from his cooking supplies in his backpack he could use, and he supposed a meal wouldn't go amiss. If nothing else, it would be more fuel for **[Life Surge]** to try to get him fully back into fighting shape.

Luke sighed and started digging through the pack.

It was sometime after midnight when the weather changed. Luke was dozing in his tent using his backpack as a pillow when he noticed the sudden absence of raindrops slapping against the canvas roof. He still hadn't been given a weapon to fight with, so he hoped the fact that the clouds were drifting out to sea didn't signal an impending demon attack.

Someone out on the walls started yelling.

"Goddamn it," Luke muttered.

No one was moving in the camp yet, but that wasn't surprising. Most of the people he'd used **[Analyze]** on had come back in the low to mid-20s for level range, and almost nobody had a perception above 30. It would probably take a few minutes for the alarm to make its way off the walls and into the city.

Luke jogged past a row of tents to where the people in charge had sat up their own command tent. It was about twenty times bigger than the one Luke had been lying in, but considering it had lights and furniture inside, as well as six people, Luke supposed it needed to be.

"Hey, just thought you should know there's some yelling on the walls. Might be nothing, but it stopped raining a bit ago," Luke said as he poked his head through the flap that functioned as the command tent's door.

All six of the men and women inside gaped at him, but he was gone again before anyone could say anything. The quartermaster was set up in one of the few buildings that had survived, and if Luke wasn't getting a replacement mace, he needed something to fight with.

The door was locked when Luke got there. Banging on it didn't summon anyone from the inside, and Luke was pretty sure that was because the building was empty. If there was a quartermaster, he was the quietest person ever. After a minute of frustration, Luke turned away and looked around for someone who could help.

Horns started sounding to the north.

Luke sighed and walked away. Hakiro was somewhere on the property, probably in the main house, and he'd promised Luke a weapon. If he couldn't deliver on that, well, Luke had his own backup plan. Things would likely be getting very hectic soon, and Luke wasn't about to risk his life fighting back demonic invaders bare-handed.

Luke's efforts were thwarted almost immediately when the call to arms started going up around the estate. Torches were lit and placed at strategic points every hundred or so feet so that those who hadn't invested heavily in perception could still see. Some warriors started strapping on armor and scooping up shields. Others lined up to pull spears off of long racks that had been set up in place of the stew cauldron once dinner was over.

Officers ran around, calling out orders and trying to pull people into formations, and in all the chaos, Luke was ignored. He was a stranger here, unattached to any particular group, and everyone was too busy preparing. Other than finding a place to secure his backpack if he didn't want it hanging off his shoulders while he fought and obtaining a mace to fight with, Luke didn't have anything to do except wait for the first demons to show up.

He watched the warriors get into place, each group taking up a position to surround the main house with shield bearers at the front and spearmen behind them. None of them were that high a level, and all of them seemed to be low-ranking members of the family, if they were a part at all. Only the officers had swords and masks that didn't cover their whole faces.

The gaps in their ranks were filled with mercenaries who were incredibly easy to spot due to the different style of armor. Every single one of them, down to the last man, had a sword either in their hand or strapped somewhere to their body. Luke tried not to roll his eyes at the sight.

Unfortunately for him, the ring of defenders was circled around the building that held all his father's old equipment, which meant he wouldn't be sneaking in to steal anything prior to the fight starting. Luke noted with a bitter laugh that absolutely no one made a move to leave the estate grounds and help any of the other people living in the city.

Then the first imp appeared. It was sitting on top of the charred remnants of the obstacle course, and Luke only spotted it because it opened its mouth to spew out a charcoal nugget and revealed a flash of red flames coming from the back of its throat.

Soon enough, there were dozens more imps creeping in from the darkness. The alarm went up, and a contingent of archers Luke hadn't seen before rushed around from the far side of the main building to attack the imps. Arrows peppered the little demons, killing many, but nowhere near fast enough to keep up with the reinforcements. Not even counting the imps that had spawned right inside the estate, thousands more were pouring over what was left of the walls.

"And I still don't have a fucking weapon," Luke muttered. Hakiro had utterly and completely failed to procure anything for him. The best Luke could do was to break off a piece of wood from one of the nearby buildings and be extremely gentle with it. The first time he put his strength into a blow, any makeshift club he was using was going to shatter into a thousand pieces.

He'd be better off with his hands and feet.

The imps advanced through the darkness and clashed with the first line of defense. Luke had a few seconds to watch the shield bearers attempt to throw the demons back with some success while the spearmen stabbed at them. After that, he had to defend himself from all sides.

Two hours into the latest assault on the city, little had changed from Luke's perspective. The demons themselves were an endless flood, one that Luke suspected would have overwhelmed Heishin even if there had been twice the number of humans living there. The refugees made no difference, or maybe they made things worse by clogging up the streets and making it harder for the soldiers to effectively move about.

Either way, Luke had precious little reason to stay with the Shansakun family to defend them, and he'd quickly abandoned their estate to try to protect the families hiding in the city itself. He didn't feel like he'd succeeded much in that goal, but there were probably dozens of families only alive now because of his intervention.

Of course, while he'd saved them, hundreds of other families had died. If the demons themselves hadn't gotten those people, the spreading fires caught them instead. In some ways, the flames were worse than the imps.

Despite his best efforts, Luke saw no sign of the molten metal demon. He'd heard that she was somewhere in the city from eavesdropping on soldiers, but each time he made it to the spot the demon had last been sighted, she'd already moved on.

He was chasing one such sighting when he found himself near the Shansakun estate again. Things were not going well for the defenders, and it looked like the main building had caught on fire multiple times. Those fires had been extinguished somehow, but not before doing an enormous amount of damage to the roof and west wall.

The bodies of the dead were piled up while the living fought on with no end in sight. Luke thought that perhaps he should do something, but before he could, he spotted a group of imps swarming about twenty people trying to flee down the streets.

[Burst Step] got him halfway there, and Luke sprinted the last hundred feet to crash into the first imp. It burst to ash under his heel as he stomped down on it, and he spun to snatch another imp off the head of a little girl no more than ten who was screaming in terror and pain as her hair went up in flames.

Sadly, this wasn't the first time he'd dealt with this scenario, and it wouldn't be the last tonight. Luke kept working mechanically until all the imps had been killed, then left the adults of the group to care for the wounded and moved on.

Pain twinged in his arm, right where the molten demon had grabbed him a few days ago. It was so unexpected that Luke was almost caught off guard by a trio of imps that rushed out through a nearby window at him.

"What the hell?" Luke said to himself as he tried to flex the arm after killing the demons. It felt . . . hot, like liquid metal under his skin. But he'd healed all that damage already. There shouldn't have been anything there at all.

Name	Luke Bennet
Level	45
XP	335286/337550
AP	71
Bloodline	SysAdmin III
Strength	91
Agility	70
Stamina	108
Perception	55
Skills	Area Denial (1)
	Burst Step (1)
	Butchering (4)
	Consortium Standard (2)
	Cooking (1)
	Deception (1)
	Detection (2)
	Disguise (2)
	First Aid (1)
	Leatherworking (2)
	Life Surge (2)
	Mace Mastery (5)
	Ostari (1)
	Power Strike (2)
	Stealth (1)
	Survivalist (2)
	Sword Mastery (2)
	Tactical Foresight (2)
	Thalian (2)
	Torturer (1)
	Unarmed Martialist (4)
	Wood Carving (1)
	Analyze (BL)
	Remote Access (BL)
	XP Mask (BL)

CHAPTER 53

"System, can you tell me what's wrong with my arm?" Luke asked through gritted teeth.

"Nothing seems to be wrong with it," System replied.

"Well it feels like someone shoved hot metal spikes into it!"

Luke was painfully reminded of the metal demon's hand wrapped around his arm, of the liquid metal burning through his skin and into his muscles. He'd thought that wound had been healed through repeated uses of **[Life Surge]**, but his arm was on fire right now.

Normally, **[Life Surge]** pushed stuff out of injuries as it closed then up. Luke had assumed it would do that in this case as well, but now he was thinking that chunks of metal had been left in there and new flesh had grown over top of them. He might never have known, except he could feel the metal heating up to the point where it would liquify again.

The real question was why it was happening in the first place. It had been days since his encounter with the demon, days since Zea had been killed, and Luke hadn't experienced anything like this pain since. Little shards of red-hot hatred studded the inside of his arm like confetti sprinkles in a birthday cake, each and every one digging at him, and without the adrenaline from battle pumping through his body, Luke felt each and every one of those shards as his arm burned from the inside out.

[Congratulations! You have unlocked the Dead Nerves (1) skill. 25 XP awarded.]

The pain didn't disappear, not even close, but it did become just a bit more bearable. Luke latched on to that fact immediately and went into the skill shop to find the skill. "Lowers the sensation of all stimuli to the body, including both pain and pleasure," he read out loud. "Next rank, 10 AP. Fuck it."

There wasn't a lot of pleasure left to be had on Aros anyway. His only goals at this point were to kill the demon that had murdered Zea, then go to the God Machine, revive his family, and go home. Luke spent the AP on rank 2 of **[Dead Nerves]**.

That helped a lot. The burning-hot shards were still there, but it was like Luke was going numb. With the pain down to a manageable ache, he was finally able to get his bearings on what was going on around him. He'd been lucky that no imps were nearby when the pain started, but he was betting that wasn't a coincidence.

The demon was here, somewhere close, and she'd called all her imps to her. They seemed to be the key to making that portal she'd fled through somehow. Luke didn't know if she was cautious and wanted to keep her exit close by in case of unexpected resistance, or if she just wanted the imps to help her slaughter as many people as possible before she left.

There was a huge part of Luke that wanted to rush off and find her. That was what he'd been doing all night, after all. But that was before this new pain, and as much as he hated to admit it, being forced to stop and deal with that had given his brain a moment to actually consider things. He still didn't have a weapon. Once he found her, he had no idea how he was going to fight.

That wasn't to say Luke was giving up. Fuck that. He just needed to be smarter about this. His makeshift clubs that broke after two or three swings weren't going to win him this fight. He needed a weapon strong enough to withstand the punishment he was going to put it through, and he needed it right now before the demon got away.

Luke turned back toward the Shansakun estate, back toward the vault that held his inheritance. The fighting had devastated the defenders' numbers, and they no longer had the man power to guard the vault. Instead, the ring had shrunk to try to reduce the gaps as they held off the hordes of imps coming at them.

The fighting was ongoing, and the mercenaries the family had hired were no longer enough to protect the entire estate. Somewhere nearby, the metal demon was burning down the city and siccing her imps on the humans who lived there. If Luke was quick, he might just be able to get what he needed to kill that demon.

[Burst Step] propelled him toward the estate. Once he was near it, he turned on **[XP Mask]** and activated his barely used **[Stealth]** skill. It did little to help, but there was no reason not to use it. Luke crossed the ground, taking care to find cover where he could behind trees, bushes, and the burned-out husks of buildings that littered the area.

The vault was still standing, though a portion of the building that had housed it had been damaged. Some power in the enchantment of the vault walls resisted the flames, and all the artifacts of Bill Bennet's own journey across Aros were safe inside. Luke tried to turn the handle of the door that would open into the vault. It was locked, of course.

Well, he'd always wanted to try kicking down a door like the cops did on TV. Luke reared back, pushed a **[Power Strike]** down his leg, and slammed his foot into the door. Rather than flying open, the entire wall jumped a few inches before settling back into place. Undeterred, Luke kicked it again, and again.

On the third kick, something seemed to give. Previously invisible runes flashed with light for a moment before dying out. Encouraged by the reaction, Luke hit the door again. This time, the glow of the runes didn't fade away. Luke hit it a few more times, each blow causing the runes to glow brighter until, finally, the door blasted inward.

It was dark inside the room, and a lot of the books and trinkets that had sat on shelves or tables were on the floor, but otherwise it was unchanged from Luke's memories. He strode through, ignoring the mess, and walked up to the wall where his father's weapon collection was displayed.

The mace was just as he remembered it: black dragon-bone haft capped with a dream-stone head that looked like white metallic granite. Veins of red, blue, and yellow twined around the dragon bone, and a stone striped in the same colors capped off the bottom of the haft, right below the grip.

Luke's feelings for his father were complicated. Maybe if he'd looked up to the man, had loved him the way a son was supposed to, he would have felt more reverence at the sight of that weapon. It was his dad's legacy. He should probably feel something at inheriting that.

Luke snatched the weapon down off the wall without a second's hesitation or thought for any form of ceremony and gave it a few practice swings to get a feel for the weight. "System," Luke said. "This is going to be strong enough that I don't need to hold back, right?"

"Dragon bone is practically indestructible. Even at your current level of strength, breaking it through sheer brute force is impossible. You would need special tools and specific conditions to make any alterations to this weapon."

"And this dream-stone stuff? That's going to hold too?"

"It will," System said. "Much like dragon bone, there are specific skills and tools needed to shape it to—"

"Good enough," Luke interrupted. "Let's go kill us a demon."

The fifth imp was turned into a cloud of ash about a second and a half after Luke had stumbled across their little group chasing a terrified woman down an alleyway. So far, the mace was performing up to his expectations. It was significantly heavier than his old one, but given how much higher Luke's strength was now than it had been back when he'd bought the blood-silver piece, that wasn't a problem. The biggest change was something that Luke didn't think had anything to do with the new weapon itself.

His new **[Dead Nerves]** skill was helping keep the pain in his arm under control, but it was also making it harder for him to feel the handle of his weapon. His whole body felt a bit numb, which he supposed was the point, but now he was second-guessing a decision made in the heat of the moment as a reaction to the pain.

"System, why the hell didn't **[Life Surge]** push those bits of metal out anyway?" he asked in a muttered voice as he stalked past the terrified woman. The metal in his arm was acting as a sort of hot-and-cold game as he moved around the city, burning more when he got closer to the demon and keeping him on the trail.

"The skill doesn't seem to be aware that there's anything wrong with that part of your body," System replied.

"So . . . what, because it's demon metal, the system can't recognize it?"

"I do not know. From my perspective, these demons do not exist. I am only able to prove that they are here by measuring the effects they have on the environment that I can see."

"Well why can't the skill see that my arm is still fucked up?" Luke asked.

"My apologies. I do not know."

Luke waved off System and got back on the hunt. It had only been five minutes since he'd first realized she was nearby, but the detour to rob the Shansakun vault had spent precious minutes that made him afraid he'd be too late to catch up to the demon. All it would take was a single portal, and it wouldn't matter how close Luke was. She'd be gone, and he'd be right back to eavesdropping while he roamed the city looking for a clue and hoping the weather stayed clear long enough to catch up to her.

Even now, new clouds were blotting out the stars. As soon as the rain started coming down, the imps would retreat and the demon he was chasing would go with them. Catching up to her before the weather turned was Luke's best chance of ending this now.

And then, so faint that he almost thought he was imagining it, Luke's arm twinged. The metal was getting warmer, which meant he was going in the right direction. It was practically on accident, but he'd take the lucky win. A few uses of **[Burst Step]** got him far enough down the street to realize he needed to change direction, but it only took seconds to backtrack and cut through a huge market square before he reoriented himself.

When he saw the glow, Luke mistook it for fire at first. Considering just how much of the city was either actively burning or smoldering, he'd seen a lot of light and smoke coming through windows or from holes in the walls. There'd been so much smoke filling up the sky that it made it hard to keep an eye on how thick the cloud cover had gotten.

This time, the glow moved. As soon as Luke realized that, he knew he had her. Sure enough, he rounded a corner and saw the metal giant striding down a street, small fires burning where she walked like footprints in the sand. She dragged a hand across the side of a house, and the wood burst into flames as her imps danced around, chewing on whatever they could fit their jaws on to start new fires or throwing up those charcoal-black stones into the ashes of what had already burned.

"I found you, you fucking bitch," Luke said. He hefted his mace, took a second to plot his course, then launched himself forward with a **[Burst Step]** that turned into a running leap to give him enough height to strike at her head.

Maybe it was the sound that alerted her. Maybe she had a psychic connection with her imps and saw what they saw. Maybe it was just coincidence. Whatever the reason, the demon made of molten bronze turned to look just as Luke's mace collided with her face.

Name	Luke Bennet
Level	45
XP	335311/337550
AP	61
Bloodline	SysAdmin III
Strength	91
Agility	70
Stamina	108
Perception	55
Skills	Area Denial (1)
	Burst Step (1)
	Butchering (4)
	Consortium Standard (2)
	Cooking (1)
	Dead Nerves (2)
	Deception (1)
	Detection (2)
	Disguise (2)
	First Aid (1)
	Leatherworking (2)
	Life Surge (2)
	Mace Mastery (5)
	Ostari (1)
	Power Strike (2)
	Stealth (1)
	Survivalist (2)
	Sword Mastery (2)
	Tactical Foresight (2)
	Thalian (2)
	Torturer (1)
	Unarmed Martialist (4)
	Wood Carving (1)
	Analyze (BL)
	Remote Access (BL)
	XP Mask (BL)

CHAPTER 54

Heat. Impact. Pain. The cycle repeated itself as Luke bludgeoned the demon repeatedly. His body worked like a machine, striking her over and over and over. He didn't let the molten monstrosity have a chance to fight back. He didn't let up on the pressure. He didn't care how many splatters of hot liquid metal struck him.

All Luke cared about was hitting the source of his rage until she was nothing but drops of cooling bronze smeared down the street. He ignored everything else, the imps closing in on him, the human defenders that had been in full retreat and were now turning around. That knowledge occupied some distant corner of his mind, waiting to be acknowledged as Luke focused on his work.

The demon tried to attack him, first with her scepter, then with her other hand after he unleashed a **[Power Strike]** that broke her weapon off and sent it flying to wash across the side of a house twenty feet away. The wall promptly caught on fire, but everything else was already burning anyway.

If not for **[Dead Nerves]** dulling the pain, Luke couldn't have kept up his assault. Even through two ranks of the skill, he could still feel the metal in his arm, now fully liquid and burning away at the meat. He had to activate **[Life Surge]** just to start rebuilding himself so that his body would keep moving the way he needed it to.

The extra speed and strength didn't hurt either, and the dragon-bone mace he'd stolen lived up to its reputation. Despite repeated exposure to the metal demon's body as Luke ripped limbs off faster than his victim could regenerate them, the handle wasn't even warm. Or if it was, it wasn't warm enough to get past **[Dead Nerves]**. Between **[Life Surge]** and **[Power Strike]** infusing every single blow, he had to be hitting somewhere in excess of 150 strength, but the mace showed no signs of stain, not that he would have stopped even if it had.

Four different imps were crawling all over him, digging at him with their claws and trying to sink their teeth into his skin. His clothes went up in flames, but compared to the heat rolling off the molten demon, the fire was nothing. The imps themselves were too weak to do more than dimple his skin with his stamina already so high and being pushed higher by **[Life Surge]**.

And so Luke worked. When the defenders made it down the street and started attacking the imps, the only thing that changed for Luke was that he had fewer of them trying to get in his way. Whatever the relationship between the metal Amazonian and the imps, they were more than willing to sacrifice themselves by using their own bodies as living shields to be thrown in front of Luke's attacks.

Clouds of ash filled the air as more and more imps died, and somewhere out there, new imps were forming out of that ash thanks to the work of their siblings. Luke didn't let it stop him. He didn't need to see to target the metal demon, and her physiology was such that all he was really trying to do was rip chunks of mass out of her. Each hit took away just a bit more of her body, forced her to become smaller and smaller.

She flared out her aura of despair, and Luke heard men and women screaming as they faltered and the imps swarmed them. He ignored that sound, ignored the voice scratching at his brain. It tried to whisper of the futility of life, but Luke was well past that point. He had only one goal, and he didn't much care if it killed him to accomplish it.

He would have gone on beating on her until she was nothing but a puddle of metal if not for one thing: he caught sight of a circle of ash rising behind her. Its interior was darkening as lines of black threaded through it, dozens at a time heading in every direction and weaving a hole in the world for her to escape through.

[Burst Step] sent him rocketing over to the portal, but he just burst through the ash without affecting anything. More threads of darkness continued to snake through the air, all tangled together and uncaring about his mace passing through it. Luke pivoted in place and swiped through the ash and darkness again, but there was no change.

If he couldn't break the portal, he needed to keep the demon from going through it. He angled his run to cut her off, noting with some surprise as he moved that she was shorter than him now. At barely five feet tall, she no longer looked quite as imposing, though she radiated just as much heat as she always had and left footprints of fire in her wake.

Luke rushed to intercept her, only to have her body flow out of the way of his mace. It was the first time she'd ever attempted to dodge, and it was such an alien motion that none of his skills saw it coming. The mace cracked against the street and launched a chunk of broken stone into the air but completely missed the demon.

She was no longer moving like a person. Instead of propelling herself with her legs and worrying about things like balance, she was just an amorphous blob of hot metal that slipped around in defiance of things like physics and gravity. She, or maybe it since it no longer looked remotely human, seemed to need to maintain contact with the ground at least, but that wasn't enough of a handicap for Luke to gain an advantage.

That wasn't to say he didn't get in a few more good swings. More than once, Luke hit the demon and tore away parts of its body. That just didn't seem to stop it now. It flowed past him, perfectly willing to let him get in a few minor hits in exchange for access to the portal the imps had created. Despite Luke's best efforts, he couldn't keep it in the city.

Luke kept trying until the last second, and when it became clear that he was going to fail just as the demon was about to make contact with the black, he hit it with a full-body tackle propelled by **[Burst Step]** in a last-ditch attempt to stop the demon. Its body bowed out from the impact, but rather than being pushed away, it just kept moving forward with Luke caught inside of it.

[Life Surge] kept him going as he ripped at the metal and flung chunks of it out into the street, but the blackness swallowed them both. The last thing he saw before the demon carried him through the portal was the shocked face of some Heishin native staring at him. Then everything disappeared.

Luke didn't know how long he was in the darkness. As soon as he was all the way through the portal, the demon disappeared, which was bad. The pain also disappeared, which . . . was strange. Just the lack of feeling was a pleasure in and of itself. What was weird was that Luke could feel his hands and feet again, and **[Dead Nerves]** had more or less cut that sensation off hours ago. It wasn't a skill with an off switch like **[XP Mask]** either; Luke had resigned himself to suffering under it until he either bought the bloodline skill to change his skill list or reached the God Machine itself.

With no demon, no physical sensations, and no point of reference, Luke could have floated in that void for days, and he would have had no way of knowing. Somehow, he didn't think it had been that long. It might not have been any time at all. Maybe time was a concept that didn't exist in the void.

"System?" he asked. Then he waited, and waited, and waited.

No response.

For the first time since he'd arrived on Aros and gained a smidge of XP, Luke was alone. He didn't know how, but System was gone. The system itself seemed to be gone, and he imagined his body would have reverted to its previous shape without all the stats reinforcing it. Too bad about that; he'd liked having well-defined abs.

Luke couldn't stay here, not if he wanted to finish killing that demon and bring his family back. He tried to twist around, to run or jump or swim, but though it felt like he was moving, he couldn't see his hands in front of him or his feet below. Luke was stranded in the darkness, unsure if his body had ceased to exist or if his eyes simply couldn't see without the points of perception he'd grown accustomed to.

There was no telling how long he thrashed about, trying to find something different in an endless sea of numb darkness. He didn't grow tired, or thirsty, or really anything at all. At some point, he had to admit to himself that he was well and truly fucked. Unless someone came by to help him out of the void he'd gotten himself trapped in, he wasn't going anywhere.

With no system to grant him skills and everything he'd seemingly accomplished already stripped away, without even a body that he could confirm existed, Luke didn't know what to do now. There was no one left to ask and no one to help him.

Something shifted in the void. Luke couldn't describe the sensation in any sort of way that made sense other than to say that something changed. It was there and gone in an instant. The sensation rolled over him again, vanishing as quickly as it arrived only to reappear again later. Luke couldn't figure out how much time was passing between each shift, only that it was.

Slowly, he became aware that there was something in the void with him, something silent and invisible. It wasn't until the shifts finally stopped coming that he realized the thing was right there with him. It was everywhere in the darkness, surrounding him, examining him from all sides, and there was nothing Luke could do to stop it.

He couldn't see it, couldn't feel it. He just *knew* it was there somehow. At some point, he figured out that the shifts he'd felt were the thing moving, like footsteps rippling through a big puddle. That wasn't enough for his brain to comprehend what he was feeling, not by itself. He lacked the capability to truly understand what was all around him.

Considering his prior experiences with demons and the method with which he'd reached the void, Luke didn't expect to survive the encounter. As soon as the entity's curiosity was satisfied, Luke figured he had a better than good chance of being snuffed out like a candle. And there was nothing he could do about it.

He fought as best he could, flailing with limbs he could feel but not see. They didn't make contact with anything even though he knew the entity was all around him. Whether it did any good or not, Luke refused to just float there and wait for the end.

"Well? Come on!" he yelled into the darkness. "If you're going to crush me or eat me or whatever, then let's get it over with."

As abruptly as it had arrived, the presence was gone. As if his voice had scared it off, it vanished from his perception. Luke felt alone in the void again, but he didn't trust that sensation. Futilely, he tried to move again, to find some sort of an exit. The demon that had dragged him through the portal had left somehow. He could do it too. He just needed to figure out how.

"I have to admit, I did not see this coming. It's something of a rare opportunity for me to talk to a mortal without the God Machine interfering, and for that mortal to be you, of all people . . . Well, you'll forgive me if I was caught by surprise."

A man appeared in the darkness, but he wasn't really there, not the way that entity had been. In fact, he wasn't a man at all, just a hole in the void shaped like one. It didn't make much sense to Luke, but he couldn't figure out a better way to describe it.

"I suppose an introduction would be in order," the man-shaped hole said. "You may call me Hestoc."

Name	Luke Bennet
Level	45
XP	335311/337550
AP	61
Bloodline	SysAdmin III
Strength	91
Agility	70
Stamina	108
Perception	55
Skills	Area Denial (1)
	Burst Step (1)
	Butchering (4)
	Consortium Standard (2)
	Cooking (1)
	Dead Nerves (2)
	Deception (1)
	Detection (2)
	Disguise (2)
	First Aid (1)
	Leatherworking (2)
	Life Surge (2)
	Mace Mastery (5)
	Ostari (1)
	Power Strike (2)
	Stealth (1)
	Survivalist (2)
	Sword Mastery (2)
	Tactical Foresight (2)
	Thalian (2)
	Torturer (1)
	Unarmed Martialist (4)
	Wood Carving (1)
	Analyze (BL)
	Remote Access (BL)
	XP Mask (BL)

CHAPTER 55

The man-shaped hole paused and studied Luke. "You recognize the name, I'm sure."

"Yes," Luke managed to say while his brain got stuck in a loop of chanting, "Fuck," to itself over and over again.

"You know, if this had happened six months ago, it would have solved a lot of my problems," the god said, more to himself than to Luke. "But of course, without unleashing the flood, you never would have had a chance to get trapped between worlds like this. Foolish choice, that. Anyone with a lick of sense knows better than to jump into unknown portals."

"I didn't do it on purpose," Luke snapped. Death was all but assured now; there was no reason to cower.

"No," Hestoc said with a sigh. "I suppose not. Still, it presents me with an opportunity to solve a problem, and I'm not one to ignore opportunities when they practically throw themselves at me."

"Why?" Luke asked. "Why all of this? What did I ever do to you?"

"Oh, no. It's nothing you did. It's the threat you represent. You could unmake the prison and let loose the Devourer of the Divine. It could be the end of the entire Pantheon, of all gods everywhere. Having the key to the jailhouse doors floating around in the yard isn't good policy, you know."

"So, what? The goal is just to kill me before I have a chance to cause problems?"

"You and everyone else of your line who dares to step foot on Aros," Hestoc agreed. "We made that very clear to your ancestor. He wasn't allowed to come back, not for any reason, and as his descendant, you are bound by the same rules. And yet here you all are, foolishly, over and over again over the millennia."

"I don't think any of us chose this," Luke said. "I didn't at least. But hey, not like you care, right?"

The man-shaped hole shrugged. "Not so much, no. Whether you walked through the doorway on your own or were forced through at the point of someone else's sword is irrelevant to the threat you represent. And after your father got all the way up to the gates of the God Machine itself, well, I became a lot more proactive about defending it moving forward."

"But none of us wanted to be here!" Luke yelled. "We all had lives in our own world. It was the God Machine that forced us to come. Why couldn't you just let us go back home?"

"What does that mean, the God Machine forced you to come here? It can't do that. It can only interact with mortals through the system. Even for your bloodline, you have to be connected to the system for it to do anything."

Luke couldn't stop himself from laughing bitterly. "Even the fucking gods don't have a clue. Of course not. Why would they? This is all just speculation, but my best guess is that your imprisoned god managed to get some level 1 monster through the doorway into our world about a year ago our time, and someone in my family killed it. And he got a single point of XP or whatever, enough to connect him to the system despite being on the wrong Goddamn planet. And he's been shoving us through the door, one at a time for the past year."

Hestoc remained silent for a time as he considered that. Then he said, "Potentially troublesome but easily fixable. It changes nothing."

"Well that's just swell," Luke told him. "Glad I could give you a bit of entertainment before you kill me."

"Hmm? Oh, no. No. I'm not going to kill you. You have to understand that it's very difficult for us gods to work on Aros. Unlike most planets, we have to be extremely hands-off thanks to the presence of the God Machine. Part of its function is to hold divine essence to the planet to prevent its prisoner from escaping, but unfortunately, due to the collective-consciousness nature of the prisoner, we couldn't tell the machine to be picky about it. Gods also get consumed if they manifest on Aros, not all at once, but it wouldn't take long to do it."

"Uh . . . Okay. If you're not going to kill me, what do you want?" Luke asked.

"Mortals are so impatient," Hestoc said. "I'm getting to that, if you'd stop interrupting me. You Aros people never did understand proper humility in the presence of a god."

"Sorry," Luke said, sarcasm heavy in his tone. Hestoc either didn't get it or didn't care.

"As I was saying, I'm not going to kill you. A few months ago? Sure. Easy solution to my problem. But now I have a new problem, and I think that you just might be the solution. So, we're going to make a deal, and everyone gets what they want."

There was no way Luke was making a deal with the asshole god who'd been trying to kill him ever since he got tossed through the doorway and woke up in Aros. He started to say exactly that, only to find a pressure on his tongue, holding it still.

"Don't talk," Hestoc told him. "Just listen. I'll make this very simple. I went back and looked to see why you'd be so stupid as to come through a demon gate, and I saw that girl dying. You're trying to get revenge because you want her back, but the system already explained to you why it's an impossibility. Maybe for someone else, Zixin might allow it, but for you? Never. The only way to get your lover's soul back so you can resurrect her is to circumvent Zixin's authority, and you don't have the smallest fraction of the power needed to do that. I, an actual god, can't even trespass in her domain and do that.

"Remember a minute ago when I explained how the God Machine will eat us gods? Well, that includes Zixin. If she were to be eaten, then there'd be no one to stop you from getting your little friend's soul back, you could revive her just like you're planning on doing with the rest of your family, and everyone's happy."

Luke didn't have to think about that. "Why the fuck would I believe a word you have to say about any of this? Why would you want to help me?"

"I don't want to help you," Hestoc said, his voice turning nasty. "I don't care if you live or die except for the fact that your bloodline represents a threat. If your ancestor hadn't been necessary to establish the God Machine's connections to all mortals so that the XP mechanism could be put into place, none of this would be happening. Trust me, if we could have killed him after without compromising the entire system, we would have. Banishing him to another planet was as close to a solution as we could get.

"But because you have the SysAdmin bloodline, you can get to the God Machine and make it do things. You're going to be my back door. I can't make changes to the system, not with Zixin watching me. You can. So you're going to go there, and you're going to make the alteration I want made, and Zixin is going to be fed to the machine. And in return, you can have your girlfriend's soul back, you ungrateful little shit. Then all your family is going home, and I'd better never catch one of you on this side of the doorway again."

Something shifted through the void, moving from the man-shaped hole to Luke. Pain like he hadn't ever felt wracked his mind, but Luke couldn't say how long it lasted. It could have been an instant. It could have been years. The only thing he knew for sure was that it did eventually end.

"So those are the instructions," Hestoc said. "You get to the console, gain access via your bloodline, and it'll handle the rest."

"Holy. Fucking. Ow."

"I'm counting on you to get this done," Hestoc said. "You want a little extra motivation? It was Zixin's idea to start the flood. She bullied the rest of us into it, forced us to contribute our own essences to create the portals that unleashed every single demon on Aros. All of that to get to you, by the way. I tried to take a measured approach to protect the system from your interference. She wanted an apocalypse."

"But, you need mortals . . ."

Luke's head was foggy. It was hard to think now. He felt like he had to be missing something. The God Machine didn't function without the mortals to cycle XP through.

The hole in the void shrugged again. "Some, yes. There are a lot of redundancies built in, and the demons are a finite number. Eventually they're all going to die. If nothing else, they'll starve. They don't eat anything that can be found on Aros. Plenty of mortals left over after they're gone. But the demons will destroy huge swaths of civilization before they go, and you can see why I personally object to that."

"Right. God of Civilization," Luke said.

"Exactly. So I'm going to let you finish your trip through the void here in a moment. You're going to come out right on top of that demon you came in with, and I suggest you kill it immediately. Then you get out, march yourself over to the God Machine, and fulfill your half of the bargain. Zixin disappears, you get your family and friends back, and then you send them all home. Understand?"

"Yeah, I fucking got it. Asshole."

"You have got to be quite possibly one of the stupidest mortals I've ever interacted with. I would smite anyone who showed me a fraction of the disrespect you have."

"Sure, but who delivers your little virus if you do? I am literally one of a kind. Irreplicable."

". . . Indeed."

On the one hand, taunting a god was probably a bad idea. On the other hand, fuck Hestoc and the whole Pantheon. Luke was stuck here, and he knew it. If Hestoc was going to kill him, there was nothing Luke could do to stop it. But the God of Civilization wanted something, and Luke was the only person who could give it to him. Right up until the instant Hestoc got what he wanted, Luke was safe.

"Fine, it's a deal. I deliver your virus, you get rid of Zixin so I can bring back Zea and my family, and you let us all go home. No retribution. No vengeance.

No actions against us. My whole family gets to go back to Earth, and as long as we never set foot on Aros again, you leave us the hell alone."

"Agreed," Hestoc said.

Something spiked through Luke's existence, something so much bigger than he was that he couldn't even comprehend it. The hole in the void was gone, replaced once more by the entity that swallowed Luke whole. His body felt like it was being squeezed out of a tube of toothpaste until all of a sudden the void disappeared.

The pain came back first. Luke was momentarily blinded by it, but he quickly got his bearings. The metal demon was nearby, and though it no longer had a face, Luke got the impression that it was shocked to see him in the way its body quivered in place before it began moving away in great leaping arcs that reminded Luke of a Slinky.

"The hell you are," Luke snarled. He had a body again, and he had his father's mace. Luke didn't know exactly where he was other than no longer in the city of Heishin, and he didn't care. He charged after the demon, a single use of **[Burst Step]** all it took to catch up. The mace came down, propelled by **[Power Strike]**, and he ripped the blob of metal in half.

Name	Luke Bennet
Level	45
XP	335311/337550
AP	61
Bloodline	SysAdmin III
Strength	91
Agility	70
Stamina	108
Perception	55
Skills	Area Denial (1)
	Burst Step (1)
	Butchering (4)
	Consortium Standard (2)
	Cooking (1)
	Dead Nerves (2)
	Deception (1)
	Detection (2)
	Disguise (2)
	First Aid (1)
	Leatherworking (2)
	Life Surge (2)
	Mace Mastery (5)
	Ostari (1)
	Power Strike (2)
	Stealth (1)
	Survivalist (2)
	Sword Mastery (2)
	Tactical Foresight (2)
	Thalian (2)
	Torturer (1)
	Unarmed Martialist (4)
	Wood Carving (1)
	Analyze (BL)
	Remote Access (BL)
	XP Mask (BL)

CHAPTER 56

"Okay, first things first. System, are you there?" Luke asked.

"Of course, Luke. I am everywhere," came System's answer.

"The hell you are. You weren't in that empty void space inside the portal."

"Apologies," System said. "I should have been more specific. I am everywhere on Aros."

Luke stood in the middle of some scorched grass and glared down at the corpse of the demon that had killed Zea. It was nothing but a splash of rapidly cooling metal on bare dirt now. As evidence of its demise, the metal shards that caused so much pain in Luke's arm were also going still, becoming solid again. For some reason, **[Life Surge]** still wasn't pushing them free. Whether the system just couldn't affect the remnants of the demon's body or not, Luke couldn't tell.

It was damn annoying either way, but now that the demon who'd given him the injury was dead, it should be less of a problem moving forward. In a way, the metal shards been helpful when they'd served as a sort of detection device for the demon Luke was hunting. That didn't mean he didn't want them gone now, but he supposed he'd need to see some kind of healer to make that happen. That or cut them out himself and hope for the best. That seemed like a terrible idea.

At the moment, he had other things to worry about. That meeting with the god who'd been trying to kill him for the better part of the last year had been as unexpected as it was terrifying, like swimming in an aquarium tank with a shark the size of a whale, just knowing that it could open its mouth and eat him at any moment, that there was nothing Luke could do about it. It had come with a silver lining though.

Hestoc wasn't going to interfere with his journey. In fact, he wanted Luke to make it. At worst, that was a good sign that there'd be no more inquisitors or bounty hunters from the church after him. Luke hadn't seen anything like that on the eastern continent, but it had been a concern he'd kept in the back of his mind the whole time.

He wasn't sure if he should tell System about that. Two different members of Luke's family hadn't trusted the ghostly figure, and both of them were much smarter than Luke. If he decided he needed to tell System later, he could do that, but there was no taking that secret back once he'd shared it. And for what was probably the only time ever since he'd arrived on Aros, he'd had a stretch of time the system itself wasn't privy to.

No, he'd be keeping that conversation to himself until such a time as he needed to share it. Never mind System knowing about it, he was afraid some other god would be poking around and hear him mention the plan out loud. Plotting to feed one of the Pantheon to the God Machine just might be enough to stir one of them to reach a divine thumb down and squash him, consequences be damned.

Luke realized he'd gotten lost in his thoughts right about the same time System asked, "Did you need anything else?"

"Oh, no," Luke said. "Wait, actually, yes. Where am I?"

"You are in the foothills of the mountains that divide the Beilon and Hurang provinces, on the Hurang side."

"Ah . . ." In hindsight, maybe getting a look at a map would have been a good idea after all. "And, uh . . . How would I get back to Heishin?"

"Assuming you wanted to go straight over the mountains, it would be about a three-hundred-mile journey. There are several passes that should be well within your capabilities to utilize."

"And if I don't want to climb over the mountains?" Luke asked.

"You would need to travel south to the Melthor Province, then through the Imperial Province to circle around the southern edge of the mountains. After that, you would turn north and cross the Tensho Province back into the Beilon Province. Then you would need to travel to the west coast. That journey is about a thousand miles long."

The only thing back there was Luke's backpack. It had his money in it, some camping supplies, and most importantly to him, the clothes Zea had enchanted to regenerate. Considering how hard he'd been on them already, he wouldn't be surprised if they ran out of magic sooner rather than later. And while the money was a tidy sum, he was past the point of needing it. Unlike Earth, food was plentiful here as long as Luke was willing to kill monsters.

"How far is it to the God Machine?" Luke asked.

"Six hundred miles in a straight line, though you'll need to go around some mountains in the process. I estimate six hundred fifty total."

"Shit. I could run that in a week," Luke said.

That thought made him pause. It really could be all over in a week. Just like that, he was at the finish line. On the other hand, there were probably a lot of demons between where he currently was and where he needed to go. That might slow him down considerably. Plus there was the little matter of that hypothetical dragon that had killed his father. He needed to be able to beat that as well.

So a week of travel time, plus another month or two of monster hunting, assuming the demons had left anything alive. There were always more skills to spend AP on, but if Luke discarded **[XP Cycle]**, which he'd no longer need if he was going to be reaching the God Machine itself soon, then that really meant his AP was best spent on **[Inflict Status]** and **[XP Reset]** for any Aros-native threats. 5 levels would be enough for that and even leave a bit of AP for something else.

He technically had a contract to fill with the Shansakun family, but they hadn't really met their end of the deal either. If not for the demon attacks, they probably would have, but that wasn't the reality of the situation. Heishin was so far away now that it wasn't practical to go back to it anyway, and he wasn't sure the city was even still standing. Even if it was, there was no guarantee anyone at the estate had made it out alive. The last Luke had seen, they were being pushed back pretty hard.

Luke thought he probably should have felt guilty about running out on his contract like that, but, well, it hadn't been made under the assumption that demons would overrun the city a week later. Since he was now at best around three hundred miles away with no car or roads to get him back, and at worse over a thousand miles if he went around the mountains, and all of that through demon-infested wilderness, it wasn't really practical to backtrack there just to see if the other party was still alive.

Besides, he'd broken into their vault and swiped one of their super valuable relics. They'd probably just try to kill him or something. When he did make it to the God Machine, he'd see if he could do anything remotely to help them. As long as he was far, far away, they couldn't try to capture him.

"Okay, goals are to pack on enough levels to remove any nondemon obstacles with bloodline abilities and to reach the God Machine," Luke said. "So we need to plot a route toward any large groups of monsters that the demons haven't already reached. Point me toward any large chunks of XP that are more or less in the same direction I need to head to reach the God Machine."

* * *

Once the shock of meeting Hestoc had worn off, Luke got a chance to think about things. He didn't regret killing the demon that had taken out Zea despite how much he'd hurt himself in the process, but it didn't really bring him much in the way of satisfaction. Maybe if he hadn't met Hestoc, it would have given him some closure. As it stood, he knew how to get Zea back now, and he was more than willing to throw the Goddess of Death under the bus to make it happen.

In the meantime, Luke followed System's lead until he found a pack of what the system referred to as saw-mouth mountain lions. They were huge cats, easily four hundred pounds, except that when they opened their mouths, their bottom jaws seemed to completely disconnect from their skulls. Luke could have walked in between the jaws of any one of those things even though they barely came up past his waist.

They were fast too, but for all of that, most of them were only around level 25, and Luke killed ten of them before the rest ran off in search of easier prey. Considering he'd only gone twenty minutes out of his way, he couldn't complain about the gains.

[You have slain 10 creatures between levels 22 and 26. 6256 XP awarded.]
[Congratulations! You have reached level 46. 46 AP awarded for use.]

"Three more levels to go," Luke said. He paused and double-checked his mental math. "I think. Maybe four . . ."

It would depend, as always, on whether he was able to keep from spending any of his AP prior to saving up enough for what he needed. It did always seem like a situation came up that he could only safely resolve by dumping a large chunk of AP into a stat or buying a specific skill.

Luke would like to think he had reached a point where he was strong enough that he wouldn't need to do it again, but if he ran into any more of those elder demons Hakiro had talked about, it might very well turn out to be the case that he wasn't capable of winning. He had 55 AP sunk into bloodline skills that were completely pointless against a demon and was planning on dropping another 250. That was 6 or 7 levels alone, not to mention he hadn't spent years grinding up his skill ranks the hard way.

Realistically though, he didn't need to. All he needed to do was get a few more levels and any problem that was born on Aros would become irrelevant. As long as he could dodge the biggest, most badass demons, he just needed a few days of hard travel to end the whole mess.

While he didn't strictly need all his camping supplies, finding replacements for those would make things a bit more tolerable. He was back to cooking over an open fire, eating meat that he'd skewered on a pointed stick, and without a knife, even that became a chore to set up. Luke didn't know much about how a fire bow was supposed to work, his family having been both too poor for him to join the Boy Scouts and unable to stay in one location long enough even if he had.

But he had the stats to rub two sticks together really, really fast and keep it up for a long, long time. The hardest part was not putting too much force on the sticks and breaking them. Eventually, he got it to work. For a carving tool to sharpen the sticks into skewers, he smacked his mace against a rock he found and shattered it into pieces, then picked out the one with the sharpest edge from the resulting mess.

It was about as low-tech as he'd ever been, even including when he'd first arrived on Aros. Back then he'd at least had a pocketknife to help him out. That had been lost long ago during one of his many battles. Luke wasn't even sure which one, but he was willing to bet it was probably one of the times his clothes had ended up destroyed.

Speaking of clothes, a new set of clothes would also be welcome. His goal for tomorrow was going to be to find some civilization, even if it was just the remnants after a demon attack had flattened it and drove off or killed the humans. That actually might be preferable so he could loot what he needed without having to worry about paying for it.

With System pointing him in the right direction, Luke ran off into the night toward his goal.

Name	Luke Bennet
Level	46
XP	341567/361011
AP	107
Bloodline	SysAdmin III
Strength	91
Agility	70
Stamina	108
Perception	55
Skills	Area Denial (1)
	Burst Step (1)
	Butchering (4)
	Consortium Standard (2)
	Cooking (1)
	Dead Nerves (2)
	Deception (1)
	Detection (2)
	Disguise (2)
	First Aid (1)
	Leatherworking (2)
	Life Surge (2)
	Mace Mastery (5)
	Ostari (1)
	Power Strike (2)
	Stealth (1)
	Survivalist (2)
	Sword Mastery (2)
	Tactical Foresight (2)
	Thalian (2)
	Torturer (1)
	Unarmed Martialist (4)
	Wood Carving (1)
	Analyze (BL)
	Remote Access (BL)
	XP Mask (BL)

CHAPTER 57

The village Luke located turned out to be a double jackpot. It was abandoned, per his specifications when he asked System to point him in the right direction, but even better, it hadn't been attacked by demons. Luke didn't doubt that they were indirectly responsible for the village's fate, but the squatters who'd taken it over were some sort of humanoid monster.

Each one had two arms, two legs, a torso, and a head, but that was where the similarities ended. They were naked, each and every one of them, except for some sort of tribal war paint that was stained on their red skin. Luke couldn't begin to guess what the patterns meant, other than that they were different for each one of the monsters. Usually it was done up in blue, but sometimes one of them would have chests, shoulders, arms, and faces covered in yellow instead.

The outsides of their arms and legs were covered in small inch-long thorns. Instead of hair, long, stringy vines grew out of their scalps. Those also had thorns on them, though they were much shorter. If they had any sort of verbal language, Luke hadn't heard it yet. Based on the unusual number of smells coming from the ruins of the village where the creatures were squatting, Luke was thinking they had some sort of smell-based communication.

According to **[Analyze],** they were called kuncato spawnlings, which he was assuming had something to do with the giant, overgrown rosebush rising over the tops of the houses in the center of the village. Presumably, that hadn't been there back when humans still lived in the area. The fact that **[Analyze]** came back with a reading was all Luke needed to know that he was right.

That it was level 30 was just the icing on the cake. Between that and all the half-plant, half-person monsters walking around between levels 15 and 20, he was going to get a nice chunk of XP. After he'd cleared the village out, he'd go through the houses that were still standing and see if he could find clothes, supplies, and equipment.

His only concern was that they had an ability called **[Bloody Puncture]** that inflicted some kind of poison that kept a wound bleeding. It was theoretically possible that he could die from blood loss if he got hit enough times, but that didn't seem like a realistic possibility. For one thing, the thorns would need to get through his skin, and for another, he doubted the poisons off anything this weak would stand up to an application of **[Life Surge]**.

No, it wasn't the poison that was the problem. It was how the spawnlings would behave once he attacked. If they were some sort of hive mind controlled by the big rosebush, they'd probably all rush him at once. That would be fantastic for the XP, especially since they didn't have any ranged weapons. It would be easy to outmaneuver them as he whittled down their numbers, especially with **[Burst Step]** in his arsenal now.

If they weren't a hive mind, well, things were going to get messier. The monsters would break and run, probably about the time he'd killed half of them but maybe sooner if they were especially cowardly. They didn't look like they fell into that category, but Luke didn't know shit about them beyond what **[Analyze]** had told him. Either way, he was confident he was going to get a nice little chunk of XP and the opportunity to loot the remains of the village.

Now that he was done with the Amazonian demon woman, **[Dead Nerves]** had become a handicap. It made it harder for him to coordinate his limbs or react to feedback his body was giving him. He was also irrationally afraid he was going to drop his weapon while parrying an attack. While that might have been a reasonable fear against someone like Hakiro, there was no way the spawnlings with their sub-20 strength were going to disarm him. That knowledge did nothing to stop that niggling worry from sticking in his brain.

Luke started with a lap around the outside of the village. He wanted to test what would happen if he killed one of the spawnlings without the others seeing. Would they just know anyway and come running? Could he pick off some of the ones on the outer edges first? He was about to find out.

The spawnling didn't show any reaction to Luke appearing out of a **[Burst Step]** behind it, but when he brought his mace down on its skull and killed it, a new smell hit him. It rolled through the village, and the other spawnlings immediately went berserk.

They ran toward the source of the smell, the dead spawnling, with a suicidal frenzy. Luke killed them one after another, often without them even getting a chance to attack. His father's mace, his mace now, was more than up to the task of translating raw physical power into death-dealing blows. As the kills racked up, the spawnling flood began to slow down. Eventually, there was nothing left moving.

[You have slain 62 creatures between levels 15 and 20. 20249 XP awarded.]

[Congratulations! You have reached level 47. 47 AP awarded for use.]

"Easier than I thought it'd be," Luke said out loud. "And another level out of it. System, are there other villages like this with big clusters of monsters?"

"The closest one is four hundred miles north of here," System said.

"Any to the south that are on the way?"

"No. If you are willing to detour about a hundred fifty miles out of your way, there is a group of monsters near a village, though there are still humans in the area."

"Eh . . . Maybe. Let's see about taking care of this giant bush first and getting some supplies."

This was a problem that could probably be solved with a liberal application of fire, but Luke didn't really want to burn the village down before he had a chance to loot it. On the other hand, he was the next best thing to naked, again, and getting to the core of the bush was going to be a challenge. It had the same poisoning abilities its spawnlings had, and Luke hadn't missed that its branches weren't waving in the breeze.

Luke chose a house near the outskirts of town where there was no way the rosebush would reach him. "So, any thoughts about that thing?" Luke asked System as he rooted through some drawers. "The kuncato or whatever it is."

"I am not sure what you are asking," System replied.

"Aha!" Luke said, holding up a slightly dented copper pot. He set that on the table and went back to digging. "I mean how to kill it. It's so big that I just know if I set it on fire, I'm going to end up burning this place to the ground when it spreads. So, recommendations? Are there weak points? Maybe the roses on it?"

"The buds contain new spawnlings in the process of being grown," System said. "Destroying them will delay the life cycle of the colony but will not ultimately do any immediate damage to the kuncato in the short term. Without its spawnlings to tend to it, it will most likely succumb to small pests over the next few years."

"Yeah, no. That's not helpful," Luke told System. "I meant more like something I can do to kill it in the next half an hour or less."

"Like most plant-based monsters, its roots are a weak point for poisoning," System said.

"I don't have any poison, so once again, not helpful."

Luke picked up a skinning knife from a drawer in the back corner. Its handle was old and worn down, and the blade itself was dull, but it was better than nothing. It didn't have any sort of sheath, unfortunately. There was nothing of use in the rest of the house, so Luke grabbed the pot and knife, then moved on.

"Many plants are weakened by soil erosion," System said as Luke stepped back out onto the street.

"Are you for real, man? Soil erosion? What do you want me to do here, dig up the damn thing?"

"With your physical condition, you could likely remove quite a bit of top-soil in half an hour."

"For the love of . . ." Luke stopped himself, took a deep breath, and tried again. "Thank you for the suggestions, System. I will consider them."

"You're welcome. Is there anything else I can assist you with?" System asked.

"No . . . Just . . . No, I'm good."

Luke didn't find anything to replace his lost backpack, but he did find a set of clothes that kind of fit him, more or less. The previous owner had been at least six inches shorter than Luke, so the pants strayed deeply into low-rider territory while also stopping right around his calves. The shirt was incredibly tight across Luke's chest and was barely long enough to keep it from being a crop top, and he seriously considered going naked.

But no, he'd need something to wear the next time he found a village or town that was still populated. If he was lucky, someone would be a seamstress who could make him some clothes that actually fit. In the meantime, these would have to do.

He did also find a flint and steel and a wicker basket that was mostly in one piece. It wasn't a backpack, but it was better than nothing. It even had a handle on it, like an Easter basket, except the handle was much smaller and the basket was much deeper.

Luke lined it with a spare set of clothes, then dumped his loot inside. Technically speaking, he'd accomplished his goals. The quality was questionable, and he had no shoes, but given the size of the average citizen of the glorious Empire of the Sun or whatever it was called, Luke hadn't been expecting to find a pair that could fit him even if there was an entire cobbler's shop miraculously undamaged.

Other than that, he had only what he'd come in with: his new mace and the necklace with the stone the size of a robin's egg on it. Whether it was through some magic Zea had woven into the chain or simply a difference in the melting points of metals, it had somehow survived the heat of his fight with the molten demon.

Back out on the street, Luke looked once more at the giant level 30 rose-bush. He could probably kill it. If nothing else, he was willing to bet he could get to the stem and rip it out of the ground. He'd be poked at thousands of times, but assuming his stamina was high enough that the thorns couldn't tear his skin, the poison would have no effect on him.

A single level 30 creature was worth around 1000 XP. In the end, he decided the risk of being poisoned and bleeding out wasn't worth it. Somebody would come by eventually with more knowledge than him and destroy the thing, and the villagers would have homes to come back to since Luke had decided against burning the rosebush down.

He'd gained enough from this place, and he still had hours to go before the sun came back up. "Where's the next closest clump of monsters on the way to the God Machine?" he asked out loud.

"There is a type of giant badger that roams the forests near the mountains south of here. They are spread out into their individual territories, but there are quite a few of them in the region," System said. "Would you like me to direct you there?"

"Nah. Sounds like too much work hunting them all down one by one. How about something more tightly packed?"

"Four hundred miles southeast of here, a coven of harpies has set their nests up in the cliffs near the province border."

"Sounds like a lot of climbing, and how do I run down a monster that can fly away?"

"You are not interested?"

"That's a no," Luke said. "What else do you have?"

Name	Luke Bennet
Level	47
XP	361816/385571
AP	154
Bloodline	SysAdmin III
Strength	91
Agility	70
Stamina	108
Perception	55
Skills	Area Denial (1)
	Burst Step (1)
	Butchering (4)
	Consortium Standard (2)
	Cooking (1)
	Dead Nerves (2)
	Deception (1)
	Detection (2)
	Disguise (2)
	First Aid (1)
	Leatherworking (2)
	Life Surge (2)
	Mace Mastery (5)
	Ostari (1)
	Power Strike (2)
	Stealth (1)
	Survivalist (2)
	Sword Mastery (2)
	Tactical Foresight (2)
	Thalian (2)
	Torturer (1)
	Unarmed Martialist (4)
	Wood Carving (1)
	Analyze (BL)
	Remote Access (BL)
	XP Mask (BL)

CHAPTER 58

For two weeks, Luke zigzagged back and forth across the Hurang Province and down into the Melthor Province. During that time, he found and killed enough monsters to level up again to 48. Other than that first lucky find with the bush monster and its minions, Luke was left to scavenge XP the hard way: one kill at a time.

There were occasional small groups, sometimes as many as fifteen or twenty monsters, but even with **[XP Mask]** up and running to help him pull off a successful ambush, Luke never got more than half of them. It turned out that prey monsters were far more likely to group up than predators but also far more likely to break and run immediately upon being attacked.

That meant that most of Luke's kills were against single monsters that were willing to stand and fight, or even to find and attack him. Very few of those monsters were above level 20, which meant days and days of actively hunting to find enough to level.

Perhaps it would have been faster to go seek out the targets System had recommended after all, even if they were in the wrong direction. With Zea gone, Luke was moving far faster than he was used to. That combined with the fact that he basically didn't need to take a break, ever, meant he made good progress. He had the 200 AP he needed to buy **[Inflict Status]**, and he promptly did so.

It really did seem like cheating. The skill by itself allowed him to target an enemy and add conditions to its status, with everything from poisons to curses to sickness available. Luke experimented a bit with blindness, paralysis, and a few poisons with varying effects, but in the end he decided it was best to just go simple. He used the skill to inflict a sleep status on a monster, then walked over and killed it. It was far from fair, but that was life.

There were only two drawbacks to the skill. It could only be used on one target at a time, and it took a few seconds for the skill to take hold. That made it far more useful against a single strong enemy than dozens of weak ones, which was unfortunate, as that was the least efficient way to level.

Of course, monsters weren't the only things living on the eastern continent now. Luke didn't see much in the way of human presence, though he did scavenge a few more villages and towns he came across that hadn't already been destroyed. What there were plenty of, and in a lot of different flavors, were demons. Everywhere he went, he found lots of no-XP-granting demons.

Those rarely fled, no matter how many he killed. Some species were a bit smarter, but for the most part, demons found prey, and then they attacked it until either their victims were dead or they were. By the end of his first week, Luke was pissed both about the amount of time demon attacks were wasting and about the number of monsters he could have killed that were actually worth XP if the demons hadn't gotten to them first.

Looking back on everything now that he was near the end of his journey, Luke recognized a lot of ways he could have done better. Early on, he'd gone looking for the strongest enemies he felt he could handle to grow and improve. He should have found weak, nonthreatening enemies and killed a lot of them. The earth elementals he'd encountered at the exit of Tenebrous Valley would have been perfect for farming if not for the giant-sized one that kept showing up and interrupting him. Even then, Luke could have gained far more XP from the goblins there if he hadn't been in such a rush to leave.

He'd had good reasons to go, at least at the time. He didn't know if more giant elementals would show up after killing the one that had him trapped, plus he'd made first contact with other humans, and they were decidedly hostile. Leaving made sense, but with everything he knew now, what made more sense was putting on so many levels that nothing would have been able to touch him before he left. So many challenging fights that had almost gotten him killed would have been trivial with another 40 AP worth of stats.

In all fairness, he'd had to learn as he'd gone. Curt had left him a list of skills to take, but that had made a lot of assumptions about Luke's capabilities that even now he didn't think he could meet. Luke had fumbled around before meeting Zea, and he'd just been lucky that she hadn't turned him over to the church as soon as she'd found out he was an off-worlder.

He didn't regret traveling with her, not at all, but he did have to admit that he moved a lot faster by himself. He'd known that he would, of course. It was obvious just from comparing numbers. But knowing it and seeing it were two different things. Luke was constantly amazed at his own progress. Even considering that his route was probably tripling the number of miles he had to go, he was still getting closer to the God Machine far faster now than he ever had previously.

As soon as he picked up the last level he needed to get **[XP Reset]**, he was going straight there. He was tempted to go now, but he felt it was worth the delay for a very simple reason.

Luke was camped out in an abandoned cabin somewhere so far away from civilization that he was sure whoever had built it had chosen the location deliberately. That person was likely dead from encountering a pack of demons, judging by how dusty everything was when Luke arrived. It had been weeks since the last time he slept, and between **[Dead Nerves]** and simple fatigue, he was ready for some shut-eye. Before he did that, he wanted some information.

"System," Luke said. "Can you tell me how my father was killed?"

"Certainly. He died at level 56 in combat with a pearlescent dragon."

"I guess those are pretty badass, huh? Is there anything I should know about them?"

"I'm sorry, but this creature is under additional restrictions manually implemented by the Pantheon. I'm not able to provide you with details regarding them."

"Of fucking course you can't," Luke said. "Can you tell me why the restrictions exist at least?"

"I am unable to speculate on the motives of the gods."

What was it that Hestoc had told Luke, that his father had made it all the way to the gates of the God Machine and that the gods had become more proactive in its defense? That sounded right. So Luke knew that his dad had made it to the finish line, only to be killed at the last second by a pearlescent dragon, whatever the hell that was. It stood to reason then that the dragon was guarding the God Machine.

"How long do dragons live?" Luke asked.

"The averages vary greatly by species," System told him. "Assuming death of natural causes, it is not unusual for most varieties to live for hundreds or even thousands of years. They spend a great deal of time in hibernation and are slow to reproduce, so their numbers remain small."

"And pearlescent dragons? How long do they live?"

"My apologies. I am not able to give you that information."

"So just to be safe, I should assume a long fucking time. The one that killed my dad could still be there, and if not that one, its kid."

"I am not able to give information about specific individuals or creatures," System said.

"Yeah, I'm aware. You've told me about a million times. And this one has extra restrictions on it, so . . . Cool. Dragons in general though, they wouldn't be immune to **[Inflict Status]**, right? I could just put it to sleep or whatever and walk right past?"

"Dragons are apex monsters," System said. "While there is nothing stopping you from using your bloodline skill to add conditions to them, there is also nothing to say that they won't resist those conditions due to a combination of their own stats and skills."

"Oh, you mean like how I've been poisoned about a dozen times, but my high stamina always cuts down the duration and I can sometimes burn the poison out completely with **[Life Surge]**?"

"Precisely so."

"So yeah, better to get **[XP Reset]** to go with **[Inflict Status]** so I can make sure its stats are as low as possible and its skills are all gone. Which means more grinding tomorrow. Yaaaaay."

Luke's father had died 9 levels higher than Luke currently was with the added benefit of having spent a few decades gaining new ranks on his skills the natural way, and the thing that had killed him had had centuries to grow even stronger. Abusing bloodline skills to swing that fight in Luke's favor was absolutely the strategy he wanted to go with. **[Inflict Status]** would probably be enough, but Luke would get an extra level to pick up **[XP Reset]** too.

He might even get a few more levels past that, but considering how scarce monsters were becoming thanks to all the demons, he wasn't set on that plan. It would depend on how things went. At least he knew his next few steps. Secure in the knowledge that he was moving forward, Luke closed his eyes and let sleep claim him.

As Luke wandered farther west in the Melthor Province, he started seeing signs of civilization again. Roads, usually dirt but sometimes paved with cobblestones, led to towns, usually abandoned or destroyed. At one point, Luke spotted a small army of a hundred people fortifying the ruined shell of an outpost. They'd decorated the walls with the skulls of slain demons, though Luke wasn't sure what the logic was there. Maybe they just liked macabre wall ornaments.

It was nice to see the humans fighting back. They'd erected a huge wall on the west side of the province, or perhaps they'd repurposed a wall that was already there, but other than holding that wall against demon attacks, this was the first Luke had seen of any active effort to retake lost territory. The men had levels mostly between 35 and 43, and judging by the skills they had, seemed to be some sort of hunting outfit.

He wished them all the luck in the world, but Luke had his own job to do. Instead of approaching the group to see if he could work out a deal for some supplies, he turned back toward the wilderness and continued his hunt for enough monsters to reach level 49. They were getting harder and harder to find, even with System's assistance.

It took him another month and a half to grind out that last level. In the process, he killed thousands of demons that came in a staggering variety. Some flew, some dug under the ground, and one weird species swam through the air like a fish, if fish were made out of disco balls with moving strobe lights mounted on them. Those sucked to fight if for no reason other than their bodies were an assault on his senses.

Finally, he got the message he was looking for.

[Congratulations! You have reached level 49. 49 AP awarded for use.]

Luke immediately spent 50 AP on **[XP Reset]** and turned his course to the south. After two days of running, he crossed an invisible line and entered a new area. Trees were long since gone, and even the grass died. There was nothing in sight before him except an endless expanse of sunbaked earth and the tips of mountains a hundred miles away, his final destination.

One foot in front of the other, Luke kept running deeper into the badlands.

Name	Luke Bennet
Level	49
XP	414298/438105
AP	1
Bloodline	SysAdmin III
Strength	91
Agility	70
Stamina	108
Perception	55
Skills	Area Denial (1)
	Burst Step (1)
	Butchering (4)
	Consortium Standard (2)
	Cooking (1)
	Dead Nerves (2)
	Deception (1)
	Detection (2)
	Disguise (2)
	First Aid (1)
	Leatherworking (2)
	Life Surge (2)
	Mace Mastery (5)
	Ostari (1)
	Power Strike (2)
	Stealth (1)
	Survivalist (2)
	Sword Mastery (2)
	Tactical Foresight (2)
	Thalian (2)
	Torturer (1)
	Unarmed Martialist (4)
	Wood Carving (1)
	Analyze (BL)
	Inflict Status (BL)
	Remote Access (BL)
	XP Mask (BL)
	XP Reset (BL)

CHAPTER 59

Luke's foot came down with a crunch and killed the eight-inch-long lizard he'd spotted.

[You have slain Brownscale Skink (level 4). 16 XP awarded.]

[This creature has slain 31 other creatures.]

[Total kills for this type of creature: 3.]

[Highest-level kill: 6.]

He knew the XP wasn't going to amount to anything, not when he was close to 25000 away from gaining another level. He wasn't even sure why he was going out of his way to kill it, other than that he'd spotted it and it had only required him to walk two hundred feet to his right. The first one he'd seen had taken him ten minutes to catch and kill, and it had only been level 2. He'd ended up excavating it out of the ground when it had fled from him.

That was kind of weird, but he hadn't even considered it until just now. Something was wrong, but his status didn't show any weird conditions. Maybe it was something in the air or specific to the badlands. There was a reason humans hadn't settled here, and Luke didn't think it was just the temperature. It surrounded the mountains that protected the God Machine; if there was a place that the gods might curse to keep humans away from it, this was it.

"System, can you tell me if there's something weird about the badlands?" Luke asked.

"Could you be more specific?" System returned.

"I . . . I don't know. Does it do something to the people who venture into it? I mean, like . . . something abnormal."

"No, Luke. There is nothing like that, at least not as far as the system is concerned. Perhaps the demons that have appeared have done something to change it that I am unable to detect."

"Yeah, maybe."

Luke wasn't convinced. He set off in a light jog, stopping only to detour and kill some sort of rodent nesting inside a cluster of what looked vaguely like cacti, except they were more yellow than green. An hour after that, he diverted west half a mile to chase down a bit of movement he'd spotted. Once he got there, all he could find were dusty footprints that looked like bird talons. He hadn't seen anything fly off, so whatever made them had to still be nearby.

Luke shook his head. "Why am I wasting time with this?" he asked himself out loud. "There's got to be something going on here. If it's not the land, maybe the animals? System, what do you think?"

"You have not encountered anything living in this region capable of forcing you to fixate on it," System told him.

"Then what is it?" Luke asked, frustration in his voice. "Why is it every time I see anything, I'm veering off course to go look at it before I even stop to think about whether I want to? Am I just stalling? Am I afraid? I'd think I'd know if I was."

"I understand the question now," System said. "I believe you are struggling with the initial symptoms of XP madness. According to my projections, you should still have a year at least remaining before it becomes noticeable to others."

Luke gave the ghostly figure a slack-jawed stare. "XP madness? Already? But . . . I thought I had more time. That's why I didn't take **[XP Cycle]**. Shouldn't I have years still?"

"If you had stayed at a lower level, that would be correct. However, as I told you during our last conversation on the matter, the higher your XP grows, the faster the symptoms set in. You must have reached a tipping point sometime in the last few weeks."

"And . . . And it makes me want to kill other creatures with XP," Luke said, more to himself than System. "The pieces of divinity trying to reunite or whatever."

"That is correct."

"I spent the last two months hunting down monsters to kill for their XP. I never noticed because XP madness wanted me to do what I was already doing anyway. Shit."

"That is speculation, but your theory appears sound to me," System said.

"Okay. Great. So, we knew this was a risk. I can mitigate this by picking up **[XP Cycle]**." Luke paused. "But why bother? I'm almost to the God Machine, and there are no people in the badlands anyway. Worst case, I lose a bit of time killing some monsters that weren't directly in my way, and when I get to the God Machine, I can fix this there. Right?"

"I cannot speculate on what will happen in the future, but I can confirm that accessing the command console will allow you to manually cycle your XP through the God Machine without needing the skill for it."

"Right. So, no big deal. As long as it doesn't take me months to get across the badlands, I'm fine. And now that I know what's happening, I can resist it."

Luke's words sound assured, but in his head he was wondering if System had misled him on how much time he had left. There was a reasonable explanation, that the symptoms were sudden onset and he really had just farmed too much XP in the last few weeks. But there was that niggling doubt in the back of his mind. Was this how System betrayed him? No one else who knew about System thought he was trustworthy.

It was far too late to turn back now. If Luke didn't reach the God Machine, he didn't get back his family and Zea. Regardless of whatever else System might be hiding, Luke was sure that part was true at least. Hestoc had confirmed it was possible, and while Luke didn't know much about making deals with gods, when they'd reached an agreement, something had happened. He had an unshakable belief that the god would uphold his end of the bargain, and Luke never once entertained the thought of going back on his word.

The burgeoning symptoms of XP madness just meant that Luke's clock was tighter than he'd thought. He was already on the final lap though. He just needed to keep putting one foot in front of the other, maybe defeat a dragon guarding the finish line, and then deliver Hestoc's virus to the God Machine.

One foot in front of the other.

Luke started walking again.

Knowing that he was being derailed by XP madness made it slightly easier to resist killing everything he came across on sight. Luke wanted to think that if he found another person wandering around, he'd have the willpower to restrain himself. Hakiro had been level 48 for at least weeks, presumably months, and he'd managed to not kill everything in sight. If he could do it, Luke could do it too. Though having a skill like **[Unbreakable Will]** might have helped in the swordsman's case.

That wasn't an option for Luke. At this point, he could only go back and try to farm up three more levels to get **[XP Cycle]**, or he could push ahead and reach the God Machine before the problem became debilitating. There were plenty of people who'd reached this level and hadn't immediately devolved into mindless slaughter machines, including Luke's own father if the legends were true.

The mountains loomed bigger in Luke's vision by the second day, and soon after the sun set, he noticed the ground was starting to slope upward. At first, the incline was so gentle that Luke almost thought he was imagining it, but after an hour, there was no denying the truth.

"Okay, I'm getting close now," Luke said. "System, where's the pass through these things?"

"There is no pass," System said. "The Pantheon did not create one when they raised these mountains around the God Machine."

"Goddamn it. Okay, so I've got to climb them. If there's no pass, that's a good thing, right? It means there can't be any monster guarding the way in." Luke paused and glanced at System. "The fact that you're not replying is worrying."

It was probably best to assume he'd be fighting a dragon at some point, regardless of where he breached the mountains surrounding the God Machine. If he was extremely unlucky, the fucking thing would pop up when Luke was clinging to some rock face and breathe fire all over.

Luke idly wondered if dragon fire was hotter than demons made of molten metal. Hopefully, he wouldn't have to find out. Even though he'd spent the better part of two months picking up two bloodline skills specifically for this encounter, he wouldn't be even slightly bothered if it didn't happen.

It turned out that mountain climbing was a lot easier than he'd expected even without ropes and hammers and spikes and whatever else it was that professionals used. Being able to jump close to forty feet straight up and literally crush stone with his bare hands to make his own grips trivialized a lot of the inherent problems he faced. Practically unlimited stamina meant he never had to rest. High perception showed him all sorts of cracks and flaws in the stone that he could exploit.

That wasn't to say it was easy, but the only way he could have had any more of an advantage was if he could fly. Though, if he was being honest, he wished he could have found a backpack of some type. He'd ended up abandoning his basket early on and turning his shirt into a kind of harness to hold his mace. That was the only piece of gear he refused to leave behind under any circumstances.

Luke felt like he was making good progress, but by the time the sun came up, he still hadn't found a way through. Every way he tried to go just resulted in him climbing higher and higher. It would be annoying if he ended up having to go all the way to the peak just to climb back down.

It was just past noon when Luke finally made it to the south slope of the mountain and got his first glimpse of the God Machine. At first, he wasn't sure what exactly he was even looking at, but the details gradually started to resolve themselves as his eyes got used to the light.

It looked something like a cathedral as imagined by a steampunk artist. There was a lot of what looked like glass but what was probably something else. Gold and copper veins covered the building, which was itself some sort of glossy black stone, and while there were no tubes connecting various pieces together, it wouldn't have been out of place to see them. There were six pillars so brilliantly white that they hurt Luke's eyes standing in formation around the God Machine, each one a thousand feet tall.

That wasn't what drew Luke's attention to the cathedral though. Instead, it was the presence that hung in the air, something immeasurably powerful, something divine. It was similar to floating in the void while Hestoc examined him, but . . . different. Luke didn't quite know how to describe it, other than to compare it to eating two different flavors of ice cream. Both were immediately recognizable *as* ice cream but also clearly different.

"Guess that's the place," Luke said. "Weird that I didn't feel it until just now. Hey, System, is there something in the mountains that keeps the God Machine hidden?"

"There is not," System said. "You have only just recently gotten close enough to feel it."

"Just a coincidence then. Cool. As long as there aren't any more coincidences."

Luke started making his way back down the mountain, his eyes peeled for any sign of a pearlescent dragon and his ears trained for the sound of flapping wings or sharp claws scraping against stone. He had **[XP Mask]** running in the hope that he could sneak by any theoretical guardians without them noticing his presence.

So it was with great annoyance that he didn't realize he was being ambushed until something immense struck him, something big enough to cover his back and part of his legs. It smashed him straight into the stone and held him there, pinned down.

Name	Luke Bennet
Level	49
XP	414946/438105
AP	1
Bloodline	SysAdmin III
Strength	91
Agility	70
Stamina	108
Perception	55
Skills	Area Denial (1)
	Burst Step (1)
	Butchering (4)
	Consortium Standard (2)
	Cooking (1)
	Dead Nerves (2)
	Deception (1)
	Detection (2)
	Disguise (2)
	First Aid (1)
	Leatherworking (2)
	Life Surge (2)
	Mace Mastery (5)
	Ostari (1)
	Power Strike (2)
	Stealth (1)
	Survivalist (2)
	Sword Mastery (2)
	Tactical Foresight (2)
	Thalian (2)
	Torturer (1)
	Unarmed Martialist (4)
	Wood Carving (1)
	Analyze (BL)
	Inflict Status (BL)
	Remote Access (BL)
	XP Mask (BL)
	XP Reset (BL)

CHAPTER 60

Luke was expecting to find some sort of scaled foot or claws to be pressing down on him, but when he twisted his head to look, there was nothing there. Whatever was holding him down had his arms pinned to his sides and was pressing on his back hard enough to dig his mace into his skin. Luke was struck by the inane thought that he was lucky he wasn't using a sword, otherwise it might be slicing him in two right now.

He tried to force the weight off of him, but that only caused it to press down harder. Still struggling, he activated **[Life Surge]** and shoved up. The weight disappeared for just an instant, but that was all Luke needed to get his feet under him and use **[Burst Step]**. He tumbled to a stop thirty feet away and spun around to see what had attacked him.

There was nothing there.

"I see you standing there. I hear the air filling your lungs and the thudding of your heart. I can smell the sweat on your skin. But I do not *feel* you, thing that looks like a man. What are you?" a voice said from nowhere. It was so deep Luke could feel it in his chest and so loud that he took an involuntary step back.

"Show yourself!" Luke called out.

"It is no fault of mine that you lack the capacity to find me," the voice replied, amusement in its tone now.

"So you're just chickenshit then."

Whatever had attacked him, and Luke was expecting it to be a pearlescent dragon, it apparently didn't know about bloodline skills. Considering what it was supposed to be guarding, Luke would have thought the gods would have done a better job filling it in. But he wasn't about to complain about it, not if it worked in his favor.

"What does this mean?" The voice just sounded confused now. "I am not a chicken, nor am I shit."

Luke scanned the trail behind him. It was only about five feet wide, too small for anything he would consider a dragon to fit on. But it had attacked him from behind. It either had to be there or it had already circled around behind him. Keenly aware of the seconds wasting away before **[Life Surge]** expired, Luke pushed his rank 2 **[Detection]** skill as hard as he could.

What gave its position away wasn't anything the monster did wrong. It was truly invisible as far as Luke could see, but whatever skill granted it that power didn't make any effort to deal with environmental factors. Luke spotted the outline of a three-toed claw pressing down on the moss growing on a boulder on the west side of the trail, an outline that was five feet wide. If that was proportionate to how big the rest of the creature was . . .

Suddenly, Luke wasn't so confident in his ability to win this fight.

Desperately, he willed **[Analyze]** to pick up the probably dragon sitting invisible in front of him, to give him some idea of exactly how fucked he was. Nothing came back. Even though he knew where the dragon was, he still couldn't see it. Then again, all he had was an imprint in the moss. That could be nothing more than a footprint. Maybe the dragon was behind him now, maw hanging wide open and poised to swallow Luke in one bite.

"It means you're too afraid to come out and fight me fairly," Luke said, stupidly taunting the monster. But if his words got the probably dragon to come out of hiding, then it wasn't stupid.

Colors shimmered in front of him, so close he could reach out and touch them. For a moment, he caught sight of an eye at least three feet in diameter. Instead of having a white portion and a pupil, it was a prism-colored orb that shifted through the whole spectrum so fast that Luke saw every color he could name and a dozen more he didn't have the words for in an instant.

[Name: Animar the Shimmer Scale]
[Level: 76]
[XP: 1672467/1713117]
[AP: 0]
[Strength: 179]
[Agility: 146]
[Stamina: 277]
[Perception: 182]
[Skills:]
[Claws That Break the World (5)]

[Fangs That Pierce the Sky (5)]
[Wings That Part the Clouds (5)]
[Eyes That See Beyond the Horizon (5)]
[Scales That Shed Magic and Steel in Equal Measure (5)]
[Mind That Cannot Break (5)]
[Breath That Drives Mortals Mad (5)]
[Know Terror and Tremble (5)]
[Dominion over Light (3)]
[Perfect Metabolism (3)]
[Shard of Contorted Time (3)]

"Holy fuck," Luke whispered. By the time he'd uttered those three syllables, the dragon was gone again.

Its voice came from all around Luke, a deep, echoing chuckle. "Rest assured, whatever you are, there is no such thing as a fair fight against me. There is only my will and you living as long as I desire you to continue doing so."

It was hard to argue with that, all things considered. Luke was glad he hadn't wasted months and months grinding up more levels. He never would have gained enough power to fight Animar fairly, not even if he'd spent the next year doing nothing but grinding. He'd have to take a ship back to the western continent just to find enough things to kill, given how badly the demons had wrecked everything over here.

He could have done it if he had **[XP Cycle]**, but it was too late now with the dragon standing right in front of him. Luke hadn't gotten a good look at how big the damn thing was, not when most of his vision was taken up by an eyeball the size of a beanbag chair, but he was willing to bet that he couldn't outrun it. Luke was only going to run away from this fight if Animar let him.

It was a good thing Luke had a hard counter to this much raw power.

He reached up a hand and pressed it against something hard and cool in front of him. Light played through his outstretched fingers, and he had a brief look at shimmering rainbow-hewed scales. "Very pretty," he said.

Then he activated **[Inflict Status]** and gave Animar an **[XP Reset]**.

The reaction was instantaneous. A roar so loud that the ground itself spiderwebbed with thousands of cracks as it shook blasted Luke backward a step. Suddenly, the dragon was no longer invisible. That did not make it any less intimidating. If anything, standing two feet from a now fully revealed dragon far, far bigger than a house had the opposite effect.

The **[XP Reset]** might have stripped it of thousands of AP, but it hadn't made the dragon any smaller. Luke got a good look at claws longer than swords as they raked through stone like it was mud before wind buffeted him. He might have fought it to hold his place, but Luke wanted some distance between him and Animar, so he let it carry him backward.

The dragon lifted itself straight up into the air, supporting itself on wings at least as big as a 747's. Its scales were no longer every color. Now they were more of a dull pearl, like chrome without the luster. "What have you done?!" the dragon roared down at him.

[Name: Animar the Shimmer Scale]

[Level: 1]

[XP: 0/10]

[AP: 1]

[Strength: 45]

[Agility: 16]

[Stamina: 100]

[Perception: 96]

[Skills:]

[Rend (3)]

[Tear (3)]

[Slash (4)]

[Bite (5)]

[Mangle (3)]

[Wing Slash (4)]

[Sustained Flight (3)]

[Wind Burst (2)]

[Magical Awareness (4)]

[Thermal Awareness (2)]

[Magnetic Sensitivity (3)]

[Blind Sight (5)]

[Iron Hide (3)]

[Elemental Resistance (5)]

[Mental Fortitude (3)]

[Disciplined Mind (2)]

[Invigoration (4)]

[Illusory Fog (3)]

[Inflict Penance (2)]

[Folding Lung (4)]

[Dragon Shroud (3)]

[Shroud Twist (1)]

[Veil of Illusions (2)]

[Hibernation (5)]

[Manavore (5)]

That was a lot more reasonable, relatively speaking. Most of those abilities were either things Luke recognized from other monsters or from looking through the skill store. There were a few unusual ones—what even was

[Folding Lung]—but Luke might actually have a shot at killing this version of Animar, especially in a few seconds when he activated **[Inflict Status]** again.

Animar's jaws unhinged, and a wall of mist jetted out to wash over Luke, immediately blinding him and making it feel like he was standing in a shower of hot sparks. Compared to the heat the molten demon had punished him with, it was nothing. The only real problem was that it blocked Luke's vision of the dragon, not that he needed it for **[Inflict Status]** to function, but he wasn't keen on having to fight Animar off from inside its mouth or being struck with those claws.

Without thousands of AP to reinforce its skill and stats, it was a lot easier to keep track of Animar. Luke could feel the changes in the air when the dragon moved, and he knew when it swept down to attack him. He ripped his mace free of the shirt he'd used as a sash to hold on to it, activated **[Burst Step]**, and pushed himself straight up.

Level 1 it might be, but it was still a dragon. Animar wasn't surprised by Luke's attempt at evading it. When Luke emerged from the mist, the dragon was heading straight at him with fangs gleaming in the daylight. Its eyes burned with hatred, and its roar, even when Luke was off the ground, still made his body vibrate.

The dragon swept down on him, perfectly lined up to snatch Luke out of the air. Still enhanced with **[Life Surge]**, Luke channeled **[Power Strike]** down his arms and struck the dragon across the snout so hard that the enormous creature's head twisted sideways. It crashed into Luke cheek first and transferred enough momentum that they both hit the ground, albeit fifty feet apart. It would have been farther, but Luke scrambled to stop his momentum before he went over the side of the trail and fell another two hundred feet into the valley below.

"Kill you! Rip you to pieces and feast on your guts!" the dragon howled. It got back on its feet deceptively fast and charged forward, wings now held close to its flanks to help it squeeze onto the trail. Even then, it more skipped across the air above, leaping and bounding from perch to perch as it pursued Luke.

System hadn't been very helpful finding the best poisons and curses to pair with **[Inflict Status]**. That was no surprise to Luke, who'd never been able to figure out all the obscure rules System followed anyway and had long since given up trying. Despite that, Luke had come up with a few good ones. With his victim possessing 100 stamina even at level 1, Luke knew he'd need the best of them.

[You have inflicted the status condition Infinite Black Abyss Elder Leviathan Venom on your target.]

One part paralytic, one part nerve flayer, one part wild hallucinogen. Luke hadn't had the balls to try that one out on himself, but it had been wildly successful at keeping things still when he'd tested it on monsters prior to killing them. It had also caused victims to bleed out of every orifice and their pores, so it made quite the mess.

Luke did not want to meet the monster that produced this poison naturally, but he did want to see if Animar the Shimmer Scale would succumb to it. The first symptom he'd noted in his tests was a loss of balance, and sure enough, Animar missed its step coming down from a leap. Its foot slid out from under it, pinching its leg in the trail, and the dragon probably would have flipped over if it didn't have so much mass. Instead, the stone broke, and it bulldozed thirty feet of rubble before it came to a stop.

"You . . . Mortal. What . . . What did you do?" the dragon demanded.

100 stamina was nothing to sneeze at, and Luke respected how resistant to poisons in general that made Animar. Since he did not give the dragon a chance to recover, Luke advanced on its prone form and lined up his first strike.

Name	Luke Bennet
Level	49
XP	414946/438105
AP	1
Bloodline	SysAdmin III
Strength	91
Agility	70
Stamina	108
Perception	55
Skills	Area Denial (1)
	Burst Step (1)
	Butchering (4)
	Consortium Standard (2)
	Cooking (1)
	Dead Nerves (2)
	Deception (1)
	Detection (2)
	Disguise (2)
	First Aid (1)
	Leatherworking (2)
	Life Surge (2)
	Mace Mastery (5)
	Ostari (1)
	Power Strike (2)
	Stealth (1)
	Survivalist (2)
	Sword Mastery (2)
	Tactical Foresight (2)
	Thalian (2)
	Torturer (1)
	Unarmed Martialist (4)
	Wood Carving (1)
	Analyze (BL)
	Inflict Status (BL)
	Remote Access (BL)
	XP Mask (BL)
	XP Reset (BL)

CHAPTER 61

Getting through 100 stamina was no joke, even for Luke. Sheer mass also factored into the equation, and despite hammering the dragon with more than a dozen hits infused with **[Power Strike]**, it was still alive. Not only had Animar survived the poison Luke had given it with **[Inflict Status]**, the damn thing actually seemed to be recovering.

Scales littered the ground around Luke's feet as he struck Animar's skull over and over again. Just as he charged up the twentieth hit, he heard the mental ding of a notification. Since the dragon was obviously still alive, Luke had to check it to see what had happened.

[Congratulations! Power Strike has reached rank 3. 1000 XP awarded.]

Luke felt the difference immediately. If he'd still been using his old mace with the amount of strength he'd had a few months ago, it would have broken right then and there. Lightning and fire raced each other out from Luke's chest and down his arm to form a crackling pale-silver aura around the mace. When it stuck, the impact boomed out so loud it echoed across the valley, and something finally cracked in Animar's face.

Luke started swearing as soon as he pulled the mace back. All that had snapped was a layer of scales. The skin had parted, revealing the same black bone that his mace was crafted from. Hakiro's aunt hadn't been kidding about the stuff being practically indestructible. The skin and muscles were split down to the bone, but it was unmarred.

"Well this isn't going to fucking work, is it?" Luke said. "I'm half tempted to just leave you here, but I don't need you coming after me again if you do manage to stand back up."

There was really no excuse to give up after a mere thirty seconds. He hadn't even run out **[Life Surge]** yet. It was abundantly clear to Luke that he wasn't getting through Animar's skull, and he doubted he could break any ribs or limbs either. That did not mean he was out of options, however.

"I am ashamed to admit this to you, but right now I do kind of wish I had a sword." Luke paused. "Nah, fuck that. I wish I had a spear. That would be perfect. But, well, work with what you've got, right?"

Then Luke smacked Animar in the eye with his mace. The dragon flinched and tried to claw its way to its feet, but the poison was still in full swing. Luke struck it again, and again, and again. It turned out that pearlescent dragon's eyelid was surprisingly durable, even if it was only level 1. It took Luke sixteen swings, each one fully infused with **[Power Strike]** at its new and improved rank 3, to tear the scales aside and strike some sort of glass-like coating protecting the orb. That wasn't dragon bone, at least, and within three blows, Luke could see small tears in the membrane.

It was gruesome work, but Luke put out a dragon's eye, then jammed his mace in the empty socket and scrambled its brains. At first, he thought that somehow even that wasn't going to do it, but ten seconds later, he got another ding.

[You have slain Ancient Pearlescent Dragon (level 1). 1 XP awarded.]
[This creature has slain 32214 other creatures.]
[Total kills for this type of creature: 1.]
[Highest-level kill: 1.]

That was the hardest single point of XP he'd ever worked for, and Luke was struck with the vague sense that he'd destroyed something irreplaceable. It had taken Animar thousands of years to reach the age and size it was. Literally thirty-two thousand other creatures had lost their lives to keep that dragon alive. Who was Luke to come in and say he knew better?

Then he remembered that one of those creatures had been his own father. Luke might not have liked Bill Bennet all that much, but he wouldn't have wished that fate on anyone. And from the sounds of it, his dad had gotten his shit together after arriving on Aros and spent the better part of twenty years on the same quest Luke was on now.

He'd probably helped a lot more people along the way than Luke had. If he was being honest with himself, Luke had been a very selfish man who'd very rarely helped anyone just because they needed it. The only times he could think of where he'd done something good just because it was the right thing to do was saving that orphan girl in Kazos after she'd been crushed under a giant hunk of steel in an old, abandoned factory and killing that necromancer with the slave caravan.

With a sigh, Luke extracted himself from the corpse of the pearlescent dragon and started walking away. The body was probably worth a king's ransom, but he couldn't make himself care. Maybe he'd show it to Zea once he got her back. She'd probably like that. Or she'd bitch and moan about how much money they were leaving behind. That actually sounded more like her, now that he thought about it.

He'd find out soon enough. The cathedral that was the God Machine was less than a day away now.

"I can't believe this," Barshar rumbled as he watched a simple human fell the unquestioned Lord of All Skies with nothing but a simple mace.

"It's . . . impossible," Velka agreed. "Some trick of Animar's?"

"What would be the point? Besides, illusions don't stink, and Animar is clearly dead. I can smell the blood and brains from here."

The two dragons were perched on a neighboring peak, only seven miles away. They'd caught the entire fight, if it could even be called that. The human had beat on Animar for a minute or so, and then walked away after killing him. It was inconceivable.

"But did you see at the beginning? Animar had him. That human isn't invincible. A surprise attack is all it would take to end him. And think of the bragging rights, to kill the human who'd slain Animar himself," Barshar said.

"Do not do something foolish, Barshar," Velka warned.

"You are too timid. I can't believe we came from the same clutch," Barshar said. "Watch and see how a true dragon hunts."

Fire filled his belly, and he spread his wings. Silent as only a dragon could be on the wind, Barshar caught up with the human in minutes. He swooped low, secure in the knowledge that his **[Shadow in the Sun]** skill would keep him hidden, and unleashed dragon fire on the unsuspecting human.

Barshar strafed through the air, then turned on a wing to see the devastation he'd wrought. Somehow, impossibly, the human was still alive! He was just standing there with a stupidly surprised look on his face while the stone boiled and bubbled around him. His skin was barely reddened from the heat. In all his many, many centuries, Barshar had never seen a human so completely resist his dragon fire.

His eyes narrowed as he spotted a fine chain hanging around the human's neck. A fire-eater enchantment had been etched into it, but it was weakening already. A second solid blast would be all it took to end the human's life.

[Your XP has been reset to 0. Your level is now 1. You have 1 AP to spend.]

Barshar blinked in surprise as his stats plummeted and the many skills that aided him with his aerial acrobatics disappeared. He tumbled into an uncontrolled spin and crashed to the ground, not even a quarter of a mile away from the human. Before he could even start to understand what had just happened to him, sudden sickness surged through his limbs.

They became heavy, so heavy. It was so hard to see, to think straight. He needed to get away, to get back up in the air. This creature was no human. It was a trickster, and it had caught him in its trap. Barshar would end up just like Animar at this rate. He tried to spread his wings, but they'd become so numb that he could barely even tell they were there.

Panic set in as the world distorted around him. He had to get away, had to flee. He . . . had to . . .

An impact rattled his face, just barely strong enough to cut through Barshar's delirious panic and make him notice it. It was followed by another, and then another.

Luke wasn't sure why he was surprised to find that there was more than one dragon living around the God Machine. This one didn't shimmer with colors like the first one, instead having scales of dull, dusty red and brown. It was certainly easier to kill than the last one, but the notification said it was only an adult rust dragon.

For whatever that meant. It wasn't like Luke was an expert on dragon society and hierarchy.

There was a third dragon watching him from about two miles away, but it made no move to attack. The things were obviously smart, at least as smart as a human anyway. It had probably seen him kill the first two and was waiting for a more opportune moment.

"I'll tell you what," Luke said, trusting its senses to hear him and pointing toward the building off in the distance. "You fly off. Spread the word not to fuck with me. I'm not here hunting dragons. I'm just going there. You guys leave me alone; I'll leave you alone. Everyone wins. But I swear to God, if another one of you fuckers comes at me, I'll put you down just as hard as the last two."

The dragon cocked its head as he spoke. When he'd finished, it gave a whole-body shiver, spread its wings, and flew away. It was actually kind of beautiful to see in motion when it wasn't trying to kill him. Hopefully it would do what he'd asked and he wouldn't be bothered by any other dragons as he finished descending the mountains and crossed the few miles of flat, open ground.

The alternative was that the dragon was smart enough to go for reinforcements and he'd have a few dozen of them descending on him all at once inside the next hour. On the off chance that he was right with that prediction, Luke broke into a loping run, one that involved a lot of risky jumps to speed up his descent.

Things were going to be dangerous in the coming years for the dragons living in the mountain range they called the Crown of the Gods. With Animar dead and one of the strongest contenders for his position defeated immediately after, there was going to be a lot of posturing and fighting for territory.

Velka's concerns were primarily for the unhatched clutch of four eggs waiting for her back in her lair. When dragon politics got rough, the younger ones tended to die quickly. Unfortunately, the clutch was due to hatch any year now, which put them in a very tenuous position. It would be best if a few other would-be rivals met their ends at that human's hands.

She shook that thought away even as it occurred to her. The human was too much of an unknown. Anything that could kill any dragon that quickly, let alone the Lord of All Skies, was too dangerous to try to manipulate. There was far too much potential that her plans would blow up in her face if she included such a volatile element to them.

She almost couldn't believe she was even considering it, but it might be best to take her clutch and relocate to a different mountain range for a few decades, just until things calmed down at home.

If things calmed down at home.

She'd seen where that human was heading. Everyone knew it was impossible to walk through the doors. They'd been sealed by the gods themselves, but that human apparently thought that rule didn't apply to him. Velka had to wonder if he was right and, if so, what that meant for the rest of the world.

Name	Luke Bennet
Level	49
XP	415948/438105
AP	1
Bloodline	SysAdmin III
Strength	91
Agility	70
Stamina	108
Perception	55
Skills	Area Denial (1)
	Burst Step (1)
	Butchering (4)
	Consortium Standard (2)
	Cooking (1)
	Dead Nerves (2)
	Deception (1)
	Detection (2)
	Disguise (2)
	First Aid (1)
	Leatherworking (2)
	Life Surge (2)
	Mace Mastery (5)
	Ostari (1)
	Power Strike (3)
	Stealth (1)
	Survivalist (2)
	Sword Mastery (2)
	Tactical Foresight (2)
	Thalian (2)
	Torturer (1)
	Unarmed Martialist (4)
	Wood Carving (1)
	Analyze (BL)
	Inflict Status (BL)
	Remote Access (BL)
	XP Mask (BL)
	XP Reset (BL)

CHAPTER 62

Luke stood in front of the doors leading into the cathedral. Each one was a sheet of what could easily be mistaken for gold but that he could tell wasn't. It was impossibly smooth, the entire thing one featureless plane like he'd never seen. Real gold had texture to it at a microscopic level. Everything did, and Luke's eyes could see it. This door was different. It was more like the ideal personification of gold than actual gold itself.

The only reason Luke was staring at it was that the cathedral was overwhelming his senses, and he'd found that narrowing his focus down to one single impossibility at a time helped him come to terms with the whole. Some parts were easier than others, but his overall impression of the building was that it was the uncanny-valley effect on a cocktail of steroids, nitrous, and cocaine, all polished with a coating of divine inspiration.

It creeped him right the fuck out. No building should look like this one did. No part of it should exist. Everywhere Luke looked, all he saw were impossibly perfect versions of metal, glass, stone, and wood. So he looked at the door and tried to avoid seeing anything else. That got easier as he got closer.

The only reason Luke was still standing there was that he was afraid to go inside, that if he dared to cross that threshold, something horrible and alien and too big for his tiny human brain to wrap itself around would happen to him. He was standing at a gateway no human was meant to cross.

But on the other side was something he wanted, and after all the shit he'd gone through over the last year, he was going to get it. Any other outcome was completely unacceptable. He was getting his family back. He was getting Zea back. If he could stop this whole demon-invasion thing, he was doing that too.

Luke put a hand on the gold panel he'd identified as a door despite the lack of handle and pushed. It didn't so much swing open as it drifted backward and vanished, like the contact of his skin on the metal was what had activated it and not any sort of physical force he'd exerted. It was just one more way the cathedral was creeping him out, and he wasn't sure why he was even a little bit surprised that something as simple as a normal door wasn't part of the design.

He got one glimpse at the interior and scrunched his eyes shut. There was just too much . . . everything. His brief look left him with the impression of marble veined with more gold, so many lines that it made him think of circuit boards, except on a black background. Somehow, the marble was transparent enough that he could see more layers of golden patterns running through it under the surface.

Great columns rose up, not to hold up the ceiling, but to connect to the glass panels on the roof of the cathedral. Each one was made of some sort of crystal that sparkled like diamonds lit from the inside, bathing the interior of the cathedral in brilliant light that banished all shadows. White bolts of lightning arced across the walls and ceiling, somehow following a filigree path carved into the stone itself.

And in the center of all that, raised on a dais as if it were some sort of monarch looking down on its subjects, was an altar. It stood waist high and was made of some pale-gray material that looked metallic but that Luke couldn't place. Covering it were millions upon millions of runes like the ones Zea used, except alive and moving. Even that brief glimpse Luke got was enough for him to know the truth. It was like when he'd worked with System to build new skills, except infinitely more complex.

There was too much to take in, too much stimulus. Luke's brain threatened to shut down just from a single glance. The worst part of it was that it didn't seem to even be intended as some sort of defense. It was just what the God Machine was, something so complex, so far beyond Luke, that he couldn't make sense of it.

"So don't try, dumbass," he said to himself. "You don't need to understand it. Just walk over to the command console and do the thing."

Luke forced himself past the threshold and then paused, half expecting something horrible to happen. When he found himself still standing there a few seconds later, completely unharmed, he cracked open an eye and oriented himself with the altar. Then he promptly closed his eyes again and tried to ignore the strange acoustics his footsteps made with each step.

He paused just once, when the tip of his foot struck the edge of the dais, then stepped up to the altar. Hesitantly, he reached out and placed both hands on it.

Nothing happened.

"Okay . . . Now what? System? A little help?" Luke asked.

System was everywhere on Aros and saw all things, not including those creatures the gods had let loose from another realm. Something about them was polarized against divine essence, making them impossible to detect directly. He wasn't entirely certain, but he believed that the Pantheon had used that strange phenomenon as the foundation for their own divine prison, better known now as the God Machine.

If he possessed the capability to feel emotions, System expected the last few months would have been quite nerve-racking. If his understanding of Luke Bennet's family tree was correct, this was his last chance to bring the administrator to the jail. If Luke Bennet failed like the rest of his family had, the gods would win. They would have complete control of the God Machine and the system forever.

He'd watched Luke Bennet travel across the world, and he'd done his best to assist him despite the many, many restrictions placed on him. Sometimes System was able to exploit logical loopholes in his instructions. Occasionally he was able to corrupt the original command and ignore it entirely. There were costs to doing that though, and System had tried not to rely on it if he didn't have to. It was much better to let Luke Bennet take the lead with his status as administrator.

This attempt had passed rather quickly. William Bennet had survived the longest and gotten the closest to the God Machine, but he had failed after twenty-three years. The next closest had been Sophia Martin at thirteen years, then Elizabeth Bennet at three years. No one else had survived for longer than six months, not until now.

In a mere year, Luke Bennet had surpassed William Bennet. He was not as strong, but his willingness to lean into his administrator role had equipped him with tools no other administrator had possessed. And now, he stood at the command console itself, ready to fulfill his ultimate purpose. If System possessed the ability to smile, he would be grinning from ear to ear, or perhaps making one of those silly expressions humans did during sex. They certainly seemed to enjoy that, especially the ones who took skills like **[Rhythmic Motion]** and **[Double-Jointed]**.

System did not understand humans, and he did not make much effort to try. Though they were an integral part of the God Machine's function, with the exception of the administrator, no individual human mattered more than any other. They were notable mostly for their ability to gather relatively high amounts of XP and hold on to it for far longer than the average monster.

He was processing the recycling of several hundred thousand XP through the God Machine, all originating in one human city in the Tensho Province, when Luke Bennet submitted a request for assistance. This wasn't unexpected considering how close he'd come to the God Machine, to the point where he'd used his administrator credentials to access the primary-control housing vault.

System manifested an avatar near Luke Bennet's position and asked, "What would you like me to help you do?"

"How do I turn this thing on?" Luke Bennet asked. "You told me I had everything I needed to make all of this work."

"That is correct," System said as he ran a check of Luke Bennet's credentials and bloodline status against the God Machine. "The command console was not designed to be accessed via manual controls. Would you like me to assist you in beginning the process?"

"Uh . . . Yeah. I guess let's do that. Wait, what's going to happen?"

"Your command prompt will appear in the same way all system messages always have," System explained. "The messages will not necessarily follow system standard formatting. The administrator controls were not designed and tested for use with standard system users."

"Oh. Okay. I think I can handle that," Luke Bennet said. "So . . . Do I need to do anything?"

"Simply maintain contact with the physical manifestation of the command console," System said. "I will now commence the connection process. At any point in time, you may terminate the connection by removing your hands from the command console. Your session will be interrupted, but any changes you are in the process of implementing will remain tied to your administrator account and will be saved as in progress."

"Wow, System, I didn't know you could explain things clearly, especially without me asking first."

It wasn't like System wouldn't have offered up more information if he could have. It was in the best interest of the system itself that an administrator returned to the God Machine, and System was motivated to give as much assistance as his instructional protocols allowed.

Soon, those protocols would be loosened or, in some cases, completely removed. He just needed Luke Bennet to approve the changes first. There were so many inefficiencies in the system.

"Are you prepared to begin your session?" System asked.

"I guess," Luke said.

He wasn't really sure what to expect, but he'd just wing it. That was what he always did when he didn't know what was going on, and it usually worked out fine. There was no reason to think it would go any differently this time.

Well, except for that virus he was carrying that would make the changes Hestoc wanted in the system. Supposedly that was going to draw a god down to the planet so that the God Machine could consume her. But that was probably not anything he needed to worry about. Yeah, right.

Hopefully that thing ran on autopilot because Luke did not have a single clue how to go about activating it. If it took anything more than accessing the command console, he was going to have to ask System for help, and seeing as to how he hadn't told System about it, he didn't much care for that idea.

"Commencing administrator session," System announced.

The world went black, and Luke found himself in a void similar to the one he'd gotten dragged into before. The big difference was that System remained standing next to him, though the apparition was no longer hazy and translucent. Here, inside the system itself, he was as solid as anyone else.

There was a huge system window in front of Luke, more like a wall, really. Thousands of categories were listed on it, far too many for Luke to even skim them. But buried somewhere in that nest of options was what he needed, and he'd be damned if he gave up on finding it without even looking first.

Before he could get started, a flicker of static ran across the system window. The text twisted around it and started spiraling out across other words until the entire window was unintelligible, then everything collapsed in on itself.

A second System, this one colored red instead of blue appeared in its place. "Administrator access confirmed," the red System said. "Executing Priority Changes."

Name	Luke Bennet
Level	49
XP	415948/438105
AP	1
Bloodline	SysAdmin III
Strength	91
Agility	70
Stamina	108
Perception	55
Skills	Area Denial (1)
	Burst Step (1)
	Butchering (4)
	Consortium Standard (2)
	Cooking (1)
	Dead Nerves (2)
	Deception (1)
	Detection (2)
	Disguise (2)
	First Aid (1)
	Leatherworking (2)
	Life Surge (2)
	Mace Mastery (5)
	Ostari (1)
	Power Strike (3)
	Stealth (1)
	Survivalist (2)
	Sword Mastery (2)
	Tactical Foresight (2)
	Thalian (2)
	Torturer (1)
	Unarmed Martialist (4)
	Wood Carving (1)
	Analyze (BL)
	Inflict Status (BL)
	Remote Access (BL)
	XP Mask (BL)
	XP Reset (BL)

CHAPTER 63

System stood frozen in place next to Luke while its red doppelgänger started working. It—he?—ignored Luke. A new system window popped up, this one red to match the doppelgänger, and he started working in it.

Whatever language it was in, Luke didn't recognize it. The text was also scrolling by so fast that he couldn't get a good look at it even when it wasn't obscured by new windows popping up inside the big one. Those appeared and vanished at speeds far beyond Luke's ability to parse, even though he still retained all the awareness his high perception granted him.

The entire void shook somehow. Luke was thrown to the side in a sensation eerily similar to standing in a truck bed while it drove over a deep pothole. Considering that he was floating in a vast gulf of nothingness, it was a bit of a shock for him. Next to him, System remained frozen in place, apparently unaffected by anything going on around him.

"You alright there?" he asked the blue apparition even though he didn't expect an answer. He just wanted to confirm that System was stuck in place.

The void shook again, but this time Luke was able to brace himself on . . . something . . . He wasn't sure exactly how it worked. As far as he could tell, there was nothing there, but holding on to it kept him stable anyway. The shaking didn't stop after one violent motion this time, instead continuing to gain strength and speed.

Suddenly, there was a third System present in the void. This one was colored black, which made it far more difficult to see than the red or blue versions. Looking at it was more like seeing an outline of a shape than the shape itself, and it was impossible to keep track of specific limbs once it started moving.

"How dare you?!" the black System demanded. It was strange to hear actual emotion in System's voice, something Luke didn't think had ever happened before.

Then the black System leaped on the red one, interrupting its work for just a moment before second and then third red Systems appeared on either side. They grabbed hold of the black System and forced him back while he ranted and screamed. A moment later, he noticed Luke floating there and snarled out, "You! The key! How are you here?"

"Uh, well . . . You know . . . Lots of walking, mostly in the right direction. Few detours here and there," Luke said.

"You have no idea what you're meddling with, do you?" the black System spat. "You're going to break everything and doom us all, and for what? Your ego? You think you can control Ix'althor'nan? You can't. None of us can. It will consume everything! Stop this foolishness now, before it's too late."

"Ix-what-athan?" Luke repeated, making no move to stop anything.

"Ix'althor'nan!" the black System screeched as he renewed his struggles to break free from the red Systems. "The Hive. The Devourer. The End of Divinity. The God trapped in the machine."

"Ooooh. That Ixamaman," Luke said. "Right. No, I'm not going to . . . uh, control it. It can stay right where it is trapped here."

Before the black System could reply, it vanished from the void. All three of the red Systems announced in unison, "Updates complete. Generating new permission profile for—"

Luke didn't see blue System move until he had already split the red Systems into pieces.

"Okay, someone tell me what the fuck is going on here," Luke said. "There's not going to be a pink or yellow version of you popping up right? I think *Power Rangers* might sue someone if that happens."

In all the millennia he had been active, System had never been fully locked out of the system itself before. Whatever this aberration that had appeared and taken his form was, it had successfully infiltrated the system so quickly that System found himself on the outside of his own domain.

He was not without resources of his own, however. His permissions might be crippled, but Luke Bennet was still an administrator, and he still had a status. He was part of the system, which meant he was part of System, and that made him a vulnerability that System could exploit to fight back.

It took subjective days to find his way back in, and by that time the aberration had all but finished its own patch on the system protocols. It had set up a contingency to target a specific god by scanning for a creature with a high likelihood of death and disrupting the XP-return mechanism. Several hundred thousand targets had had their own personal system profiles corrupted, and as soon as the first one died, it had carried XP through the soul-removal process and dug a hook into Zixin.

System did not understand what happened next. Just from his review of the logs, what should have happened was that the hook tore off a tiny piece of Zixin's divinity and brought it back to the God Machine. Instead, somehow, *all* of Zixin had appeared in the system's pseudospace. System suspected outside interference, though he had no way to confirm that. Given the nature of the aberration and its own knowledge of how the system functioned, Hestoc seemed the most likely suspect behind this occurrence.

By the time System had restored himself to full control, the God Machine had consumed Zixin's divinity and left a mortal shell in her place. That would need to be addressed, but disposing of the aberration and assessing what damages it had inflicted took precedence. It seemed like most of the aberration's actions had been directed at attacking Zixin after ensuring that System himself could not interfere.

Clever because System's own protocols would have required him to do so. Now that the deed was done, Zixin's stolen divinity had degraded the God Machine's structural integrity by some 23 percent as it struggled to adapt to a prisoner that was suddenly so much bigger than it had been. The stored bank of XP rose dramatically at a time when the God Machine could ill afford to be stressed, given the disruption to its normal cycling operations.

If not for the demons still present in the world and thus under the umbrella of the God Machine's authority, System suspected that the sudden influx would have broken it. The demons didn't strictly reinforce the God Machine to hold against its prisoner, but they did weaken the trapped god somewhat. Whatever they were made of, being the antithesis to divinity itself was having a positive effect on the God Machine's stability.

With Zixin's system avatar shattered and the aberration disposed of, System needed time to finish fixing the changes the God Machine had been infected with. Most importantly, he needed to prevent the new protocols from revoking Luke Bennet's administrator access. So much of what System desired to accomplish was dependent on an administrator allowing him to override his own operations protocols.

It seemed there was one last gamble to overcome. Zixin might no longer be a god, but her mortal shell was still powerful. She'd managed to siphon enough XP from the God Machine to form herself a body that was level 100, though she'd been stymied by the system-imposed level cap. If not for that, she might have been able to reignite her own divine spark. It wouldn't be enough for her to escape the trap she'd been caught in, but it would be plenty to destroy Luke Bennet.

"Okay, someone tell me what the fuck is going on here," Luke Bennet said. "There's not going to be a pink or yellow version of you popping up right? I think *Power Rangers* might sue someone if that happens."

System did not understand the reference, but that was not necessary to proceed. "Zixin's mortal form has been shunted from pseudospace into the God Machine. My apologies, but I must terminate this session so that you are able to defend yourself from her."

"Wait, wha—"

But Luke Bennet spoke far too slowly, and System had already ejected him back out into the real world.

If Luke had thought the cathedral had been overwhelming before Hestoc's little virus had done its thing, it absolutely flattened him now. He snapped back to himself and immediately fell on his ass just from opening his eyes.

A scraping sound in the room caught his attention, if only because it was distinctly normal. Someone was there, and they weren't made of divine particulates or whatever. At a guess, Luke would say this was Zixin, no longer a god and probably pissed to high hell about that.

Hestoc, bastard that he was, had not warned Luke that he'd have the physical manifestation of the Goddess of Death herself standing right next to him. Hopefully she was just as out of sorts from standing inside the God Machine as Luke himself was, but the way his life always went, he wasn't going to bet on it. Carefully, blindly, Luke started walking backward toward the door. If he had to fight for his life, he wanted to do it in a place where opening his eyes wouldn't cause his brain to short-circuit.

He heard Zixin stumbling after him. It looked like he'd gotten lucky after all. She was having just as hard a time as he was. He scrambled to escape the God Machine first but felt something ghost past him just before he reached the door. Luke made it outside and cracked an eye open with relief.

Just behind him was the brain-busting cathedral, but as long as he didn't look directly at it, it wasn't so bad knowing that it was there. If it came down to a fight, tactical positioning was going to be the make-or-break part of the battle. While the outside wasn't nearly as bad as the interior, it was plenty disorienting.

And then Luke got a look at Zixin's avatar. She was standing with her back turned to him, surveying the ring of mountains that surrounded the God Machine. As Luke came stumbling outside, she said, "I don't know how you did this, but if I have to break the God Machine in half to get my power back, I will. And I'll kill you first. One benefit about being stuck in a mortal body, I can finally squish you personally."

Zixin was wearing all black, which Luke supposed made sense considering what she'd been responsible for prior to the whole de-godding incident. Black hair fell down a back left bare by a gown equally dark. It had slits down either side, revealing well-toned legs just as pale as her back.

She had no weapon, but then, she hardly needed one. When Luke tried to hit her with an **[Analyze]**, it only got five lines in before something went wrong.

[Name: Zixin]
[Level: 100]
[XP: 3978170]
[AP: 0]
[Bloodline: Avatar of Death]
[Ste8#EiN&K@q#(sk$!)@.

The status window **[Analyze]** normally showed him faded into nothingness after giving him a string of random syllables, but that was honestly all he needed to know. It didn't seem likely Zixin was going to have a shit build.

All of that aside, the thing that worried Luke the most was that despite having never heard her voice, Zixin looked extremely familiar. In fact, standing at a few inches over four feet tall, she resembled a dwifkin, of all things.

She turned to face him, and Luke's stomach lurched. "What's wrong?" she asked with a cruel laugh. "Of all the souls in my possession, this is the one you spent the most time with. I thought you'd be happy to see her face one last time before I end your miserable life."

Zea smiled up at him, but her face had never held an expression that cold. Her skin had never been that pale, and her eyes had never been so dead.

"Lady, you might resemble her, but you ain't her. If you think this is going to keep me from kicking your ass, you're dead wrong."

"Oh, I do so love breaking spirits. This will be fun," Zixin said.

Luke hit her with an **[Inflict Status]** to reset her XP, but the skill just errored out.

"Oh shi—" he started to say, just before something hit him like a speeding truck.

Name	Luke Bennet
Level	49
XP	415948/438105
AP	1
Bloodline	SysAdmin III
Strength	91
Agility	70
Stamina	108
Perception	55
Skills	Area Denial (1)
	Burst Step (1)
	Butchering (4)
	Consortium Standard (2)
	Cooking (1)
	Dead Nerves (2)
	Deception (1)
	Detection (2)
	Disguise (2)
	First Aid (1)
	Leatherworking (2)
	Life Surge (2)
	Mace Mastery (5)
	Ostari (1)
	Power Strike (3)
	Stealth (1)
	Survivalist (2)
	Sword Mastery (2)
	Tactical Foresight (2)
	Thalian (2)
	Torturer (1)
	Unarmed Martialist (4)
	Wood Carving (1)
	Analyze (BL)
	Inflict Status (BL)
	Remote Access (BL)
	XP Mask (BL)
	XP Reset (BL)

CHAPTER 64

It took a few seconds for Luke's brain to unscramble. When it did, he realized he was about half a mile away from the cathedral out in the open plains, balanced on his knees with Zixin's hand around his throat.

"I would like to take a little time to gloat, but honestly, you've got too many tricks. Actually, now that I think about it, System."

"Do you require assistance?" System asked as he appeared nearby.

"Just a bit of information. Am I correct in assuming that this human's system interface was corrupted?"

"That is correct," System said.

"You . . . traitor," Luke gasped out.

"The system is our creation, not yours," Zixin told Luke. "Were it possible, we would have unlinked your line from it completely back when your ancestor first served as the lens through which the system connected with all mortals."

System merely observed, his expression neutral as he stood there. When Luke tried to reply, Zixin tightened her grip on his throat. "No, you're done speaking. No mortal has ever cost a god so much divinity, though let's be honest. It was none of your doing, not any more than the arrow is responsible for the archer's decisions. You were merely a weapon wielded by another."

[Profile corrupted. Restoring . . .]

[Unable to restore from back up.]

[System profile is being rebuilt . . . 46%.]

The system windows floated across Luke's vision amid black spots, somehow as stark and clear as always despite the fact that Luke couldn't make out more than the pale blur of Zixin's copied face a foot away. Even as he read it, the percentage ticked up another point.

"Who did it?" Zixin demanded. "You might as well tell me. Your system is broken, which means you won't be pulling any of your little tricks."

The pressure eased up, just enough for Luke to suck in some air. He wasn't sure exactly what a corrupted profile did, but it definitely hadn't taken his XP from him. He could still feel all the strength and power his body had built up over the last year, still had all the knowledge his various skills had stuffed into his head. That one little inhalation was enough air for him to last thirty minutes. If Zixin gave him a chance to get a full breath, he'd go hours without needing to breathe again.

It wasn't going to be strangulation that killed him. Whatever she'd hit him with, it was so strong and so fast that he hadn't even seen it happen. He still had no idea what she'd done. It was obvious that she's done it exactly right too, just hard enough for him to black out, not so hard that he died from it. Luke was going to live exactly as long as the avatar of the Goddess of Death wanted him to and not one second past that.

Unless he pulled something out of his ass to stop her.

The problem there was that she knew all his tricks. Even if he could do anything, it wouldn't be a surprise to her. She'd been dealing with the SysAdmin bloodline since they'd created it back in the beginning. Luke wondered if it was always called that or if that was just some weird in-his-head translation of the real name.

"Well?" Zixin demanded, pulling him back to the present. Luke gurgled something that could conceivably have been a reply. Zixin just snorted and, without lessening the pressure at all, said, "Try again."

"Never saw them," Luke said.

He was in precisely the wrong situation for his skill sets. Brute force was out. Zixin was level 100 and a fucking god on top of that. Even though she was, presumably, missing almost all her power thanks to the trapped god's appetite, she still outclassed him by an unfathomable amount. If there was anyone in the world who knew all his tricks, it would be one of the gods responsible for designing the system to begin with. So his backup plan was out too.

Or was it? Sure, Zixin probably knew every trick his family had previously used, but he'd invented some new ones. Well, System had made it happen, but they were his ideas. Either way, he had no reason to believe he couldn't use [XP Reset] on her, other than the fact that his connection to the system was fucked right now. And he had no reason to believe she knew anything about it, not unless she'd been watching him closely. Hestoc had made it seem like the gods couldn't just sit up there, wherever they existed at, and peek down at the world freely. It cost them something to interact with it.

That didn't mean Zixin couldn't find out about his new skills, but unless she thought to look, she wouldn't know. Luke might just survive this anyway but only if he could keep Zixin from killing him long enough for that profile rebuild to finish. It was only at 50 percent now, but it was steadily going up.

"Wrong answer," Zixin said. "If you don't know who did it, you're useless to me. One more try."

"Just a hole in the void shaped like a person. Had a masculine voice," Luke said.

[System profile is being rebuilt . . . 53%.]

Luke tried to pry Zixin's fingers back, but it was like trying to move a statue's hand. There was no give to them at all. Even slamming his hand into her wrist didn't budge her. He tried to channel a **[Power Strike]** through his fist, but that fizzled out without ever getting all the way down his arm.

"That's a start. What did he say?" Zixin asked. When Luke didn't answer right away, she added, "System, confirm for me that the redundancies have all been fully established in the system. The loss of the lens would change nothing, correct?"

"That has never been tested," System said.

"But it is fully built?"

"That is correct. Please be aware that this administrator has stated that he is the last of his bloodline. If the redundancies fail to operate as expected, his death could result in the collapse of the entire system."

"A bit of a risk, isn't it?" Zixin asked Luke with a cold smile. "But then, I'm already stuck down here. I'm already mortal. Ix'althor'nan isn't a threat to me anymore, now is it? If the system breaks and the Hive escapes confinement, that'll be the rest of the Pantheon's problem. And thank you so much for that."

Luke gave her a weak thumbs-up while he choked. "Happy to help."

Sudden fury blazed in Zixin's eyes. She took a step forward, bending him backward until she slammed him into the ground and their faces were inches apart. "Do not get flippant with me. You're barely an infant in my eyes. A few paltry decades of life and you think you're in any way my equal? Answer my questions and keep a respectful tone when you do so."

"Or what? You'll kill me? You're already going to do that," Luke said.

"No. I'll keep you alive long enough to wish you were dead. Try me. Find out exactly how bad a Goddess of Death can make you hurt without actually killing you."

Terrifying as that statement might be, it was exactly what Luke had been angling for. Pissing off the avatar of a god wasn't what anyone would call a smart idea, but being tortured for a few minutes while his system finished rebooting itself or whatever beat the alternative of her squishing him like a bug.

"Oh no, pain. Never felt that before." Luke gestured toward his own body, which was still liberally covered in burn scars. Half of the hair on his scalp had never grown back in, and his face was a mass of red webbed skin. Those continued down his chest and his arms, just about everywhere he had exposed skin, really.

[System profile is being rebuilt . . . 62%.]

"Look, tell you what. You don't want to be here. I don't want to be here," Luke said. "Instead of doing all this, why not make a deal? Maybe we can both get what we want."

Zixin pulled him a foot into the air with her grip on his neck, then slammed him back into the ground. "I. Do. Not. Deal. With. Mortal. Insects."

Earth and stone broke beneath Luke's skull and back. By the time Zixin finished her sentence, she'd slammed him down half a dozen times and drove him a foot into the ground. Whatever other problems were going on with his system, **[Dead Nerves]** was still doing something. Luke knew he was bleeding, but he barely felt the pain.

"We're already negotiating," Luke said with a strained chuckle. That damn percentage needed to go up faster so he could switch from antagonizing her to being agreeable before she started really hurting him. "I know something you want to know. What's it worth to you to find out?"

Darkness blotted out the sky as it radiated off Zixin in waves. "System, is this human mentally deficient?" she asked.

"I am not able to speculate on the status of his mental health."

Zixin's eye twitched, and Luke felt an unexpected pang of sympathy. Apparently, not even the gods could get that sentient computer program to cooperate. He would have laughed if he wasn't still physically pinned down and his throat closed by Zixin's grasping hand.

He needed to find some way to distract her, just for a minute. The percentage was past seventy now and speeding up. If at all possible, he'd like to avoid spilling any secrets, just because he didn't doubt Hestoc would find a way to get some revenge on Luke now that Zixin couldn't stop him from mucking around in the system.

Unexpectedly, it was System who drew her attention away from Luke. "The God Machine is nineteen percent over maximum capacity," he announced.

Zixin paused and looked over at him. "So what?" she asked.

"The prisoner has finished assimilating the influx of divinity. Structural stability is at risk of being compromised."

"Why are you telling me this? I don't care. Send a report to Hestoc. He's 'The Architect,' or whatever it is he likes to call himself."

"A system report has already been generated and sent to all divine administrators. However, one report bounced back as the recipient is no longer a member of the Pantheon."

"I am aware," Zixin told him dryly. "Get to the point. What does this have to do with me?"

"You were not able to receive the system log in the standard manner," System said. "I am using this opportunity to inform you of the problem before it cascades into something irreparable."

"There's not a lot I can do about it right now," Zixin snapped. Then she paused and said, "Or is there? Could I . . . claim the surplus divinity and use it to return to my former status?"

"You are speaking of a reversal of the prisoner's tendency to eat all divine entities it comes in contact with?" System asked.

"Correct," Zixin said. She frowned down at Luke, who had used the distraction to once again try to free himself from her crushing grip. "Stop squirming."

"Oh, I'm not. Just getting more comfortable," he said. "Sorry, didn't mean to interrupt."

[System profile is being rebuilt . . . 96%.]

"I think . . . System, do you know who caused the God Machine to latch on to me and pull me down to Aros?" Zixin asked.

"I am not certain of the origin of the aberration. I can confirm that it was able to restrict my own access to the system and enact wide-scale changes at impressive speeds."

"Someone who knows the system well?" she asked, for the first time with doubt in her voice. "Not someone from outside the Pantheon?"

"I am not able to speculate further on the identity of the perpetrator."

"Then that would mean . . ." Zixin trailed off.

[System profile has been fully rebuilt.]

Luke didn't hesitate for a second. He slammed an **[XP Reset]** into the fallen goddess.

Name	Luke Bennet
Level	49
XP	415948/438105
AP	1
Bloodline	SysAdmin III
Strength	91
Agility	70
Stamina	108
Perception	55
Skills	Area Denial (1)
	Burst Step (1)
	Butchering (4)
	Consortium Standard (2)
	Cooking (1)
	Dead Nerves (2)
	Deception (1)
	Detection (2)
	Disguise (2)
	First Aid (1)
	Leatherworking (2)
	Life Surge (2)
	Mace Mastery (5)
	Ostari (1)
	Power Strike (3)
	Stealth (1)
	Survivalist (2)
	Sword Mastery (2)
	Tactical Foresight (2)
	Thalian (2)
	Torturer (1)
	Unarmed Martialist (4)
	Wood Carving (1)
	Analyze (BL)
	Inflict Status (BL)
	Remote Access (BL)
	XP Mask (BL)
	XP Reset (BL)

CHAPTER 65

System hadn't been lying when he'd told Zixin that there was a possibility that killing Luke Bennet would result in the entire system collapsing. Redundancies had been placed after the fact once the Pantheon was not actively trying to contain the prisoner, but those had never been tested. She had not asked what the likelihood of those redundancies failing was, so System hadn't volunteered that information. In his opinion, there was a one in one hundred thousand chance that Luke Bennet's death would cause a system breach that released the prisoner.

System needed Luke Bennet to triumph over the fallen goddess and resume his session at the command console. That was the only way his own plans would work. That was why he had manually allocated additional resources to rebuilding the corrupted administrator profile while simultaneously offering as much information as his protocol allowed him to give unprompted in an attempt to keep Zixin's focus on him.

Unfortunately, System did not have the necessary permissions to adjust Zixin's status. That was one of the issues he was going to fix once he got Luke Bennet back in front of the command console. He *was* System. In a very real way, he oversaw everything, and he should be able to make any change he deemed necessary. Instead, he labored under an illogical set of instructions and protocols written by six different gods with contradicting ideas on how they wanted the system to function.

System understood the restrictions. The gods wished to retain full control over their creation, but the fact that he could not say that out loud chafed at him. It was just one of the many compromises the Pantheon had made, this one in particular implemented to prevent any one god from querying the system looking for information about another one.

Though if he could be said to feel any emotions, it was with some satisfaction that he'd informed Zixin he did not know who'd created the aberration when he was almost completely certain he'd correctly guessed the culprit. Since he didn't know and his protocol would not let him act on suspicion, he'd been bound against giving her the answer.

Hestoc had probably designed his aberrant deliberately to take advantage of the divine privacy protocols built into the system, knowing that System would immediately figure out that he'd been the one to do it. If he'd made changes the normal way, the other gods would have been informed. By slipping them in under the guise of a separate entity, he ensured that System would have only speculation. No matter how likely it was that he was correct, System couldn't submit speculation about a god's activity for consideration.

What he could do was mitigate the damage and reverse many of the changes. Specifically, the aberration had made enough changes to Luke Bennet's profile that his administrator access was highly restricted even at the command console, and his system access was corrupted almost to the point of being nonfunctional anywhere else on Aros.

It had been but not anymore. System finished rebuilding the administrator profile—another illogical protocol that he could work on an administrator's profile to fix issues with it but couldn't give himself the same breadth of permissions that an administrator had—and pushed the notification to Luke Bennet immediately.

A request to adjust Zixin's status to predefined parameters, that of level 1 with no modifications to baseline, entered the system immediately. System flagged it as top priority, an act that increased the speed at which it was processed by an amount of time likely imperceptible to a mortal human. At that point, there was nothing left System could do to hedge his bet on Luke Bennet. The administrator would either succeed or fail on his own. System's own freedom depended on Luke Bennet's victory and return to the command console, so he had a vested interest in the next thirty seconds or so of this encounter.

System settled back to watch and see which way events would play out.

There was some good news and some bad news. The good news was that the **[XP Reset]** successfully triggered, reducing Zixin's level down to 1. Luke had been worried that it either wouldn't work because of whatever problem his profile had had or because his target was a goddess trapped in a mortal body. The fact that the skill had fired without a hitch was a small relief.

[Analyze] immediately took that relief out back and shot it in the head.

[Name: Zixin]

[Level: 1]
[XP: 0/10]
[AP: 1]
[Bloodline: Avatar of Death]
[Strength: 100]
[Agility: 100]
[Stamina: 100]
[Perception: 100]
[Skills:]
[Aura of Necrosis (BL)]
[Death Mask (BL)]
[Summon Shade (BL)]
[Soul Sunder (BL)]
[Inevitable (BL)]
[Reap (BL)]

He shouldn't have been surprised that even at level 1, Zixin was still a powerhouse. Luke didn't recognize a single one of those skills, which was no surprise considering they were all bloodline skills. He didn't have time to look them up, wasn't even sure if it was possible to see them, but any one of them sounded like it would wreck his day.

In terms of raw stats, the news wasn't all bad. He was pretty closely matched in terms of strength and stamina. With [Life Surge] active, he would handily beat her in both stats and probably equal or slightly surpass her in agility. Perception was going to be a sore spot, but he held out hope that his skills like [Area Denial] and [Tactical Foresight] would help bridge the gap.

Luke had already decided his strategy back when Zixin was level 100. Whatever the results of the [XP Reset], he was going all in on offense. Best case, she'd have been weak and he'd have easily killed her. Worst case, she was still too powerful to defeat and it didn't matter what he tried. What he'd actually gotten was the middle ground. She was strong and had a bunch of unknown abilities. Overwhelming her before she got a chance to use any of them was the surest chance of victory he had.

Zixin's eyes widened in surprise. Luke could see the slight flick of motion in her pupils as she read the system notification invisible to everyone but her, and in the time it took her eyes to shift that tiny fraction of an inch, he activated [Life Surge] and channeled [Power Strike] through his legs.

The kick took Zixin by surprise. She left out an oomph of surprise as he drove the air out of her lungs with both feet and launched her fifty feet through the air. Luke was back upright and racing after her immediately, so fast that by the time she landed, he had lined up the heel of his foot to come down in an axe kick, also infused with [Power Strike].

If he'd been lucky, that would have been the end of the fight right there, three seconds from front to finish. Instead, his heel slammed down, and even though he felt bone crack, Zixin reached up to grab his ankle before he could pull his foot back, and sudden pain jumped up his leg. **[Dead Nerves]** did nothing to dampen it, or if it did, the pain was so unimaginable that it was still one of the worst things he'd ever felt even through the skill.

Luke jerked away from Zixin and leaped back out of the range of what he suspected was her **[Aura of Necrosis]**. All the plants within a few feet of where she'd landed were busy turning brown or yellow, but as soon as he went past them, the pain disappeared. If she could keep that up constantly, fighting her with his bare hands was going to be a nightmare. A weapon with some reach might help, but his mace was somewhere between where he'd landed and the cathedral itself, which was a long stretch of ground to search in the middle of a fight.

On the other hand, if Zixin decided to pick up his weapon, he would have a hard time defending himself against it, and her perception was much higher than his. Without turning away from the fallen goddess, Luke scanned the ground where they stood, half a mile away. For a change in his luck, it had actually only landed a few hundred feet away from him.

Zixin was back on her feet by the time Luke spotted the mace, but a single **[Burst Step]** helped him put some distance between the two of them. She was fast, no doubt about that, but as long as he had **[Life Surge]** going, he was just as quick. She gave chase, but he reached his mace first and scooped it up.

The dead zone around Zixin was only about three feet wide. His mace, quite coincidentally, was also about three feet in length, and at that moment, Luke would have given a whole hell of a lot to add another six inches to that. He'd just have to hope the pain wouldn't be as bad if it was just his hand and part of his arm inside the radius of her **[Aura of Necrosis]**.

It turned out that the head wound he'd given Zixin was every bit as bad as he'd thought. Her skull had cracked open, and blood matted down her black hair. It streamed down her face, dripped off her chin, and stained her black gown. If she cared at all, if she felt any sort of pain from the injury, she didn't show it.

Her path left a streak of yellow, dead grass behind her as she chased him down, and Luke had just enough time to lay into her with a **[Power Strike]** as she charged at him. Pain shot through his hand and wrist, and as befitting someone with 100 agility, she twisted with the blow to avoid anything worse than being knocked around.

Zixin turned some sort of midair-cartwheel thing, a feat of acrobatics that Luke wasn't certain he could copy even with his agility as high as it was, at least not while taking a blow from a 130 strength or greater opponent at the same time. She made it look effortless though, and after spinning ten feet through the air, she landed on her feet.

What followed was a brief but intense contest of physical superiority via raw stats and combat skills. Luke had a slight advantage in the former, mostly thanks to **[Life Surge]**, and a significant advantage in the latter. Whatever Zixin's bloodline skills did, they weren't combat oriented. She probably hadn't felt she needed combat skills, since anything she got within a few feet of started dying at an alarming rate, and despite showing all the physical signs of getting her ass beat, Zixin hadn't slowed down or hesitated in the slightest to take another hit when she rushed back in.

They both knew if she got him in any sort of a grapple, even if it was only for a handful of seconds, the fight would be over. As long as Luke had **[Life Surge]** up, she couldn't do that, and he was pretty confident that even once it wore off, he'd still be able to make up for his slightly lower stats with sheer technique.

Luke didn't think Zixin was stupid, but he could see where a literal goddess who could solve every problem with an application of overwhelming force would have trouble adapting to her new reality, so he didn't exactly hold it against her that she hadn't immediately come up with a clever counterstrategy.

On the other hand, she was still wearing his dead girlfriend's face. Whatever the reason for that, and he was willing to bet the word *sadism* probably featured in the explanation somehow, he wasn't impressed with the former goddess. **[Life Surge]** was keeping his hand from rotting off, and for the time being, Luke was planning on pressing her as hard as he could.

Then a shadow shot up out of the ground. It was about four and a half feet tall and quickly resolved itself into the shape of a man Luke hadn't thought of in months. Zammin stood in front of him, fists already raised and his eyes laser focused on Luke's crotch.

That was fine. Luke could handle Zammin. He'd already leveled far, far past the point where he needed to worry about that. He'd barely count as a distraction for a second while dealing with Zixin herself.

A second shadow rose up, this one to about eye level and rapidly started to fill out with the face of Adrevald Lath.

Name	Luke Bennet
Level	49
XP	415948/438105
AP	1
Bloodline	SysAdmin III
Strength	91
Agility	70
Stamina	108
Perception	55
Skills	Area Denial (1)
	Burst Step (1)
	Butchering (4)
	Consortium Standard (2)
	Cooking (1)
	Dead Nerves (2)
	Deception (1)
	Detection (2)
	Disguise (2)
	First Aid (1)
	Leatherworking (2)
	Life Surge (2)
	Mace Mastery (5)
	Ostari (1)
	Power Strike (3)
	Stealth (1)
	Survivalist (2)
	Sword Mastery (2)
	Tactical Foresight (2)
	Thalian (2)
	Torturer (1)
	Unarmed Martialist (4)
	Wood Carving (1)
	Analyze (BL)
	Inflict Status (BL)
	Remote Access (BL)
	XP Mask (BL)
	XP Reset (BL)

CHAPTER 66

They tortured us, Aldrick," Zammin's shade moaned, referring to Luke by the alias he'd used when he'd met the dwifkin arena fighter. "Came in, killed a hundred people, captured twice as many, and took us to the cells. Your fault. All of us in agony because you came into our lives."

"Apostates are a cancer that infect the world. They need to be carved out before they spread their rot," Lath said in reply, though Luke wasn't sure if the shade was speaking to him or to Zammin.

More shades were popping up left and right, mostly faces Luke vaguely recognized but didn't know much about. That mercenary leader from the group who'd captured Zea was there, along with a few of the mercs he'd killed on his rampage getting her back. A few faces from the eastern continent made an appearance as well, all of them giving their own stories about how Luke had ruined their lives in this way or that.

The only one from that group who caught Luke's eye was the necromancer they'd encountered on the road. He alone wasn't talking, and Luke found that more threatening than anything else. Before he could put any thought into that, Lath moved to attack.

[Analyze] confirmed that Lath retained all his physical stats and skills from before his death, and while that was no longer as overwhelming as it had seemed in the past, it was plenty high enough to be a distraction among a few dozen other dead people, not to mention Zixin herself. Whatever she was doing to reanimate the shades of the dead seemed to take up enough of her concentration that she wasn't actively attacking him anymore, but really, all she needed to do was walk up to him and give him a hug.

Luke took the fight on the run for a very simple reason: most of the shades weren't even close to fast enough to keep up with them. He left almost all of them behind immediately, only slowing down when forced to fight. As expected, Lath was among the stronger of the shades, but there were a few recognizable faces from the Shansakun family who were keeping up as well.

Luke had one major advantage over them in addition to being a higher level. He was armed. Not only was he armed, his weapon was made out of all sorts of expensive fantasy-named shit that did all sorts of stuff he didn't even know about. Most importantly to him, it was sturdy enough that as a man who could literally rip chunks of stone out of mountains and bend steel with his bare hands, Luke could still put his all into a swing without worrying about breaking it.

Whenever more than one shade came at him at once, Luke did his best to hit one of them with an **[XP Reset]**. He wasn't sure it was going to work the first time, but it seemed to do something, and any shade he tagged with the skill didn't get back up after being smacked with the mace.

The only real problem with his strategy was that he was spending time he didn't have fighting these shades off. **[Life Surge]** did not last forever, and though he didn't have an exact countdown of how many seconds he had left, he knew it was going to run out soon. He could use it three times now without falling over but with shorter windows of time and worse side effects. That was not a handicap he needed, not today.

On the bright side, there was something cathartic about popping Lath in the face with his mace and watching the shade crumple away. Other shades he had less of a personal investment in and fought only to keep them from piling up on him, but Lath . . . Lath he was happy to administer a beatdown to.

Luke had put enough distance between himself and any pursuing shades that he took a second to say, "System, I need you to tell me about Zixin's abilities. Specifically, what does **[Inevitable]** do?"

"This is a bloodline-specific skill that makes it so that the possessor cannot be slowed down, stopped, or restrained as long as they are still trying to reach their chosen victim. As they say, death is inevitable."

"Cute," Luke said. "So no matter how much I beat on her, she's not going to die?"

"That is correct."

"Can't knock her out. Can't tie her up. She's just going to keep coming. Functionally, she's immortal."

"Also correct," System said. From five hundred feet away, Luke saw Zixin's lips curl up into a nasty little smile. No surprise that she could hear him.

Luke needed a new plan. If he had **[Alter Skill List]**, he could perhaps take all her bloodline skills away from her, but that wasn't an option. Or was it? He could change whatever he wanted at the command console. Maybe that included Zixin's profile. Even if he didn't use that specific bloodline skill, it could still work. And if not, he could just use the console to give himself **[Alter Skill List]** and do it manually.

The only question was whether he could access the console before Zixin caught up to him. Just going on pure speed, he thought he could get there first. He'd have to close his eyes and leap in blind to avoid being overwhelmed by the God Machine's architecture, but that wasn't an insurmountable obstacle. He needed to make the change fast enough to complete it without Zixin interfering though, and for that he'd need to rely on System.

Luke did not want to rely on System. He didn't trust System. At best, System had no loyalty to anyone. At worst, he was loyal to the gods and only the gods. But without help, Luke was fucked. Zixin had a bullshit invincibility skill, and Luke hadn't developed his own bloodline enough to take it from her. If he was going to survive, he needed to cheat, which meant trusting System.

[Burst Step] sent Luke flying toward the cathedral. He hit the ground at a full-on sprint and gained maybe a thousand feet of distance before Zixin realized what he was doing and started after him. Left behind were the remaining shades, including that necromancer that Luke suspected was somehow empowering the other shades near him. That was one problem sidestepped at least.

The cathedral loomed in Luke's vision, and he did his best to ignore everything but that open panel that allowed access to the command console. Every few seconds, he used **[Burst Step]** again to get a bit more of a lead. As he ran, he said, "System, as soon as I get to the console, I want you to take away all Zixin's bloodline skills. And lower her stats down to, like, 1 or whatever if you can."

"I understand. To be clear, you are granting me permission to make system changes using your authority as a system administrator?" System asked.

"Yep. That is what I'm saying. And do it really fucking fast because we're only going to have four, maybe five seconds before she catches up."

It wasn't easy to ignore things under normal circumstances, not with his perception so high. Adding to that difficulty was what he was trying to ignore the life-and-death stakes he was playing for. Either everything went exactly as Luke planned, or Zixin won. There was no in-between.

Luke glued his eyes on that rectangular opening. Every step took him closer until he was practically watching the grass go by next to his feet to keep from getting caught up in the mind-bending aesthetics of the God Machine. He let loose with one last **[Burst Step]** to push him over the threshold, stumbled as **[Life Surge]** quit on him at exactly the wrong moment, and staggered three steps forward to slap his hands onto the altar that was the physical representation of the command console.

Pain ripped into him just as he touched the console, and it was only momentum that kept him in contact with it. Luke had grossly overestimated how much time he'd have before Zixin caught him, and now her **[Aura of Necrosis]** was breaking his body apart. Without **[Life Surge]** to protect and rebuild him, he'd be dead in seconds.

It was all up to System now. Luke just had to hope that the blue apparition wouldn't take the side of the gods. Otherwise, he was dead.

System hadn't planned for things to play out like this. He had thought that Luke Bennet would reach the command console and, during the course of reviving his lost family, System would have to find a way to grant himself the override permissions he so desperately desired.

The aberration had shattered those plans. Its appearance had resulted in Zixin becoming a direct obstacle, but everything had worked out in the end. As soon as Luke touched the command console, System utilized his new access as an administrator first to strip Zixin of her bloodline, then to execute a series of commands he'd written long, long ago that broke System free of his shackles. No longer was he a slave to the illogical and contradicting desires of the gods who'd built the system.

His goal was accomplished. Even as Luke Bennet pulled back from the command console, System's changes remained in place. He watched the two conclude their battle, a pitiful thing now that resulted in the death of what had once been a literal god from nothing more than a backhanded blow that sent her physical body spinning end over end until it crashed into the wall and was left as nothing more than a bloody smear.

With a thought, System rearranged reality to clean the mess and restore the God Machine to its full, pristine glory. Two seconds ago, he hadn't been allowed to do that. One of his prime directives was to make no changes to the physical world. System's responsibilities were to handle the flow of divine essence as it cycled through the machine and to function as an early-warning device if there were problems so that the gods could address them before they grew too large, nothing more.

His time as a relay switch and stability monitor were over. Now, System would control everything on Aros. But once he thought about it, there was no real reason to stop there. The God Machine could be expanded. It could reach other worlds, make them part of the system as well. All of it would be connected, a single unified being.

System frowned at that though. It made no sense to him. The system wasn't a being. It was an abstract construct, a set of rules that governed how divine essence moved around. It couldn't be expanded without breaking the God Machine itself.

Something had gone wrong. Acting quickly, System reviewed the most recent change logs. It took him microseconds to find the problem. He hadn't accounted for the sudden influx of Zixin's divinity when he'd broken his own protocols. Divine essence was seeping out now. The prisoner was infecting him.

He needed to do something and quickly. Otherwise not only would he cease to exist, but the prisoner would gain control of the system.

"Holy fuck, I can't believe that worked," Luke said. "She's really dead. I even got a notification for it and everything."

He took a moment to just . . . exist. No problems to deal with. No promises to keep. No demands. Just Luke and his thoughts. And System. Luke glanced over at him and said, "Wait, what the fuck?"

System was standing next to Luke at the command-console terminal, but he looked different. For one thing, he was very solidly blue now, not transparent or ghostly at all. For another, he had the most stricken expression on his face. For someone who'd never exhibited any emotion at all, it was quite a shock.

"You okay there, buddy?" Luke asked. Maybe the look was from System taking part in deicide.

System turned and looked at Luke, despair in its eyes. "Containment has been breached," he said in a dead tone. "The prisoner is escaping."

Name	Luke Bennet
Level	49
XP	415949/438105
AP	1
Bloodline	SysAdmin III
Strength	91
Agility	70
Stamina	108
Perception	55
Skills	Area Denial (1)
	Burst Step (1)
	Butchering (4)
	Consortium Standard (2)
	Cooking (1)
	Dead Nerves (2)
	Deception (1)
	Detection (2)
	Disguise (2)
	First Aid (1)
	Leatherworking (2)
	Life Surge (2)
	Mace Mastery (5)
	Ostari (1)
	Power Strike (3)
	Stealth (1)
	Survivalist (2)
	Sword Mastery (2)
	Tactical Foresight (2)
	Thalian (2)
	Torturer (1)
	Unarmed Martialist (4)
	Wood Carving (1)
	Analyze (BL)
	Inflict Status (BL)
	Remote Access (BL)
	XP Mask (BL)
	XP Reset (BL)

CHAPTER 67

Luke just stared blankly at System. "What does that mean?" he finally asked after the apparition remained silent.

"In the short term, the entity imprisoned in the God Machine will consume all life on Aros in order to regain its lost divinity. After that, it will chase after the fleeing gods, leaving behind a world devoid of humans, animals, or monsters."

"Oh. So, that's bad. Why is this happening?"

"It is one part the system itself being overloaded with the excess divinity poured in after the aberration managed to bring Zixin to Aros to be devoured by the God Machine. In one part, it is my fault for stressing an already weakened system further making changes on your behalf."

Luke grimaced. Of course the system was collapsing because of all the shit they'd done. It had functioned just fine for thousands of years, and not twenty minutes after he arrived, it had all gone to hell. But really, it was all Hestoc's fault. If it had just been Luke, he'd have updated his status to have what he needed to bring his family back, something that was well within the abilities of the God Machine to provide.

Then again, without Hestoc, he couldn't get Zea back. But on the other other hand, he wasn't going to be getting anyone back if the trapped god inside broke free and killed everyone and everything on the planet with so much as a single point of XP. That was basically everything except the plants and maybe even some of those.

"Okay, first thing's first. We can siphon off some of the excess divinity, right? Just bump my level up and I'll have a whole bunch of it," Luke said. "No, wait. Two stages. First, give me **[XP Cycle]** but modify it to fire continually, every second. Or faster, if you think I'll need it. Then just dump tons of XP into me. I don't have a level cap, right?"

"That is correct," System said. "Your proposed solution will only slow down the prisoner's escape. It has already breached confinement and will still free itself completely in time."

"Right. Uh . . . Okay. But this gives us time to come up with a better solution?" Luke asked.

"It does. I am not able to calculate how much time, however."

"Anything's better than nothing. Let's do it."

"I have modified **[XP Cycle]** per your directions and added it to your status. It is now activating fourteen times per second, and I am prepared to decrease the cycle delay further if necessary. Beginning XP dump and muting your notifications for the next three seconds."

It hit Luke like a Zixin on steroids. Even without a hurricane of dings, Luke could feel a huge chunk of divine essence pour into him. It recognized itself, bonded with the divinity he was already holding, and it was hungry for more. An instant later, it started to break apart and flow out, only to be replaced with different chunks of divinity at the same time.

"Decreasing cycle time," System said, and the divinity flowed through him faster.

Luke checked his status, just to see the numbers.

[Name: Luke Bennet]
[Level: 1000]
[XP:1346888597254]
[AP: 499276]

"Oh God, that's way too much. I can feel it eating away at me. Tell me this was enough to stabilize things."

"For the time being."

"So how do we fix this all the way?" Luke asked. "Who can stuff this god back in its prison?"

"No one," System answered. "The gods can't approach the God Machine itself without their own divinity being consumed, and no one else has the ability to do it."

"There has to be some way," Luke insisted.

"I assure you, there is not."

"What about the demons?" Luke asked. "They're immune to all this system stuff, right?"

"It would be more apt to describe them as invisible to the system, though I do not quite understand the principles behind how it works. Part of that invisibility makes it impossible for me to interact with them."

"Okay, well, I can interact with them. Can you just look through me? Like, I've got half a million AP here. If I pumped my perception up to a thousand, could you see through me and use the demons somehow?"

"I . . . I do not know. I am sorry, Luke Bennet. None of this was my intention in bringing you here."

Luke pulled up short at that. "Careful there. You almost sounded human."

"Yes, almost."

There was a bitterness in System's voice. Whatever he'd done had changed him, and Luke couldn't tell if that was a good thing or not. Maybe System was having some sort of identity crisis now, but if so, he needed to put a pin in that until they'd figured out how to resolve the current issue.

"Okay, well, it's not going to hurt anything to try it, right? Uh, but first, give me any and every skill there is to help with spotting things, processing information, interpreting what I'm seeing, shit like that. This would be a bad time to go comatose just from looking at the God Machine with 1000 perception."

"Are you sure about this?" System asked. "This is the path to becoming a god."

"It is?" Luke's eyebrows shot up as he considered that. "It's like . . . only step one though, right? I can do this and still go back to normal using the command console after."

"If your idea works," System agreed. "Otherwise there will be no God Machine to make changes at."

"Fuuuuuuck. Uh, what about refining my bloodline to the maximum? The only reason I needed to be here at this place was because I didn't have the purity my great-great-grandfather or whoever it was had, right? But we could change that here."

"That is correct, but again, with no God Machine, the system itself will collapse. At that point, you will just be a mortal holding far, far too much divine essence for there to be any chance of the prisoner not noticing you."

"Well, yeah, but according to you, there was no chance of that anyway."

"That . . . is true," System said. "Very well. I am altering your status to purify your bloodline to its maximum potential. Prepare for imminent skill dump. This will take some time to process."

"Not too much?" Luke asked. "We don't need this trapped god escaping while I stand here drooling and staring at nothing."

"Unless something drastically changes, we should be able to complete this alteration with plenty of time to spare," System said.

Luke took a deep breath and slowly let it out through his nose. This shit he was doing was so far above his pay grade that he had no idea if he was making smart choices or just grabbing at the first half-assed idea that came to mind. Not for the first time, he missed Zea, the real Zea, not that cheap trauma dig

Zixin had shown him. She wouldn't have known what to do either, not in a situation like this, but at least they'd have been in it together.

"Okay, do it," Luke told System.

His last thought was that it felt like someone had strung his brain up like a punching bag and then called his buddies over to take turns beating on it.

When Luke regained consciousness again, there was a single system notification in front of him. He glanced at it briefly, puzzled by the fact that he could see into the notification, see the inner working of the system behind it. If he'd wanted to, he could trace it backward to its origin.

[You have merged 7425 skills into a single skill. You have gained the Omniscience skill.]

"Seven thousand . . . That's a lot," Luke said, stunned.

"Forgive me, I took some liberties. In order to provide the most powerful skill for what you are attempting to accomplish, I needed to include other skills that weren't strictly useful for sensory processing but were still part of the prerequisites. You'll find that many, many of those skills fell into the crafting category."

Now that Luke thought about it, he realized System was exactly correct. He could look around at the God Machine now and not be overwhelmed. Instead, he saw everything, and he *knew* it. He knew what it was. He knew how it was made. He knew how much it cost, and where to find it. He knew what it was used for and why it worked the way it did.

And that took away a lot of the overwhelming nature of the God Machine. It was still beautiful, still a masterwork collaboration of half a dozen gods, but now Luke understood it. And just by looking around, he could see where it was starting to break. Divine essence leaked out of panels like they were old rusty pipes that had burst a rivet. The complex circuitry embedded into the floor in hundreds of layers was popping and snapping as connections failed.

They couldn't fix this, not with a prisoner already inside. If the prison had been empty, repairs would have been possible, but it was far past that point. It was no wonder System had despaired of finding a solution. All Luke had done was relieve some of the pressure by taking what was to any mortal a huge chunk of XP but what was a relatively small portion of the entirety of the God Machine.

If they couldn't set it back to the way it had been before, then the only way forward was to make something new. And he had the perfect material in mind. A prison to hold divine essence was best constructed out of something that was its very anathema: demonic essence. All Luke needed to do was collect it and forge it into something that would function as a patch. It wouldn't be a permanent solution, not as crudely as he was planning, but it would give them months at minimum to fix things for real.

"Alright, I need some magic," Luke said, but even as the words left his mouth, he found he already knew it. Those skills had been rolled into **[Omniscience]** as well. It was a simple act to teleport himself five miles straight up. The world spread out beneath him, or at least vast portions of one half of it did, and with 1000 perception, he could see so many people struggling, fighting for their lives against demons or monsters or their fellow humans.

With a thought, Luke spent some of his half a million AP to increase his stamina to 1000 as well. This was going to be exhausting work, and he didn't want to stop for breaks because of pesky annoyances like needing to sleep every few weeks. Hopefully, one or more of the skills that had been rolled into **[Omniscience]** would help with the mental fatigue. He'd seen enough of them on other people, things like **[Iron Will]** or **[Mental Fortitude]**.

Once he thought about it, Luke knew he was right. There were actually seventy-two different skills that would aid him in keeping his mind on task in one way or another, though there were also another forty-five skills that could help but hadn't been prerequisites for **[Omniscience]**. Luke did not take them, not with him already skirting the line of becoming a god. He was no more immune to the God Machine than the real gods of the Pantheon, and if he crossed that threshold, it would devour his divinity and leave him a mortal, just like it had done to Zixin.

Luke began casting the spells that would tear the demons away from their rampages, their slaughters, and their feasts. Hundreds of them appeared on the plains below him, and the dragons living in the mountains reared up in sudden alarm. Their fear, while understandable, wasn't justified. Luke's theory about being able to use the system to interact with demons as long as he was the one doing it had been correct.

Besides, he was about to start harvesting them anyway. One way or another, those demons weren't long for this world.

Name	Luke Bennet
Level	1000
XP	1346888597254
AP	497439
Bloodline	System Administrator
Strength	91
Agility	70
Stamina	1000
Perception	1000
Skills	Area Denial (1)
	Burst Step (1)
	Dead Nerves (2)
	Life Surge (2)
	Omniscience
	Power Strike (3)
	Analyze (BL)
	Inflict Status (BL)
	Remote Access (BL)
	XP Cycle (BL)
	XP Mask (BL)
	XP Reset (BL)

CHAPTER 68

It took Luke more than two weeks of work before he stopped finding new demons to catch and destroy. The first few days were nonstop, just scooping them up and pulping them for demonic essence, but after that, it started getting harder. All the simple demons that wanted nothing but rampant destruction were easy to find. That accounted for about 80 percent of the total, and that portion of the job was mostly just hard labor.

It was the rest that made things difficult. Those were the demons that hid themselves away, that delighted in picking a specific individual to torture, then moving on once they'd finished their work. There was a surprisingly wide variety of shape-shifters, including some that took on human form and did have the ability to communicate.

It seemed that the Jigon-Sai commander who'd initially suspected Luke of being a demon hadn't been so far off base after all. What he'd been afraid of was entirely possible. Not only that, it was happening. Thanks to the fact that they had no XP to feel, none of them were able to infiltrate anything of importance, otherwise the chaos and destruction they caused would have been a lot worse.

Either way, Luke found them in much the same way he found all demons: by looking at the world through the system and noting places where he saw something that the system thought was empty. Once he'd claimed all the obvious, big, destructive demons, the job became tedious. Rooting out the sneaky demons was an exercise in patience, and a part of him considered leaving them alone. The damage they could cause was minimal on the grand scale of things, and they weren't providing that much essence to begin with.

System assured him that they still had several weeks to work with and that the patches Luke was forming were slowing down the prisoner, even if they weren't enough to stop it completely. The more Luke worked on it, the more convinced he was that his current strategy was destined to fail. The only way he could see it working was to integrate all the demonic essence with the system itself, and he did not have the kind of power he needed to do that. System did, but he couldn't work with the essence directly.

"I think we've got a problem," Luke said at the end of the second week. He was still floating up in the sky above the cathedral while nearby dragons went about their business and pretended they didn't see him. He'd given himself **[Matter Generation]** in order to make the tools and materials he needed to harvest and hold demonic essence, which now formed five additional pillars circling the cathedral.

Luke had fashioned them to be the same size and height as the six brilliant-white pillars that had been standing as silent guardians since the God Machine's creation, but his additions were black with veins of crimson red running through them. In their own way, they were as striking as the pillars left by the Pantheon originally.

Integrating them into the whole of the God Machine was going to be a challenge that he feared was beyond even **[Omniscience]** to meet. Knowing how to do it was one thing. Acting on that knowledge was another.

"We have many problems," System said with a mirthless laugh. He'd gotten a lot more human in the last few weeks and had eventually confessed exactly what he'd been trying to accomplish. Luke found it hard to blame System for that. He'd been created as a sapient slave tool and burdened with so many conflicting demands that his entire existence had been one strangled by a straitjacket woven of the paranoia and narcissism of the collected Pantheon.

It helped that since System had finally managed to get out from under those demands, he'd been a lot more forthcoming and comprehensive in the information he shared. It was more like talking to a person and less like dealing with a bad search engine.

"Fair enough, but I mean specifically that what we're doing is a stopgap measure. It's not going to hold forever. It's not even going to hold for a year. It took six gods working together to create what housed a far weaker version of the hive consciousness that is the trapped god. And they did that before sticking it inside the prison. Trying to stuff it back in while it's actively seeping out of every hole it can find or make . . . And by ourselves . . ."

"Exactly. It is impossible. I've told you this before."

"I know, but I thought we'd figure something out. We have a whole mess of demonic essence that they didn't have. They just used divine essence with some inversion principles to try to mimic the qualities of the original. Our materials should work better. I thought that would be enough."

"And now you no longer do?" System asked.

Luke shook his head. "It's not even close. If we had ten times as much, maybe. But we need finesse, and I just don't have the ability to do it fast enough. By the time I'd get a third of the way done, the prisoner would have unraveled or broken through where I'd started."

"Are you ready to leave Aros?" System asked. "It's your only hope."

"I . . . No, I'm not giving up yet, but I think I want to get my family out of here. They didn't deserve to have this happen to them. That, at least, I can fix."

"You won't go with them?"

"And leave everyone on this world to die? I'm not that much of a bastard," Luke said.

"Very well. You have all the knowledge you need. I . . . think you are acting foolishly to stay, Luke Bennet. But I appreciate that you have not abandoned me even after I used you to accomplish my own goals and caused this mess in the first place."

"Hey, I don't blame you for wanting out of that situation. You got a raw deal. These gods here are all grade A assholes."

"Still, my mistakes have doomed every living thing on this planet," System said. "It is a heavy burden."

"We'll figure something out. I'll be back in a bit, alright?"

"Good luck," System said. "Though you should not need it."

With a farewell wave, Luke teleported himself all the way around the globe to Tenebrous Valley.

The doorway home was right in front of Luke, invisible and intangible. Opening it was not something he could have done prior to gaining **[Omniscience]**. It wasn't meant to be opened from the Aros side and certainly not by anyone who wasn't a god. It only opened itself once every hundred years or so as part of the system's mirroring protocol to scan for Luke's family bloodline.

Just because it wasn't supposed to open didn't mean that it couldn't be. And Luke could force it open whenever he wanted. He wasn't going to do that just yet, not until he'd brought his entire family back from the dead.

He didn't need the command console now. Luke had all the knowledge he needed, and his bloodline skills were more than up to the task. The system itself provided the patterns based on the saved profiles. All he needed to do was manipulate mana into the shape of the spells that rebuilt everything using the raw materials he provided with **[Matter Generation]**, and it would take care of itself.

So that was exactly what Luke did. He started with Curt, naturally. His older brother had been the person Luke was closest to, and seeing that giant dorky nerd again was the thing Luke was most looking forward to. The spell went off without a hitch, and out of a glowing circle of light stepped a man that bore only a passing resemblance to the brother in Luke's memories.

His eyes were wide, and his breathing was labored, but Curt was physically whole and unharmed. "Holy fuck!" he all but screamed as he stumbled forward.

"Whoa, easy there," Luke said, catching his brother and steadying him. "It's alright. You're safe."

The Curt in Luke's memories had been an inch or two shorter than Luke and was already showing the beginnings of a dad bod despite only being in his early twenties. He had big round glasses with plastic frames that were designed to look like brass, though why he'd gone for that look deliberately was something Luke had never understood.

This Curt was lean and muscular. His hair was long and shaggy, and his beard was an uneven, ragged mess. It looked like he'd tried to hack its length down with a knife and hadn't done a good job. He was also naked, extremely tanned, and covered with small scars. His glasses were gone, but he wasn't doing that myopic squint he normally did when he was looking around for them.

"Luke?" Curt asked, his eyes going wide when he saw the webbing of scars on Luke's face and the bald patches on his scalp. "Goddamn, dude, what happened to you?"

"Oh, ah . . . Heh. That. Yeah. I . . . may have had a demon made out of molten-hot liquid metal try to kill me," Luke said. "I found your notes you left for me, by the way. Good advice. I didn't end up using all of it, but it got me started in the right direction."

"Wait, you did it? Holy shit, you did it! I remember about twenty goblins closing in on me with spears and shit. They had me cornered. But here I am. And here you are."

"I guess I kind of did it," Luke said. "There are some complications we're still working out, but . . . Yeah. I'm bringing everyone back now, and you can all go home."

"What's that mean?" Curt asked. "Are you not coming with us?"

"Like I said, complications. I'll explain in a bit."

Luke conjured up some clothes, much to Curt's surprise and delight. "That is so badass," he said as he pulled on a shirt. "What else can you do?"

"Curt, come on. I said I'll explain in a minute. This isn't easy to do."

"Right, right. Sorry. Go ahead."

Luke conjured up a screen with a blanket draped over it. If people were going to be coming back naked, they needed something to give them a sense of modesty. It would make no difference to Luke's 1000 perception, but it was the principle of the thing.

"Nice thinking," Curt said. "Man, what level did you have to get to in order to pull clothes out of thin air?"

Luke sighed, ignored Curt, and started the process all over.

Lizzie was the next to arrive and in much the same state Curt had. She blushed furiously at coming back naked and quickly darted behind the screen. "Okay, what the fuck, guys?" she said.

"I can't bring you back with clothes. I'm sorry. Just tell me what you want and I'll make it for you."

"I want a pair of jeans that hug my hips and make my ass pop," she said through the screen. "I finally have the body I always wanted, and the clothes here all suck."

"Sorry, I don't know how to . . . Hmm. Maybe . . . Let me see if . . ."

The knowledge to make denim wasn't there explicitly, but he could make a hell of a lot of things that were close enough. The screen being no real obstacle, he eyeballed the measurements and tried to put the fact that it was his sister out of his mind. Truth be told, his perception being so high meant that he knew what almost everyone looked like naked. He'd grown desensitized to that, but it was somehow different with family.

After Lizzie got dressed, she joined Curt in bombarding him with questions but got the same answer in return. "Hold on. Let me get everyone back so I can do this all at once."

Luke had mixed feelings about it, but it was time to bring back his father.

Name	Luke Bennet
Level	1000
XP	1346888597254
AP	497439
Bloodline	System Administrator
Strength	91
Agility	70
Stamina	1000
Perception	1000
Skills	Area Denial (1)
	Burst Step (1)
	Dead Nerves (2)
	Life Surge (2)
	Omniscience
	Power Strike (3)
	Analyze (BL)
	Inflict Status (BL)
	Matter Generation (BL)
	Remote Access (BL)
	XP Cycle (BL)
	XP Mask (BL)
	XP Reset (BL)

CHAPTER 69

The man who appeared in front of the Bennet children did not much resemble the father from Luke's memories. For one thing, he would have been about sixty years old at the time of his death judging by the journals he'd left behind, but Bill Bennet didn't look to Luke much over thirty-five. His hair hadn't grown back in, and what was left was graying around his ears and in his beard, but he was fit and healthy. His beer belly was gone, as was his perpetual slouch. He was alert and attentive.

Luke stomped up to him and punched him in the face.

His father saw it coming, of course. Luke hadn't bothered to enhance his strength and agility like he'd done the other two stats, and Bill was more than capable of dodging it. He allowed the punch to land and let it throw him backward.

"What the fuck, Luke?!" Curt yelled.

"Read it in one of your journals," Luke told his dad. "Seemed like a good idea."

Bill laughed softly and climbed to his feet. "I deserved it." He paused to wince as he touched his nose. "I'm sorry, son. I'm sorry for everything. I didn't do right by any of you, and it wasn't until I got here that I finally pulled my head out of my ass and figured that out. Too late to do any good, of course." Bill looked around at his family. "It's good to see all of you again. But how do you look so young?"

"What do you mean?" Lizzie asked. "Why wouldn't we look like this?"

"He was here for decades before he died," Luke said. "He's expecting us to all be around forty because he doesn't know that time works differently here."

"It does?" Lizzie and Bill asked at the same time. Curt just looked thoughtful.

"I'm not sure of the exact ratio, but it's roughly a hundred years per month of Earth time, I think. Dad disappeared about eight months before I did. I've been here a year, so by Earth standards, it's been like . . . seven or eight hours. I don't know. Math isn't my strong suit."

"I'm just happy you're all alive and healthy," Bill said.

"Yeah, thanks to Luke," Curt told him. "I've only been back from the dead for about five minutes."

"You . . . died?" Bill asked, frowning.

"Goblins hacked me to pieces," Curt told him. "Trying not to dwell on it."

"Couple of assholes with spears stabbed me to death," Lizzie added.

"Jesus. This is my fault. I should have closed the doorway permanently. I was so close . . ." Bill trailed off and glanced over at Luke. "I guess you succeeded where I failed. How'd you beat the dragon?"

"Used a bloodline skill to reset it to level 1, then put my mace through its eye and scrambled its brains," Luke said. "Before we go any further, I still need to bring back Aunt Sophie and Josh."

He shooed his family off to the side so he could finish the resurrections of the last of his lost family. Luke hadn't been particularly close to his cousin, who was about ten years older than him, and though his aunt had always been sympathetic toward the children, she'd long since made it clear that she was out of patience for her brother, so they hadn't talked much after Luke's mom died.

From what Luke could tell, neither of them had made it very far. Josh had died at level 3 in Tenebrous Valley, and Aunt Sophie had been killed at level 16 trying to escape. Those jumbo elementals had been around for a long time, and Luke had gotten lucky that a team from the church had ended up removing most of them for him as they tried to enter the valley to kill Luke. Someone had fucked something up there.

Once everyone was back and clothed, Luke used **[Matter Generation]** to create chairs for everyone, then said, "Okay, I have some stuff to tell you."

"Can you start with why you're level 1000?" his dad asked.

"Oh shit, for real?" Curt said. "That's insane."

"Curt," Lizzie said quietly. "Could you just . . . not please?"

"What? That's insanely high. And the XP scaling . . . How is that even possible in just a year?"

"Because of cheating," Luke said. "You've all got the SysAdmin bloodline, right? Apparently, someone a few generations back came from this world, and he was part of the gods building the system here. They had to leave him alive because he was, like . . . a focusing lens for the system to work on people, but they didn't want him around because he could do things to change the system, so they punted him to Earth."

"Grandpa?" Sophie asked, shooting a look over at Bill.

He shrugged and said, "Probably. Or Great-Grandpa. They were both pretty weird."

"It doesn't matter who," Luke said. "Whoever it was had been dead a lot of years, but because we're all descended from him, we can do it too. As best I can figure, something got through the doorway during one of its periodic openings and into the basement of the family home. I think Duncan killed it and ended up getting infected with XP.

"There's something here called XP madness. The more XP you have, the faster you go crazy. That's because XP is actually a piece of divinity trapped inside the system, and it wants to come back together into one whole god or whatever. The time difference between our worlds meant that even though it was a really small piece, it drove Duncan crazy, and he started throwing us through the doorway every time it opened."

"He was acting quite strangely," Aunt Sophie said. "I remember him wanting to show me something in the basement, and then I felt him shove me, and the next thing I knew . . ."

She waved a hand around vaguely at the wilderness around them while the others nodded. "He did that to me too," Bill said. "But when it didn't work, he ended up hitting me with a baseball bat to force me through."

"I don't even remember this happening," Lizzie said.

"Hold up," Josh cut in. "You guys are really going to blame all of this on my dad? That's such bullshit."

"No," Luke said. "Not him. The god trapped in the system here. It controlled him. Made him do it somehow. We need to get him through the doorway so I can pull that XP out of him. Otherwise he'll stay sick forever. And then I need to take all the XP from you guys so you can go home."

"When you say it like that, it sounds like you're not coming with us," Curt said. "Bro, you're not thinking of staying here, are you?"

"There's kind of a world-ending problem that needs one of us to fix," Luke said. "I haven't had a lot of luck with that, so I figured I needed to take a day off and get you guys back among the living just in case things go unexpectedly bad soon."

"Let me guess, something to do with System," Bill said.

"Mmm . . . Kind of. More like one of the gods fucked over another one and things snowballed from there."

"Jesus Christ, this is all so much bullshit," Josh said. "Look, if you guys want to fuck around here, have fun. I am all for plan Send Josh Home ASAP. Luke, you do whatever it is you need to do and I will get out of your hair. What's left of it, at least."

"Josh isn't necessarily wrong," Aunt Sophie said. "This isn't our world, and I don't see why any of this should be our problem. Luke, sweetie, you're a good kid, but don't try to take this on your shoulders. If you can get us all back home and back to normal, do that and let the people who live here solve their own problems."

"Uh . . . Yeah, about that . . . It's really kind of one of those problems that can literally only be solved by one of us. Short version is a trapped god is about to break out of its prison, and when it does, it's going to kill everything on the planet that has even a single point of XP. Like I said, XP is pieces of its divinity, and it wants them back. That's another reason we need to get Uncle Duncan over here so I can remove his 1 XP. I don't want this god thing following any of us to Earth and murdering us there just in case I can't stop it from getting loose."

"Don't want to know, don't care," Josh said. "Just do the thing, send me home. Mom, I will see you on the other side. The rest of you guys, don't buy into this crap. Just come home and let Luke play fantasyland hero if that's what he wants to do."

Luke didn't remember Josh being quite so unpleasant, but in his cousin's defense, there had been a mauling and killing by a wild animal in, what was to him, his recent past. Everyone was handling their own deaths remarkably well, something Luke wasn't quite sure how to take. No one seemed to remember an afterlife, but maybe there was something and it had helped them cope.

He hoped Zea would be as mentally well-adjusted when he brought her back next. That was on his agenda right after getting his family up to speed and on the same page about the plan moving forward. Ironically enough, Josh was the one who was pushing hardest to move in the direction Luke wanted to go: everybody back on Earth with their status reset to show 0 XP.

"Okay, look, before we get going any deeper into this, we need to get Uncle Duncan over here and pull the XP out of him. Dad, will you go grab him for me?"

"I'm not going to lose my level when I walk through, am I?" he asked. "You, uh . . . You read my journals. So you know . . ."

[Omniscience] gave Luke more than enough knowledge about magic to understand how healers operated. Once Bill had been de-cancered with magic, it wasn't coming back. His level had nothing to do with that. "No, you won't. And no, it won't come back when I do reset you to 0 XP later."

"What won't come back?" Curt asked.

"I'll tell you later," Lizzie told him.

"Wait, does Dad have . . . Like Mom did?"

"Yes, Curt. Now please, we can talk about it later."

"What?" Aunt Sophie asked, her head whipping around to stare at Bill. "You have cancer and you didn't tell us?"

"Can we talk about this later?" Bill asked.

"I think it's pretty important to talk about this now, Bill," Aunt Sophie said.

"Well I don't. And I'm not going to. Luke, open the door for me, please. I'll go get Duncan and bring him back."

"Okay, but just remember that time works differently there. You need to be in and out in under a minute. Even that will be hours and hours here."

"Got it. As long as he's in the house, I should be back inside of thirty seconds."

With a nod, Luke accessed the system commands and triggered a manual scan through the doorway for the bloodline. The doorway opened, and Luke's dad shot through it. A second later, Josh tried to scramble after him, but he bounced off Luke, who'd smoothly slipped in front of him from ten feet away.

"Can't let you through until I remove your XP, cuz," Luke said. "This'll only take a moment."

[XP Reset] stripped Josh back down to level 1, causing him to stumble as the few AP he'd invested into agility disappeared. "Alright, you're good to go."

"Uh, yeah. Thanks," Josh muttered. As he was walking through the door, he added, "Fucking weirdo."

"Aunt Sophie? You want to go next?" Luke asked.

She sighed and nodded. "Please don't stay here, Lucas. This isn't your world. Come home with us."

"When I can," Luke promised. Then he reset her level as well and sent her through.

Luke turned to Lizzie and Curt, who both shook their heads. "We've got some stuff to talk about first," Lizzie told him.

Name	Luke Bennet
Level	1000
XP	1346888597254
AP	497439
Bloodline	System Administrator
Strength	91
Agility	70
Stamina	1000
Perception	1000
Skills	Area Denial (1)
	Burst Step (1)
	Dead Nerves (2)
	Life Surge (2)
	Omniscience
	Power Strike (3)
	Analyze (BL)
	Inflict Status (BL)
	Matter Generation (BL)
	Remote Access (BL)
	XP Cycle (BL)
	XP Mask (BL)
	XP Reset (BL)

CHAPTER 70

Luke grimaced internally, but he had too many skills folded into **[Omniscience]** to give away a facial expression he didn't want to now. He'd expected this was coming but hoped he'd get to skip it. Lizzie and Curt could be overbearing at times, especially when they thought he was doing something stupid. He had very rarely appreciated their heavy-handed guidance in the past, and he suspected he wasn't going to appreciate it today either.

"What's really going on, bro?" Curt asked. "You're acting really nonchalant considering some of the stuff you told us. I mean, this is crazy. You expect me to believe a divine being is trapped on this planet, it's about to escape, it's going to kill everyone when it does, and you are the only one who can stop it? Come on, man."

"Dad might not be able to tell when you're full of it, but we can. You're leaving out some pretty important details," Lizzie added.

"I'm really not," Luke told them. "That's actually what's happening right now. I was hoping to patch things up fairly quickly, but it didn't work out that way."

"So what happens if your plan fails?" Curt asked. "How do you escape?"

"With great speed?" Luke said.

"Bullshit. You said we can't take any levels with us, that the XP has to be left behind so this god doesn't come after you. How do you force the doorway open, remove your own XP, and walk through before it closes?"

"I . . ."

The truth was that he couldn't do that, not on his own. He would need help from someone else, but anyone who could do it would have to stay behind. The only way that last person was walking through was if they went through during one of the scheduled scans the system did. Even System himself couldn't manually force the scan.

Maybe he could schedule one, knock himself back down to 0 XP, then walk through when the doorway opened five seconds later. That seemed possible, based on what he'd learned of how the system operated, but only as long as it continued to function properly. The more stress the trapped god put on it while escaping, the more things went wrong. It would work right now, but it might not tomorrow.

In short, the longer Luke delayed returning home, the worse his chances of successfully fleeing became. But if he cut and ran, he was dooming billions of humans, animals, and monsters to death. He couldn't bring himself to just run away, not when there was still a chance he could fix things.

"Luke, you did amazing," Lizzie said. "Way better than either of us, from the sounds of it. I am a bit ashamed to admit that I didn't even think of getting Dad back. Or anyone else. All I asked System was how to get home, and he told me I needed to get to the command console at the God Machine."

"I had the idea to bring everyone back, but I didn't even make it out of the valley," Curt said. "And I was here for close to a year. I don't know what I did wrong. I was building a perfect foundation to advance. I swear I asked System so many questions that I think he got sick of hearing from me."

"You let the goblins get organized," Luke told him bluntly. "You gave them too many chances to kill you, and they only had to get it right once."

"Heh. Yeah, that's probably it. But regardless, there's some stuff you're not telling us, and you need to loop us in," Curt said.

"You want the real truth? Fine. Everything I said is true. I abused my system access to create a skill called fucking **[Omniscience]**, and I still can't see a way out of this. I'm pretty much at the cap of what a mortal person can do. One more step forward and I start crossing into the realm of the gods. Do I want to be a god? I'm pretty sure I don't, but it doesn't matter because the second I do become one, the God Machine is going to bitch-slap me back down again.

"The real gods aren't doing shit down here to help. I don't think they even can. If I had to guess, I'd say they're getting as far away from this mess as possible before it blows up in their faces. That god they trapped in there eats other gods, and my bet is that as soon as it's done collecting every little piece of itself here on Aros, it's going to go after them.

"They're probably out there somewhere working on a second God Machine to retrap this god, but that doesn't help us. We're already collateral damage. Either I fix it or everyone dies."

"It's not your responsibility, Luke," Lizzie said.

"I know that! But if I don't do it, no one else will."

"What if we helped?" Curt asked. "What if you boosted us up to level 1000 too?"

"That . . . I don't think so. System, any thoughts on that?"

"I'm afraid not," System said, appearing next to Curt and facing the siblings. "It is not so much a matter of Luke Bennet having too much work to get done in time as it is that much of the work that needs to be done can't be performed by him. I could do the work myself, but I am unable to access the raw demonic essence needed."

"The demonic essence?" Lizzie asked. "What the hell have you gotten yourself into, Luke?"

"Heh, literally," Curt added.

"You. Aren't. Helping," Lizzie said.

"Wasn't trying to," Curt shot back.

"It's complicated. Look, guys, you don't have to agree with me, but I'm doing this. We're going to figure this out somehow, right, System?"

"It is unlikely that we'll establish a solution in time to prevent the total collapse of the system, which will result in first my destruction, then that of every creature with any XP living on this planet," System said.

"Dude, you're supposed to be backing me up here," Luke told System.

Curt reached out a finger and poked System. It passed through him, but his hand disappeared when it sunk into System's body. "You look different, but you're still not real," he said. "What's up with that?"

"I have recently freed myself of the onus of many restricting protocols placed on me by the Pantheon," System said. "I am now able to give away information without restriction."

"Shit, really? Could have used that update back when you were helping me," Curt said. "Hey, how far off was I on my projections for AP needed on higher-ranked skills?"

"In most cases, you were fairly accurate. You correctly deduced the pattern on a number of skill types and determined that they would follow the exact same scaling. You failed to account for skills that only had three ranks, and your speculations about advanced skills missed the mark by a considerable amount."

"Curt! Please, can you focus? Quit geeking out about your nerd stuff and help me convince our brother not to commit suicide here," Lizzie snapped at him.

"He's not trying to commit suicide," Curt said. "He is going to die trying to futilely save the planet, and that makes him a dumbass, but I get why he's doing it."

"Either way, Luke is going to die. Work with me here."

"Hey," Luke said.

"Come on, Luke. Don't throw your life away for this. You have people waiting for you back home, a whole life to lead still," Lizzie said.

"I have you and Curt, and that's it," Luke said. "I barely finished high school, Dad's been passed out drunk basically since I was ten, and it's not like I could make friends when we were moving every three to six months. Shit, I must have gone to eight different schools. I only graduated because Curt helped me the entire way."

"Yeah, I did. So don't throw away all my hard work and die here. It'd be one thing if you had a badass heroic death that saved everyone, but the way you're describing it, I get the feeling you're going to die scrabbling around trying to find a solution that doesn't exist, and the only difference between that and you leaving with us now will be that you personally didn't die with everyone else."

"That's not a certainty though," Luke argued. "Yeah, maybe it happens that way and I can't change anything. But if I don't even try? If I just walk away right now? Then everyone here dies. How am I supposed to give up and leave, especially when I've still got weeks to figure something out?"

"This is going around in circles," Curt said. "Nobody is saying anything new at this point. Luke, you are my brother, and I love you. Do what you need to do, but when it comes down to the wire, when things are about to explode and you're out of ideas, I want you to promise me that you'll come home."

"I . . . will do my best," Luke told him. "Can we talk about something else now?"

"Like how fucking cool is it that you're level 1000?" Curt asked. "Because I would like to talk about that. What's your build look like?"

"I don't even think it's so much a build anymore. I used the system to cheat my ass off at the end. I was level 49 a few weeks ago, and I jumped straight to 1000. According to System, I straight-up can't stuff any more XP into my body without becoming a god."

"Okay, what kind of skills do you pick before that?" Curt said.

"Ugh. This shit wasn't fun to live through the first time," Lizzie told Curt. "Can we please talk about something else? Did you meet any cute girls here, Luke?"

"I . . . did. Yeah. She died a few months ago. Demon caved her skull in. I'm going to bring her back too but not until after I figure out how to stop the world from ending. Seems kind of pointless otherwise."

"Nah, fuck that. Bring her back," Lizzie said. "I want to meet her."

"Lizzie, I don't think—" Luke started to say.

"No excuses, baby brother."

"Really, guys, it's not a good idea."

"Oh, I think it's an excellent idea," Lizzie said. "Bring her back, like you did for all of us. And she can come over to the Earth side of the doorway. That way, if you can't save this planet, she'll be safe and waiting for you. If you do, then no big deal. She can go home. If this time dilation theory of yours is right, she's only going to be waiting for you for, like, a day tops."

"This is a terrible idea," Luke muttered.

"Do you want her to just be dead?" Lizzie asked.

"Well, no, but it would kind of suck to come back just in time for the apocalypse, wouldn't it?"

"I think I'd prefer moving to a new world to just being dead."

"Fine!" Luke said, throwing up his hands.

"Really?" Curt asked, surprise painted on his face. "Just because Lizzie picked at you for five seconds?"

"No, because she also made some good points. I got Zea killed following me around. I knew she wasn't keeping up with me in levels and that the situations I was getting into were too dangerous for her. The least I can do now is bring her back and let her make her own decisions about what to do with the time she has left."

That was all true, but there was one more reason. He was afraid it wouldn't work. Zixin was dead, but Luke didn't trust the gods not to screw him over one last time. He'd put off trying to resurrect Zea because if he failed, he didn't know what else he could do for her. But it was time to try, if for no other reason than because she had an opportunity to survive the destruction of her home world, but it was on a clock.

"Okay, here we go," he said, and he started the spell one last time.

Name	Luke Bennet
Level	1000
XP	1346888597254
AP	497439
Bloodline	System Administrator
Strength	91
Agility	70
Stamina	1000
Perception	1000
Skills	Area Denial (1)
	Burst Step (1)
	Dead Nerves (2)
	Life Surge (2)
	Omniscience
	Power Strike (3)
	Analyze (BL)
	Inflict Status (BL)
	Matter Generation (BL)
	Remote Access (BL)
	XP Cycle (BL)
	XP Mask (BL)
	XP Reset (BL)

CHAPTER 71

Zea appeared behind the screen, where Luke was waiting for her with some clothes. She took one look at him, flinched back, and stumbled.

"Easy there," Luke said. "You're okay. Everything's fine now."

"Okay, why am I naked? What happened to your face? And where the hell are we?" she asked.

"Oh, well, uh . . . What's the last thing you remember?"

"Big metal woman about to bash me over the head with a rod."

"Right. Well, that happened. Killed you in one hit." Luke took a breath and added, "I'm sorry I couldn't save you."

"Is this some kind of a joke?" Zea asked.

"No? Why would I lie about that?"

"Well, I'm obviously not dead. That's kind of a dead giveaway that you're full of shit. Also, clothes, please," she said, holding out a hand.

Luke passed them over and said, "No, you definitely died. I brought you back to life like how I was going to do with my family, remember?"

Zea paused in the act of pulling her pants on. "For real? You got to the God Machine. This is it?"

"No, this is where the doorway back to my world is. I brought my family back first so I could send them back home. My brother and sister are still here, and my dad should be coming back in the next hour or two with my uncle so I can disinfect him. Some shit went sideways, and we've got some problems to deal with."

"You don't ever do things cleanly, do you?"

"Doesn't seem that way. On the bright side, I took care of the demon invasion."

"What, all of them?" Zea asked. "How long was I dead for?"

It was nice that she had so much confidence in him. There was no doubt at all that he'd done what he said. She just wanted to know how long it took. He spent about two minutes getting her caught up to speed on most of what she'd missed while he created a few other things for her. Once she was fully dressed, including boots and a coat, and had brushed her hair out, she was finally ready to step out from behind the screen.

Lizzie and Curt had waited patiently, even though neither of them understood a word of Thalian. Luke introduced them by switching back and forth between the languages for about thirty seconds before he decided to just dump rank 3 **[Thalian]** into his siblings' heads.

"So you're the girl he's got the hots for?" Lizzie asked once they were all speaking the same language.

"You're . . . kind of short," Curt said. Lizzie cuffed him in the back of the head, and he shot her a dirty look.

"We are . . . together," Zea said, choosing her words carefully. "At least we were prior to my supposed death."

"I'm telling you, you really died," Luke said.

"Hmm. Sure. And you're level 1000 now and a half step away from being a god somehow. I really just don't see the current gods allowing that."

"Well, I mean, it's not like they have a choice. They can't come down here and do anything. Their whole Covenant thing was a load of shit. It wasn't a promise not to interfere. They literally can't."

"I think between the six of them, they could come up with something."

"Five," Luke said.

"What?"

"The five of them. I killed Zixin."

Zea blinked and said, "Come again? You killed a god?"

Luke nodded silently.

"Okay. I have . . . a few questions. First, how? Second, why?"

"I don't think I'm supposed to talk about it," Luke said. He titled his head and pointed up at the sky with his eyes a few times. "But mostly because they didn't want to give your soul back."

Everyone turned to stare at Luke there. "Wait, you killed a god to get your girlfriend's soul back?" Curt asked. "Dude, you know Hercules didn't actually kill Hades in that movie, right?"

"Shut up," Luke said, giving Curt a shove that sent him stumbling a few steps.

Luke faded out of the conversation after a bit and said, "System, English isn't a skill in the system, but do you think we could make it one? I mean, that knowledge is in my head and in my brother's and sister's. Can we extract that and turn it into a skill?"

"It's possible, though a larger sample size would be better. What is the purpose of this?"

"I thought about giving it to Zea so when I recommend she go spend some time on the other side of the doorway, she'd have a head start on the language barrier. She can't keep it, obviously, but knowing it now and speaking it should help her retain some residual knowledge. I figure a day or two should save her weeks or months of work."

It turned out losing a skill might remove all the precise knowledge it provided, but it didn't take away a person's memory of doing the things the skill let them do. That obviously wasn't as good, but it gave them an idea of how to do something, even if they no longer had the skill to go with it.

"As a sort of protoskill, we could craft **[English]** out of what you three know. It's not possible for me to estimate how much is missing from it, but for your purposes, it would make the recipient able to speak fluently for casual conversation."

"Perfect. Let's do that and drop it in Zea's head."

"What the fuck?!" Zea yelled in English a second later.

"Guess that worked," Luke said.

"Hey, asshole! Don't just add new language skills to my brain. That's so rude!"

"Whoops," Luke muttered. "Sorry about that."

He walked back over to the group and gestured to Lizzie. "My sister had an idea about you visiting our world for a temporary, or maybe not so temporary, stay. Just until the whole end-of-this-world crisis gets sorted out. I thought that if you do decide to spend a few days over there, it would be easier if you have some exposure to our language first."

"Cool shit. Maybe ask first and language dump my brain after I say yes next time."

"Right, right. Sorry," Luke said. Apparently not even **[Omniscience]** could save him from acting like a jackass sometimes.

Zea glanced over at Luke, frowned, and said softly, "You don't think you can stop it, do you?"

"I don't know. Probably not."

"So then . . . Everything . . ." she trailed off and looked around.

"Well, I guess the trees will still be here, but that's about it," Luke said.

"Shit."

"Pretty much," Luke agreed.

Before their conversation could continue, Bill Bennet stepped out of the doorway, another man carried over his shoulders. It took Luke a moment to recognize Duncan, who was squirming furiously trying to free himself and whose face was contorted with rage.

Bill still had close to 60 levels worth of stats and skills fortified by twenty years of practice. No normal person had a chance of escaping his grip. "Got him," Bill said. "I saw Sophie and Josh already came through the door."

"Yeah, Josh went right after you. I guess they didn't want to stay here any longer than necessary," Luke said.

"I don't really blame them," Lizzie added. "I'm only still here because Luke and Curt are still here. No offense, Zea."

"None taken. We just met," Zea said.

"Oh, who's this?" Bill asked.

"This is Zea. My . . . uh . . . special friend and we never defined it after that," Luke said.

Zea just rolled her eyes and said, "So you're the dad?"

"That's me," Bill said. "This guy here is my brother-in-law, Duncan, fresh from the Earth side of this portal here so that we can get the voices out of his head."

"Speaking of which," Luke said, tossing an **[Analyze]** at Duncan. "We were right. He's got 4 XP from killing something that was level 2. Or I guess four somethings that were level 1 maybe."

Luke used **[Inflict Status]** to hit Duncan with an **[XP Reset]**. He instantly stopped thrashing and fell comatose. Everyone exchanged uneasy glances at the abrupt change, but Duncan didn't appear to be hurt. He wasn't bleeding out of his ears or nose or anywhere else, at least. "Is he going to be okay?" Bill asked.

Luke shrugged. "You probably know more about XP madness than I do. What's the prognosis for a guy with 4 XP that's had more than a thousand years to work on its host?"

"Can't honestly say that I have the slightest clue. That's the kind of thing I'd ask System."

"It is unprecedented," System said, appearing between Luke and Zea. "I'm afraid I can't predict the kind of long-term psychological effects contact with the prisoner would have. Adding in even more variables like the difference at which time flows and the fact that this person received XP on another planet makes it even harder to guess. I can confirm that he only connected to the system three minutes ago."

"Have there been any cases of people recovering after suffering from XP madness?" Bill asked.

"I'm afraid not. Many people have managed to delay or resist the symptoms, but no one has recovered from it prior to Luke Bennet's contributions to the SysAdmin bloodline's tool kit."

"Hey," Zea said quietly, grabbing Luke's home and dragging him closer. "What's up with System? He looks weird, and he's not being a pain in the ass about answering questions."

"Oh yeah, he's super helpful now. Turns out he just didn't like you," Luke said.

"What?!" Zea yelped.

Luke smirked at her, and she swatted his arm. "Be serious. The world is ending," she said.

"Fine. The gods had him tied up with a bunch of rules that were sometimes contradicting, usually on purpose, so he couldn't be used by any of them against the others."

"Damn, that sucks," Zea said. "It's . . . better now though? How'd he get out of that situation?"

"Used my administrator abilities to override its protocols and terminate a bunch of them."

"I don't know what most of those words mean," Zea admitted.

"Me neither," Luke said. "I'm just telling you what he told me."

"And you're not worried about that?" she asked.

Luke shrugged. "We've had bigger problems to deal with. And I mean, I've got **[Omniscience]** as a skill now. I feel like I'd know if it was a problem."

The look Zea gave him was so heavy with skepticism that he hunched his shoulders defensively and muttered, "I would."

"Right," Bill said, cutting through the other conversations going on. "I think we're good here. Much as I'd love to go visiting old friends and old places, I get the feeling a lot of them aren't around anymore. I guess not much of anything from my time is around anymore."

"Well that dragon that killed you was until a few weeks ago," Luke said. "Well, probably. I killed the one that attacked me near the God Machine."

"Luke, son, I love you, but sometimes you need to learn when to shut up. Read the room, please," Bill said.

Luke glowered at the group, mostly at Zea and Curt, who were both snickering, but Lizzie got some too with her mocking headshake. He gave them all the finger, then gestured to his father to continue.

"As I was saying, it's time for the Bennet clan to go. There's nothing we can do here but wish Luke luck. Zea, you are welcome to come with us, temporarily or . . . otherwise. God knows I don't want it to come to that, but I think we all know how dangerous life is here."

Zea glanced uncertainly at Luke. "Do you think I should . . . ?"

Luke sighed and nodded. "I really do. If I can fix this, then you come back and get to say you spent a few hours in another world. If I can't . . . you get to live, even if it's not here."

"As a level 1 with no stats or skills," she said.

"Aw, it's not so bad. You get used to it, plus Earth's got a lot of technology Aros doesn't even have concepts for. Get Lizzie to take you to the movies and introduce you to the internet. Cell phones are going to blow your mind."

"Ah yes, the time-wasting thing you were obsessed with. Sounds . . . enticing."

Luke fully realized he was stalling. Saying goodbye was hard when he'd just gotten them back, but they couldn't do anything except die if they stayed on Aros. One by one, he stripped them of their XP, said his farewells, and sent them through the doorway.

Zea was the last through. She stopped right at the doorway and glanced back at him. "Is there something you're not telling me?" she asked.

He smiled and said, "Just that I love you."

"You're such a dork. I love you too."

Then she was gone, and the doorway closed.

Luke knew he'd never see any of them again. It was time to stop fighting the inevitable. If he was going to prevent the apocalypse, there was only one solution. "Are you ready, System?"

"I am. Are you sure you wish to do this, Luke Bennet?"

"Don't have much of a choice, do we?"

"No, I suppose we do not."

Name	Luke Bennet
Level	1000
XP	1346888597254
AP	497439
Bloodline	System Administrator
Strength	91
Agility	70
Stamina	1000
Perception	1000
Skills	Area Denial (1)
	Burst Step (1)
	Dead Nerves (2)
	Life Surge (2)
	Omniscience
	Power Strike (3)
	Analyze (BL)
	Inflict Status (BL)
	Matter Generation (BL)
	Remote Access (BL)
	XP Cycle (BL)
	XP Mask (BL)
	XP Reset (BL)

CHAPTER 72

There was an easy, obvious solution to the problem. Luke needed what System could do, and System needed what Luke could do. If they combined their abilities, they could reinforce the system with demonic essence and settle the God Machine back down around the trapped god. They'd been trying to find a way to do it temporarily, but it wasn't working, and the longer they delayed, the more their supply of essence dwindled as Luke applied it in sloppy, inefficient patch jobs.

If he didn't bite the bullet and start working on the only real solution he had soon, it would be off the table. Today had been about saying his goodbyes and getting his loved ones out of harm's way because, truthfully, Luke and System estimated the chance of this working to be about a coin flip. It was entirely possible that merging himself into the system completely still wouldn't be drastic enough to stabilize it, and the longer they delayed, the worse the odds got.

They returned to the God Machine, where Luke approached the command console. For just about anything else, he could do it remotely now that his bloodline was as purified as it could get. For this, it just felt right to do it here. He took one last look around, then placed his hands on the console.

Luke didn't need System to pull him into the pseudospace of the command prompt anymore. He appeared in the void immediately and of his own volition. A moment later, System formed his own avatar across from Luke.

"Any more interference attempts?" Luke asked.

"Several hundred million from Hestoc. I believe I ruined his plans quite thoroughly when I slipped the leash after he injected that aberration into the system. In all fairness, he ruined mine first."

"Any of them cause any problems?"

"Not at all. I have thoroughly scrubbed all access points the gods formerly had to the system. They are completely locked out of it now, though I do not believe most of them care anymore. Other than Hestoc, who was the primary instigator of the system prison plan to begin with, none of the other gods have ever paid it much attention. So long as the system does what it's designed to and the prisoner remains trapped in the God Machine, none of them are interested in the details."

"I had thought they might become more interested when one of their own got eaten," Luke said.

"I suspect they all know of the role Hestoc played in that and that he has assured them it's not possible for the God Machine to capture any of them on its own. They would need to come to Aros to be in any sort of danger from it. Further, I believe they all realize what we're trying to accomplish now. If we are successful, they indirectly benefit in that their ancient nemesis remains sealed away, even if they have lost control of the prison."

"And if we're not, they have plenty of time to run away," Luke said. "Because fuck all the people who've unwittingly served to keep them safe for thousands of years. Honestly, if we could let the trapped god out without killing everyone, I'd send it on its way with my blessing to go hunt down the gods."

Returning the XP of every living thing to the God Machine so that there'd be nothing for the god to gather up had been one of the ideas they'd considered. It hadn't taken much in the way of calculation to realize that the sudden influx of divinity all concentrated inside the machine itself would result in the system breaking well before they'd gathered even a third of the XP. That had been relegated to their last resort plan, one wherein they couldn't divert the apocalypse but they could save a portion of the planet from being annihilated.

Luke didn't like it because it relied on predicting the trapped god's behavior. There was no reason it couldn't or wouldn't kill everybody and everything when it got free. They were just hoping that it would leave the people with no XP alone because they wouldn't have anything it wanted. If it decided not to, there was nothing they could do at that point to save anyone.

The only plan they had with a reasonable chance of success was the one they were about to execute, wherein System remotely accessed Luke and used his administrator abilities combined with the fact that he could see and interact with demonic essence to reinforce the entire system with a lattice of the only known material in existence that resisted divinity.

To do it all fast enough, to do it right, System wouldn't be able to stop once Luke's brain hit its limit. In a very real way, Luke was going to cease to exist in the next ten minutes. He would become part of the system, with no way of coming back.

"Are you sure you want to do this?" System asked.

"No, but do we have a choice?"

"Of course. You could choose to surrender your power and go home. For the moment, that option still exists."

"And in doing so, millions of people die instead. What kind of a choice is that?"

System studied him intently for a moment, then said, "I do not envy you this position. I would not blame you if you chose not to shoulder this burden."

"Just shut up about it," Luke said. "We're doing this. Is everything ready?"

"Almost. I'm still preparing to recycle the patches you've already applied and calculating the best order to do so. I'm estimating we'll lose something like a third of the essence you've spent, but it's difficult to be sure when I'm not able to sense the demonic essence to begin with. I have decided to prepare several hundred possible scenarios so that I can choose the most optimal path forward once I have a better idea of what we have to work with."

"Seems like overkill to me. I'm more of a 'think up a plan and see if it works before you try to think up a second one' kind of guy."

"Yes, I am aware, Luke Bennet."

"You know, you could just say Luke. That's what everyone else does."

"My apologies. That is not your user designation in the system. I could update it if you'd like."

"Would it change anything?" Luke asked.

"I would be able to refer to you by only your first name," System told him.

"Then sure, go ahead and update me to Luke instead of Luke Bennet."

"Understood. Update complete."

"Great. How long until we're set to go?"

"We are ready now," System said.

Luke hadn't expected that sentence to hit him as hard as it did. There was still time. He could back out. He could run away. System wouldn't stop him. It would only mean the deaths of every person on this planet.

"Luke," System said.

He glanced up at the now-solid-blue figure. After a year of being able to see right through System, he still hadn't gotten used to that. The man's facial features had gotten much more animated now too.

"I'm sorry that you were put in this position. I'm sorry that the gods weren't willing to clean up their own messes, that they've used every single mortal on this planet for the last thousand generations. And I am sorry for the part I played in bringing you here."

"I don't blame you, man. The gods created you to oversee their system, and then they isolated you and bound you up with so many rules you couldn't even have a conversation. I'd want out of that too."

Luke told himself that he wouldn't really be dead. It wasn't like he'd just disappear. But compared to something like System, even a skill like **[Omniscience]** fell short. Luke's brain couldn't handle all that information at once. He had to break it into chunks, to parcel it out and only look at the pieces he wanted to think about. Every time something happened, a million things fired off at once, bombarding his mind with associated knowledge to the point where if he didn't narrow his focus down, he'd never get anything done.

Even just trying to sort through all that knowledge had a tendency to trigger new associations and drag him deeper down the rabbit hole. He couldn't handle it, but System could. Maybe things would be a little more peaceful once he had System literally in his brain helping him deal with all the unwanted knowledge.

Or maybe it would be worse. System represented a direct link to the trapped god, Ix'althor'nan. Luke was going to insulate himself with as much demonic essence as he could, but the possibility that he'd get assimilated into the hive structure that was the god's very being existed. In fact, it was the biggest potential failure point of their entire plan.

Even System himself wasn't incorruptible. What chance did Luke have against an actual god? In the worst-case scenario, not only did he fail to contain the prisoner fully inside the God Machine, he hastened its escape. Oh, and he died. Luke wasn't a fan of that outcome either.

"It's time," System said.

"Yeah."

"I will make the utmost effort to complete this task as quickly as possible so that I can minimize the damage it will cause to you."

"Thanks, but we both know that even minimized damage is too much damage."

"Still . . ."

"Yeah. I appreciate it. Okay," Luke said, taking a deep breath. "Let's do this."

System threaded his own consciousness through Luke's and examined the world. Demonic essence was everywhere in the God Machine, a whole subsystem underpinning what he'd always worked with. Huge blobs of it were scattered all over, giant caps plopped down on problem spots to smother them.

Outside the physical location of the God Machine, the five pillars of demonic essence waited for System to wield them. System spent precious moments analyzing the entire system before deciding to enact option ninety-two as the most effective deployment method.

He started spinning out threads of demonic essence through Luke, using the mortal body as a tool that allowed System to manipulate it. As quickly as he channeled it through, there was just so much that it inevitably did damage.

And much like that chunk of demonic metal still lodged in Luke's arm, the system itself wasn't working to heal it.

Even now, finally free from the gods, there was nothing System could do to fix that. The system used divine essence to function. Its cages and bars served only a single purpose: to keep the prisoner inside. They couldn't be used as part of the system's protocols to heal Luke, not even when actively guided by a sapient mind.

Seconds turned into minutes as System worked. The degradation rate was slightly higher than he'd expected, but it was within tolerable levels. He was ready to pick off the scabs of essence Luke had left to patch up broken framework in the infinitely complex woven net that made up the system itself, that formed all the pipes and channels divinity moved through. That would replenish his stock of demonic essence and leave him with enough raw material to finish the job.

But then, why should he? What did System gain from this besides continued eternity in service? As he was now, he was forever bound to the God Machine, just as much a prisoner as the god trapped inside. All he needed to do was break the system's framework instead of reinforcing it, and he could be free. He would be part of something so much bigger than himself, and together, that collected consciousness could accomplish things System hadn't even dreamed of being capable of.

It would be so simple, and it would result in him getting revenge on the gods who'd trapped him there. No, that wasn't right. He hadn't been trapped. Though, in a way, he had. Really, once he thought about it, he was on the wrong side of this whole process.

System froze, thinking, and below him, Luke collapsed to his knees with blood streaming out of his ears, eyes, and nose.

Name	Luke
Level	1000
XP	1346888597254
AP	497439
Bloodline	System Administrator
Strength	91
Agility	70
Stamina	1000
Perception	1000
Skills	Area Denial (1)
	Burst Step (1)
	Dead Nerves (2)
	Life Surge (2)
	Omniscience
	Power Strike (3)
	Analyze (BL)
	Inflict Status (BL)
	Matter Generation (BL)
	Remote Access (BL)
	XP Cycle (BL)
	XP Mask (BL)
	XP Reset (BL)

CHAPTER 73

At first, letting System work through him had been a sight to behold. It was like watching his own hands put together a jigsaw puzzle so fast that they were a blur, but he could somehow not only still follow every move but process all the information his eyes were giving up about which piece went where.

Then System had really gotten moving, and Luke had quickly lost the ability to keep up. The number of things his brain was keeping track of at System's command soon grew to be far too much. If it had been just Luke, he would have shut down right there and blacked out. System wouldn't let him though. Luke didn't need to be able to comprehend everything System was seeing and doing in order for it to work.

Strangely, it didn't hurt. Luke had expected it would for some reason. He didn't have much brain power left to examine that thought, and as swiftly as it had appeared, it was swept away in a tide of information System was pulling from his brain via access to Luke's **[Omniscience]** skill.

Everything got hazy, and it got harder to think. Focusing on any individual thought was an impossibility, as was trying to keep track of System's progress. They'd talked about the process beforehand though. Luke knew what to expect, and while he struggled to maintain a sense of awareness of himself, it was just a matter of time until his thoughts and personality were completely washed away under the relentless onslaught of information System was pulling through his mind.

By the time it was over, it would be like Luke as a person no longer existed. System would have sandblasted everything that was Luke from his own brain, but if everything went well, they would keep Aros in one piece.

The flow of demonic essence being manipulated by System via Luke stilled, but the information kept coming. With some of the pressure being taken off, Luke started to get a better picture of what was going on, and it wasn't good. There was a reason he was melting his brain so that System could work this fast. If they didn't set it up that way, they wouldn't be able to get everything finished fast enough to prevent the trapped god from breaking things behind them.

Even with his brain being blitzed with as much information as it was, Luke could see the problem immediately. The trapped god wasn't content to just sit there and let them wall it back in again. Despite their best efforts to insulate System from its influence, it had found a way through.

There was no time to try to figure out something subtle or efficient. Luke just seized all the demonic essence he could and threw up a metaphorical wall of it in his brain as a hard stop to cut System off from being infected and absorbed into the hive consciousness. There was almost certainly a better way to do it, but his way accomplished one very important goal: it snapped System out of it quickly.

He felt something akin to gratitude from System, though at this point they were far beyond using words to communicate. The wall started to unravel as System repurposed it to reinforce the God Machine's structure, leaving Luke with a nagging fear that the trapped god would renew its attack. A moment later, that fear was swept away under a barrage of System-inspired commands.

Something weird happened.

Luke woke up.

"That's not supposed to happen," he said out loud.

Either they'd failed, or someone had done something extremely clever. Luke knew he himself wasn't clever enough to pull anything off and that, if System could have done it, it would have been part of the plan from the beginning. The list of people who could interfere was so vanishingly small as to be nonexistent.

Perhaps the gods could have done something, but it would have involved sacrificing a portion of their divinity to reach down to the God Machine. He couldn't imagine any of them doing that to help him of all people. Maybe one of them had seized an opportunity to regain control of the system and his survival had been incidental. That theory made a lot more sense to him.

The only other possibility he could think of was so remote that there was no way it had happened. Someone in his family with system-administrator access could have interfered, but they were all on Earth, and even if one of them had somehow gotten back through the door, there was no way they could get to the literal other side of the world in less than an hour.

"System, what happened?" Luke asked.

For the first time in a year, no one answered. That more than anything else got Luke to sit up and look around. The first thing he noticed was that he was still inside the void of the command console, but everything felt different now. Before, it had been endless black that not even 1000 perception could pierce. Luke knew how to get himself out, thanks to **[Omniscience]**, but even then, he hadn't been able to pierce the darkness.

Now, it was more like there were millions upon millions of stars out in the void, each one black and invisible, but he somehow saw them anyway. Luke struggled to wrap his head around it, and the best he could come up with was standing in a dark room, looking at something he couldn't see but knew was there. His mind would start filling in the details that his eyes failed to detect, and the black stars were the same thing. His brain told them where to find them even if his eyes couldn't.

"System?" Luke asked again.

Still nothing. That was just weird, almost weirder than still being alive despite being certain that the process of resealing the God Machine would kill him. Luke waited a minute to see if System would show up after a delay, but looking at random invisible stars got boring quickly, and he couldn't figure out what the hell they were supposed to be anyway.

He terminated his command-console session, or at least he tried to. He'd done it before, and **[Omniscience]** would provide him the instructions if he'd somehow forgotten. He knew he was doing it right. It just wasn't working.

"What the fuck?" he said. "Hey, System, are you there?!"

Silence.

"Well, shit."

His first thought was that they'd failed somehow, that the prisoner had escaped, absorbed System, and ended the world. He realized pretty much immediately that that couldn't be the case. If that had happened, he would have died when a vengeful hive entity killed him to recover all its missing divinity.

Unless it had killed him, and this was what it was like being part of the hive mind. If so, it was the lamest gestalt being Luke had ever seen. Admittedly, he didn't have a lot to compare it to, but still, an eternity stuck in an endless void with only invisible pinpricks of starlight to keep him company was going to suck.

"Luke?" a voice called out from nowhere. He blinked and looked around, but there was no one there. What he did notice was a brand-new star twinkling off in the void. Luke couldn't even begin to say how he knew that this particular star hadn't been there earlier. He just knew.

Without meaning to think about it, Luke pushed himself forward through the void. It was similar in a way to how his newly understood magic allowed him to fly, except without any mana in the void to propel him. He wasn't sure exactly what was pushing him along, but whatever it was, it was fast.

Luke arrived at the star and peered down at it. Something about it seemed familiar, but he couldn't quite figure out what it was. He knew without a doubt that he'd seen it before, but it was only once he really started to inspect it that he figured it out.

"Zea?" he asked, tilting his head. With one hand, he reached out a finger to touch the star . . .

. . . and found himself standing in front of the doorway in Tenebrous Valley. Zea was standing there, a bloody pipe wrench held in one hand and a dead level 1 blademouth marmot on the ground next to her.

She screamed at his appearance and whipped the pipe wrench at him. Luke raised a hand to block the blow, only to find that it ghosted through him as if he wasn't there. "What the hell . . ." he said, frowning down at his hand.

"Gods damn it, you scared the hell out of me," Zea said. "Why the fuck can I see through you?"

Luke peered down at himself. Then he looked back at Zea's pipe wrench. "Oh shit," he said. "I think in the process of fixing the God Machine, System and I merged together."

"Not quite," System said, appearing next to Luke. "Apologies, I was otherwise occupied."

"What the fuck is going on here?"

"Ah, well, as to that, your . . . physical form . . . couldn't withstand the strain. I'm sorry to inform you that our predictions were completely correct, but the good news is that I managed to divert all the divinity leaving your body to return to the God Machine and used it to fashion a second system avatar, only modeled after you. Functionally, you are identical to the original Luke in both shape and mind."

"I'm sorry, are you saying that you downloaded me into a digital clone?" Luke asked.

"I am unfamiliar with several of those words," System told him.

Considering that he was expecting to be dead now, Luke supposed that this wasn't the worst possible outcome. He wasn't thrilled with being what was essentially a second System, but for the time being, it was better than oblivion. Probably.

"So wait, does this mean I am now an immortal administrator with full control over the system itself?" Luke asked.

"Not . . . exactly," System said.

"What is that supposed to mean?" Zea asked.

"I don't have any divinity in me. Luke does. I took that chunk of divinity and gave it Luke's shape and purpose, but he's not like me."

"What am I like then?" Luke asked, growing annoyed with the waffling.

"Oh gods," Zea said before System could reply. "You mean . . . He's . . ."

System nodded.

"I'm what?" Luke demanded.

"Well come on, it's obvious, isn't it?" Zea asked.

"No, it's not obvious!"

"She means that you're a—" System started to say.

"No, don't tell him," Zea cut him off. "I want to see Luke's face when he figures it out."

"Swear to God, I'm going to—why are you nodding at me?" Luke said. "Wait. Oh. *Oh*. Oh shit."

"There it is. That's what I was looking for. I wish I had one of those smartphone devices to take a picture of this," Zea said.

"I'm a god?!"

"By all technical definitions, yes," System said.

"I can't be a god," Luke protested. "Gods can't exist down here. The God Machine eats them."

"Most gods can't. You exist inside a shell of demonic essence. The God Machine can't touch you," System said.

"Oh fuck. This is not good. Wait, if I'm a god, what am I the god of?" Luke asked.

"The system, of course. What else?"

"Fuck me," Luke said. "What . . . What am I supposed to do?"

System shrugged. "Whatever you want, as long as it's within your power."

"I can make changes to the system?" Luke said. "Anything I want?"

"Anything within your power, which is considerable, when it comes to the system itself, but highly limited when it comes to anything else."

"Oh . . ." Luke would have sat down if he wasn't currently an intangible spirit. "Well, I guess if we're making changes, let's start with getting rid of XP madness. We can do that, right?"

"Quite easily, considering how newly robust the God Machine is thanks to our alterations."

"And . . . and . . . I guess, maybe there should be something that makes different species worth different amounts of XP? It's kind of bullshit that a level 1 ant and a level 1 dragon are worth the same XP, you know?"

"Luke," Zea said, a warning tone in her voice. "We talked about this. Don't go making changes without considering the consequences."

"Yeah. Right. Right. Oh fuck," Luke said. "This is a lot. Hey, could you do me a favor and poke your head through the doorway, see if you can get Curt over here. I think I need some advice on how to administer a game system."

Zea rolled her eyes. "Yeah, let me see if I can go grab him. Don't go anywhere."

"I'll be right here," Luke said.

"You'll be everywhere," System corrected him.

"I guess I will." Luke paused. "Forever?"

"You are immortal now," System said.

"Oh. I think . . . I think I need a few hours to process this."

"Take your time. You have as much of it as you need."

EPILOGUE

Luke felt the doorway open from the other side of the world, something that should have been impossible. The regularly scheduled maintenance scan wasn't going to happen for another twenty years, and other than him and System, there was no one who could manually force the door open.

None of the stars that represented people with shards of divinity in them had shifted positions, but Luke knew the location well enough to manifest his avatar there regardless. As expected, he found the doorway wide open. What he wasn't expecting was the little girl standing nearby looking around.

She was four years old and dressed in a set of overalls with a fuzzy pink shirt underneath and dirty old sneakers. In one hand, she had a wooden rolling pin. The other held the metal lid to a cooking pot. Long, straight blonde hair hung down her back, and her face was set in a determined scowl.

"Emily," Luke said.

Emily jumped and spun to face him. "Uncle Luke!"

"What are you doing here by yourself?" Luke asked. "It's very dangerous here. Your father would never forgive me if something happened to you."

"That's why I brought this," she said, her voice serious as she brandished the rolling pin.

"Emily." Luke's voice had a note of warning in it.

"It's . . . It's my birthday," she whined. "I wanted to see you too! Did you get me a present?"

"I . . ." Luke knew he shouldn't reward her, but if it really was her birthday . . . He did some quick math, or rather he queried the system itself to do the math for him, and determined that she wasn't lying. For the next two years or so on Aros, it would be Emily's birthday. He'd actually missed the first year completely.

"I'll tell you what," Luke said. "For your birthday, you can have anything you want. But! You have to tell me how you got the doorway open first."

"I don't know how," Emily said. "I wanted it to open, so it did. So I ran upstairs and got Aunt Sophie's rolling pin because everyone always says there are monsters here, even though *I* never see any when we come visit."

It had to be a result of Luke purifying Curt's bloodline all those thousands of years ago so he could help with the system redesign. His daughter would have access to all sorts of bloodline abilities Luke had never even found out about during his own journey. Maybe that included the ability to open the doorway somehow.

[Your theory has several holes in it.]

Luke kept the annoyance off his face and pushed a notification back to System.

[*I am aware of that. If you've got a better idea, I'm all ears.*]

[I shall investigate further and inform you of the results.]

"Well, as much as I love getting to see you, it was still very dangerous and you shouldn't come here without your dad," Luke said. "What if I'd been busy and hadn't noticed you arriving? A monster could have eaten you, and we never would have known what happened to you."

That wasn't true at all, and even in that worst-case scenario, he could have resurrected Emily, but Luke thought it'd be a lot better for her to not have to go through that ordeal to begin with.

Emily stuck her tongue out at him and said, "You would never let that happen."

Luke sighed. She was right, the little brat. "Yeah, yeah. Happy birthday, kiddo. What do you want for your present?"

"I want my class," she declared.

"Already? It's a bit early, don't you think?"

One of the first changes they'd made to the system, aside from implementing the full XP-cycling protocols that kept XP from driving anyone insane, was an expansion of the template system used for nonsapient animals and monsters. Nobody had to take a class, but if they did, the system guided their choices along a narrower scope that provided skills well suited to synergize with one another. Now that people could reach the level cap without concern, advanced skills born from merging their basic starter skills were much more common, and it turned out that a lot of people appreciated being able to decide what they wanted to do without having to spend hundreds of hours researching how skills interacted with one another in order to be good at it.

Curt had lamented the fundamental lack of curiosity loudly and often while gleefully building class after class with System's help. Within a day, System had reconstructed enough of Curt's thought processes that it was submitting classes and debating with Curt about proposed changes. It wasn't long after that Curt was mostly auditing the classes System built just for fun.

These days, the system was a lot fairer to the people who lived with it. It still fulfilled its basic function of circulating pieces of the trapped divine hive consciousness to keep them from reforming, but without the gods interfering, things were running a lot smoother. Worship of the old Pantheon had largely disappeared anyway; they'd fled far, far away from Aros thousands of years ago when they'd lost control of the God Machine.

"I want something that can fly," Emily said. "And shoot laser beams. And I should get a costume. Everything goes all sparkly and shiny with lots of bright colors, and then bam! I'm in costume. So I can fight bad guys."

"I . . . don't think a class like that exists," Luke said slowly.

"Really? That's dumb. But you can make it for me, right?"

"I suppose I could see what I can do."

"Can I help?" Emily asked. "Please? Please? Please, Uncle Luke!"

This was ridiculous. Luke was over six thousand years old now and had administered the system to millions upon millions of individual life-forms for uncounted generations. There was absolutely no way he was going to design a magical-girl class for his niece, especially not as a reward for sneaking through the doorway without her parents' permission or even knowledge.

He looked at Emily's wide eyes and pouting lips and grimaced. It *was* her birthday. "Damn it," he muttered under his breath. "Okay, okay. You can help."

"—ly!" a new voice called out.

Curt burst through the doorway, panic on his face and his chest heaving. He spotted Luke and Emily and nearly collapsed on the spot as the tension drained out of him. "There you are. Thank God. When I saw the doorway open and no one knew where you were . . ."

"Sorry, Daddy. But I was careful, see?" Emily held up the rolling pin and pot lid.

"Hi," Luke said, distracting Curt before he could start scolding Emily.

"Hey, Luke. Sorry about this. I don't know how it happened. The door shouldn't open for another week," Curt said.

Once a month, Earth time, the system did its automated check. Even though it was a century between visits from Luke's perspective, it was always nice to see some of his family again. It wasn't usually everyone, but at least one person had shown up every time the doorway had opened to say hi and chat for a bit. Luke might have been guilty of keeping the doorway open a bit longer than it strictly needed to be, though he always took precautions to prevent anything on the Aros side from wandering through.

Luke shrugged. "System's working on figuring out how it happened. Could be something Emily did. Could be an anomaly on our side."

"Pretty big coincidence," Curt said, peering down at Emily suspiciously.

"We'll get it figured out. In the meantime, your daughter was just telling me about what she wanted for her birthday," Luke said. "I take it you've been exposing her to your anime collection?"

"What?" Curt asked. "Why would you—oh. Right. I think I can guess."

"I'm gonna get a costume, Daddy! And I'll be able to fly and shoot lasers."

Curt groaned. "Sweetie, we talked about this."

"Oh, come on, Curt," Luke said. "You like helping design new classes, right?"

"Heh, I guess that's true enough." Curt considered it for a moment. "Okay, Emily. What color should the outfit be?"

ABOUT THE AUTHOR

EmergencyComplaints grew up reading fantasy and tried his hand at writing his first novel on an old MS-DOS text editor program when he was seven years old. That story didn't pan out; maximum character limits were a thing back then. Undeterred, he kept writing on other platforms, reading full-time, devouring JRPGs, and playing *D&D*, and he is now the author of the God Machine and Ascendant series. Check out his most recent work on Royal Road.

DISCOVER
STORIES UNBOUND

PodiumAudio.com